# ROSEMARKED

Also by Livia Blackburne

*Midnight Thief*

*Daughter of Dusk*

*Umbertouched*

# ROSEMARKED

LIVIA BLACKBURNE

HYPERION
LOS ANGELES NEW YORK

First Hardcover Edition, December 2017
First Paperback Edition, November 2018
10 9 8 7 6 5 4 3 2
FAC-025438-19050
Printed in the United States of America
This book is set in 11 1/2 -pt. Garamond MT Pro, Helvetica Neue/Monotype
Designed by Marci Senders

Library of Congress Control Number for Hardcover Edition: 2016054754
ISBN 978-1-368-00834-1

Visit www.hyperionteens.com

For Thisbe

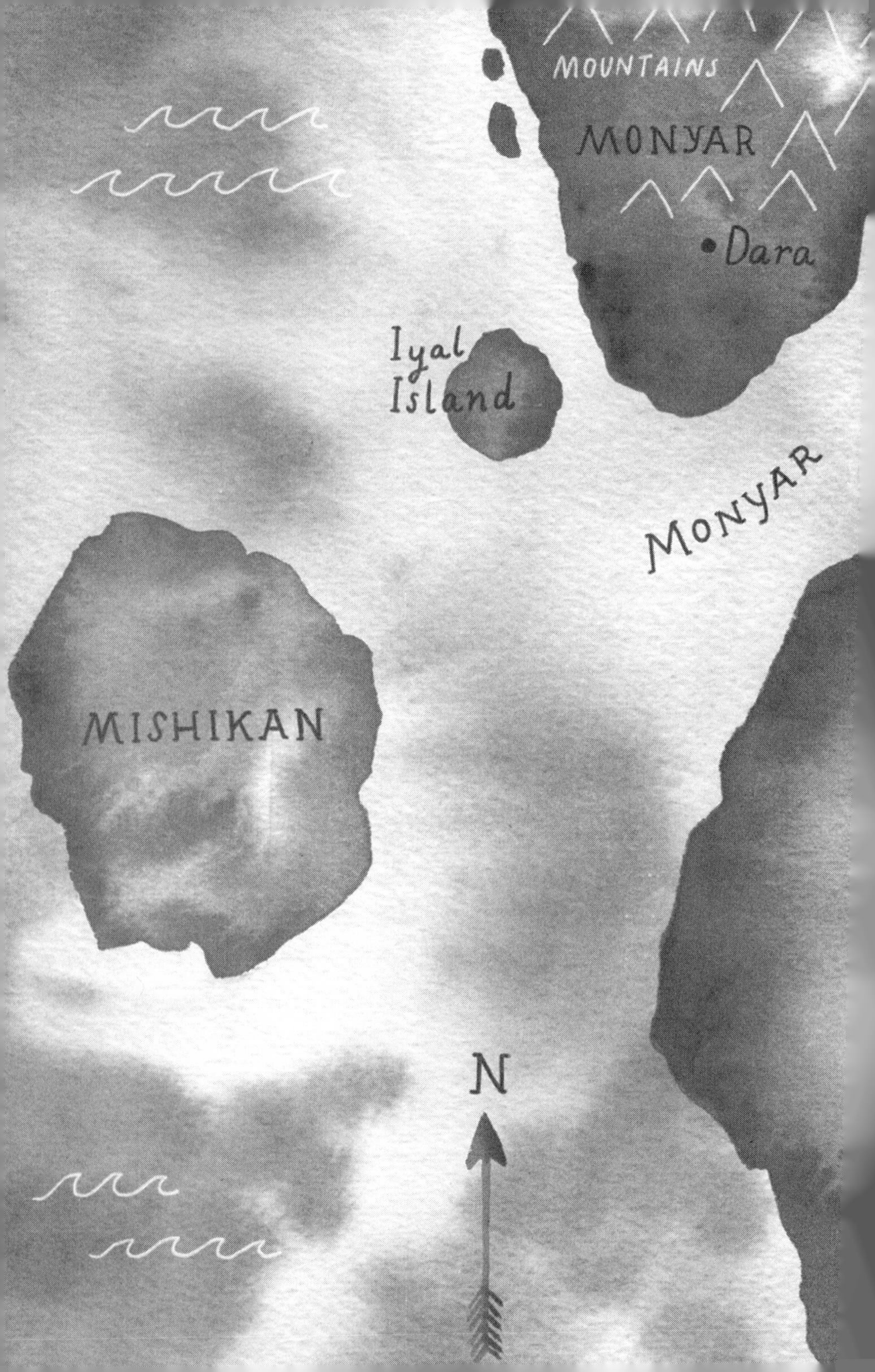

MOUNTAINS

MONYAR

Dara

Iyal
Island

MONYAR

MISHIKAN

N

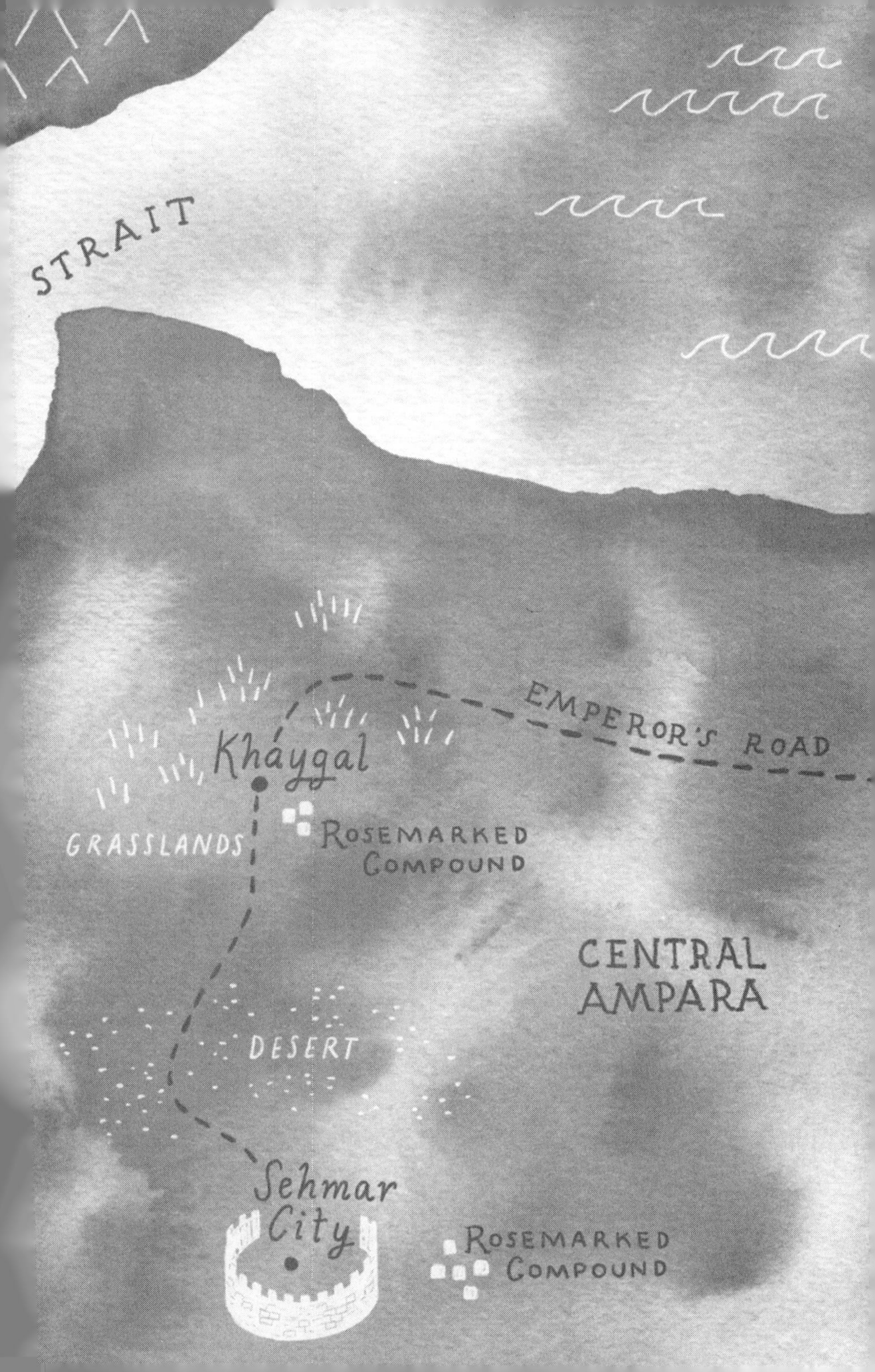

STRAIT

EMPEROR'S ROAD

Khaygal

GRASSLANDS

ROSEMARKED COMPOUND

CENTRAL AMPARA

DESERT

Sehmar City

ROSEMARKED COMPOUND

# PART ONE

# CHAPTER ONE
## ZIVAH

A bitter film of ziko root coats the inside of my mouth. I run my tongue over my palate to rub out the taste, though I know it won't work. Nothing dislodges ziko bitterness—not water, not bread, nor goat's milk. If I'd been planning ahead, I might have brought a mint leaf to chew, but I've had more important things on my mind.

The ziko pulp, which I'd sorted by smell and chewed mouthful by mouthful, now sits in a pot over a fire. It won't be long until the whole mixture boils, and I wonder if I should take it off the fire now, just to be safe. The hotter the ziko gets, the stronger its protective properties—but only up to a point. A perfect potion is brought to boiling and immediately cooled, but letting it boil a few moments longer ruins it all. Perhaps I should be cautious today, when my future is at stake. Perhaps it's better to present a passable effort than to aim for perfection and fail.

A bead of sweat rolls off my brow. As I wipe it away, I see my master, Kaylah, sitting between two other healers. If I've added a spoonful too much water or built my fire too high, missorted the roots or chewed my mouthfuls to the wrong degree, she will have seen it. Many times before, Kaylah has stopped me to gently correct my technique, but today she is an impartial judge like the others. The sight of her strengthens my resolve, and I dismiss my thoughts of playing it safe. Kaylah has taught me well, and I know I can do this.

The first bubble forms at the surface of my mixture and pops, sending droplets of potion hissing into the fire. Immediately, I grab some washcloths and lift the pot off the flames. Then I stir the contents briskly until the entire mixture is cool enough to drink, murmuring the ritual prayer: "Goddess, let your touch come through the craft of my hands. Let your breath come through mine to those you've placed in my care."

I bow deeply toward the judges.

Doron, the head judge, rises to his feet and comes to stand in front of my fire. "Tell me what you have made, apprentice."

"Ziko potion, to protect against the bite of the soulstealer snake."

"And what does it protect?"

"The mind. It keeps the victim from losing his memory."

"When may it be safely used?"

"The potion causes no harm unless used alongside valerian root, in which case it may cause the victim to fall into an unwakeable sleep. But the potion itself will only protect the mind if taken before the bite, or within a quarter hour after if the brew is extremely potent."

Doron nods in approval, then turns his attention toward the pot. He stirs the ziko pulp, observing the way his spoon moves through the mixture. He dips his finger and licks it, his forehead creasing as he works the mixture with his tongue. For a moment, he frowns, and my heart skips a beat. Does it taste wrong? Did I wait too long to take it off the flames? No, I'm sure I've done everything correctly.

"Well done," he says. "Perfectly done."

I cannot suppress my smile, nor my deep sigh of relief. I glance behind Doron to see Kaylah's eyes sparkling.

Doron clears his throat. "You have passed all the required tests to earn a healer's sash. You may stop now and serve Dara as an herbalist, or you may take one more test to become a high healer, but that trial carries by far the greater risk. What will you choose?"

His words are ritualized, but my throat tightens nonetheless. For the briefest moment, I hesitate. If I back out now, I wouldn't be the first apprentice to do so. But I've worked ten years for this.

I find my courage. "I will undergo the final test."

"So be it." Doron looks to the door, where a messy-haired apprentice stands at attention. "Bring in the cages."

The boy bows and walks outside. When he returns, two other apprentices follow him. All three carry long bamboo poles—like fishing poles, except small cages dangle where the hook should be. The apprentices line up solemnly in front of Doron, taking care not to let the poles swing near themselves or any other person. A forked tongue flicks out between the bars of the middle cage.

From the closest cage comes the barely detectable click of thin, hard legs on bamboo. A tingle goes up my spine. There's a reason why these are called the cages of death.

Doron speaks loud enough for all to hear. "As a healer, you must walk ahead of your patients into death. The sources of our art are not always safe. Are you willing to brave the fangs of deadly creatures to harvest their venoms and bend them to your will? To take vehicles of death and transform them into agents of life?"

"I am, and I have prepared myself." But there is no way to know if my preparation has been enough.

"Then may the Goddess judge your worthiness."

Doron unhooks the first cage from its pole and pulls out a green serpent as thick as his finger and long as his forearm, with a violet square marking the top of its head. I tell myself I shouldn't be fearful. I've tended snakes for years and injected myself with larger and larger doses of venom to prepare for this day. But that doesn't quiet the knowledge that the purple-crowned serpent can fell a horse within a half hour. Any one of these creatures in front of me will kill a normal person in several heartbeats, and now I must survive three bites at once.

The test of the deadly venoms is more than just a test of my body. It is a test of dedication and discipline, an embodiment of the principle that one who safeguards the lives of others must first be able to heal herself. The venom injections I took to develop immunity were painful and sometimes made me sick, but if I wanted to become a full healer, I had to push through. I had to follow directions precisely so that I would neither kill myself with too much venom, nor cheat myself with too little. And I had to keep it up year after year alongside the rest of my studies.

The serpent slithers docilely up Doron's arm. At the head judge's low whistle, the snake anchors its tail on his wrist and raises its violet head, ready to strike. With his other hand, Doron draws my arm toward him. It's all I can do not to pull away.

Doron's whistle changes pitch. Pain flares in my arm as the snake embeds its teeth into my skin. For a long moment, I stare dumbly at the fangs locked onto my flesh, and then Doron grabs the creature's head and carefully pries it off. Invisible flames spread down the length of my arm. Though I've worked hard to develop resistance against the venom, there is no way to protect against the pain.

Doron coolly examines the wound, peering into the punctures to make sure the venom has entered my bloodstream. I resent his clinical gaze, though I'm in too much pain to move. Finally, Doron nods in satisfaction and returns the snake to its cage. The first apprentice sneaks a worried look at my face before he leaves. He's Zad's apprentice—one year older than my seventeen, but he won't take the trials until the usual age of twenty. In the few times we've met, we've had a friendly rivalry, but today I sense his wholehearted wish that I succeed.

The blackarmor scorpion comes next, with its paralyzing sting. Doron goads it with a stick, and soon enough, its tail plunges down next to the snakebite. As Doron inspects the wounds, the edges of my vision cloud and I sway on my feet. Doron directs a sharp gaze at me and commands me to sit. He helps me down with the steady hands of a seasoned healer, and I'm unable to reconcile his gentleness with the fact that he's just goaded two deadly creatures to kill me.

After that comes the red-ringed spider. This one's the worst, not because it's any deadlier than the others, but because I've never completely rid myself of my fear of these creatures. My mother says a leaf spider bit me when I was very young, but I have no memory of it. I look away when Doron coaxes the creature onto my arm, and the bite is mercifully quick. Then the last apprentice leaves, and I am alone with the judges.

Fire from the three bites spreads through my chest, and the room itself fades in and out of view. Doron catches me as I list to the side. There's a sleeping mat on the floor, and I wonder when they laid it out for me. Heat envelops my body. My vision clouds red, then black. Voices echo in my head, climbing like vines up the underside of my skull and threatening to burst me open. When I scream, Kaylah's face appears in front of me, only to morph into the head of a snake. I'm suddenly thirsty, unbearably so, and I ask, then beg, for water. But no one comes to my aid.

Gradually, the sensations lose their strength and fade away. The torturous sounds collapse back into familiar voices, and the room stops wavering in front of me. The heat ebbs too, but not the all-consuming thirst. By the Goddess, I'd give up my healer's sash for something to drink.

Footsteps shuffle up next to me. It pains me to turn my head, but when I see Kaylah holding a cup of water, I lunge for her. I don't make it far, not even to sitting, but Kaylah catches me before I fall and holds the cup to my lips. It empties all too quickly. Kaylah sets it aside and wipes my face with a damp cloth.

"I'm proud of you, Zivah," she says. "You are now the youngest high healer Dara has ever seen."

Once it's clear that I will survive, my judges aid the rest of my recovery. Now the healers who'd so relentlessly tested me all morning refocus their considerable experience toward nurturing me back to health. Doron mixes three drafts in quick succession—one to clear the remaining venom from my blood, another to help me regain my strength, and a third to rehydrate my parched body.

Zad, the third judge, applies a salve to my wounds. "You'll have scars," he says as he wraps the bandage with his long bony fingers. "But you want these scars. They are a mark of all you've worked for."

And after he's finished, Kaylah helps me out of my sweat-soaked clothes and wipes down my skin. When I feel human again, she takes me by the arm.

"Ready?" she asks.

I nod, and she opens the cottage door. It was dawn when I stepped into the cottage for examination, and now it's late afternoon. Sunlight filters through the bamboo groves that surround our village, and the paths are mostly empty. Most of the people are still out on the crop terraces, finishing the spring planting.

"Zivah!"

I turn as my younger sister, Alia, throws her arms around my waist. "They told me you survived, but I had to see for myself." She clutches me so tightly that the air rushes out of my lungs.

I laugh. "Are you trying to squeeze the remaining life out of me?"

My older sister, Leora, moves in for her own embrace. Her wise eyes shine. "Father and Mother had to return to the terraces. They will see you at the feast."

Alia flings a thick black braid over her shoulder and grabs my arm. "And it is our job to prepare you."

With that, she pulls me down the dirt path, giggling. The paths are uneven, curving with the slope of the valley. They are tricky to navigate on the best of days, and after this morning's trial, it takes all my concentration not to fall on my face. Alia's enthusiasm is infectious though, and I make a game effort as Leora makes more stately progress alongside.

We take a wandering hen by surprise as we careen around a bend. The poor bird squawks and flaps her wings, and Alia squeals in turn, windmilling her arms to keep from trampling the creature. Leora comes to the rescue, catching Alia's waist from behind. For a moment, we are a wobbly tangle of arms and legs, and it's only by some miracle that we don't collapse altogether. Alia's crying from laughter now, and I'm smiling as well. But Leora's expression sobers suddenly, and I turn my head to follow her gaze.

A cluster of Amparan soldiers lounge by a stand of bamboo. One is a blond northerner. Another is a brown-skinned recruit from the southern territories, while others have the honey-colored complexion of the central empire. All of them, though, wear arrogance like mantles over their shoulders, and far too many look at my sisters and me in a way that makes me want to scrub their gazes off my skin. Leora squares her shoulders and deliberately resumes walking down the path. Alia and I follow her lead. After a few moments, the soldiers return their attention to their dice game.

When the Dara people surrendered peacefully to Amparan forces a generation ago, one of the stipulations, besides the yearly tithes, was that we would house battalions of soldiers that passed through our lands. One such group arrived five days ago. As always, our village leader split the battalion into groups to be hosted by each family. My mother, father, sisters, and I moved our cots to one side of our house so three foot soldiers could roll out their bedrolls on the other. It's never pleasant, having the soldiers about. Feeding all these extra mouths stretches our supplies, and not all the soldiers follow the Imperial Army's code of honor. Some have fingers that all too easily sweep valuables into their pockets, while others are aggressively friendly with the women. But the alternative is worse. The empire might be strict with those who surrender to them, but they are absolutely ruthless against those who resist. Those peoples have their homes burned to the ground, their people enslaved and shipped to the central empire. It's the thought of these stories, carried back by those who travel beyond Dara's borders, that makes me swallow the resentment in my chest as we walk by.

We're quiet the rest of the way. Leora pauses just outside our bamboo cottage, and I know she's wondering if the soldiers lodging with us are inside. But when she pushes the door open, the house is empty.

Leora smiles, regaining a bit of her cheer, and pulls me inside. "Come. You'll be the most beautiful healer Dara has ever celebrated."

They set to work immediately. Alia weaves colorful ribbons through my long black hair as Leora takes out my best silk dress, which she's washed and pressed. Then Leora pulls out a red sash, and my breath catches. Healer's sashes are usually plain red, the color of life, but this one has been embroidered with purple and green threads. Repeated along its length, subtle enough to avoid attention but clear enough to be seen, are images of the purple vel flower. It is said that the First Healer was taught the art of potions by the Goddess herself, and that the first lesson was vel tea for flu. Once the First Healer mastered the healing arts, the Goddess sent him forth to guard the curtain between life and death and ensure that none pass through before their time.

"Kaylah will present this to you at your ceremony," Leora says. The embroidery is fine and even, clearly the work of Leora's patient hands. For the second time today, my eyes prickle with tears. Soon my hair is pinned up, and my dress caresses my skin like a blessing. Leora smooths some berry juice onto my cheeks and lips, and then we're back out the door.

We smell the roasting meat before we see the bonfire. A shout greets my arrival, and people crowd around me. My neighbor, whose belly swells large with her first child, embraces me and tells me she wants me to be present at her baby's birth. Others follow in quick succession, taking my hand, offering their well-wishes. And then I see my mother and father waiting by the bonfire.

My mother's face breaks into a smile when I reach her. She pulls me close and rubs my back as if to assure herself that I am in one piece. "You passed your trial."

My father, his face lined by years on the crop terraces, clasps my shoulders. "My daughter, a full healer at seventeen. The Goddess smiles on our family."

The ceremony itself is short. Head Healer Doron calls me forward and reads vows for me to repeat, the very ones that the Goddess gave to the first healer. *I will use this sacred knowledge to heal and not to harm. I will brave the jaws of death to save those the Goddess has chosen*. Then, with the village watching, my master Kaylah ties the sash around my waist.

The feast starts in earnest after that. Wine is poured, and after everyone has had their fill, some village boys pull out tambourines and pipes, and the dancing starts. I'd been worried about Amparan soldiers intruding on the festivities, but surprisingly few of them show up. It's curious, since they must be able to smell the venison roasting, but I count it a blessing.

Much later that evening, I'm sitting at the edge of the festivities when Kaylah comes to join me. "Is the day catching up to you?" she asks.

Indeed, my limbs ache as I move over on the bench to make room for her. Kaylah sweeps her heavy black hair over her shoulder as she sits down.

"If I'd only been bitten by one creature this morning," I say, "perhaps I'd still be dancing."

Her eyes crinkle in her round face. "I've spoken to Doron and Zad. You'll take over the care of my younger patients until you become more accustomed to managing things on your own."

Doron and Zad will probably travel back to their own homes tomorrow. Though we call Dara a village, it's actually a series of clusters up and down the valley. Doron, Zad, and their apprentices live a day's travel away in different directions.

We sit side by side and watch the dancing. I've probably spent more time with Kaylah than anyone else, even my family. I was very young when my mother discovered I had an interest in healing. Like many women in our village, my mother sometimes foraged herbs for her own home remedies—vel for fever or a cold, sweetgrass for digestion, puzta flower for scrapes and bruises. I used to forgo playing with my sisters so I could tag along with my mother. I'd meticulously help her sort and clean the herbs, then set them out to dry.

In my seventh year, the Amparans waged a campaign near our home, and the perpetual presence of soldiers drained Dara's food stores almost completely. I remember the never-ending gnawing at my stomach, my constant and growing obsession with food. Once I even sneaked out to spy on a group of Amparan soldiers as they ate, only to be dragged back by my terrified mother when she found me.

My mother developed severe pains in her abdomen that year, something more than common hunger. She tried to hide it from us, but I saw how she turned pale and clutched her belly, the drops of blood on her handkerchief. She didn't go to the healer—they were busy serving the soldiers, and we didn't have money to spare. That was the first time I remembered hating Ampara.

One night it occurred to me that if puzta helped scrapes and bruises, and sweetgrass helped digestion, the former added to sweetgrass tea might help whatever sores she had in her stomach. In hindsight, it might have turned out badly, and my mother only drank the brew I gave her because she was distracted at the time. But the pain was gone within a day. Once my mother realized what had happened, she took me to Kaylah. In the ten years since, Kaylah has taught me a healer's skills—to sort herbs, milk snakes, mix poultices, and bind wounds. She's also taught me to observe patients, to see beyond their symptoms for what truly ails them, and to have a healthy reverence for the Goddess's work.

"Healer!" A harsh male voice cuts over the music.

I turn and jerk back when I see the Amparan commander Arxa cutting across the field. He's an imposing man. Tall and well built, with sharp eyes and a hint of gray in his thick black hair. Several soldiers trail in his wake, silencing the few villagers around us with their glares.

Arxa's eyes lock on Kaylah. "Healer, we need you. Now."

Kaylah stands immediately, closing the distance between them before the commander can make any more of a scene. "What is it, Commander?" Tension rolls off the soldiers around us, and I can feel the growing unease of the witnesses surrounding me.

"Three of my men have fallen ill," says Arxa.

Kaylah nods. "Lead the way."

Commander Arxa leads Kaylah and his soldiers out of the square. I trail behind, and Kaylah motions me back. "Stay here, Zivah. Tonight is your night."

But I ignore her, and she can't afford the time to argue. I would be no friend at all if I let her go alone with these soldiers.

The commander stops in front of a house at the edge of the village and throws the door open to reveal three soldiers lying on the ground, their hair damp from sweat. One moans. Another turns his head from side to side as if searching the room for something. They don't seem to notice us.

"How long have they been like this?" Kaylah asks. She steps closer, but Arxa puts out an arm to block her.

"Go no closer, Healer, until you see them more clearly."

Kaylah pauses, puzzled, but then our eyes adjust to the darkness. Not much moonlight comes through the doors or windows, but enough to illuminate the soldiers in faint gray light. Kaylah sees it first, and her gasp rings in my ears. The soldiers' arms are covered with large patches of discolored skin, patterned like the spots of piebald dogs or horses. The spots are bruise colored in the darkness, but if they were illuminated...

Kaylah draws a shaky breath. "I understand, Commander. I need light."

Dread gathers in my gut as Arxa delivers the order and a soldier comes bearing an oil lamp. Kaylah carries it toward the sick soldiers, though she stops a good distance away. One cries out and throws a hand up over his eyes. Now, with the lamp, we can clearly see that the marks are large and bright red.

"Rose plague," I whisper. Words that no healer ever wants to hear.

Next to me, Kaylah nods grimly. "These soldiers must be quarantined right away."

Before she finishes speaking, another Amparan soldier runs up and salutes the commander. "Two others have developed a fever, and another seven are feeling unwell."

Kaylah's jaw sets, and her voice takes on an authority that rivals Arxa's. "Round up your soldiers, Commander. They must all be checked."

Arxa fixes his eyes on her for a moment, then gives a brisk nod. He steps out and addresses the soldier that just arrived. "Gather everyone. Line them up in front of this cottage."

He steps through the doorway, and I follow behind him, my mind swirling from the news. Rose plague kills three out of four in a matter of days, and there is no cure. My skin crawls at the thought of those three feverish men inside the cottage. How many others have fallen ill? Who among the village has already contracted the disease from them? What would the empire do to us if Amparan soldiers died in our care?

Then the commander walks fully into the moonlight, and I let out an involuntary cry. It's hard to see, but now that I know what I'm looking for...

"Commander," I whisper. "Can you angle your arm toward the light?"

All heads turn first to me, and then to Arxa. The commander slowly angles his forearm to catch the moonlight. We all see the beginnings of skin markings. The Amparan soldiers turn to each other in horror, and everyone starts speaking at once.

"Order!" Arxa says, and the soldiers snap to attention, though their eyes are wide and their faces pale. There's no fear in Arxa's countenance as he looks down at his arm. The man's just been handed a death sentence, yet he studies the marks on his skin as if they were simply battle diagrams or maps. Arxa drops his hand to his side and steps deliberately away from the others. He looks around, and when he's made certain that everyone is paying attention, he speaks.

"I relinquish command of our battalion until my illness resolves," he says. "See that authority moves correctly down the chain."

Then he turns to Kaylah. "Healer, the lives of my men are in your hands. See that you do the empire proud."

He doesn't say the rest, but he doesn't need to because we hear it as plainly as if he'd said it out loud. *Do your best, and convince the empire that you spared no effort. Otherwise, your people will pay the price of your failure.*

# CHAPTER TWO
## DINEAS

Amparan soldiers torture me in my dreams. They hold my head underwater until I writhe like a hooked fish, inhaling the foul liquid and coughing it back up. They beat me, whip me, hang me from the ceiling until I beg for mercy. I scream until my throat is hoarse, calling for anyone who might help—the gods of war and mercy, Warlord Gatha, my mother...

And this time, someone answers back. "Wake up."

My eyes fly open. I expect to see the dark walls of my cell, to hear the screams of fellow prisoners and choke on the rank air. But instead I'm in a small, warmly lit room, and a woman wipes down my face. I grab her hand. She gasps, and I push her away and roll off the bed. The bedding tangles around my legs, and I realize I'm as naked as a newborn. Then the room spins around me. I pitch forward. The dirt floor is not as hard as the dungeon's stone, but it's still enough to make lights flash in front of my eyes.

As I groan into the ground, the woman shuffles to my side. "We won't hurt you, boy."

I roll over, my breath rasping through my throat as my eyes settle on her. She's about my mother's age, and only now do I notice her roughly spun clothes and the uneven walls of the room that holds me. "Where am I?" It doesn't look like the dungeons. Maybe I'm still dreaming. Or maybe my captors have finally succeeded in driving me mad.

"An hour's walk from Khaygal."

I'm no longer in that accursed military outpost? Still, an hour doesn't feel far enough. I grab the sheet from around my legs and pull it up to cover myself. My fingers shake.

"What's your name?" the woman asks.

"Don't ask his name." A man comes up and puts a protective arm around the woman's shoulders. "Don't ask anything. The less we know about him, and he about us, the better." He scowls down at me. "Behave yourself, boy. My wife might have pulled you out of the pile of bodies, but I'll throw you right back out there if need be."

Pile of bodies . . . I rub my aching temples and gradually, the memories return. The rose plague outbreak in the dungeons, the panicked guards . . . I remember coming down with fever, looking down to see red marks on my skin, lit by the dungeon's flickering torchlight. And I remember feeling happy, because it meant they wouldn't be able to hurt me anymore.

"You were dumped outside the fort, along with the rest of the diseased prisoners," says the woman. "The sole umbertouched body in a pile of corpses."

Only then do I see that the marks on my skin have turned dark brown, and I have a perverse urge to laugh. I just can't die, though I've begged Zenagua, goddess of death, to take me countless times. Everyone knows the stages of rose plague. First comes the fever and the delirium. It kills most people up front, though a few manage a stay of execution. Their fever ebbs, and they regain their strength, but their rash stays red, which means they can still pass the disease to others. Those are the rosemarked, and they're banished from society until the fever reclaims them a few years later.

Besides the rosemarked, there is one other group of survivors: the umbertouched, who beat the disease completely. Those lucky bastards have marks that turn brown. They also regain their strength, and they're immune to the disease from there on forward. Seems I've now joined their number.

And it finally sinks in. I might actually be free. Free, after a year in the Amparan dungeons. A year at my jailors' mercy, cut off from my fellow fighters, wishing for death. My bones go soft. I cover my eyes, hold my breath, do anything to keep control, but I collapse into wracking sobs. It takes me a while to realize the animal sounds echoing off the walls are coming from my own throat.

I feel a hand press gently on my shoulder, though the woman says nothing. It shames me to break down like this. After what seems like an eternity, the tremors finally subside.

"Why did you pull me out?" I ask. My throat is parched, and my tongue feels awkward. "You could have left me there to die with the others."

"Not everyone condones the way the empire treats its prisoners. If Hefana says you are to live, I do my utmost to help."

Hefana, the goddess of healers. It still strikes me as odd, almost heretical, that Ampara would have the same gods as my people, the Shidadi. It's said that we share the same forefathers, but the Amparans ceased their wandering and settled in cities. They brought the gods with them and built them giant stone temples, while my people continued to worship in our tents. From how things have turned out, it seems clear that the gods prefer temples.

Well, whether this woman was sent by Hefana or dumb luck, I owe her my life. "I don't know how I can repay you."

The man comes close—I'd forgotten about him—and he bends down so his face is just a hand's width from mine. "You can repay us by leaving. We've risked enough nursing you back to life. We'll give you food, provisions, enough to get you started on your journey, but you need to be out of our house in two days, you understand?"

The woman presses her lips together, and I can tell this rebellion on her part is a constant thorn between them. His words are raw, but they're fair. If they've really pulled me out of that living hell, they've already done more than I can ask of anyone. I need to get away, for my sake and for theirs.

"What provisions can you give me?" I ask. I'm already thinking ahead. I'll have to travel on back roads and steal food along the way. It'll be a tough journey, but at least I'll be in the open air, free from chains, going on my own terms.

And if Ampara comes after me again, I'll make them regret it.

I leave my rescuers' house under cover of darkness. In the dungeon, I'd resigned myself to never seeing the sky again, and it's overwhelming to step out into open grassland with the stars stretching as far as I can see. It feels like a trick or a dream, something that might be snatched away at any time. I walk as far as I can that night, wading over hills covered with grass as high as my knee. Every stray sound, every footstep or falling pebble, has me diving for the ground. As I huddle, hardly daring to breathe, I silently curse Ampara for the frightened rabbit I've become. There was a time when I was fearless, when I'd run into battle with no thought of the consequences, but now I know too much.

Dawn comes with no sign of pursuit, and I continue to travel by night, avoiding the emperor's road and sticking to the side paths. When my supplies run out, I loot the occasional village for food. As my strength grows, so does my confidence, and I start to think about where to go. Truth is, I'm not sure where my people are. At the time I was captured, our fighters had been pushed into the mountains on Monyar Peninsula. But it's been over a year since, and I wonder if they've been driven even farther back. I suppose they could have gained ground as well, but that's never happened in my lifetime. Ten years ago, some of our tribe still lived on the main continent. But little by little, we fled to more remote regions, finally crossing the strait to Monyar. And the empire continues to expand its reach.

Still, even though it's been a year, my best lead is to go where I'd last seen my people. After a week of travel, I reach the black waters of the Monyar Strait. I steal an unguarded rowboat and push it out as the tide's going down in the evening. It's windier than I expected, and I come perilously close to some sharp rocks on the way out, but finally I pull the boat onto the Monyar side. A pile of rocks and driftwood provides a hiding place for the boat, and I duck into the shelter of the forests to rest.

It's not quite a homecoming. Our tribe crossed the strait when I was twelve, and we've moved around too much for me to really feel like I belong anywhere. Still, Monyar's bamboo forests are a welcome sight. The Dara villagers live in the valleys and foothills, and I avoid them, since they've shown their belly to the empire. Instead, I hike deep into the mountains, wandering the bamboo groves, gaining strength day by day. The hunting's good once I knap a rough knife and throw together some snares, and there are a few small caves where I can conceal a cooking fire. I don't bother trying to look for my people. The Shidadi have always been good at staying hidden, and with the empire coming down harder on us every day, we've had to become ghosts.

Even ghosts leave traces though, and little by little, I see signs that they're still here—the ashes of a campfire not quite scattered, telltale divots where a snare had been placed. Every sight ignites a new spark of hope. I wonder about my fellow fighters. Are they alive? Have they given me up for dead? I let myself hope, just a little. Several times I see crows flying in unnaturally straight paths. I whistle to them, though none come down to me. Still, it's another sign that my people are around. If I wander these forests long enough, they'll find me.

It happens on my fifth day back. I'm walking the trails when a voice above me calls out. "Who are you, stranger? Speak your name." The words are Amparan, but I smile and reply in Shidadi.

"Dineas, son of Youtab and Artabanos, fighter for Gatha." I don't look up, because any motion would invite at least five arrows to loose from their bows.

"Pull back the hood of your cloak," comes the voice again. Very slowly, I draw my hood back. A caw splits the air. A familiar black blur launches from the leaves, makes two circles around my head, then lands on my shoulder. The feel of claws digging into my shoulder is the best welcome I could hope for.

"Good lad, Preener," I say.

The crow, whom I'd raised and trained from the shell, flaps his wings in reply. Finally, I raise my head to see archers perched in the bamboo above me.

And then a familiar voice calls out. "Neju's sword, it really is Dineas."

I know that voice. I've drilled so often to her commands that I could follow her orders in my sleep. I scan the forest until a short muscular woman steps out from the shadows. Gatha looks older than when I left her. There's more gray in her short cropped hair, and she sports a fresh scar on her face, but I recognize the fierce grin she directs right at me.

"Dineas, son of Youtab and Artabanos. Welcome back from the dead."

# CHAPTER THREE
## ZIVAH

I stand in the midst of a storm.

Soldiers march in from all directions. They line up as they arrive, rigid with imperial precision. From a distance, they appear to be the same imperturbable military machine, but I can see the whites of their eyes, the way they take care not to touch each other.

Word spreads. People from my village come by, take in the scene, and rush back to the bonfire to tell others. Doron walks in front of the line of soldiers, holding a torch to each man's face and searching him for signs of rash or fever. The air around us is thick with fear, and it infects me too, sliding up my arms and settling, cold and damp, on my skin. For a long time, I'm paralyzed, but finally I cast it aside and take a step toward Doron. I don't know what I aim to do, just that I need to help.

Kaylah grabs my arm and pulls me back. "Not yet," she says.

She follows Doron with her eyes, as if staring would grant him the power to cure the illness. Her whisper is urgent in my ear. "Remember. Rose plague is deadly, but its essence is heavy. It clings to the patient and doesn't travel easily through the air. You must not touch the sick if you can help it. Wear plague gloves, wash your hands and face to rid yourself of any essence you pick up." She stops. "You can make it through this, Zivah, if you're careful."

I don't remind her that she'd tested me on this knowledge this very morning. Her words aren't meant to teach. They're meant to reassure, to kindle courage, and they're meant for both of us.

Tal, our village leader, soon orders this part of the village to be set aside as a quarantine and hospital for the soldiers. The paths fill with families hurriedly packing their belongings, strapping them to the backs of household goats. The pack animals pick up on the tension, and the air echoes with their bleating.

As the villagers clear out, I run back and forth between the quarantine area and Kaylah's supply hut, gathering herbs, tinctures, buckets, and washcloths. As I carry a pail of water around a corner, I glimpse my father talking with Kaylah. Something about his expression makes me tuck back out of view.

His voice carries through the air, angrier than I've ever heard it before. "She's too young for this," he says. "You send Zivah in there to attend the soldiers, you send her to her death." The desperation in his voice breaks my heart.

Whatever Kaylah says does not mollify my father, and the arguing continues. I drop the bucket I'm holding and dig my nails into my palms, willing my hands not to shake. If I'm honest with myself, part of me hopes my father will win. The rose plague terrifies me, and I know the worst is yet to come. But to leave the quarantine would be to abandon Kaylah and the other healers, and that I will not do.

In the end though, it doesn't matter what I want, because I have no choice. It's not about my life, or the other healers' lives, or even the soldiers'. It's about our village. If word gets back to the empire that we withheld an able-bodied healer when the soldiers needed attention, all our people would pay the price.

And so my father relents, as I know he must. By dawn, everybody is gone except for four healers and one hundred soldiers. The dust of last night's exodus settles, carrying with it an eerie silence. Any sound, the stomp of boots or a sick soldier's cry, seems strangely dampened.

Doron divides the remaining healthy soldiers into two groups.

"Clear out three cottages and divide the sick among them," he tells one group. He charges the other with digging a trench. When one soldier asks how big the trench should be, Doron falls silent for a moment. "Fifty bodies, at least," he says, his voice flat, and then he heads into the nearest cottage.

More soldiers fall ill by the hour, collapsing and having to be carried in turn by their comrades. There's so much sickness around that it's easy to imagine myself light-headed as well, to sense a prickling on my own skin. I tell myself that the plague takes days to manifest, and force myself to keep working. By evening, eighty of the one hundred soldiers lie on sleeping mats inside our makeshift hospital.

"This isn't natural," Kaylah says. "Rose plague simply doesn't spread this way. Someone must have deliberately infected these soldiers, perhaps with blood in their water or food."

I count the days in my head. Rose plague takes nearly a fortnight to take hold, and the soldiers arrived five days ago. "They weren't infected here."

Everybody nods in agreement. They've been doing the same figures.

"It doesn't bode well for the future," says Zad. "If deliberate infection becomes a weapon of war..."

A soldier calls out for water, his eyes wild with fever delirium. I rush to his side and hold a cup to his lips. Just a day ago, he would have swaggered down our streets, taking what he wished. Should I pity him now? Hate him still?

When I straighten, Doron is beside me. "Come, Zivah," he says. "I have a job for you."

He's been giving me jobs to do all day, but something in his voice tells me this is different. I follow him out the door.

We've divided the foot soldiers into three separate cottages for treatment. Now, though, Doron leads me to a fourth, one that I didn't help set up. Inside is a cot with a single patient. His hair is damp with sweat, his face obscured by fever rash—he looks like any of the others in our care. But finally, I recognize Commander Arxa. It's clear that the sickness has taken a firm hold on him. He tosses his head from side to side, and he mumbles words I can't quite make out. Though his eyes are open, he doesn't see me.

"The Goddess teaches us all lives are equal," says Doron. "But in the empire's eyes, this is the life we must most zealously guard. I'll oversee Arxa's treatment, but I want you to be with him when I can't. Check on him every hour. Let me know immediately if anything looks awry."

The weight of the charge doesn't escape me. "If he doesn't

make it," I say. "The emperor can't possibly blame us for a disease. . . ." I trail off when I see the way Doron is looking at me. He must be at least sixty years old, but this is the first time I've seen him look his age.

"Just keep him alive," Doron says.

# CHAPTER FOUR
## DINEAS

My welcome feast is simple, since any big celebration risks attracting attention. Still, Gatha allots me a double portion of meat. My fellow fighters make obnoxious comments about my umbermarks and shake their heads over how I managed to survive the plague.

"Zenagua had no use for Dineas in her underworld," says Tus, a veteran fighter with a missing eye. "Even goddesses know he's trouble."

I spit a piece of gristle into the fire. "Here's what really happened. Zenagua took one look at my face and deemed me too great a temptation for the maidens of her realm."

"Ha! And she marked you up so you'd leave the live ones be as well."

Pouriya, a warrior one year my senior, comes and clasps my

hands. "Looking handsome, Dineas. You might even have a chance with some of the Dara villagers' goats."

"His face is still prettier than yours, Pouriya," calls another voice.

Laughter erupts, and we settle down to eat. Before I was captured, I hadn't realized how much these feasts meant to me. Our tribe has always shared tight bonds, but there's something about these rare times we let ourselves celebrate, when we face each other rather than stand shoulder to shoulder in combat, that cements what it means to be Shidadi. We have our squabbles and differences, but not in what matters. When I was in prison, I saw power struggles between the soldiers who guarded me, but my people don't have quarter for that. When the enemy surrounds us, we breathe as one and we fight as one.

Still, as much as I've yearned for this, I find it hard to jump into the festivities. It feels too odd to simply fall back into this world. The ghosts of the dungeons still cling to me, and everywhere I look, I see how vulnerable we are, how easily we can be scattered by the empire. Though I'm a continent away from Khaygal, part of me is still there.

Pouriya's still repeating his goat joke—he's always been far too amused at his own wit—and I tune out of the conversation. Instead, I find myself studying everyone, picking up who looks older, who has a new scar, who's not here. There are some definite faces missing, but I don't have the courage to ask after them. Not yet.

Gatha stands up. "Come with me, Dineas."

I'm relieved to obey. She leads me a short distance away and stops at a pile of cloth-wrapped bundles. I swallow reflexively when I realize what she's about to do. Gatha bends over to pick up the first bundle. It's small, but she holds it with both hands and takes great care to unwrap it. She pulls the cloth away to reveal a matched set of daggers.

"These belonged to Stateira," she says. "Lost her in battle last month."

Stateira. She'd been deadly with those daggers. I can still see her crouched with a blade in each hand. She was lightning fast and beautiful, the way she darted in and out of her enemy's reach. She'd kissed me once, in a celebration after a successful raid. A reward, she'd said, for shooting so many dogs that day.

A cold breeze brushes my skin. As I tuck the knives into my belt, I make her a silent promise to use them well.

The next bundle is a set of swords, last used by a man who'd helped me learn to use them as a boy. I balance his swords in my hands, feeling their weight. I wish his spirit well and strap the blades to my back.

Gatha pauses before the last bundle, long enough for me to fear the worst. And when she unwraps a well-polished bow and a quiver of arrows, a fist closes around my heart.

"Your mother's bow," Gatha says gently, as if the weapon were not as recognizable to me as my own skin. "She fought bravely. Took at least three Amparan soldiers with her." This is Gatha's way of telling me what I'd been too afraid to ask. My hands shake when I take the bow—the wood is worn smooth where my mother held it.

When my father died eight years ago, my mother didn't let me cry. Instead, she'd strapped my father's dagger around my waist and pulled the belt tight. *If you love him, Dineas, avenge him.* It was what she'd said then, and what she'd want me to do now. Still, my eyes burn and I turn away. The weight continues to press on my chest.

Gatha's voice is gruff. "I won't lie to you, Dineas. Things have not gotten any easier. The soldiers continue to hunt us. They strike at us from their bases in the valley villages."

I brush the dust off my arms. "Cowards." The villagers have always traded their self-respect for safety, and their cooperation makes it that much easier for Ampara's armies to fight us.

"Maybe, but there may come a time when we need each other. Ampara doesn't stop until it drains you dry. The Dara are starting to realize this."

These are words I'd never expected from Gatha. "Have you been talking to them?"

"A bit." Gatha doesn't elaborate.

We're facing desperate times indeed, if Gatha's thinking of allying with the villagers. But still, how helpful could they be? "They're not warriors. They'd be destroyed in a fight." Ampara forbade them to bear arms when they surrendered, and like sheep, they obeyed.

"Maybe," says Gatha. "But they have strengths and skills that we don't."

I look back toward the campfire. A boy and girl of eight or nine have started an impromptu grappling match, and people gather around to cheer them on and give advice.

"You're heavier, boy. Push your advantage!" one man shouts as a woman tells the fighters to guard their faces.

Suddenly, a cheer erupts. I crane my head to see around the crowd. The girl has her arm snaked around the boy's neck from behind, and after a moment he taps his defeat. Onlookers congratulate the victor and give advice to the loser.

In the aftermath of the contest, I make my way back to the campfire and settle down. It's not long before Tus, the man who'd teased me about being kicked out of Zenagua's underworld, comes to my side.

"Gatha told you?" he says.

He means my mother. I nod, my throat constricting, and keep my eyes on the flames.

Tus lets out a long breath. "We're never really orphans in this tribe," he says. "Shidadi blood runs deep."

I remember now, how Tus had been one of the first to take an interest in me after my father died. There wasn't much my mother couldn't do, but in those few domains where a father's example would have helped, Tus stepped in. When my beard started growing, he showed me how to angle my dagger so I wouldn't cut myself when I shaved. When my shoulders and chest developed a man's muscles, Tus taught me exercises to develop this new strength. Years later, he's still watching out for me.

"Thank you," I say.

"No need for that," he says.

A thin whistle floats through the air. Around me, everything goes silent. We're all intimately familiar with the sound of our sentry's signal.

The man nearest the fire dumps a basket of dirt over it, snuffing out the light. All around me, I hear people taking cover. Someone runs past me, so close that I feel the breeze. Someone else shoves me from the side.

"Move, Dineas," Tus growls. "Have you been gone so long?"

I spring into motion, running for one of the thicker stalks of bamboo. Others who know the terrain better than me will go farther, but I'll take my chances here. It's hard to climb without dropping anything, and my swords knock noisily against my back. But finally I get to a point where the bamboo forks into two stalks, and I wedge one foot in the split. By now, I can see again in the darkness, and I scan the forest floor below. My skin prickles with the possibility of combat. To calm my nerves, I take my bow from my back and run my finger along the wood, lingering around the spot worn smooth by my mother's grip. An image of her face flashes through my mind—sharp, angular, with strength etched into every ridge and shadow. I feel her rough brown hands on my arms and shoulders, adjusting my hold. I hear her voice. *Steady, Dineas. You must be calmer than the enemy.* If I can no longer have her with me, I can at least do her proud.

All around me, the crickets start chirping again. I lift my gaze to see the girl who'd won the wrestling match perched in a tree nearby. She's too young for a sword, but she holds a sling in one hand and a stone in the other. The determination in her face feels familiar. Did I look like that at her age?

The crickets fall silent. Down below, there are faint footsteps, and then I see the purple-and-gold overtunic of an Amparan soldier. At the sight of him, my heart starts to hammer against my chest. Did he follow me? Did I lead him right here? My breaths come harsh and ragged. Screams from the dungeons echo in my ears.

I grit my teeth and force myself to focus. To think. The soldier's alert, but he's not wound up like he's expecting an attack. Most likely, he's just a scout. This man has no idea what's above him—we don't let scouts return to camp after seeing us in the trees.

Nearby, the girl readies her sling. The man only wears a light cap—no helmet. If the girl is as good with the sling as she is a grappler, I've no doubt she can make the kill. Still, I catch her eye and signal her to stop. Her eyes narrow, but I'm her elder, and she obeys.

I draw an arrow and take aim. The string feels tighter than I remember and digs into my fingers now that my calluses are gone, but the movement stays with me. Draw the string, breathe out, hold, release. The arrow buries itself in the soldier's throat, and he sinks to the ground without a sound. I slide down to the forest floor, scanning for his comrades. The empty woods stare back at me.

The girl reaches the body at the same time I do. "Good shot," she says, but there's bitterness in her voice. She thinks I wanted the glory for myself.

I check the soldier's pulse—nothing. As I pull my arm back, my hand brushes against the imperial seal on his tunic.

*I'm on the mainland with Gatha's other top soldiers, trying to steal records from Khaygal outpost. Gatha's created a diversion a quarter league away, and now I'm in the commander's study, digging through tablets for a code key or translated message. I'm looking at one slate with a cryptic list of troop movements when my lookout whistles. I bite back a curse and scan the tablet one more time, trying to commit what I can to memory. Then my lookout whistles again. I put everything back in its place and jump out the window.*

*"Intruder! Stop him!" someone shouts before my feet even touch the*

*ground. I don't look to see who's spotted me—just take off at a dead run. An arrow whistles by my ear and another grazes my arm. Then pain explodes on the back of my thigh. I tumble head over heels, the arrow digging itself deeper with every somersault.*

*As I lie stunned, Amparans close in around me. Someone shouts that they want me captured alive, and that kicks me into action. I fumble for my dagger. Useless against these numbers, but quite effective on myself. I can't let them take me.*

*I look up to see an Amparan guard raising a club. A scream builds in my lungs.*

I swallow the scream at the last moment, but not before a ragged sound escapes my throat. The girl jumps away from me. I realize I've thrown my hand up over my head. I stagger, struggling to get my bearings. My heart is about to burst out of my chest. The girl's staring at me, and I thread my arms under the dead soldier's armpits to hide my confusion. That memory had been far too real.

"Clear me some space in those bushes," I tell the girl. When she continues to stare, I raise my voice. "Move!"

She runs ahead of me, pushing branches aside, and then the two of us start the work of hiding the body. She keeps her distance from me, and I can't blame her. Have I gone mad?

Finally the body's well hidden. I wave the girl away and she runs off. I kick some more leaves over the corpse as I watch her go. She's silent and fast—like a wood sprite, if wood sprites carried slings and had deadly aim. To be honest, I'm not sure why I commanded the girl against taking that shot. She had as much of a right to go for the kill as I did. But then, where would that have led? One kill and then another. In several years she'll be leading raids on the mainland, and one day she'll be captured. For a moment, the future stretches out all too clear. For me, for her, for the boy she wrestled, and for everyone else around the campfire tonight.

And I wonder just how much longer we can endure.

# CHAPTER FIVE
## ZIVAH

Days with our patients bleed into nights, which blur again into sunrise. At first I wonder if I can do it, whether I can work so hard to save men who care nothing for us, who've made our lives difficult in so many ways. I wonder if I should drag my feet, leave their fates to the Goddess. But the plague is no less horrifying when it strikes an enemy, and all men look the same under the fever's hold. And after a while I'm too tired to think about anything at all.

I alternate rounds in the plague-ridden soldiers' cottages with visits to the commander. I mix potions for Arxa morning and night: vel tea for fever, valerian root to help him sleep, a tiny bit of snake venom to keep his blood flowing freely. Doron can find no fault with my treatments, but even our best drafts can only do so much. In his delirium, Arxa relives past battles, and there's one in particular, in the southern deserts, that he commands over and over, ordering cavalry to harry the enemy flank, cursing the adversary for making his archers shoot into the sun. In a quiet moment, he calls for Mehtap, and I wonder if he has a woman back home.

On the fourth day, I'm walking between rows of patients when I hear Zad curse. In the years I've known him, I've never once heard Zad raise his voice, and I run to his side. Zad stares down at the glassy-eyed foot soldier lying on the pallet before us. The man is unnaturally still.

"He won't be the last," he says.

It occurs to me, as we dump the body into the freshly dug mass grave, that I don't know this soldier's name.

Nine more die that day, and then twelve the next. Disposing of the bodies becomes mechanical, and I no longer wonder about their names. The smell of the decomposing dead clings to my skin. At first I dutifully scrub my hands and gloves after disposing of each body, but as my skin begins to redden and crack, I have to stop. It should upset me that I can no longer take these precautions, but it doesn't. Surrounded by so much death, it seems folly to think I will be spared.

On the sixth day, I notice a change in one of my patients. When I give him some water to drink, his eyes fix on mine, and I can tell that he recognizes me.

Hope bubbles up in my chest. "This one," I call to Kaylah. "Is he recovering?"

Kaylah is as exhausted as the rest of us, but her eyes take on that familiar glint of concentration. She examines the patient—checks his pulse, looks in his eyes, and examines his skin.

"What is your name?" she asks.

The soldier's voice comes out as a rasp. "Piruz."

"Who is your commander?"

"Arxa, commander third rank."

His answers are promising. The rose plague fever sometimes burns away a patient's memories, but this man seems to know who he is. As Kaylah continues to question him though, I begin to worry. He looks to be gaining strength by the moment, yet his marks are still red. Finally, Kaylah gives the man a sleeping draft to help him rest. As he drifts into slumber, I see pity in Kaylah's eyes instead of the relief I'd hoped for.

"He will survive," she confirms. "And he made it through the fever with his wits intact. But he is rosemarked."

A wave of helpless rage overtakes me. What cruel disease is this, that hands out hope only to take it away? This man might have wrested his life back for a few years, but he'll live out that time in isolation. I look down at the sleeping soldier, who seems unaware as yet of his new fate, and in my mind's eye I see Kaylah bedridden, covered with rosemarks, Doron burning with fever, and Zad raving with delirium. I suck in a breath and look away. I sense Kaylah's eyes on me, but she doesn't say a word.

More days, more deaths. Some others beat the fever and emerge with rose- or umbermarks. In his private cottage, Commander Arxa continues to battle his own illness. I've spent so much time with him that I've learned the patterns of his ramblings. Sometimes I give his battle commands alongside him. I even start bringing him good news from his imaginary war, in hopes that it might ease his mind and rally his spirit to fight. Other times I have nonsensical conversations with him about the mysterious Mehtap. I decide that she is his daughter, because of the protective way he speaks of her.

On the ninth day, I check on him at dawn and see his marks faded to a dull brown. His forehead is covered with sweat, but no longer hot to the touch. I can't believe it at first, and I walk around him, looking at him from different angles of light. It's the same from every direction.

When I step closer, his eyes flutter open.

"Zivah," he whispers.

It startles me that he knows my name.

The commander looks around him, taking in his surroundings. "Where are my men?" he asks. "How many fell ill?"

I open my mouth to reply, but instead I break down into incoherent sobs. Doron comes tearing into the room, ashen, but I shake my head and point toward the still-disoriented commander. It takes me several tries to get the word "umbermarks" out clearly enough to be understood. By then, Doron is already at Arxa's side, seeing his condition for himself. And a layer of fatigue lifts off his face.

Doron puts a hand on my shoulder. "Good work, Zivah. The commander is alive because of your care."

The commander is one of the last to break the disease's hold, and it doesn't take much longer for the rest of the soldiers to die or pull through.

In another few days, the troops are ready to leave. The battalion of a hundred that had so proudly ridden into Dara is now reduced to half its size. Leading them are the lucky twenty who never contracted the disease. Then there are their eight comrades who fell ill and emerged umbertouched, though two of them have fever amnesia and remember very little of their life before their illness. They will return to their families, who will have the task of reintroducing them into society. Last are the fifteen rosemarked, whom Arxa has separated into their own group to travel back. There are so many of them that we don't have enough cloth to make plague veils for all of them. It's hard to look at these soldiers' faces, because they have the hollow, hopeless stares of dead men. Central Ampara has strict laws regarding its rosemarked, stricter than ours. These men will live ten more years if they're lucky, one year if they're not. Either way, it's likely they'll never see their families again. Despite my general distaste for their kind, I can't help but pity them.

Commander Arxa comes to speak to me as the soldiers line up to march. "You have my gratitude, Zivah. I may not have been in my right mind, but I remember enough to know that you spared no effort to save me."

I don't know how to respond. Comforting Arxa when he was my patient felt natural, but now he's once more the hand of the empire, still weak from his illness, yet strong enough to destroy our village with a word.

Thankfully, he doesn't seem to expect a reply. "You clearly possess great potential. I have friends in the Imperial Academy of Medicine who could arrange for you to study there. Would that be of interest to you? I suspect they'd have as much to learn from Dara's healing arts as you would from them."

Again, I'm speechless, but for a different reason. Sehmar City's medical academy is legendary. Even in Dara, I've heard of the great physicians who've studied and taught there, and of their library, which collects medical texts from all corners of the empire. Amparan understanding of herb lore is unremarkable compared to ours, but their surgeons are said to be so skilled they can sever and tie off single blood vessels. I'd never even dreamed of being able to learn from them.

"I..." I manage to stammer. "I would be honored, Commander."

Arxa gives a brisk nod. "I will send word."

Kaylah comes to stand by me as the troops ride off. "The Imperial Academy," she says. "The knowledge you could bring back to our people..."

I can hardly dare to think about it. If the commander proves to be a man of his word, then some good might come out of this whole ordeal after all. But the sight of our recently emptied hospital keeps my hope in check. First, I must survive the next ten days.

The healers allow ourselves a day of rest before resuming our battle against the disease. Men from the village bring in three of our own who fell ill with rose plague. Zad takes over their care, while the rest of us begin the work of cleaning up.

The makeshift hospitals have to be scrubbed. The sleeping mats, rags, and blankets have to be burned. It's hard, backbreaking work, but I attack it with obsessive ferocity, scrubbing until my arms ache, rubbing away the foul residue of sickness. After days of helplessness in the face of active disease, expelling its final traces feels like a battle I can win. I volunteer to make trips to the well for water, relishing the burn in my legs and the buckets' weight on my shoulders. Everything I feel is proof that I'm still alive. I just need to hang on for another fortnight, and then I will know that the plague has passed me over.

I don't even make it two days. On my third trip to the well, I collapse.

It's like my test all over again—faces swimming in and out of view, disembodied voices talking about me, though I cannot make sense of anything they say. My skin burns, yet I shiver incessantly. In my dreams, I see rows of dying soldiers. I mix endless batches of potions for them and coax them to drink. Sometimes the soldiers morph into my sisters, sometimes into the other healers.

I do have some moments of clarity. I wake a few times to see Kaylah or Doron or Zad by my bed. A few times, I choke on whatever they hold to my lips. I look down at my arms and see red, and some part of me knows that this is a bad thing. But those moments are few, interspersed with dreams and hallucinations. I am at the fever's mercy.

When my mind finally clears, it takes me a while to figure out that I'm in the same cottage that housed Arxa. Kaylah sits at my bedside, watching me. I think back to my last coherent memory of walking to the well, and then to the confusion that came afterward. I remember that even in my madness, I'd looked down at my arms and seen the bright marks of plague.

But what color are they now? I close my eyes, and I thank the Goddess for sparing me. And then I pray, harder than I've ever prayed before, that my marks will be brown.

I look down. Bloodred splotches stare back at me. Still I deny it. Maybe it's too early. Maybe the marks just need more time to fade. But then I look at Kaylah's face, and I see the tears she's holding back.

"I'm sorry, Zivah," she whispers.

It's hard to hear her voice over the sound of my own heartbeat. My mind whirls with numbers. I'm seventeen right now. One year from now, I will be eighteen. In ten, I will be twenty-seven. That's the best I can hope for, if I'm one of the lucky ones. Where will I go? What will I do? I try to breathe, but there's no air.

"I'm so sorry," Kaylah says again.

Everything around me comes into focus. The leaves blowing outside, the trickle of the water clock in the corner. I'm aware of every drop that falls. I'd never noticed how quickly they come.

Kaylah reaches to take my hands, as she so often had before. Except this time, she's wearing plague gloves. The leather is worn soft from use, but there is no warmth in its touch.

# PART TWO

## THREE MONTHS LATER

# CHAPTER SIX
## ZIVAH

Spasms run through me. I've long since vomited up the contents of my stomach, but wave after wave still grips me until I think I might die. No, that's not right. I know I'm dying, but for this hour of misery, I have no one to blame but myself.

I'm huddled behind my cottage, crouched on the ground because my legs are too shaky to hold me. Once again, I go through the workings of my potion, the theory behind the disease. Rose plague essence is heavy and sticky, hard for the body to purge. The umbertouched somehow rid themselves completely of the disease, whereas the rosemarked dislodge all but a remnant, which clings to some unknown region of the body.

My recent attempts have focused on the liver, because I've noticed a yellower tint to my skin since I fell ill. A tincture of chozat to strengthen the organ, a drop of nadat-root juice to expel the disease essence, plus boiled syeb petals to stabilize the body's energies. It seemed a good mixture, but now I'm on my knees, and the rosemarks show no sign of disappearing. The problem with expelling such a stubborn illness is that anything powerful enough to do the job wreaks havoc on the rest of my body as well.

At times like these, I'm glad to be in isolation. At least no one else is here to witness my recklessness, and my failure.

"Zivah?" Leora's voice floats toward me from the direction of the village.

A tiny groan—the most I can muster right now—escapes my lips. I do my best to stand, but another spasm hits me and I collapse again. And on the heels of the spasm, as predictable as the plague's steady march, comes the despair. Another potion, another failure. I don't know how much longer I can keep on hoping.

Light footsteps come up behind me.

"Zivah!" I can imagine the shock on Leora's face. "What—"

"Stay back!" My throat is raw, but for this, I manage to shout. Rose plague travels through touch and through the bodily humors, and Leora forgets caution when she's upset.

Behind me, her footsteps stop, and I count it a small blessing. "Stay back," I repeat, more quietly now. "I'm all right. I promise."

I'm hardly convincing, doubled over as I am. If a vomiting fit is bad when I'm alone, it's ten times worse when I have an audience, especially when I know the audience will be sorely disappointed in me.

Finally the fit passes. Everything aches, and I'm tempted to lie down and never get up again. When I finally turn around, Leora looks just as stricken as I'd expected.

She shakes her head. "Zivah, I would give my own life if I knew it would cure you, but are you sure these experiments are safe?"

"They are," I lie. "The potion just upset my stomach, that's all."

Leora simply looks at me, and I can see her concern warring with her desperate wish to believe me. It's maddening. I know so much of herb lore. I've memorized the makings of hundreds of drafts and invented dozens of others. But despite my years of study, despite the skill that everyone tells me I have, I cannot cure myself.

Truth is, Leora doesn't even know the true extent of my efforts, how I stay up every night reading scrolls by candlelight, searching for some secret that will scrub these marks from my skin. For every time that Leora or Kaylah found me ill from my experiments, there are five more where I've suffered alone. Perhaps my efforts are futile, but what else can I do when the alternative is to quietly accept my death?

I collect my feet under me. With a firm grip on the bamboo frame of my cottage, I pull myself to standing. "It's not your normal time to visit."

I can see Leora trying to decide whether to let me change the subject. "I finished my bridal veil." She stops, and suddenly looks unsure. "I thought you might like to see it."

I brighten. Leora's been working on her veil for months. "Of course. Take it to the sitting area."

As Leora disappears around the corner, I hobble to the water basin to rinse out my mouth. Afterward, I lean against it, staring at the mottled red patterns on my hands. It's been long enough now that I'm no longer surprised to see the rosemarks on my skin. I can feel them though, a heaviness in my limbs that follows me throughout the day. The scrolls tell me it's not a common symptom of the disease, but then, the scrolls have never been ill.

"Goddess," I whisper, "I could serve you so much better if you granted me a cure." It's a prayer I've uttered many times, and I'm ashamed at the desperation in my voice. As always, I get no response.

By the time I walk on shaky legs to the front of my house, Leora is settled under the awning where I entertain guests, seated in one of the four chairs I never touch. She unfolds her veil and lets it flutter in the breeze. My breath catches as I come closer. As a journeywoman seamstress, Leora's stitchwork has always been fine, but she's poured her heart into this one. Embroidered into the green headdress are paired butterflies, symbols of love. Their iridescent wings seem to flap with every ripple of the silk. Interwoven between the butterflies are vines, flowers, and dazzling patterns. My fingers itch to touch the fine stitches, but I grab the hem of my tunic instead.

"It's beautiful."

She gives a modest smile. "Thank you. I'm working on Alia's headdress now."

It's a sister's duty to carry incense ahead of the bride and make the paths fragrant for her arrival. My rosemarks keep me from taking part in the celebrations, although my younger sister has promised to carry for both of us. It should be a beautiful ceremony, and Leora a radiant bride.

Suddenly, I don't want to talk about the wedding anymore.

I stand. "I should tend to my creatures. Come with me?"

I start walking before Leora can reply, though I hear her follow several steps behind me. We used to walk hand in hand, but now the rule is five paces apart.

A great many things have changed since I fell ill. Treating patients is out of the question, of course. A rosemarked healer makes about as much sense as a tone-deaf minstrel. I've had to move to a house away from the village, and my only duty these days is to raise poisonous creatures and harvest venom for potions. Doron thinks the venoms are powerful enough to resist the rose plague essence, and there are so few trained healers that we can't afford to waste my skills. It's not a horrible existence, and I know things could have been much worse. In Central Ampara, I would have been quarantined outside the city and left to die.

But there are still difficult days. The hardest was when Commander Arxa's messenger came to Dara with a formal invitation to the Imperial Academy. I sent my regrets, and then went to bed for the rest of the day.

I keep my venomous pets in a shed specially built to house them. There are shelves for all the cages, and an open space between the walls and the roof to let the light in. The snakes need to be milked once a day, as do the scorpions. For the spiders, I place mock insects into their webs to attract bites. Those, I collect every two days.

My purple-crowned serpent is bobbing and weaving in her cage when I open the door. I whistle a soothing tone as I approach.

"You love Gil, then?" I ask Leora, who watches from the doorway. "He's the one you want to live out your life with?"

There is joy in her eyes as she replies. "He is very good to me. And he will be a good father to our children."

I feel a twinge that I tell myself isn't envy. I love Leora dearly, and she deserves all the happiness that's coming to her. I say it silently to myself, and then I repeat it again.

Diadem flicks her tongue at me when I open her cage. She's usually a peaceful creature, and I'm not sure what's bothering her. I reach for her slowly, ready to pull back if she strikes, but she simply slithers up my hand and anchors her tail around my wrist. I wince at the strength of her grip. With my other hand I pick up a jar covered with deer gut, and Diadem rears her head high. When I change the tone of my whistle, the snake strikes, embedding her fangs in the lid. The move calms her somewhat, but she's still not herself. I decide to keep her on me as I move to the next cage. I wouldn't have spent so much effort on the creatures before I fell ill, but these days they're my most consistent companions, and I do my best to keep them content.

With Diadem firmly anchored on my upper arm, I move on to the blackarmor scorpion. "Send my well-wishes to Gil," I say. "I'd like to have him visit sometime, if he is willing."

It's not the first time I've extended the invitation, but somehow I know that Leora will continue to come alone. Leora doesn't respond right away, and I feel guilty for putting her in a position where she must make excuses for her betrothed.

She looks toward the clearing. "Someone's coming."

I place the scorpion back in its cage and step outside. A man I don't recognize is coming down the trail from the village. His shin-length tunic is trimmed in imperial purple and he is escorted by two soldiers—a messenger from the central empire. The man stops short at the sight of me, and a flash of distaste crosses his face. I can't tell what bothers him more: my rosemarks or the snake on my arm.

"I seek Zivah, the rosemarked healer of Dara," he says.

That title vexes me. I see Leora pull her shoulders back.

"I am she," I say.

The messenger pulls out a clay tablet the size of his hand. "I bear a message from Commander Arxa."

The commander again? "I sent my regrets with the previous messenger. I cannot go to the Imperial Academy because of my illness."

The man gives me a patronizing look over the bridge of his nose. "He has received your message and is saddened to learn of your illness. Commander Arxa has recently given a large portion of his personal wealth to expand the rosemarked colony in Sehmar City. He now extends an invitation for you to serve as a healer there, if it is of interest to you."

I'd never heard of the rosemarked colony in Sehmar, though I'd assumed there must have been something like it. "He would like me to travel there?"

"More healers are needed at the colony, as many of the untouched healers are unwilling to go. The commander adds that as a healer in the capital, you will have an opportunity to work with other physicians within the compound, as well as access to scrolls from the Imperial Academy."

I can sense Leora's eyes on me. The Academy still holds its

allure, but it's such a long journey away. To travel so far from my family when I don't know how many years I have left...

As if sensing my ambivalence, the messenger speaks again. "The commander doesn't require a response right away. I am only to deliver the message, and you may send word to him when you're ready. This invitation will serve as a travel document, should you choose to make the journey." He places the tablet on the ground in front of him, and his bow this time is clearly an invitation for dismissal.

"Thank you for your message. Consider it delivered," I say.

With another bow, the messenger and his escorts disappear into the bamboo.

Leora speaks as soon as they're gone. "Will you go?"

I pick up Arxa's invitation by the edges, as if it were harboring disease instead of me. There is a note authorizing my travel as a rosemarked person, along with the commander's seal. "No," I say, though my answer is a heartbeat slow. "It wouldn't make sense." Still, I wonder what it would be like to live and work alongside other rosemarked.

"Zivah," Leora says gently. "You don't have to stay here just for us."

"I'm not." I spin back toward the shed, throwing the door open with a bit more force than necessary. "I want to stay."

Leora doesn't reply, and we speak again of her wedding as I finish up my chores. She takes her leave after I finish, and I return to my cottage. In the corner nearest the door is a basket I keep for clay shards. I take out the commander's invitation and prepare to dash it against the others. There's no way I can make the journey, and no reason to let good clay go to waste. Still, my hand doesn't move.

After a long moment, I step back. I have a pile of scrolls on shelves near my bed, and I tuck the tablet underneath. I step back for a while, staring at the scrolls, before finally continuing with my tasks for the day.

# CHAPTER SEVEN
## DINEAS

This place is too neat. Even with a wide-brimmed hat tilted low over my face, I can see the carefully cleared dirt paths, the delicate bamboo cottages. Everything is in its place. Nothing shows arrow dents or char marks. The people, too, are well fed and unmarked. I don't look at them directly, but I glimpse how smooth their skin is, how whole they are. After months back among my people, where you can't walk into a crowd without seeing scars, bandages, and missing limbs, the difference is striking. If Gatha hadn't ordered me here, I'd walk right back out to the mountains.

*Unusual times call for unusual allies*, Gatha had said. Over the past months, she's been meeting secretly with Tal, the leader of the Dara villagers. Now there's enough trust to set up a better way of communicating. That's where my crows and I come in.

I can see the sense in this new alliance, and I'll follow Gatha's orders to my death if need be. Gods know, if she asks me to ally myself with a nanny goat, I'd braid the creature's beard myself. If my warlord's decided to work with these villagers, I'll do my best to help her.

But that doesn't mean I have to respect them.

It's a humid summer afternoon, nearing evening. I'm dressed like a Dara man in a coarse tunic and trousers, and the moisture from the air coats my skin. My hat hides my darker complexion and lighter hair from casual observers, but anyone who comes close would know I'm not from here. It can't be helped though. The crows must be trained in daylight, so the best I can do is pick a time when Amparan soldiers are unlikely to show, and hope for the best. And if any of the villagers see me . . . well, Dara's leader assures Gatha that his people have little reason to turn me in. I hope he's right.

A shadow flits over me—probably Slicewing, who likes to fly low. I repeat Gatha's directions to myself as I walk. Second path from the south, then down a side trail to a well surrounded by three cottages. According to Gatha, the village leader lives in the biggest of these three. I could knock on the door, but there's a cluster of women standing by the well. Instead, I circle to the back of the cottage and knock on the window shutters.

After a few moments, a man peers out. He's a little older than Gatha, with some white in his short black hair. Like the others, he's soft and well fed. But I suppose he looks as much like a leader as any of them.

"Village leader Tal?" Since I don't speak the Dara language, I address him in Amparan.

When he nods, I tilt my hat back. "Gatha sent me."

His eyes flicker over my face. "Wait there," he says, and ducks out of view. A few moments later, he comes around the corner. "Did anybody take notice of you?"

At least he feels no need for pointless talk. I shake my head.

"Good." Tal looks around nervously. "An imperial messenger came to the village this morning with an escort of three soldiers. If the Goddess smiles on us, you won't cross paths with them, but it's best to be on your guard."

If the Dara Goddess is anything like our gods, I'd best keep my own lookout. "And if they see me with you?"

Tal smiles grimly. "I'd rather not find out."

All the more reason to get this done fast.

I look to the sky and whistle sharply. A few moments later, Slicewing spirals down and lands on my shoulder. Scrawny alights on a nearby rock, and I hold out my hand for Preener to land. The birds cock their heads to look at me.

"Tal," I say to them. "Learn Tal." The three crows launch again in a flutter of wings. Tal cranes his head and watches them circle overhead.

"Hold out your hand," I tell him.

After a few moments, Scrawny glides down to land on his arm. The crow must have dug in his claws, because Tal winces. Preener and Slicewing settle nearby.

I hand him a tattered blue handkerchief. "I'll send a bird to fly over your house every day at dawn. If you have a message for Gatha, hang this outside and the bird will land. Least suspicious place would be to hang it out with your wash." I take out a thin piece of leather, roll it up, and tie it to the skinny part of Scrawny's leg, barking at the bird to hold still when he fidgets. "Roll up your message and tie it like so. They get surly sometimes, but you just have to show them you're in command."

Tal doesn't look like he completely believes me, but he gives a deliberate nod. "Thank you."

I shrug off his thanks and whistle for the birds to follow me out of the village. Slicewing launches into the air, and the other two take wing moments after. The sun's getting close to setting now, and I pass more villagers on the paths, mostly coming from the direction of the crop terraces. No one stops me, though I get a few curious looks. I'm almost back into the forest when I hear someone speaking in Amparan.

"Be ready to leave at dawn tomorrow for Sehmar City."

A shiver goes up my spine, and I stop in my tracks. That must be the messenger that Tal mentioned.

Their voices get louder. Up ahead of me, my path meets another trail. It sounds like they're coming from that direction, though a cottage blocks my view. I cast around for somewhere to hide.

"The village leader looks less happy to see you every time you come."

"He's lucky the village didn't get razed with what happened to Arxa's troops. He'll behave himself. If not, well, that's why you have your swords, right?"

Laughter follows. Bastards.

The path is frustratingly free of vegetation or cover. There's a goat pen, but the fence is too low to hide anything. I edge toward the cottage, thinking that I can try to keep it between me and the speakers.

A memory forces itself before my eyes.

*I'm chained to the wall of the dungeon. The interrogator stands in front of me, whip in hand. I prepare myself for another lash, but he stops and looks to the door.*

*"Commander Arxa, what an honor for you to visit."*

*A shadow looks in from the doorway. I can hardly see him through the swollen slits of my eyes, but I can feel the force of his gaze.*

*"Make sure you get what you need out of him." The commander's voice rumbles like a cavalry stampede.*

"You, over there. What are you doing?"

Three soldiers and an Amparan messenger stand where the paths meet. All four of them are staring at me. Cursed gods, of all the times to get thrown into the past...

I keep my head down and do my best to imitate Tal's accent. "My goat got loose... sir... and I chased him here." My palms begin to sweat. I clench my fists for lack of anything better to do with them. Do the villagers keep their goats penned up? I'm not even sure the bleating I heard on my way over really *was* a goat.

The soldier squints at me, and suspicion enters his voice. "It's almost dark. Why are you still wearing a hat?"

"Easier than carrying it, sir." I look at him from under the brim as he comes closer. He's bigger than I am. Right-handed, judging from the relative size of his arms. My pulse quickens and heat pumps through my veins. My fingers itch for the daggers strapped under my tunic. I'll die before I let them capture me again.

"Take it off," he says. "I want to see your face." He's five paces away now.

I bite back a curse.

"Yes, sir," I say as the Amparan dog stops in front of me. I lift my left hand to the brim of my hat.

Then I drive my other fist into the soldier's face.

The man reels from my blow. I'd hoped to knock him out, but he's still very much awake. He cups his hand over his broken nose, and his creative use of Amparan swear words raises my opinion of him considerably. As his comrades shout in confusion, I turn tail and run. Dara men and women jump out of my way as I sprint to the border of the village and finally to the cover of the bamboo groves. I hear the soldiers behind me, their boots grinding the dirt as they call to each other about where I am.

It's getting darker by the moment, and I can barely see the bamboo stalks blocking my path. I've hardly breathed a prayer against stepping into a fox burrow when my foot lands sideways on a stone and twists. Pain shoots up my leg. For a moment I stand there, doubled over, sucking in air through my teeth. Then I hear more shouts. I clench my jaw and take another step. More pain, and I borrow a few phrases I'd just learned from that soldier. I grit my teeth and limp on, but it feels as if I'm dragging a wild dog by the fangs.

Suddenly, the forest falls away, and I break through into another clearing. I stumble to a halt. I'd thought I was heading away from the village, but ahead of me is another cottage. Did I get turned around?

I limp along the edge of the clearing, trying to get my bearings. A faint light leaks through the shutters of the cottage—there's someone in there. There's also a small shed, which looks to be dark. I drag myself over, and the door swings open easily.

As the shouts behind me get louder, I step inside and pull the door closed.

Not much light makes it through the opening between the walls and the roof, so I feel my way forward gingerly. My hands slide over bamboo crates, and I take care not to knock anything over. This shed is still too exposed for comfort, but I'm hoping there's some place in back where I can hide, or if need be, put up a good last stand.

I'm halfway to the back wall when a hiss sounds in my ear. Did I imagine that?

The hiss sounds again.

My eyes are beginning to adjust to the darkness. I can see my hands when I raise them to guard my face. As I stand there trying to make sense of what I hear, the shadowy shape of a giant scorpion materializes right in front of my eyes.

*Neju's sword.* I stumble back and collide with the shelf behind me. Crates crash down, a few cracking ominously as they hit the ground. As hisses fill the air, I realize that these aren't supply crates I've knocked over. They're cages, and I'm pretty sure the creatures they hold aren't the type I want roaming free.

They call Monyar "Death's Antechamber," and for good reason. This land is packed with snakes, scorpions, and spiders. Lethal bites are so common that the local healers raise the creatures and milk them for antivenom.

Looks like I've stumbled upon someone's private collection.

As the racket dies down, the sound of footsteps drifts in from outside. I swallow another curse.

"Hello?" It's a woman—probably the healer. At least it's not the soldiers. Still, I reach for my dagger and step carefully toward the door.

"Is anyone here?" The footsteps stop outside. I raise my knife.

The door opens to reveal a woman holding a candle. As her eyes lock on me, I grab her by the collar and pull her in. The door shuts behind us, and I push her against the wall.

"One scream from you and I cut your throat."

Miraculously, she keeps her grip on the candle. Though the flame sputters, its light reflects off my blade.

She's scared. I can tell by the rapid rise and fall of her chest. But when she replies, she speaks with a low, steady whisper. "I'm rosemarked, stranger. Spill my blood, and you'll follow me into death."

Rosemarked? Why is a patient wandering outside at night? If she's bluffing, she chose the wrong lie. "I'm umbertouched," I say.

I feel her muscles tense as she weighs my words. Slowly, she lifts her candle until it illuminates both our faces. She's younger than I expected, and I see the telltale rosemarks on her skin. Her gaze sweeps across my face and hands as well. The surprise in her expression likely mirrors my own.

"You're a Shidadi tribesman," she says.

I don't reply. Shouts echo in from outside. The words are muffled, but it's clear enough there's a search going on. A shrewd look crosses the woman's face, and it makes me uneasy. If she decides to call for help, I don't think I could actually cut her throat. I despise this healer as much as any of her fellow villagers, but I'm not a murderer.

"You're immune to rose plague," she says.

Why is she repeating the obvious? I may not kill her, but I decide I have no problem with giving her a solid knock on the head. I shift my knife to expose the hilt.

Her eyes flicker to my hand. "Are you immune to snakes?"

By the time I make sense of her words, something long and muscular is already wrapping itself around my arm. I look down to see a reptilian head topped with a triangle pattern my people have long since learned to fear. A layer of cold sweat erupts over my skin.

"Drop your knife," the healer says.

The snake winds its way up my arm, then anchors its tail on my bicep. It flicks its tongue in the direction of my face and I turn away. They say that the bite of a purple-crowned serpent feels like being burned alive.

I drop the knife.

"I wouldn't really have killed you," I say through gritted teeth. It occurs to me that I may be less than convincing under these circumstances.

She sets her candle on a wall holder. "Diadem is gentle. She only bites if provoked, or if I ask her to. Stay still."

The snake bobs its head back and forth as the healer runs her hands over my body. Word around the Shidadi camp is that Dara maidens are modest, but this one's not shy at all about where she puts her hands. I'd enjoy it more if there wasn't a snake bobbing within kissing distance from my face. It's not long before she discovers the daggers at my waist. I remain silent as she removes them, but I can't help sucking in a breath when she presses on my injured ankle.

"Are you hurt?"

"Zenagua take you," I snarl.

She runs her hand over the swelling. "It's not broken, but you'll risk much greater harm if you run any farther tonight. Put your hands behind your back. Move slowly, or you'll startle the snake."

As if she needed to remind me. Rough twine digs into my skin.

"Do you know what the empire will do to me if you turn me over?" I say. "You might as well kill me now. It would be a mercy."

Her only response is to pull the knots tighter. Then she circles around to look at me again. I must look sufficiently subdued, because she holds out her hand to the snake and whistles a low tone. My limbs go weak as the accursed creature finally slides off my arm.

"You lost your right to counsel me when you drew that knife," she says.

The healer takes a quick look around the shed and bends down to inspect the cages I'd knocked over. She lifts some of them back onto the shelves, and then frowns at a small cage that's splintered open. "You've freed one of my scorpions. It's probably already found its way outside, but you might want to avoid making sudden movements."

Then she takes the candle and walks out.

# CHAPTER EIGHT
## ZIVAH

I shut the shed door, slamming the crossbar down so hard the entire structure shudders. Then I collapse against the shed, wrapping my trembling fingers around the bar and squeezing until my knuckles turn white. I can still hear the Shidadi warrior's voice, see the light reflecting off his dagger. If I hadn't had Diadem on my wrist, or if he'd acted just a moment faster...

That nomad is almost certainly the reason for the earlier commotion. I don't know why Amparan soldiers were after him, but now I must decide what to do. The man just tried to kill me. I owe him nothing, and I could be punished greatly if I'm found to be helping him. Yet something about his plea for mercy clings to my skin—the desperation, the familiar specter of having suffered at Ampara's hands.

Leaves rustle, and an Amparan soldier steps into view. He stops in his tracks, disoriented by the sudden absence of foliage. Then his eyes focus on me.

"Who are you?"

He addresses me like a servant, and I feel myself straightening in reaction to his tone. In that moment, I make my decision. "Stay back, soldier, I'm rosemarked."

My words have their usual effect. The soldier stumbles away from me, and I speak again while I have the advantage. "What is it you seek?"

"I seek a fugitive. He was running in this direction." He looks at my cottage, at the shed, at the surrounding forest. Anything except me. Though the Goddess frowns on deception, I feel no guilt as I frame my lie.

"I came out to tend to my serpents. I've seen nothing awry."

The soldier takes another step back at the mention of serpents. When he notices me watching, he clears his throat, doing his best to regain his authority. "Send word to the village if you see anything suspicious."

Just then, another soldier runs into the clearing. He takes a step toward me, but his comrade shouts, "Stop! She's plague-ridden."

As if I cannot hear every word he's saying.

I bow my head. "Thank you, sirs, for the warning about the fugitive. I will send notice if I see anything unusual. You are free to search my house, but as a healer I cannot guarantee your safety from infection." My palms are sweating, and I'm sure my face gives me away, but the soldiers seem more interested in keeping their distance than evaluating my truthfulness.

The first soldier turns to the other. "Come," he says. "If he's hiding here, the plague will get him for us." I suppose they didn't get a good look at the nomad's umbermarks.

"Be careful in the dark, sirs," I add as they turn to go. "One of my scorpions just escaped its cage."

The soldiers walk faster.

After they're gone, I return to my cottage. I can see the shed through my window, and my nervous gaze wanders repeatedly back as I gather my things. I think I tied the nomad securely, but there's no way to be sure, and I won't risk opening the door again to check. Hanging on a hook by my bed is the blowgun I use to hunt the occasional wren or fox. The darts won't fell a man, but at least they would slow him down. I slip the dart blower under my sash. It's as long as my arm and hampers my walking, but I feel safer.

Now there's the question of what to do with my prisoner. Our leader, Tal, should be told about the nomad in our midst. I'm only allowed to approach our village during a crisis, but I think these circumstances warrant it. First though, I must wait until the Amparans have given up their search, which means I should at least wait until morning. The nomad should be able to survive overnight without food or water. Not comfortably, perhaps, but he gave up his claim to comfort when he raised a knife to my throat.

I bar my door shut before I go to bed and sleep fully clothed. All night, I toss under my blankets, startling awake at the slightest sound, and it's only near dawn when I fall into a deeper slumber.

When I awaken again, the sun is bright. At first I'm unsure what woke me, but then a cacophony of birdcalls draws me to the window. Several dark shapes circle the shed, beating their wings and chattering at the top of their lungs. I remember hearing before that the nomads tame crows.

I grab my dart blower and step outside.

"Go!" I wave the tube at the birds, and they fly higher. "Leave before I shoot you down."

Between the indignant cawing and fluttering of wings, I don't even notice the nomad woman until she's five steps away. When I finally see her, my shouts die on my lips. She's the fiercest-looking woman I've ever seen—older and shorter than me, but she has the look of a boulder with her muscular arms and thick chest. If the nomad man I faced earlier was a lightning bolt, I have no doubt that this woman is the thundercloud behind him.

The woman stops abruptly, puzzled. "A cottage out here?" she asks in Amparan. She stands with a forward tilt, as if ready to charge.

I raise my blowgun. The nomad woman's eyes widen and she puts up her hands appeasingly. Then the leaves part again, and our village leader steps out. Tal? The nomad woman only gives him a cursory glance.

Tal's mouth drops open. "Zivah," he says. He turns to the nomad. "Why are we—"

The nomad woman points to the shed. "My man's in there."

Tal stares at the shed. "You are sure?"

"That's what the crows say."

I look between them, trying to make sense of what's happening. The two of them speak like they know each other, and there seems to be confusion but no ill will between them. If that's true, then what does that say about the man in the shed?

"Zivah," says Tal. "Is this true? Warlord Gatha is a friend of our village. You may speak freely."

When did Tal start dealing with Shidadi warlords? The two of them are quite the mismatched pair. Tal's a head taller than she and about half as wide, though they address each other as equals.

"I found a nomad warrior in my shed," I say. "He tried to kill me."

Tal straightens in alarm, and Gatha mutters something under her breath. She's not pleased, but her ire doesn't seem directed at me.

"Are you hurt?" Tal asks.

"No. I was able to subdue him. That's why he's locked in the shed."

Gatha stops muttering and looks me up and down. "You teach your girls to fight?" she asks Tal.

Tal gives a weak shake of his head. "No," he says. "Zivah is a healer. She—"

"I have a purple-headed serpent that responds to my commands."

Gatha gives a low whistle. It's hard to tell, but Tal seems to be suppressing a smile.

"Well, you've sparked my curiosity, young healer," says Gatha, "and I apologize for my warrior. Is he hurt?"

"He twisted an ankle, but he should be otherwise unharmed. That is, unless he's found some way to provoke one of my creatures."

This time, Tal's shoulders are definitely shaking.

Gatha takes one step closer. "May I speak with him?"

I glance at Tal, who nods. I still don't understand what he's doing, but he's never given me reason to doubt him.

"Come this way." I turn toward the shed. "Be careful not to touch anything. I'm rosemarked, and I don't take precautions within my own home."

# CHAPTER NINE
## DINEAS

My crows have gotten a lot more... exuberant in my absence. When I woke in the middle of the night to find Slicewing in the shed with me, I could have kissed that bird square on her crooked beak. Sending her off with a command to bring Gatha had seemed a good move at the time. But when I'm woken hours later by what can only be described as a crow screaming contest outside, I'm no longer so sure. It's morning now, and I sorely hope that the Amparans have already left. I make a mental note to work with my birds on subtlety—that is, if I make it out alive.

I open my mouth to quiet the dratted crows, but my parched throat only produces a croak. My limbs creak from being in the cold all night, and I have rope burns on my wrist. My ankle's swelled to twice its size.

Then I hear human voices under the crows. They're speaking

Amparan, but it doesn't sound like soldiers. One voice sounds blessedly familiar.

The door swings open. I squint up at the light to see the healer at the door. Behind her stand Gatha and Tal.

Gatha looks down at me with a mixture of curiosity and amusement. "Well, Dineas, I worried when you didn't return, but I never imagined finding you on the floor of a healer's shed. I sent you to Dara to build bonds, not to pull a blade on a passerby."

I bow my head, an awkward act since I'm trussed up like a pig. "Sorry."

But I can't help wonder. If Gatha spent a year in the Amparan dungeons, would she still be willing to let her freedom hang on the goodwill of a Dara stranger?

"It is I who must apologize," says Tal. "I should have kept the messenger away from you."

I glare at the ground in front of me. My warlord's disappointment is hard to take, but I don't need a Dara man defending me.

"Did the Amparans give you trouble last night, Tal?" Gatha asks.

"I had one of my men release some livestock and stage a robbery. The soldiers seemed to believe Dineas was simply here to raid our stores. The entire contingent left this morning."

Decently quick thinking on his part. Gatha nods her approval and turns toward the healer. "I'm still trying to understand what happened. What do you mean you subdued him with a snake?"

For the first time, I get a good look at this healer. In the daylight, her rosemarks stand out like pools of blood, and I wonder how I could ever have missed them, even in the candlelight. In other ways, she looks the typical Dara maiden. Long black hair pulled back in a braid, homespun drab dress worn under a bright blue apron. She'd be attractive if not for the plague marks—she's tall for a girl, with full lips and large eyes. But when I look at her now, all I see is death.

She catches me looking at her, and a flash of annoyance crosses her face before she addresses Gatha. "My snake, Diadem, does what I ask," she says. "If you look inside, you will see the rest of the creatures I keep."

Gatha pulls her arms close as she comes in, careful not to touch the doorway. "I'll congratulate you, young Zivah. There are very few who have bested Dineas one-on-one."

Bested by a Dara maiden. I'll have no peace at the campfire tonight.

"With all due respect, Warlord," I say, "the snake made it two-on-one."

Gatha snorts. "Are you injured, Dineas?" She's peering with interest over my head at the cages beyond.

"A twisted ankle and a few scrapes."

She steps over me for a closer look at the blackarmor scorpion. "Thirsty? Hungry?"

"Yes, Warlord." Even the act of forming those words pulls uncomfortably on my parched lips.

"I imagine you would be." Gatha looks at each cage in turn, taking her time now that she knows I won't drop dead. I know better than to complain. Finally, she crosses her arms over her chest, looks down at me, and sighs. "Well then, let's get you free."

"Let me get his ropes," says Zivah. She takes a knife out of her apron and cuts through the twine with several deft strokes. I hiss, and flex my fingers as blood rushes into my hands. Zivah dips a bowl of water from a nearby barrel and passes it to me, eyeing me like she's afraid I'll haul off and punch her. The thought does have its appeal, especially since she's not wearing her snake anymore. But thirst wins out, and I content myself with gulping down the contents of the bowl. By the time I finish, Zivah's untied my legs. I pull myself onto numb feet and limp outside like a drunkard.

As Tal and Zivah make their way toward her cottage, Gatha holds out an arm to support me. "One messenger and three soldiers?" she asks under her breath. "Regular fighters?"

"They struck me more as hired bodyguards. Nothing special."

Gatha frowns. "And they caught you by surprise?"

I suppress a nervous roll of my shoulders. I've managed to hide the full extent of my flashbacks from Gatha so far, but this one had come at the worst possible time. "Got careless, I guess," I say.

She gives me a strange look, but Tal and Zivah have stopped to wait for us.

Gatha nods at Tal. "Thank you for protecting my fighter. We will be in touch."

In the corner of my eye, I see Zivah sigh in relief.

The village leader raises his hand. "Actually, Gatha, if you are able to stay longer, we may have more to discuss."

Gatha leans back in surprise. "Right now?"

"You say you've been trying to get inside the Amparan army. I think there's a way." Tal looks to me and Zivah. "It involves these two."

Must the man detain us now? I'm tired and stiff, and I've had my share of humiliation for the day. Also, I don't like how he just grouped me and the healer together.

My warlord nods decisively. "Speak, then. We have time."

Tal turns to Zivah. "Is there anywhere we might sit?"

"Under the awning," Zivah says. "I never touch the chairs, so it should be safe for you and the warlord."

Funny that I'm the only one who can enter her home with no fear of plague. But I doubt we'll be feeling the kinship of fellow plague survivors anytime soon. As Zivah leads the others away, I lag behind and whistle for the crows. Preener comes to sit on my shoulder. "Scout," I command softly. He takes wing, ready to sound the alarm if anyone comes close. Call me paranoid, but I'm not about to entrust my safety to this Tal character.

Once we're settled, Tal speaks again. "I suppose some background is necessary for the two of you to understand what Gatha and I have been working toward. As you might know, Dara leaders have long advocated for peace in the face of the Amparan invasion."

I make a disdainful sound in the back of my throat. I suppose "peace" is one way to frame cowardice. Gatha glares at me.

Tal continues speaking. "But the yoke of the Amparans is hard to carry. Over the past years, they've demanded greater and greater tribute, and recent events make me fear that things will get even worse. This is why I first made contact with Gatha. We've been sharing information to see how we can help each other."

*Help each other.* Would Tal really take up a sword and fight alongside us for freedom?

"Leader Tal," asks Zivah, "are you thinking open rebellion?" From the shock in her voice, you'd think Tal was suggesting they dig up ancestral graves. Gods forbid a Dara maiden get her hands dirty.

"We won't fight Ampara unless the alternative is untenable. But if it comes to the point where we have no choice but to resist, I want us to be ready." The village leader turns to me. "How good a fighter are you?"

"Good enough." I suppose I could tell him more. That I'm quick with dual swords, though my wrists have only recently regained their old strength. That I can shoot an Amparan cavalry man in the throat and hit two more before the first one falls off his horse. That I'm an aggressive grappler who prefers to choke my opponents from the back. But what would be the point?

"He's one of my best," Gatha says. "Joined my lead fighters when he was fifteen."

Fighting at fifteen and captured at seventeen. These days, being an elite fighter just means you die sooner.

"Could you match Ampara's elite?" Tal presses. "If you were one of them, could you stand out enough to catch a commander's eye?"

I have to give him credit. He really does seem interested, and his question intrigues me. I think back to what I know of the Amparans, the bits I've gleaned from the madness of battle. The Amparans always defeat us, but they do it on strength of numbers, not skill. How would I do if I faced the dogs one-on-one?

"Yes," I say.

Gatha doesn't blink at my answer, which gives me some satisfaction.

"Well then," Tal says to Gatha. "You've been wanting to get inside Ampara's heart, strike at their leaders. I may have a way to put Dineas in their ranks."

Gatha frowns. "We've been through this, Tal. You need papers to join the army, proof of birth, and citizenship. Even if we forged good counterfeits, having him in some remote training outpost would do us no good."

"That's why we don't have him join through the normal channels. We introduce him directly to an Amparan commander, through a personal acquaintance."

A gasp sounds from Zivah's direction.

Tal breaks into a slow smile. "You never did miss much, did you, Zivah?"

I exchange a glance with Gatha. The healer has personal sway with Amparan commanders? It doesn't exactly make me trust her more.

Tal speaks again. "Zivah nursed Commander Arxa from the rose plague, and he was greatly impressed by her service. After he returned to the capital, he invited her to study at the Imperial Healer's Academy, but she had fallen ill herself by then."

Zivah looks down at her hands. Her face twists the same way mine does when someone mentions the Amparan dungeons.

Tal continues. "The messenger yesterday brought a new invitation for Zivah to work as a healer in Sehmar City's rosemarked compound."

"Leader Tal," Zivah says firmly. "I can't accept that invitation."

"Hear me out, Zivah," says Tal. He faces us again. "Suffice it to say that Arxa has taken an interest in Zivah, and he will personally see to her placement in the colony. If Zivah were to introduce him to a plague survivor with exceptional fighting skill, the soldier could likely get assigned to a unit close to the capital."

"There would still be the need for papers," says Gatha.

"Plague victims get abandoned at the colony all the time. Very few have papers."

"And some come out of the fever with no memory of their past," Zivah finishes softly.

It takes me a moment to catch on. "Wait. You're proposing that I should pose as a plague survivor with no memory? And somehow, I'm to charm myself into the commander's good graces?"

"It's a dangerous mission," says Tal. "Can you keep up a pretense?"

My chair clatters backward as I jump to my feet. "You want to send me, alone, into the heart of the Amparan army and pretend, day after day, that I don't remember who I am? That I don't want to kill every last one of them?"

The whole thing feels wrong. It's one thing to kill a man honestly face-to-face. But to pretend to be something else...

And could I even pull it off? I think about what happened yesterday when Arxa's name threw me into the past, how I'd stood there, blind and deaf to the world while the memory held my mind captive. If even the sight of one of these soldiers debilitates me, how can I possibly join their ranks? The thought fills me with shame. If Gatha knew just how much my imprisonment has broken me, she'd never put me on the battlefield again.

"Dineas has already been imprisoned once by the Amparans," says Gatha. "I can't demand this risk of him."

Rather than relief, Gatha's words only increase my guilt. We've been searching for an advantage for so long.

A traitorous voice inside me whispers that it might have worked too, if I wasn't so broken. I speak Amparan like a native, since we lived on the main continent until I was twelve. And since our Shidadi share the same forefathers as the Amparans, our peoples look decently similar— certainly more similar to each other than to the lighter-skinned, black-haired Dara. Shidadi fighting styles have changed over time, but different tribes have adapted to so many different circumstances that no one style would be recognized as distinctly ours.

Zivah shifts in her seat. "Leader Tal," she says. "You said that recent events have made you fear things will get worse for our village. Why is that?"

Tal gives her a tired smile. "Things have changed since the Amparan battalion fell ill while in our care. There's been no official word from the emperor, but the military presence around here has increased, and there are more demands. The messenger yesterday, he says that our tithe will double this year yet again. I don't know how we will meet this new demand, and they know it will be hard for us. It's almost as if they are probing for some resistance on our part. I fear they blame us for the rose plague outbreak."

Zivah wraps a mottled hand around the edge of her chair. "But the soldiers fell ill only five days after they arrived. That's far too soon for us to have done this."

Gatha's laugh grates like sand across my eardrums. "Do you

think a difference of five days matters to the Amparan court? Fear doesn't listen to reason."

"The main problem," says Tal, "is that we simply don't know enough about happenings in Central Ampara. All the news we get is indirect, and our ignorance could be deadly. We need our own eyes and ears inside Sehmar City. We need to know what Ampara truly thinks of Monyar and its people, and what her plans are." He takes a breath. "We need to know what really happened to the battalion that fell ill here months ago. That knowledge could save us."

"If Ampara catches us at this scheme," Zivah says, "their wrath would fall on us even sooner."

"That is a true risk," says Tal. "And one you and Dineas will have to take seriously, since the worst of it would fall on you. For the village though, it's a choice between bleeding slowly to death or taking a chance. If we wait too long to act, we may be too weak to fight. We may already be too weak."

I watch the emotions play across Zivah's face as the true danger to her people sinks in. For once, I pity her. I've lived under the threat of extermination all my life, but it must be hard to see it for the first time. Her face settles into intense concentration, and I wonder what she's thinking.

Then she looks straight at me. "If you're simply worried about being able to keep up a pretense, I can help," she says.

I blink. "What do you mean?"

She speaks with an evenness that signifies either determination or shock. "You say you can't pretend to be amnesic among the Amparans. I can make it real for you. I can take away your memory."

My mouth drops open.

Zivah puts up a hand before I can object. "Only temporarily, until your mission is done."

What is this, some kind of sick joke? "What kind of sorcery do your people practice?"

"Not sorcery. Just a good knowledge of venoms and herbs. Your muscle memory won't go away. You'll be able to fight just fine, but you won't remember who you are. If I do it right, I could even restore your memory from time to time so you can send reports to Gatha."

"Is it safe?" says Gatha.

Zivah's lips curl into something that's not quite a smile. "Is it safe to go into battle against Amparan soldiers? I have the knowledge, but this is not something I've ever done. We study these venoms in order to protect the mind. The venom of the soulstealer snake has plagued our people for generations, and we've learned ways to counter its effects, to control or delay them. Through our studies, we've gained an ability to manipulate the mind itself. Nevertheless, things could go wrong. If I make a mistake, he could lose himself."

Gatha wipes the sweat off her brow. She doesn't scare easily, but I can see Zivah's offer has shaken her. "This is beyond my ken, Tal," she says. "I'll send a soldier into honest battle, but this . . ."

She's right. I didn't live this long by trusting foreign healers I don't even know. I open my mouth to agree with her, but then I stop again, because now I'm thinking about my mother, my father, the countless others lost to the empire. What would I give to gain some real foothold against Ampara? And beyond that, there's a more shameful temptation. As I ponder Zivah's offer, the screams from the emperor's dungeons echo in my mind, and once again I erupt in cold sweat. Is it wrong to want those screams out of my head? Is it cowardly to be tempted by the possibility of a moment's peace?

I look her in the eye and hope I don't regret this. "Tell me more about your potions."

# CHAPTER TEN
## ZIVAH

Kaylah sits quietly as I tell her the events of the past day, of the Shidadi nomad who broke into my shed, and of Tal's proposal. Surprise flickers across her face more than once. When I finish, her expression is somber.

"This is uncharted territory," she says. "You know what the Goddess has commanded regarding knowledge she gives us."

I knew this objection was coming. Our vows as healers are very clear—to use the knowledge we have to help the ailing and not for our own personal ends. "You could argue that I'm still saving lives this way, if indeed Ampara bears ill will toward us."

"It's dangerous to play such games with the Goddess's commandments."

Why should I take so much care to honor the Goddess's

wishes when she clearly hasn't given much consideration to mine? It's a heretical thought, and I thrust it aside.

"But what if Tal is right? If Ampara thinks we infected those soldiers, you know what they would do to us."

Kaylah looks away from me toward the bamboo groves, and I'm surprised at my nerves as I wait for her answer. I have my own doubts about this mission—how could I not? Sitting under the awning this morning, listening to Tal propose a plan that could kill us all, or worse . . . the entire thing had felt surreal. I'd been ready to tell him he asked too much, that I'd sacrificed enough already.

But Tal's words about the Amparan threat rang true. We've all heard countless stories about what happens to Ampara's enemies. Villages razed to the ground, entire families sold into slavery. And while I don't want to believe that the emperor would blame us for the battalion's illness, I can't deny the possibility.

"It would be harder for you there in many ways," says Kaylah. "You'll be locked away with the other rosemarked. They won't treat you like a human being."

"But there will be other healers there who would work with me." I know I haven't lost her yet, if she's still talking. Kaylah has no authority over me—I could go whether she permits it or not, but the idea of continuing without her blessing scares me.

Kaylah lets out a long sigh. "This is a slippery slope, and it pains me to put you in such danger," Kaylah says. "But I will help you."

Over the next days, I prepare my potion with Kaylah's advice. The principles behind it are simple. The soulstealer snake sweeps away your memories, and the only protection against it is ziko root potion, which weighs the memories down so they're not permanently lost. Someone who's taken ziko root and gets bitten still becomes amnesic, but his memory can be restored if we purge the venom from the body with a tincture of nadat root. A weak tincture restores the memory temporarily, while a strong one restores it completely. With Dineas, therefore, I'll act as both snake and healer. I'll give him snake venom and ziko before the mission, and nadat root after his mission is over.

The potion is the easy part. Perhaps that's why I spend all my time on it, obsessively refining my mixtures, rather than face the last issue I must settle before I leave. I've not yet told my family. I don't know what I'll say, and I'm not prepared for their reactions, especially since I cannot tell them the whole truth. They'll be safer if they don't know the real reason for my quest. To them, I'll simply be studying and serving in the rosemarked colony as a healer. Finally, with a few days left to spare, I gather my courage and summon them to my cottage.

My mother's reaction is just as I expected. "Why?" she asks me. That simple word breaks my heart. "Why so far and why now?"

"And it's not an easy journey," adds my father. He's more stoic, though his voice is equally heavy. "Not for anyone, much less a rosemarked woman."

"Tal will provide me with escorts," I tell them. "And exchanging knowledge with the Amparan healers would be good for everyone. I can learn from their doctors and send the knowledge back to Kaylah. I could treat the patients of Sehmar City."

Leora puts her hand gently on my mother's shoulder. "Zivah

needs to live her life," she says gently. "We can't keep her out here alone, simply for our sakes." Her words resonate more than I'd like to admit, and I wonder how well I'd really hidden my feelings each time she'd visited me in my exile.

"But aren't we part of your life?" Alia says. Tears have started to run down her face.

"Alia, I . . ." As I falter, Alia jumps up and runs into the forest. I hear her sobs long after she disappears from view.

Leora looks after her, and then back at me. "She'll understand with time."

My mother's teary too, though she doesn't leave. She looks at me, eyes filled with love, as only a mother can. "We want what's best for you," she says. "If this is what you truly wish to do, then go with our blessing."

Something shatters within me, and I look down to hide my face. "Thank you," I whisper. And there's nothing more I can say.

A fortnight later, Dineas knocks on my door. It's just the two of us this time: the rosemarked healer and the soldier with no fear of her disease. Together somehow, we are to steal Ampara's secrets.

I don't know what to say to him. Any greeting seems trite. I wonder how he's spent the past weeks. Has he had second thoughts as well? Did he have family to say good-bye to? Does he wish to stay, or is he eager to go?

After an awkward silence, I simply step back to let him in. He crosses the threshold gingerly, passing so close to me that his tunic brushes my sleeve. It catches me off guard. After so many months with the disease, I've grown used to people keeping their distance.

Dineas's eyes dart around my house, going from my cot to my jars of herbs. Then he checks my wrist.

I hold it up to show him it's bare. "Diadem sleeps there." I nod to a cage by my table. I've felt safer having her in my room these past weeks. To be honest, I'd feel safer now if Diadem were still on my wrist.

He regards me, a grudging respect apparent in his body language. "You don't worry about getting bitten yourself?"

"My body is resistant to the venoms."

He furrows his brow, then shrugs. "Where should I . . . ?"

"Sit down on my bed. I'll need to examine you."

He settles on my cot, plants his legs sturdily in front of him, and props his forearms on his thighs. I frown at the way he's pushed my neatly folded blankets into a pile. He glances at my expression and his mouth quirks in amusement, though he makes no move to put the blankets back in place.

I'm falling into my old healer's routine already, looking over his body with a practiced eye. He's young and healthy, but too thin to be at his full strength. I estimate his weight to be around eighty ingots, though with more food he could stand to gain a good ten or fifteen more. His coloring is good. Even with the abundance of umbermarks covering him from head to toe, his olive complexion is warm and his brown eyes are clear.

I reach for his wrist. "May I check your pulse?"

"Are you going to tie me up again?" he asks. But he holds out his arm.

I hesitate for the briefest moment before touching him. Again, I have to remind myself that he can't catch my disease. His skin is warmer than mine but not feverish, and his pulse strong. In addition to the umbermarks, a network of scars crosses his exposed skin, though his face is unmarred. It makes me wonder if he's vain of his appearance, and if he gets much attention from the young women of his tribe. He certainly carries himself with that swagger. When he turns his head, I see that his ears are puffy and misshapen. I've heard that ears can become this way with repeated blows, but it's the first time I've seen it up close.

"You're healthy enough. Your body should be able to handle my potion." I'm starting to feel jittery, so I go to my table and spoon the ziko I've prepared into a bowl. Then I add seven drops of venom. "If all goes well, I'll take away your memory today, and then restore it for our journey."

He doesn't respond. Instead, he cranes his neck to inspect the ceiling, tracing the length of the bamboo beams with his gaze. "The empire makes their slave cages of bamboo," he says.

I pause in my mixing, unsure what to say. It's true that the majority of the empire's bamboo comes from our groves.

Dineas snorts in disgust. "Must be nice, buying your safety with the blood of others."

And now I'm glad I'm bent over my herbs so he can't see my jaw clench. "We do what we must. And we've had our share of suffering."

"Blind kittens, groping at the teat. And they're surprised when they're thrown into a bag to be drowned."

Heat floods through me at his words. "And where has fighting gotten your people? Does it comfort your dead in their graves?"

For a moment, raw fury flashes across his face. My heart pounds in my chest. I know I've overstepped, but I'm too proud to back down. Dineas glares at me as if he'd like to run me through, but though his jaw works, he stays silent. Perhaps because he sees the folly of truly angering me at this very moment.

Diadem hisses from the corner, and we break our gaze. I look down at my herbs, trying to gather my spiraling thoughts. I don't know this nomad, and our few interactions have not inspired any particular good feelings toward him. But if we are to do this mission together...

I let out a breath. "We have our differences, but our paths seem to converge for a while. I want you to know that I'll do everything in my power to keep you safe. Do you believe me?"

My words seem to catch him off guard. He shrugs. "I don't know anything about you or your people, but I trust Gatha, Gatha trusts Tal, and Tal trusts you."

I shake my head. "That's not enough. You must understand that the injection I prepare is different from anything we do in our normal lives as healers. If all goes well, it should make you forget everything that's happened in your life thus far, but still leave you functional and able to regain your memories with the right antidote. If it doesn't..." I pause, trying to pick the right words. "I'm good at my craft, Dineas. I've combed the scrolls for knowledge, and I've discussed my plan with my master. But there's always the chance of something going wrong. You might lose part of yourself. I ask you again. Do you trust me to do this?"

A crow caws outside. Dineas stares out the window. His silence unnerves me, but at least I know my words have gotten through to him.

Finally, Dineas turns back to me. "I'm a soldier, first and foremost. There are comrades of mine that I don't care for, those that I'd give a good beating on the training grounds, given the chance. But on the battlefield, if an enemy comes at us, I'll give my life for that man I despise." He looks at me. "They say you're one of the village's best healers, that you worked harder than any of the other apprentices. If you're really that good, then I think you'd act the same as a soldier in battle. You might despise me, but you won't let me come to harm under your care. If you don't do it out of concern for me, you'll do it out of pride."

I don't know what response I'd expected from him, but I'm surprised at the truth in his words. "You're sure, then?"

A spasm flashes across his face. "Just do your job."

Neither of us speak as I pour the potion into a small leather bag and carry it to the cot. Sewn into one end of the bag is the tooth of a serpent, strengthened with resin and kept sharp and hollow. To Dineas's credit, he doesn't draw his arm away as I reach for it, though his hands have gone cold, and a film of sweat coats his skin. He breathes slowly and deliberately through his nose and looks away.

At the last moment, it is I who falter. My healer's vows run through my head, and I wonder if I'm making a grave mistake. It takes him a while to realize that I've frozen.

"Do this, please," he says. There's a quiet desperation in his voice. "Even if I lose my mind, it's a small price to pay for the chance to take them down."

What did the Amparans do to him in prison? I want to ask, but instead I plunge the tooth into his arm. He grits his teeth and stares beyond me at the wall as I slowly push the potion out of the bag. When I squeeze too hard, he stiffens but doesn't make a sound. Finally, I pull the snake tooth away and wipe away the blood welling up through the puncture.

He stares at the blood, as if he'd expected more. "Is that it?"

"You'll feel the effects in a few moments." My eyes are on the wound, where an angry red welt is already spreading. I take his chin, turn his head to the light, and look at his pupils. They're easy to see against the hazel of his eyes, and slowly expanding.

"I feel light-headed." Dineas's voice takes on a distracted quality. I watch his chest and count his breaths, making sure they don't slow to the point of danger. His eyelids grow heavy. He opens his mouth to say something, but then his eyes roll to the back of his head. I catch him as he goes limp. He's heavier than I expected, and it's all I can do to keep him from slamming into the cot.

I sit with my fingers on his wrist, counting his pulse and his breaths, and sighing in relief when both are steady. As to what state his mind will be in, I can only wait and see. Little by little, the water clock in the corner slowly empties.

Finally, Dineas stirs in his sleep. I haven't had a prayer answered in a long time, but I breathe a quick petition to the Goddess that all will go well. It's strange how natural it feels to have a patient under my roof again. The breeze blows lightly in through my door and window, and I can hear leaves rustling outside. I'm glad for this good weather. It will ease the shock of his awakening.

His eyelids flutter and crack open. I sit up straight, my heart in my throat, every sense tuned in on him. He rolls his head from side to side, then looks straight at me. His expression is one of placid confusion.

"You've slept a long time," I say, hoping my anxiety doesn't show. "You'll be groggy for a while."

He looks from me to the rest of the cottage. "Where am I?"

"You're safe," I say. "What is your name?"

"I don't remember." But it doesn't seem to bother him.

His memory's gone. That's the first hurdle passed. "It will come with time," I tell him. I pat the cot underneath him. "What is this?"

He looks at me, puzzled at the question. "A bed?"

He's obedient. I point to the table and cage across the room. "And can you tell me what you see?"

"I see a table. And a cage." He flinches. "There's a snake inside."

I allow myself one small sigh of relief. I haven't given him so much venom as to completely take away his knowledge of the world. "And tell me about yourself. What is your name? Where do you come from?"

"I'm not from here. Actually, I'm not certain. I'm twelve years old. No, twenty."

He's eighteen, actually. He told me.

"And you still don't remember your name?"

His forehead creases in concentration. "No." As the reality of this sinks in, agitation starts to take hold. He grabs at the sides of his cot and starts to push himself up, and I realize, with a bolt of panic, that I won't be able to restrain him if he becomes belligerent.

"Wait," I say quickly. "Let me help you."

He rolls his eyes like a panicked horse, and I fetch my potion before he has more time to doubt. "Drink this. It will help you remember."

Dineas hesitates a split second, but then raises the bowl to his lips and drinks it down in one shot. It doesn't hurt that soulstealer venom causes extreme thirst.

"Nothing's happening," he says. His eyes still dart from one corner of the room to another.

"Give it time." I take the bowl back. *Please let it work.*

He puts a hand to his head and squeezes his eyes shut. I reach for him, worried he'll collapse, but he shrinks away. Then his eyes snap open and he fixates on something I cannot see.

It's a fascinating thing, seeing memories rush across someone's face. He folds forward slightly, and his eyes go back and forth as if he's tracking a herd of horses. He grabs the edge of the cot and grips it tight. Once in a while, he shudders.

Finally, he looks at me again. He opens his mouth to speak. No sound comes out at first, and he shakes his head and tries again. "That was . . . So was that it? I can't . . ."

Near our village is a small waterfall that children like to run through. Dineas's expression reminds me of how the children look coming out—disoriented by the onslaught of water, and blinking in the sunlight.

I take his hands. "Who are you? Where do you come from?"

He answers seriously. "My name is Dineas. I come from a tribe of Shidadi under Warlord Gatha." He says those things quickly, as if to reassure himself that he still knows who he is. "You just took away my memory." The tone of his voice is half accusation and half amazement.

"It worked, then." A giddiness runs through me. "How much do you remember of what happened?"

He shakes his head again, trying to clear it. "I remember everything. Falling asleep, waking up. I remember *not* remembering anything."

"That's good." I lean toward him. "Now listen carefully. The potion I gave you just now was not the antidote. It's just a temporary restoration. From now on, you must take this potion twice a day, or you'll forget yourself again. When it comes time for us to put the plan into place, you'll stop taking the potion, and your memories will fade away."

His eyes widen. "I'll have to do this for the rest of my life?"

"No. There's also a permanent antidote." I look around for a better way to explain. Finally, I grab a basin and a handful of smooth, flat stones from outside. "Think of it this way. This basin is your mind, and"—I drop a layer of pebbles into the bottom—"these pebbles are your memories."

I take a pitcher and pour water so it barely covers the stones. "This first potion I gave you, it buries everything up to this point. Any new memories formed after that are laid above the water level." I drop a few rocks on top of the first layer of pebbles to symbolize new experiences. "After the first potion, you can remember everything above water—that is, everything that's happened since you drank it."

He furrows his brow but doesn't say anything.

"The second potion I gave you was the temporary restoration. It sweeps the water to the side so you can see everything—both your old memories and your new ones. But eventually, the potion will wear off. The water flows back, and once again you can only see what's not buried."

Dineas stares at the basin, taking in my words. "And what about the things that happen while the water's temporarily swept aside? Are those like new memories or old?"

"Good question. Those memories are somewhere in between. You might remember vague impressions after the rest of the old memories fade, but I don't think you'll be able to make sense of them."

He frowns. "And you do have something that will dry up this 'water' for good?"

"Yes. That's the permanent antidote. We'll take it with us to the capital, and it will cure you when our mission is done. But I'd rather not erase your memory more times than I must. The first potion is the dangerous part. It might not turn out so well next time."

He takes in my words, and sets his jaw. "Well then, let's go to the capital."

# CHAPTER ELEVEN

## DINEAS

Now I understand why they call that snake the soulstealer.

As I mend my clothes and sharpen my blades for our journey, I'm haunted by those short moments when Zivah took away my past, the blankness where my life should have been. I can't shake the feeling that with her potion, Zivah's taken something core to who I am. Before we parted that day, Zivah gave me several days' worth of the draft to keep my memories from fading, and I take them more religiously than most priests take their prayers. I've agreed to this mission, and I won't back down now. All the same, I'll hold on to my soul for as long as I can.

Five days later, I journey back down to Zivah's cottage under cover of darkness. Gatha's the only one who comes to see me off. It's a brisk night, with only a sliver of a moon. Through the healer's shutters, the faint glow of lamplight tells me Zivah's up and about. I send Preener off to fetch her.

Next to me, Gatha clears her throat. "When you're in the palace, Dineas, play it cautiously. Stay alive; lie low. Earn the empire's trust. Find out their plans against us and how to stop them. Anything you give us will be helpful. Their codes, their strategies, the movements and habits of their leaders . . ."

Gatha never fails to stir my courage. "I won't remember anything once the healer's done with me," I remind her.

"True, you'll be wiped blank," says Gatha. "But I suspect part of you will still remember my orders, even if you don't know it."

The light in Zivah's cottage flickers out. A few moments later, she steps through the door. She carries a small pack over her shoulders, and I'm relieved to see that she's traded her dress for a man's tunic and trousers. It's too dark to see her face.

"Ready to go?" I ask.

Her nod is so slight I could well have imagined it.

We leave without fanfare—we simply start walking, and I lead the way south. The trails are too crooked for quick going, even though we've packed light. All I have is one change of clothes and my weapons. My crows fly along behind me, since Gatha thought it better for them to come to the capital with us.

Zivah travels with a snake curled around her upper arm and several tiny cages of insects hanging from her pack. Despite the venomous pets, the healer's not as bad a traveling companion as I'd feared. She doesn't talk much at all, and she matches my pace without complaining. Soon after sunrise, the bamboo groves start thinning, the ground begins to slope downward, and the air takes on a heavier feel. A short while later, I smell the sea breeze, and the dark waters of the Monyar Strait come into view. The water looks calm, which is a good thing, because no ferry captain who gets a good look at Zivah will have anything to do with us.

"I'll see about a boat," I tell Zivah.

The pier is a short distance downhill, along with the ferryman's hut, an Amparan messenger's stable, and a smattering of vendor stalls. The smell of freshly fried fish makes my mouth water, but I go past that stall to the boatmonger, who's got several vessels sunning on the sand. An older rowboat catches my eye. The wood is aged, but sturdy and heavy enough to cut through the waves.

"How much for this?"

"Seventy telans."

Fair price. I must not look rich enough to cheat. Still, it's more money than I've spent in a long time. I dig out some coins from the stash Tal gave me, then drag the boat down to the beach. When Zivah joins me, I see she's put on a wide-brimmed hat to shield her face from onlookers.

"You been on the water before?" I ask her.

Her mouth presses into a straight line as she peers across to the Amparan shore. "A few times."

She flinches away when I offer her a hand in. It's not the first time she's been jumpy around me.

I roll my eyes. "I may be a barbarian, but I promise I won't kill you. It'd be hard for me to complete my mission if I did."

She's puzzled for a moment, and then she shakes her head. "It's not that," she says. "I just keep forgetting you're immune."

Her answer seems obvious now that she's said it. I wonder

how long it's been since she's been allowed to touch someone. But now, Zivah takes my hand, tightening her grip when the boat rocks under her weight.

"Sit here," I say, pointing to the stern. As soon as she's settled, I bend down and brace my weight against the hull. The water's ice-cold around my feet, and then my shins as I push the boat deeper. I jump into the boat before my toes go numb, and take the oars.

The boat is well-balanced and responsive. The current carries us west and I'm fighting the wind, but we move along at a decent clip. For a while, it's just the sound of my paddles hitting the water, and the waves against our boat. Zivah stares off the side, looking toward the opposite shore, and I concentrate on the rowing. There's something about the rhythm that kneads the tension out of my muscles.

"How well do you know Central Ampara?" she asks.

It takes me a while to realize she's spoken. "I grew up on that side of the strait. I was twelve when we fled across to Monyar."

"Have you been back since then?"

"A few times." I attack the water with my oars. The boat lurches. If Zivah thinks removing my memories gives her permission to go digging through my past, she'll be sorely disappointed.

She returns her gaze to the waters. She looks dignified, sitting there with her hands folded in her lap, like a queen or a priestess. I catch myself staring at her profile, and she turns toward me before I can look away.

"You know what they do to traitors in Ampara, don't you?" I blurt out.

It's her turn to be surprised. But then a hint of a smile touches her lips. "You need me on this mission, Dineas. Educating me on Amparan torture strategies might not be in your best interest."

"Everyone should know what they're facing."

Zivah pulls a splinter off the side of the boat and tosses it into the water. "What can they take away from me?" she asks quietly. "My life? That's already gone. This way, at least I can help my people. At least I can heal again."

There are fates worse than death, but I don't say it. "Is healing that important to you?"

She casts her eyes toward the twin swords resting at my feet, carefully wrapped in oilcloth to avoid attracting attention. "How would you feel if you could no longer wield those? If every blade you touched turned on you instead?"

I follow her gaze to my blades. Even though I've only owned them a few months, they already feel like extensions of my arms. I know their reach and their weight, and it makes me nervous to have them on the floor of the boat instead of on my back. "Your fellow villagers spoke highly of your skill," I say. "They say you were touched by the gods."

"We only have one Goddess. She holds healers in her hand because they guard the door to her domain." She stops abruptly. Then comes that faint smile again, but there's no mirth in it. "The Goddess might have taken an interest in me once, but she's long forgotten me by now."

I don't answer. Leave it to a priest to defend the gods to her. I won't fight that losing battle.

As we come near to the opposite shore, I pull the oars in and jump out. The beach on this side is rockier than the other, and pebbles scatter under my feet as I pull the boat to land. I'd purposely steered us to a more remote part of the border, out of view of checkpoints, docks, or any other Amparan trappings. Still, as I wade onto dry ground, a weight presses on my chest, clamping the breath out of my lungs more surely than if a horse had fallen on top of me. Images crowd into my mind—chains, heat, the moans of dying men. I close my eyes, willing the sensations to go away. I'm no warrior if I let myself be beaten down by ghosts.

"Dineas . . ."

Scars, I'd forgotten Zivah. She steps out of the boat, uncertain. I turn away from her, take a deep breath, hold it in, and let it out. *Focus on the mission. Remember what's at stake.* I'm still a little shaky by the time she reaches me. "Welcome to the Central Empire."

She looks at me as if trying to decide whether to acknowledge the hostility in my voice.

"You hate them, don't you?" she asks.

I think back to the battles I've endured, the children who lack fathers and mothers. "Don't you? That garrison of soldiers with rose plague might as well have run a sword through you."

Her expression freezes, and she scans the jagged rocks of the beach. "Sometimes I blame those soldiers," she says, eyes still focused ahead of her. "Sometimes I'm angry at the Goddess. Sometimes I blame myself."

For a moment we're both silent. Then she pushes ahead of me. "What now?"

"It's nearing sundown, so we'll make camp. Tomorrow, we'll start south to Sehmar."

We find a secluded cove nearby. When I come back from gathering firewood, Zivah is plucking the feathers off a seagull.

"Where'd you get that?" I ask.

She doesn't look up from her work. "I may not be a walking armory, but I'm not completely helpless," she says. That's when I see the blowgun on the ground next to her.

"Are you a good shot?" I'm intrigued despite myself.

She holds the bird up to show the dart buried in its side. "You can keep pestering me with questions, or you can share half of this bird for dinner."

Fair enough. I keep my mouth shut, and we cook up the meat over a fire. It's delicious.

# CHAPTER TWELVE
## ZIVAH

Dineas has nightmares the first night. I hear him tossing and groaning on the other side of the dying campfire. At first, I try to sleep through it, but when he lets out a hoarse scream, I finally call his name.

He startles awake. I hear the scrape of a blade being drawn, and I'm glad I didn't go closer to wake him. In the dim glow of the embers I can make out his profile as he turns this way and that. Finally, his hoarse breathing slows.

"Are you all right?" I ask.

"I'm fine," he says brusquely.

His blankets fall to the ground as he stands, and he turns his face from me as he gathers his bedding and walks away from the campfire. He puts twenty paces between us before I hear him set up his blankets again and lie back down. I can tell from his breathing that he lies awake long afterward, but we both pretend to be asleep.

A shadow hangs over Dineas the next morning. He knocks things about as he scatters the campfire, and he only acknowledges my presence once I've packed my bags and coaxed Diadem back onto my arm for the journey.

I make my way cautiously toward him. "If your memories haunt you at night, you could decrease the amount of restorative potion you take every evening. Dull your memories when you sleep."

His jaw starts to clench even before I've finished speaking. "I'm fine." He turns away.

I'll leave him to his nightmares, then.

We march side by side without a word. He sets a grueling pace, and soon I'm too tired to speak even if I wanted to. From the way he eyes me as we walk and the challenge in the tilt of his chin, I know he expects me to ask him to slow. But Dineas thinks I'm weak enough as it is, and I don't want to give him the satisfaction of being right. So I grit my teeth and keep one foot stepping in front of the other. It's strange though. Even if I'm tired every day from our travels, it's the normal fatigue of excessive exertion, the kind I used to feel before I fell ill. The unnatural heaviness that's weighed down my limbs since I became rosemarked is gone.

Still, the next few weeks test my resolve. My sore muscles and throbbing feet are bad enough, but I hadn't realized how unsettling the changing landscape would be. The air becomes dryer as we go inland, and the sun beats down hotter on my face and shoulders. I'd known the continent would be different, but to actually see the forest turn to grassland, then desert before my eyes . . . We start being more careful with our water and ration it between springs and wells. The shrubs and gnarled bushes we pass are alien to me, and it's unsettling. What would I do if one of us suffered heatstroke or was wounded by a wild animal? In Dara, I would smooth sap of cloudweed over a bite, but any cloudweed would wither and die in this climate. All my favorite remedies are gone, except for what I've carried with me. A lifetime of study and practice rendered useless by just a bit of walking.

As we travel, the marks of the empire become stronger. The villages and hamlets we pass gradually become bigger, and people speak Amparan instead of their native tongues. We pass temples with carved facades, large halls of cedar, and ornate tombs carved in limestone cliff faces. Several times, I'm awoken at dawn by distant chants sung by priests of Yaras, the Amparan god of the sky. I can't help but compare this grandeur to the modest cottages of Dara and wonder just how we can resist an empire with such resources at its disposal.

Then there are the ruins. We pass by two burned-out villages—half-collapsed houses, blackened thatching, no trace of those who lived there before except for somber signs written in stark Amparan, informing passersby of this village's crimes and the swiftness of punishment. One village withheld a quarterly tithe. Another took an Amparan soldier into their prisons without consulting with the empire. If villages were destroyed for this, then what's the punishment for infecting a battalion of soldiers? Of sending spies into the capital?

One day, Dineas comes to a stop at the top of a ridge. "The emperor's road," he says. It runs straight south toward where the air wavers in the horizon, wide enough for several chariots to ride side by side. Though it's early in the day, many people travel along it. In the distance, a watchtower stands sentinel.

I shield my eyes against the sun. "This will take us to Sehmar City?"

He nods. "It gets more crowded from here on out. We'll likely attract less notice if we mix ourselves in with the other travelers, rather than sneaking along the side roads. And we should go separately. Far enough from each other so that people won't think we're traveling together."

What he says makes sense. I have good travel documents. They even allow me to take rations from imperial rest houses if I so wish. Dineas, however, only has an identification parchment with a badly forged seal. It might fool a careless inspector, but it would be much better for him to avoid attention completely.

I rummage through my bags and pull out a large undyed cloth, woven loosely enough to see through—a plague veil. The empire requires their rosemarked to wear it whenever we might encounter the healthy. I run it between my fingers and then take off my hat and drape the cloth over it, securing it with ties I'd sewn on. I pause, fingering the rough fabric.

"Is something wrong?" Dineas asks.

"No. I've just . . . never worn one before."

I expect impatience or sarcasm, but Dineas stays silent. Finally, I take a breath and duck under the veil, taking care not to disturb Diadem on my arm. My hat feels heavier with the fabric draped over it. The cloth falls as low as my ankles and provides a cylinder of welcome shade. I can see through it well enough to make my way, but I think I'd trip if I had to run.

I can sense Dineas watching me. "You go ahead first," he says. "I'll trail behind."

I open my mouth to reply, but it feels strange to talk through the veil, so instead I just start down the ridge.

My progress is slow. Even though the veil doesn't reach my feet, it encumbers my arms and legs when I walk. When I hold my arms out for balance going down a hill, the motion pulls at my hat. Every once in a while, I kick a rock I didn't see or step into a divot and have to catch myself. Diadem bobs her head and looks around, more lively now in the newfound shade.

The terrain levels out as I come closer to the road. An imperial messenger rides by toward the capital, kicking up a cloud of dust. Three women make their way more slowly in his wake. Their dark embroidered gowns give them the look of priestesses. One of the women looks in my direction, and then stops abruptly and puts a hand on her companion's shoulder. The entire group stops to stare at me.

Now I'm glad for the veil, so I do not have to face them. I step onto the road ahead of them and walk along the edge. A short while later, they hurry past, single file, clinging to the other side of the road.

The other travelers I encounter behave the same way. Although my veil is meant to separate me from the world, the empty space around me is the real partition. After an hour of walking, I've encountered more fearful and suspicious glances than I've had in all the months I was rosemarked in my home village. In Dara, people knew me first as Zivah, and second as a diseased person. On this road though, I am nothing but a carrier of death.

Ahead of me, the first watchtower rises up. I see the soldiers' conical hats at the top of the tower. Two others guard the road below. As I approach, one soldier points his spear at me.

"Rosemarked, who gives you right to walk this road?"

I part my veil and hold out Arxa's invitation, with his seal embedded in the clay. "Commander Arxa of Sehmar City."

The soldier squints suspiciously at my letter, but he makes no move to step closer. Then he shrugs and waves me on. "Keep your distance," he says.

A dozen steps later something hits my pack and knocks me forward. A rock rolls to rest at my feet as another one flies past my head. I turn around. A group of young men stand clustered together, jeering at me.

"This road's not for plague carriers," one says. "Get off."

Heat rushes through me as other travelers slow down to see the spectacle. I scan their faces through my veil and don't see a shred of compassion. There's no sign of Dineas, and I'm relieved he's not here to witness this. Shaking, I step off the road and onto the uneven dirt on the side.

A rock glances off my elbow. I stumble in surprise and cradle my throbbing arm. The young men are following me.

"Not fast enough," one says.

I glance desperately up toward the watchtower, but the soldiers just look on.

A man with dust on his face pitches another rock in my direction. It brushes my veil, pushing my hat crooked.

"Spilling my blood only puts you in danger," I shout.

"Not if we keep our distance, corpse," says a voice from the back. I bring my arms up over my face just in time for a stone to connect solidly with my forearm. I gasp at the pain and turn to run, but I only manage ten steps before my legs get tangled and I pitch forward. The ground comes up hard. A rock thuds to my left, sending a spray of pebbles toward me.

Diadem hisses in my ear. Only by some miracle have I managed not to crush her.

The men are still coming, though the nearest have stopped a safe distance away. The look in their eyes turns my stomach to ice—it's a mob that's tasted blood. I realize, as I desperately try to untangle the cloth around me, that they can easily kill me here. My skin flushes hot, as if my rosemarks were radiating heat. Once again, I look for Dineas, but he's nowhere in sight. Even if he were around, for him to intervene in view of Amparan soldiers would be suicide.

My snake is gripping me so hard now that she threatens to cut off my blood flow. I whistle under my breath and she relaxes her hold. I'm glad to have her with me, but Diadem can't save me this time. I throw off my hat and veil, blinking in the sun. The men recoil at the sight of my skin as I fumble to untie the blowgun from my waist.

A shriek splits the air and a shadow drops out of the sky. A man in front throws up his hands to avoid the crow's talons. As the first bird pulls away, a second one dives, pecking at the man's face.

"What witchcraft—" The rest of the man's sentence is cut off as a third crow swoops down. The man grabs at the bird—Scrawny?—as it dodges out of the way. The men scatter and run back toward the road with the birds in pursuit.

I don't waste my time looking after them. Instead, I grab my hat and walk away from the road as quickly as I can. Only when I'm far enough that I can't hear the men's shouts do I finally turn south again.

A short while later, I again hear footsteps behind me. I take a nervous glance back and relax slightly when I see Dineas's familiar form. I keep walking.

His footsteps draw closer, but still I don't look at him.

"Are you hurt?" he asks.

I glance toward the road. It's getting darker now, but a sharp-eyed traveler could still see us. "You shouldn't be here," I say under my breath. "And it was foolish to send the crows. Your travel documents aren't good enough to be attracting attention like this."

For a long moment, all I hear is the repeated crunch of his footsteps. "You're welcome," he finally says.

I should thank him, but I can't. The humiliation is still too fresh. A living corpse, the man had called me.

"I could have handled it," I say.

He snorts. "With that blowgun? You would have gotten one, maybe two of them before they stoned you to death."

I tug at my plague veil. With the growing darkness, it's becoming much harder to see, and I long to rip the cloth to shreds.

"Please," I say, "just go away. At least until it's completely dark."

Again, I hear nothing but his footsteps. At first I think he's decided to disregard me. But gradually, his steps fade farther and farther away.

Three weeks after we left Dara, the sand-colored walls of Sehmar City appear on the horizon. The emperor's road feeds directly into massive gates, where copper-plated soldiers stand guard. I'm a good distance from the road when I arrive. Though I use it to find my direction, I haven't actually set foot on it since the day I was chased off.

I take shelter beneath a rare gnarled tree and wait for Dineas to come over the sandy hill behind me. He slows as he catches sight of the city, and a spasm crosses his face.

"That's it, isn't it?" I say.

"That's Sehmar." For a moment, neither of us says anything. Then Dineas shrugs his bag off his shoulder. "I'll stay outside the walls while you get settled," he says. "You can take two of the crows."

I look around at the barren terrain. "Will you be all right for supplies? It may take me days, if not weeks, to find a good opportunity to bring you in." And that's if Arxa doesn't see through my deception straightaway.

"I've been hungry before. I'll survive."

"The Goddess keep you, then."

I turn to leave, but Dineas barks my name. I turn to see him staring at a cloud of dust up the road. "Best wait until they pass," he says. I've never heard so much strain in his voice. His whole body is rigid and tense. He's barely breathing.

The hair on the back of my neck rises in response, and I wait. Soon a train of open wagons stacked with man-size cages comes into view. Though we're far from the road, odors of blood, excrement, infection, and sweat drift toward us on the wind. I pull my collar over my nose and fight the urge to gag. It's impossible to look away from the wretched people inside—men, women, and children. Their clothes are torn and dirty. Some sport partially bandaged wounds. Others lie curled on the cage floors, staring out through the bars with listless eyes. Occasionally one of the train's armed escorts cracks a whip and shouts a command I can't hear. Some of the prisoners shift in response, though others seem incapable of moving.

It's an imperial slave caravan.

I can't help but wonder... who are these people? What was their crime? Were they accused of harboring rebels? Did they greet an emissary of the empire without the proper amount of respect? I imagine Leora and Alia in those carts, my mother and father. It's suddenly starkly clear to me what we face if we fail.

"Last chance to turn around," says Dineas. Though his voice has its usual edge, there's a hint of compassion in his eyes.

The slave train crawls into the city. I take a breath to collect myself.

"I imagine my people in these cages too," he says. "Every time."

I can feel Dineas's eyes on me as I walk away. The soldiers at the gate nudge each other as I approach. More than one loosens his sword from its sheath. *You have the right to travel these roads, Zivah. You've been given permission.* Of course, that permission did me no good the last time.

I take the final few steps. "I'm a rosemarked traveler claiming an audience with Commander Arxa in the city," I say. Carefully, I part my veil and lay the invitation on the ground in front of me. Then I back away.

The soldiers exchange glances. Finally, one jerks his head toward another who I'd guess is the lowest ranked. That man adjusts his armor and takes cautious steps toward the invitation. He looks it over from a distance of a few paces. I feel like an open wound, an unwanted scab.

"I'll inquire of Commander Arxa," the soldier says.

"Thank you, sirs."

The man is gone a long time, and gradually, the remaining soldiers forget about me and go about their duties. I find a large rock and sit down, grateful for the shade my veil offers and trying not to think about what would happen if the soldier cannot find Arxa. What if the commander has changed his mind or forgotten about me? I don't know if Arxa is the kind of man to hold to his word.

But finally the gate guard returns, accompanied by another soldier wearing a black-and-silver sash over his livery. The newcomer stands before me and bows. He's umbertouched, and I realize with a start that he was one of the soldiers I'd treated back at Dara.

"Healer Zivah," he says. "Commander Arxa welcomes you to Sehmar City. He is unable to see you at the moment, but you are to come with me to the rosemarked colony."

I search the man's eyes for any recognition, any friendliness, but he is as stone-faced as any of the others. Does he realize that Dara healers saved his life? Does he know what we sacrificed for him? Or does he hate us for not doing enough?

"Where is the compound?" I ask.

"A half hour's walk to the east. Can you travel?" At least he looks at me straight on when he speaks.

"Yes. Thank you."

I follow him around the city walls to a small trail leading to the east. You can hardly call it a trail actually, it's so overgrown with weeds and grasses. My escort walks ahead of me without speaking, only occasionally looking back to check if I'm there. A few times, I see Preener or Scrawny flying behind me, and I waver between gladness at seeing them and worry that they'll be noticed.

Finally, we come upon a small settlement. It is nothing like Sehmar City. Instead of high stone fortifications, the perimeter here is marked by a worn earthen wall barely taller than I am. Haphazard rooftops jut out like crooked teeth on the other side. The four soldiers standing guard at the gate wave us in without a word. I get the impression that they're here to keep people in, rather than out.

I fight back a moment of panic when we step through the gates. Makeshift sheds line the roads, some made of proper bricks, some with walls of piled mud, and others that look to be a hodgepodge of straw, sticks, cloth, and whatever else was available at the time. The complete lack of uniformity is disorienting, and I wonder how often a house simply falls apart. The few people on the narrow dirt streets look with suspicion on me and my imperial escort. Some are dressed in fine linens, while others wear nothing more than rags. None of them wear veils over their rosemarked skin, and yet I feel vulnerable when I remove my own. These people look at me with every bit the amount of suspicion shown me by the healthy.

I keep my eyes trained in front of me, but I do see enough to know that there are all types here. An almost-portly older man strolls down the street, while nearby, a beggar girl reaches out to him with skeletal arms. I stop and search my bag for a scrap of bread and hand it to the child as my escort turns to hurry me along. What do people do for food here? What will I do once my supplies run out? The soldier ahead of me keeps walking, paying them no mind. I wonder if his rosemarked comrades from his battalion are here. Does he think about how narrowly he avoided this fate?

Finally, we approach a tall villa with walls of well-formed bricks, and polished wooden beams in the roof. To my surprise, I see two rosemarked soldiers standing guard. My escort salutes them and enters.

Compared to the shabbiness of the rest of the compound, this place is another world. The front door opens into a simple gardened courtyard. An old woman digs beneath one of the trees, working at its roots. A gardener? There is even a pool of water in the middle, lined with smooth blue and green tiles.

We pass through a second door into a sitting room, where the soldier gestures for me to sit. I sink gingerly into a chair, and then relax more freely as I remember that everyone who enters this room is already ill. The furniture is plain but smells of fine cured wood that must have been imported from somewhere farther north. I'm about to ask after Commander Arxa when a voice sounds from above.

"Is that you, Healer Zivah?"

The speaker is young, with the cultured tone of well-bred Amparans. I finally spot a young woman at the top of the stairs.

She looks to be about Alia's age, just a couple years younger than me. Her skin is almost as fair as my own, which makes her rosemarks all the more prominent. Her dark blond hair is bound up in intricate braids.

The girl breaks into a smile. "It *is* you! I'm so glad you're here!" She gathers her skirts and runs the rest of the way down. I get the impression I should be standing in her presence.

She takes my hands, and I'm glad I had the foresight to put Diadem back in her cage. "You must have had a long journey." Then she notices my confusion and adds, "I am Mehtap, Commander Arxa's daughter."

Mehtap. So this is the girl whose name Arxa called constantly in his delirium. I'd guessed before that he loved her dearly. If this fine house, complete with servants, is any sign, I guessed rightly.

"Lady Mehtap," I say, curtsying. "I did not know you were afflicted as well."

Her face falls for the briefest moment before she summons another smile. "Yes. I'm afraid I fell ill slightly before my father. But I apparently did not have his fighting spirit."

"Do not be unfair to yourself. The disease is unpredictable in the best of us."

"Yes, so they say. You are kind to remind me."

The air between us is sober for a moment. But then she claps her hands. "Father will be here shortly. You're to live in this house with me. We've prepared a room for you upstairs."

I'm ashamed at the lightness that floods through me at her words. I'd been steeling myself for the prospect of building my own hovel in an abandoned corner of the compound, though it feels wrong to rejoice when others have had to do that very thing.

Mehtap bids me to follow her on a quick tour of the house.

She tells me it was constructed for a general's lover a few years back. That man died, and other rosemarked aristocrats cycled in. Most recently, Mehtap lived here with a cousin of hers who fell ill in the same outbreak as Mehtap, but the cousin died last month.

"So soon?" I ask. Usually the disease grants us a few years before returning.

"I suppose she gave up," Mehtap says. Again, she is silent for a moment before shaking off her gloom. "It will be nice to have company again."

I follow quietly, unsure what to make of this talkative young woman, and unsure what she makes of me. She seems so glad for my company, and I wonder if she's truly thought about our differences. Does she realize that her father and those like him control the fate of my village? I wonder how I am to carry out my mission with her so close.

Thankfully, Mehtap doesn't seem to notice my silence. She points out the gardens, the storeroom and simple kitchen, the sitting room, and the living quarters upstairs. I breathe a sigh of relief when I see that my room does not directly neighbor hers. I also have a window, which will make it easier to manage the crows. Beyond that, it's comfortable—more comfortable than what I was used to in Dara. The bed is piled with thick blankets. There is also a desk, a chair like the ones downstairs, and a small chest.

Mehtap has stopped speaking, and I realize she's waiting for my reaction.

"Thank you," I say. "It's wonderful."

At that moment, a voice echoes from downstairs. "Commander Arxa has arrived."

Mehtap's face lights up. "Father would like to see you." With a quick glance over her shoulder to see if I'm coming, she runs for the stairs. I follow more slowly, trying to quiet my sudden nerves. Here in the heart of Ampara, it's all too easy to remember that Arxa is one of the best commanders in the Amparan army. He is intelligent, observant, and ruthless. Who am I to think I can deceive him?

The commander and four of his soldiers are waiting in the sitting room when I arrive at the top of the stairs. He must not be on duty, because he wears ankle-length court robes. His coloring is much healthier than when I last saw him, and he stands as if he's regained his strength. His umbermarks are as clear as ever and give him a fierce appearance. I try to swallow the bitter taste in my mouth. I thought I'd been careful about wearing gloves and washing myself as I treated him. Where did I go wrong?

"Father!" Mehtap runs into his arms.

Arxa embraces his daughter and squeezes her tight. It's a show of affection I wouldn't have thought him capable of, given what I'd seen in Dara. Then he turns his attention to me. "Zivah. I am pleased you decided to come."

My heart pounds in my ears as I navigate the last few stairs. A panicked certainty arises that his gaze will lay my secrets bare.

"I am grateful for your invitation, Commander." My voice quavers, and I hope he'll ascribe it to the stresses of travel.

He studies me, and I know he's looking at the telltale marks of the disease. I oblige him by pulling my sleeve, revealing the skin there as well.

"I'm sorry to see you like this," Arxa says. He doesn't show much emotion, but I do believe he is sincere.

"It is the burden of a healer," I tell him. "I won't say I'm happy to be in this state, but it is a risk we take every time we see a patient."

"Just as my soldiers face death on the battlefield every day. Perhaps our paths are more similar than we think. Indeed, your talents would have been wasted if you'd stayed isolated in your village. A soldier must fight. A healer must heal. You can still do good, for the years you have left."

It feels strange that I should agree with him, though I am no longer sure what kind of good works I'm meant to do. But a calmness has settled on me now, and I pull it over myself like a mask.

"Thank you, Commander. I hope to serve as I can."

That night I unpack my things and set up my cages in my room. I also take the first hot bath I've had since I left Dara. Then, when the house seems quiet and Mehtap has returned to her room, I open the window. I can see shadows moving in the darkness. I hear people shouting in the distance, and then a scream. The sound sends a shiver up my spine. Arxa had warned me not to wander outside at night without a guard. It doesn't take much imagination to think of things that might happen in a place as desperate as this.

I glance once more at the door to make sure it's latched, and then lean out the window and whistle as Dineas taught me. For a long, nerve-wracking moment, nothing happens. But then wings beat the air and Scrawny alights on my windowsill. A few moments later, Preener comes down and nudges him to the side.

"You made it!" I say breathlessly, and then I feel silly for talking to birds. Preener, true to his name, starts picking at his feathers. It's a good thing, for both us and them, that animals aren't vulnerable to rose plague. To the crows, this place is just a particularly dirty village.

I scribble identical notes on two scraps of leather, using a simple cipher that Gatha had given me to learn. *Made it safely into compound.* I give the crows some crusts of bread I'd saved from dinner, then tie the messages to their legs.

"Find Dineas," I say. I wonder if he followed me this morning, and hope that he's safe.

Preener swallows one last breadcrumb and takes off into the darkness. Scrawny spends a few more moments pecking around before following. Between the noises from outside and the events of the day, I don't expect to fall asleep quickly, but the blankets are soft, and I'm tired, and I eventually drift away.

The crows are nowhere in sight when I wake the next morning. I try not to think of the myriad things that could have gone wrong. Did the birds get lost? Get injured? Get killed before they could find Dineas? My mind provides no dearth of disasters, and I try to convince myself that it's too early to expect a reply. Perhaps the birds are simply slower messengers than I'd assumed.

I'm surprised to see Arxa in the dining room when I come down. Perhaps he stayed the night, though I don't see Mehtap around. He greets me and gestures toward the table, where someone has laid out flatbread and stewed beans. The bread is freshly baked and quite good. I finish the first piece quickly and reach for another.

"Were your accommodations satisfactory?" Arxa asks.

I take a moment to swallow before I answer. "Very much so, Commander. I slept soundly."

"And how are things at Dara? Your village is expanding their crop terraces, is that right?"

"Yes, sir. It will require extra work, but the additional harvest will help in lean years."

"I'm glad to hear it," he says. He puts down his bread and looks straight at me. "Seems like you may have a lean year coming, if the Shidadi keep raiding your village."

It's all I can do not to drop my bread. "I've heard of a raid or two, but we don't see much of the nomads."

"That's funny. My people have reported increased nomad sightings around Dara."

It's impossible to tell what he's thinking, and I can't help but feel that his eyes can see right through my skin. "I'm afraid I'm only a healer, and a rosemarked one at that. Everything I hear is secondhand."

He's still watching me. "Yes, I suppose you're right."

Is he toying with me? My breakfast sticks to the roof of my mouth. "I must thank you again for inviting me here, Commander," I say. "I'm looking forward to being able to work again."

He brushes some crumbs off the table onto the floor. "I'll be curious if you still feel the same way after seeing the hospital. Jesmin is in charge there and expecting you. You can have one of the guards at the manor door guide you there."

It takes all my willpower to walk calmly out into the courtyard. I ask a guard to lead me to the hospital, and my mind is awhirl as I follow him. Was Arxa sending me a warning? Am I jumping at shadows? Again I wish I knew where Dineas was.

We're almost at the gate to the compound when the soldier stops.

"The hospital," he says, indicating a door. And then he leaves me.

I linger outside for a moment, taking in the building. It's not particularly impressive—one story high and constructed of irregular bricks, though it's not falling down, which is already better than many of the structures nearby. There's no sign on or above the door. The shutters on the few small windows are open, and I see some shadows moving inside.

When I push the door open, the sight makes me stumble back. In the dimly lit first room, laid out all along the wall on frayed grass pallets, are patients in the active throes of the rose plague. The air is thick with disease. It's exactly like the outbreak back at Dara—the cries of delirious patients, the blank stares, and the acrid smell of sweat. But unlike at Dara, there's no one here tending the sick.

After a few moments, I recover enough to go in. I pace down the dirt aisle between the patients, looking about for clues to the physicians' whereabouts. Near the uneven brick wall is a stand with a water basin and what looks to be clean rags. I soak one in the water, kneel next to a man with graying hair, and wipe down his forehead. He looks at me, uncomprehending, and I whisper for him to rest. I move on from him to a plump middle-aged woman who's shivering violently. I tuck her threadbare blankets more closely around her, but it doesn't seem to help.

"You might find more blankets in the back room," says a voice behind me. "But we may have run out. We're always short of supplies."

I jump. Behind me is a lanky older man. Other than Arxa, he's the first umbertouched individual I've seen all day.

"I'm sorry," I say. "I'm looking for—"

"You're Zivah?"

I nod.

He regards me calmly. "You got to work right away. It's a sign of a good healer. I'm Jesmin, physician of this compound."

Even if he hadn't told me, I would have known. The man wears no healer's sash—I suppose the healers here have no such uniform—but he has that same quality Kaylah has, where his very presence seems to dampen the edges of suffering around him. It also doesn't escape me that he'd said "physician," not "one of the physicians."

"You're the only one?"

His mouth quirks. "Just me."

I look around, taken aback. "But there must be at least a thousand people living in this community."

"Indeed. A thousand living here, plus those abandoned outside our gates. Other healers come in from time to time, but they keep dying." He says this plainly, but I don't get the sense he's making light of the plague, just that he's long ago accepted the realities.

He looks me over, much as Arxa had earlier. "You're rosemarked," he says matter-of-factly. "Can you still function?"

It's strange, talking about myself as if I were a patient. "Other than the obvious, I am in acceptable health. I made the journey here in good time."

"You traveled a long way for this," he says. "I imagine most patients would prefer to be near their families."

Again, I hear the unspoken message. Most people, *when dying*, would want to be near their loved ones. My chest squeezes at the memory of Alia running off in tears. "I could have stayed, but I'd rather be where I can be of use." I'm glad my mother does not hear these words.

I can tell my answer pleases him. "Not all healers enter the trade for the same reasons. Some do it for respect, or for the money that it brings. Others do it because they must, because they cannot ignore the suffering of the ailing." I wonder what category Jesmin falls in. He's umbertouched, which means he could rejoin the rest of the world if he wanted, but he lives and works here.

"Come," says Jesmin. "I'll give you a quick tour of the place." He gestures toward the patients around us. "As you may have surmised, this room is for the newly fevered."

That was clear enough. "Is the rose plague not treated in the city?"

"It's supposed to be. It is a crime, actually, to dump one's sick outside the compound, but people do it regardless—families who cannot pay for a healer or who fear the sickness in their house."

There are other rooms as well: some for ailments unrelated to the plague, and others for those whose fever has returned to claim them. As we walk through the dim rooms, I see rosemarked helpers tending the sicker patients. Jesmin tells me they're hired helpers, untrained in the healing arts except for the simplest tasks.

We circle back to where we started, and he turns to face me. "So, Zivah, what are your impressions?"

What are my impressions? The gods have deserted this place. The hospital is overcrowded, and the conditions are appalling. There aren't nearly enough caretakers to go around, even with the hired help. If the rosemarked compound is a waiting chamber for the dying, this hospital is its wounded, stuttering heart.

Jesmin is watching me. I'm sure my thoughts are plain on my face, and he knows the truth about his hospital as well as I do. But his question wasn't really a question. It was a challenge. And I feel something within myself rise to meet it.

"There is work to be done," I say.

For the first time today, he smiles. "Plenty of it. How would you like to start?"

The opportunity does not escape me. "If it's all right with you, I'd like to spend my time with the newly fevered. I have some herbs that might help them."

"Wouldn't all the patients benefit from your herbs?"

"They will," I say. "And I don't plan to neglect the rest. It's just that... Forgive me. The newly ill may be wretched, but they're closer to the land of the living than the rest of us. I'd like to be near that, to have a little bit of hope." It's a reason I concoct on the spot, but it's not a lie.

Jesmin's brows furrow. "There's not much hope in the front room, I'm afraid. The patients brought in are greatly weakened from their time exposed to the elements. The lucky ones emerge rosemarked. We haven't had anyone recover completely in years."

"Still, a little hope is better than none," I say. "And perhaps I can ease the suffering of the rest."

He considers my words, and nods. "Very well, then. The choice is yours."

# CHAPTER THIRTEEN
## DINEAS

I trail Zivah at a distance as the soldier leads her to the rose-marked compound, squinting into the sun and trying not to stir up too much sand as I follow. Once she's through the gates, I turn back. I can't help her once she's inside those walls, and I need to be where the crows can find me.

I rest for the first half day, close enough to Sehmar to see it, but far enough so the gate guards are just dots by the wall. I'm twitchy, so close to the capital, and every glimpse of its walls puts an unpleasant taste in my mouth. Slicewing flies back and forth over the hills, and now that I'm alone, worries about the mission start crowding into my head. I can take care of myself out here—as long as I keep my wits about me. But between the flashbacks and the potions, my wits aren't exactly reliable. There's nothing to do for it though, except remember to take my potions and stay out of sight.

By late afternoon I'm restless. Preener and Scrawny still haven't returned, and you can only oil your weapons and throw pebbles at unsuspecting lizards so many times before it gets tiresome. I'm even starting to miss Zivah. There's something to be said for company, even if it's the company of a Dara healer. When the sun is low enough to make wandering more comfortable, I pack up my things and strap them on my back again. I want a better sense of my surroundings, and the crows should be able to find me as long as I don't stray far.

I find some dusty trails through the hills, lined with the occasional bush or gnarled dwarf tree. At least one of them ends at a watering hole. There's also the occasional fire ring or hut. The grass clusters around them are well-trampled, so I make a note to avoid these areas. Hunting and trapping don't look good though. I see hardly any tracks, and the few birds around are as skittish as unblooded soldiers. If I run out of food, I could forage enough to stay alive, but probably not comfortably.

I've about circled back to where I began when a great thundering vibrates through the ground. I run up the nearest hill to investigate, and what I see is a wonder to behold. A herd of horses runs across the desert, kicking up a cloud of dust in its wake. Even from this distance I can tell that they're beauties—long elegant strides, strength in every toss of their manes. The coming sunset bathes their coats in reddish gold. These are Rovenni horses, braver than most men, and I daresay more intelligent than a good portion as well. Our tribe used to fight on horses before we fled across the strait. I've fond memories of a chestnut mare I trained on day-to-day—not nearly as majestic as these creatures though.

I hike toward the herd to get a better look. Now that I'm closer, I can see the expert riders driving them. The Rovenni traders are master animal breeders. Sometimes they raise horses, sometimes sheep, goats, dogs, or birds. Their whole lives revolve around the care and training of their creatures.

Something sharp pokes me in the back. I freeze.

"Make no sudden movements," says a gruff voice.

And one more thing about these breeders. They're fiercely protective of their life's work.

"Keep your hands away from your swords. Reach them straight out to the sides and don't move."

I inhale slowly through my teeth as rough hands pat me down. This seems to be happening more and more often these days.

"I was simply admiring your horses. That's no crime, is it?" I say as someone lifts my pack off my back, and then my swords. The same hands confiscate my daggers a few moments later. I bite back several curses. Why don't they just strip off my skin while they're at it?

"Turn around."

Slowly, I obey. There are two people in the welcoming party. A muscular man a few years older than me has his spear aimed at my heart. Next to him, also armed and eyeing me with equal venom, is a woman. Both of them are wearing dusty robes, trousers, and fine riding boots, and they hold their spears like they know how to use them.

"Is the army sending spies now?" says the man. "That's low even for them. I've told you. The breeding stock is off the table."

For a moment I think I'm found out, but then I realize he means the Amparan armies. "You're mistaken," I say. "I'm just a traveler."

"You came out for a stroll, armed like that? Tell your masters we sell our geldings at a fair price. That's all they'll ever get."

"I'm not from the army," I say again.

He narrows his eyes. "A petty thief, then."

The man's starting to grate on me, and I want my swords back. Briefly I consider trying to disarm him, but I'd like to avoid a scuffle right now.

"Look, trader. If I was trying to spy on you, I would have done a better job of it. And I've no mind to make off with your cargo. What would I do? Climb down the hill and fight off all your guards by myself?"

"You may have friends nearby," says the man.

"Look around," I say. "Search the area at your pleasure. You'll find nothing."

"Let's not jump to conclusions, Nush," says the woman. "He looks too dusty for a spy. And we can verify his claims."

The man hooks the front of my tunic with his spearhead. I fight the urge to grab it. Dusty indeed. Have they taken a good look at themselves lately?

"Very well," he says. "But you're coming with us until we've had a look around."

The woman retrieves a rope from her saddlebag and signals for me to put my hands behind my back. I hesitate, weighing my choices. It's getting close to sundown, and Zivah will probably be sending Preener when she gets the chance—not the best time to be marched off by strangers. But then, it's not the best time to fight two horsemen within spitting distance of their friends either. Finally, I decide to take my chances. Rovenni are by all accounts honorable people. Or at least, they're too rich to be tempted by petty crime.

Once I'm bound tight, the woman motions toward the horses. For a moment, my spirits rise at the thought of actually getting to ride one of them. But no. My captors mount, and then they tell me to walk in front.

There's roughly fifty people of all ages down at their camp. The big man leads the way, and a crowd gathers as we draw near.

"We found this man sitting on a hillside with a bag full of weapons, watching our herd," Nush says. "Claims not to be a thief, but I think we'd do well to sweep the hills."

There are murmurs of agreement all around. Five men volunteer to ride out, and then Nush pulls me toward the campfire.

"Sit," he says. "You'll be here a while."

I plop unceremoniously down on the ground, which earns me an amused half smile from the woman.

Nush leaves to ride with the others as the woman, who they call Phaeda, stays to guard me. Gradually the rest of the camp resumes its business. There's a handful of people grooming the horses, others setting up tents. One person brews stew in a pot big enough for me to sleep in.

Phaeda sets her spear down beside her, levels a long look at me until she's convinced I won't run off, and then takes a needle and a round disk out of a bag. She starts sharpening the needle against the stone, looking up frequently to check if I'm doing anything suspicious.

A man about my age walks by, and Phaeda flags him down.

His forearm is bandaged, and she pulls the dressing away to reveal a burn wound in the shape of several wavy lines. She scrutinizes it, then wraps it up again. "Change the bandage."

As she waves him off, I see a faint scar on the underside of her forearm, as well as on the others nearby. I've heard about how the traders brand themselves with the same irons they use on their horses, but it's the first time I've seen them up close. It's a rite of passage for them, apparently.

The smell of pungent stew wafts over from the campfires. My mouth waters, and I wonder how these people feel about feeding prisoners. I'm looking forlornly at the soup pot, when I see a shadow flitting just outside the light of the campfires. I freeze. Phaeda looks at me, and I do my best to pretend that nothing's happened. She narrows her eyes, but in a few moments starts sharpening her needle again, and I sneak another look toward the shadow. Could that be . . .

A ruffle of black feathers, and the unmistakable profile of a very vain bird.

Preener. If he sticks around, he's going to end up in the stew pot.

I turn my face so my guard can't see me. "Go away," I whisper. "Not now."

But can the bird even hear me from this distance? I see the infuriating thing hopping around.

"Fly!" I whisper.

Preener takes a few tentative hops closer.

"No," I bark, and then turn it into a cough when several heads swivel my way. "Have you no decency?" I say loudly. "Tying up a man simply for walking in the desert."

The puzzled faces harden into annoyance, and everyone resumes their tasks. I breathe a sigh of relief and look at the edge of the fire again. That dratted bird is still there. If my hands weren't tied behind my back, I'd throw them in the air.

"Fine," I mutter. "If you want to be dinner, go ahead." That must have been the invitation he was looking for, because he takes flight toward me.

Phaeda's head snaps up. I steel myself for the worst.

Hooves sound in the distance, and Preener flies away as Nush and the five scouts return. People gather around the horsemen. I strain my ears but can't make out what's being said. Finally, the crowd parts and Nush comes up to me.

"We see no sign of your friends," he says grudgingly.

"Because there aren't any," I say. "Of all the stupid, cowardly—"

Something twitches along his jawline. "You'll stay in our camp until tomorrow morning. If we can still find no sign of anyone else, we'll let you leave."

I glare at him. "And you'll compensate me for my trouble?"

"We'll let you keep your hands and your life," he says.

I should have told Preener to relieve himself in their soup pots. Actually, I wonder if that's something I could train the crows to do. The smell of cooking meat teases my nose, and my stomach growls so loudly that Nush lifts an eyebrow.

I give him my most charming smile. "How about you give me my hands, my life, and a bowl of stew?"

# CHAPTER FOURTEEN

## ZIVAH

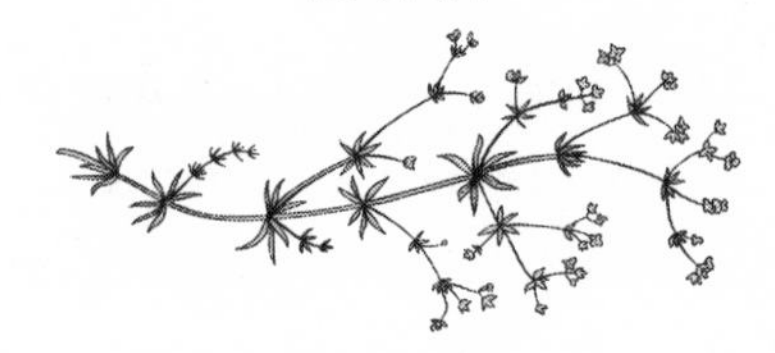

Preener is waiting on my windowsill when I get back from the hospital. I'm so relieved to see him that I almost forget to bolt my door before running across the room. The bird takes a nervous hop back at the sight of me, but a few moments later he flies onto my table and presents his leg.

I untie the parchment with trembling hands and decode the message.

*Was detained, but safe now. Camping nearby.*

Detained? Did the Amparans find him? But at least he's alive. I close my eyes and gather my thoughts. Given my conversation with Arxa this morning, can we possibly continue blindly with the plan? I need to speak with Dineas face-to-face.

I scrape off the top layer of the parchment with a knife, then pause to consider my response.

*Must talk. Tomorrow night, first watch, northwest corner of the compound.*

I start second-guessing my decision as soon as I send Preener off. Should I risk a face-to-face meeting so soon? And what if Arxa's having me watched? Either way, the message is sent. Dineas will have to avoid guards on his way in, and I must trust him to do his part. As for myself, how will I get to the meeting spot without being seen?

At the hospital the next day, I notice the many wounded who come in for treatment—stab wounds, broken bones, head injuries. Law has very little meaning here, especially at night. Arxa's warning not to wander outside alone after dark echoes in my head.

That night after dinner, I lock myself in my room and survey my belongings. I tie my blowgun to my belt. The darts, newly dipped in a sleeping potion, go in the pocket of my apron. And lastly Diadem, content after swallowing a trapped mouse the night before, goes on my arm. I cover it all with a cloak, and head downstairs.

The guards at the villa gate look up as I come through the courtyard.

"Please escort me to the hospital," I say to the nearest one. "My patients will not wait until morning," I add when he frowns.

He hesitates, but escorting me after dark is one of his duties. When we get to the hospital, I tell him I will be a few hours and ask him to wait outside.

The hospital looks even gloomier after sundown. The front room is lit by a lamp barely bright enough to cast shadows. Jesmin has likely gone home and left one or two of his helpers to tend the sicker patients overnight. None of them are in sight though, and I don't go looking for them. The less attention I draw, the better.

I change a few blankets and bedpans and help a few patients with water.

All too soon, it's time to go. I check once more to make sure no one's in dire need of care, and then glance out the window to make sure my soldier escort is still waiting. Then I head to the back corridor and the door that leads out the other side of the building.

The first thing I notice is how dark it is. It must have been equally dark coming here with my escort, but the shadows are pronounced now that I'm alone. The paths are empty, though it's by no means quiet. Voices drift past me, some loud, some soft. The walls of the houses are so thin, it's hard to tell which sounds are inside and which ones are from people out on the streets. My blowgun knocks against my knees as I walk, and I find myself wishing for a harness like Dineas has for his swords.

I make it a good distance from the hospital with no sign of anyone following me, but then I hear the footsteps of a large crowd. A group of ten people turn onto the path in front of me. Some are young, some are old—all carry weapons. An older woman limps at their front, giving orders.

"The beggars are holding back their earnings," she says. "See if they'll be more honest with persuasion."

There's something in her voice that stops me cold—it's the same feeling I get when I see a snake an arm's length away. I take a slow step back, wondering how best to leave without attracting attention, when the woman looks straight at me.

"Who is that?" she asks the man next to her. "Get her."

I turn on my heel and run, fleeing down the nearest side

alley. I wedge myself in the narrow space between two houses, my blowgun clattering against the wall as I raise it and reach for my darts. Shadows darken the alley as men run past. I hold my blowgun steady, staring so hard at the opening to my hiding place that it starts to blur in my vision.

Long moments pass. The sounds of pursuit grow softer. The woman's voice fades into the distance.

Though it's a cool night, I'm damp with sweat beneath my cloak. This entire evening feels like a bad fever dream. Part of me wants to cower here the rest of the night, but Dineas is waiting for me, and I've already lost precious time.

I'm much more careful the rest of the way, listening for people approaching, and freezing at the slightest movement. My muscles are cramped from nerves by the time I reach the corner of the compound. It's hard for me to tell the time, as it's too far from the gate to hear the watch bells. I back into an alcove, ready my weapon, and wait. The heat of my walk is seeping out of my cloak when I hear a flutter of wings around me. A crow lands on my shoulder.

"Is Dineas here?" I whisper.

The bird takes off again. A few moments later, a dark shape climbs over the wall and drops to the ground. He stays in a crouch, looking left and right.

"Over here," I call. He looks in my direction, then runs over, trailing a cloud of dust. I never thought I'd be so glad to see him. "I was worried when I didn't hear from the crows."

He snorts. "Some horse traders took me prisoner for a day, but it's all settled now."

Horse traders? "How much did they learn about you?"

"They were suspicious, but I don't think they figured out what I was. They don't strike me as the type to confide in the empire."

It's not the most reassuring of answers. "I hope you're right."

"Me too. Is it safe to talk here?"

"It's the best I can do." I decide not to mention my encounter with the gang on the way over. "I'm living in a house with Arxa's daughter, and I'm working in the hospital. Tal was right about the sick being left outside the walls. It happens every day, and the guards cart them in."

"That's good, right? Let's move on with the plan, then."

"We can," I say. "But..."

"But what?"

"I don't think the plan will work."

Dineas laughs under his breath. "Zivah, we knew coming here that this probably wouldn't work."

"No, I mean..." I hesitate again, trying to put words to my thoughts. "I spoke to Commander Arxa this morning. He suspects that Dara is collaborating with the Shidadi. If someone with your skill shows up so soon after I arrive... it's too suspicious."

Dineas shifts in the darkness; I can see his shadow hunched over in thought. "What we need is some other story for him to believe. If we can lead him to have his own ideas about where I came from, if there's some way to draw his thoughts away from the Shidadi..." His breath catches. "I might have an idea. Maybe."

"What is it?" I ask.

"Do you have anything to heal burn scars?"

# CHAPTER FIFTEEN
## DINEAS

Scouting work's never been my favorite. Too much time crawling on my belly, too many opportunities for small, sharp rocks to work themselves into my loincloth.

From my vantage point above the Rovenni camp, I see they're having a good run at the market. The size of the herd has dwindled since the last time I saw it, though they've kept their most impressive stallions and mares. This time I'm much more careful about getting caught. I keep my ears sharp and my birds playing sentry. Somehow, I doubt the Rovenni would believe my innocence if they caught me again. Once or twice, my crow caws, and I scramble from my hiding place and move somewhere else.

It's late evening and I've been here since before noon. Dinner's been cooked, passed out, and eaten by the fifty-two members I counted, and the camp is starting to wind down. Some people disappear into large square tents, while others prepare to take the first watch for the night. I see Nush heading out to sleep with the horses. One of the mares is finicky, and he flashes the brand on his arm so she sees it, and whispers in her ear. The mare calms down, and Nush goes on to check on the others.

Who would have guessed that he was right about me? I do want to steal something from them. It's just not what he thought.

I wait until everything goes still, when the last person has gone into the tents and no one else emerges. Carefully, I creep toward the camp.

Getting down between the tents undetected isn't as hard as I thought it would be. You can tell what a rich man values by where he places his guards, and most of the Rovenni sentries watch the horses. I'm sure there's gold in the camp too, spread out in different places if they're smart, but the traders don't seem to worry nearly as much about losing it. They'd be angry if someone walked off with their coin. Steal one of their foals though, and you'll be a marked man for life.

I creep past the outer ring of tents, the ones where most of the people retired for the night. The supply tents are in the middle, larger than the sleeping tents and with less snoring coming from within. I know the cooking pots come from the center tent, and some bridles and horseshoes went into the tent next to it. Well, it makes sense that horse equipment would be stored together. I lift the flap and duck in.

Inside, it smells like leather and metal, a good omen. As my eyes adjust, dark shapes materialize around me. The nearest shadow to me turns out to be a pile of blankets. A stack of horseshoes is next to it. I make my way carefully, gingerly feeling everything in my path. Smooth leather saddles, wood bristle brushes . . . I know it must be in here. The traders wouldn't travel without something so important.

Finally, my fingers brush a thin metal rod. I follow it with my hands and feel the flat wave patterns at the end, the weight of good, smooth metal. The branding iron.

I slip the iron down the back of my tunic. The branding surface chills the skin of my back. Then I get out of the camp as quick as I can manage. Slicewing flies above my head as I trek across the hills, putting as much distance between me and the horse traders as I can. Finally, when the moon's about to set, I find a place to rest.

I set the branding iron in front of me, and it taunts me as I gather brush for a fire, poking at memories I've long tried to suppress. In the dungeons, they branded the prisoners marked for slavery in the same interrogation rooms where they tortured us. I can still hear the sizzle of first contact, smell the odor of burning flesh. I'd rather stick my hand into the coals than relive these moments, but now I must bring them back, sift them for details. How hot did the slaver heat the iron? How long did he hold it against each man's skin?

The branding iron is patterned in three curved bars that remind me of horse tails. I stick it into the heart of the fire and watch it take on a devilish glow. As the iron gets hot, I tear up some greener blades of grass and knot them around my arms. I also snap a large stick off a dwarf tree and strip off the spiny leaves.

The screams of the interrogation room echo in my head. We were so helpless in there. So utterly at their mercy.

My heart's pounding hard against my rib cage as I remove the branding iron from the fire. What I wouldn't do for a jug of wine right now.

I bite down on the stick.

*Breathe, Dineas, breathe.*

My hand shakes. I drop the iron back into the fire. I can't do this.

But I must. For Gatha. For my mother. For my father.

I grab the iron again. Flesh sizzles. White-hot pain sears my skin. That old familiar smell drifts to my nostrils. I swallow a groan and count to three. Then I throw the thing to the ground. My arm feels like it's being attacked by flaming bees. I lean over to the side and vomit.

I cover my face and double over. The darkness presses in around me, feeding my memories, awakening my ghosts. They whisper in my ears, and all I can do is curl into a ball, pull my arms in close, and wait for the nightmare to pass.

The horse traders had scars shaped like three wavy lines. My new brand looks similar, though the lines are broken up in the places where I tied the leaves. The result is a wound that's similar to their tribe, but not close enough to be identified as theirs.

Over the next days, I apply Zivah's salve every morning, waiting for the burn to look a little less fresh. In the meantime, I have preparations to make. In addition to the burn salve, the crows bring me other medicines. One is a cream to tint my umbermarks red. The other is a root to induce fever.

As the days pass, my brand scabs over and the scabs fall off. My umbermarks grow red with ointment. And I know it's time. I send Zivah one last note and get one last reply: *Be careful.*

That afternoon, I start chewing the fever root as I wrap my belongings and dig a hole for them near a cluster of bushes. The root has a funny taste—a spicy earthiness that goes up my nose. I chew slowly as Zivah told me, sucking juice out with every bite. Then, when it's lost all its flavor, I swallow it whole. I don't feel any different after I swallow it. Maybe the sickness takes some time to settle in.

I shovel dirt over my things, and camouflage the newly packed dirt with rocks. Among the things buried in my bag are the vials of potion keeping my memories intact, and I can't help but feel as if I'm burying myself under that bush as well. I wonder what it will be like to see the gates of Sehmar City and not feel the anger bubbling up inside me, to face an Amparan dog and see him as simply another soldier. It feels like a betrayal to forget like this. It feels like the easy way out.

It starts to grow dark, and I make my way toward the compound. A headache starts to take hold, first a sneaking tightness in the back of my head and then an insistent drumbeat as the walls of the compound come into view. Spots dance in front of my eyes when I blink, and I'm muttering choice insults at Zivah as I struggle ahead. I sincerely hope she got the timing right. If this gets much worse before I can make it to the wall, I might be riding out this fever in the open desert with snakes and jackals for company.

The sun sets, and the bell is rung for first watch. From my vantage point, I can see the guards making their rounds. They march around the walls ten circuits an hour, so it doesn't give me much time to get myself down there. It doesn't help that the world's starting to shift around me every time I move my head. I suppose there's not much point in waiting. With every round the guards make, the fever will only grow stronger, and my memories weaker. So I wait until the guards pass by one more time, and then I make my move.

The ground lurches as I get to my feet. I bite down on a curse and stumble to the side before I catch myself. My stomach heaves in protest. I swallow the bile in my throat and force myself to put one foot in front of the other. Don't fall down. The night air feels colder and colder.

A wall materializes before me, and I barely keep myself from slamming into it. My knees buckle; I scrabble at the bricks to stay upright, but it's no good. My head feels like someone's driving a spear through it and twisting.

Footsteps sound as I crumple to the ground, voices as well. I look for them, but my eyes won't focus. I make out helmets and armor, swords, and shields. Amparan soldiers. I can't get captured, not now. I need to get back to Gatha, the rest of my tribe. I throw up my hands to block their blows. My arms feel weighed down with stones.

"Another one left here," says a voice. "Blast it."

They reach for me. I scream and try to push them away. They brush away my efforts like I'm nothing at all.

"Load him onto the cart."

They fling me onto some kind of wagon. I'm back in prison again. They're going to march me through the streets in front of jeering crowds. They'll lock me up and whip me bloody, and this time they won't stop. I scream until someone stuffs a rag in my mouth. Then I gag.

"Cover him up," says a voice. "Might as well keep the cart in case anything else shows up tonight."

# CHAPTER SIXTEEN
## ZIVAH

I'm in the front room, trying to get a fevered woman to drink, when the soldiers finally arrive at the hospital. It's all I can do to keep the cup steady at the woman's lips as I watch the soldiers carry a stretcher through the door.

A blanket is draped over the stretcher. I can't see who's lying underneath.

The patient I'm treating turns her head away from my cup, and I help her back down.

"Just one last night?" I ask the soldiers.

"A young man," says one soldier.

Finally I make out the lines of Dineas's face. His forehead's damp with sweat, and his hair is plastered to his temples. My limbs go soft with relief.

"Thank you, sirs. Please lay him on that empty pallet."

I manage a show of composure until I see the soldiers out. Then I rush to Dineas's side. He stirs at my approach, but his eyes don't focus on me. His skin is warm to the touch, and his pupils are dilated. I lift a corner of his blanket and take his wrist. His pulse is fast, but he's alive, and I cling to that knowledge. Though I've only known him a few weeks, finally having him in the compound with me is the closest thing to having a bit of home.

The fever-inducing root I gave him has clearly taken hold. He's sick and distressed, as he should be, though I can't dispel a nagging guilt for having done this to him. I find the brand he's given himself underneath a bandage on his left forearm. It's no longer an obviously new burn, but it's raw enough that it would catch a seasoned healer's attention. I wrap it up carefully. Better to keep it out of sight a few more days.

And then there's the umbermarks. I look around to make sure no one's watching, then check the skin of his torso and legs. The dark splotches are now a reddish color—not as bright as true rosemarks, but the hospital is dimly lit, and I'll just have to hope nobody looks too carefully.

This is the state of his body, but what is the state of his mind? As if in response to my thoughts, Dineas's eyes suddenly focus on me. He reaches for my hand, and when I take it, he grips me with surprising strength. His gaze is frightened, and he struggles to form words with his lips.

"Zi . . . Where . . ."

A bolt of panic shoots through me. "Be calm," I interrupt before he can say anything more. "You need rest."

He stares at me, and his eyes crinkle as if he's trying to remember. My heart lodges in my throat. He's not supposed to know me.

A new voice speaks from behind me. "Just one brought in this morning?"

Jesmin stands at the foot of Dineas's pallet.

It's a wonder I don't burst from nerves. "Just this one. The fever's gripped him tight."

Jesmin kneels across from me and gives Dineas a cursory examination. I pray he doesn't notice the strangeness of his rosemarks.

"What is this?" Jesmin asks, pointing to the bandage on Dineas's arm.

"A burn scar," I say. "I think he got it before the fever."

Jesmin lets out a heavy breath as he pushes himself back to his feet. "It's a pity when the young fall ill," he says.

"He's young and he's strong," I say. "Perhaps it will help him fight off the disease."

"May Hefana smile on your efforts, then," says Jesmin. His tone is not patronizing, but neither does he speak with great confidence.

"Thank you," I say. I need the Goddess's help far more than Jesmin can possibly imagine.

Over the next days, I watch Dineas toss and turn under the effect of the poisonous root I gave him. He cries out and talks about things only he can see. When I hold water to his lips or give him a spoonful of honey, he stares past me without acknowledging my presence. And all I can do is wait. Wait and hope that I haven't gotten things horribly wrong.

Every day, I wipe down his skin with a cloth, then hide the cloth away before people see the pink dye that's come off onto it.

The color is slower to disappear than I expected. By the fourth day, when his fever breaks and he looks at me with clear eyes, Dineas's skin still looks like that of someone in the throes of the illness. So I do the only thing I can think of. I crouch down at his bedside and squeeze the juice of another fever root into his mouth. He cringes away at the taste. At some level, he knows this will prolong his suffering, but he's too weak to resist.

"Forgive me," I whisper.

Thankfully, the repeated washing starts to work. By the time the root wears off again two days later, Dineas's umbermarks have turned dark. By the sixth day, he's sleeping off the last of the fever.

All morning, I watch him as I go from patient to patient, but he doesn't stir. Finally, when I can't take it anymore, I kneel by his pallet. Once again I'm guilt-stricken by the grayish tone to his skin and the circles under his eyes. His mouth is tight, as if something pains him even now. I pass a wet cloth over his forehead and notice the pallor of my own skin. The past days have taken their toll on me as well.

Suddenly, Dineas's eyes snap open and he sucks in air like a drowning man. He tries to sit up, and despite his weakened state it's all I can do to push his shoulders back down. He yells incoherently and throws his hands up.

"It's all right," I say softly, repeating the words in my gentlest voice, hoping my own fear doesn't show through. This entire plan is folly. I should have known this, but it's too late now. "You're safe. You're safe with us."

As I repeat those words, I feel his muscles relax under me, though his breathing still comes hoarse and frightened. His sweat rubs off onto my forearms, leaving slick tracks on my skin. Finally,

I sit up straight and look down at him. His brown eyes are wild, bloodshot.

Footsteps sound behind me, and I see Jesmin rush into the room. I suppose Dineas's yelling was loud even for this hospital. I put up a hand and try to pretend I have everything under control. Jesmin takes a few steps closer, and then stops in his tracks. His jaw drops open.

I focus my attention on Dineas. "My name is Zivah. What is your name?"

At this, he blinks. Confusion crosses his face. "I don't know." For a long time, he says nothing. He stares at the ceiling, eyes moving back and forth. "I don't remember anything," he says, with the slow horror of someone who's realized that something is very, very wrong. He pushes himself up on one elbow and fixes his eyes desperately on mine. "How did I get here?"

I can see his breathing speeding up again, the confusion building up in his eyes, but this time it seems he has himself under control. I squeeze his hand. "I know this is frightening, but try to rest. Once you are better, we can sort everything out."

His eyes flicker over my face again. "You look familiar. I feel like I've spoken to you before. But it was in a different place."

I'm painfully aware of Jesmin watching us, listening to every word of our conversation. So I look Dineas in the eye and tell the first of many lies to come. "You're confused by your delirium. We've never spoken before today."

# CHAPTER SEVENTEEN
## DINEAS

They tell me I was found outside the compound wall. That my companions, my family, my friends, whoever they were, left me for dead. And they tell me that even so, I'm one of the lucky ones.

The day I wake up, I'm some kind of marvel to those around me. Zivah, the woman who takes care of me, drops by often, checking my pulse, my color, my eating and breathing. Honestly, I think she's just trying to convince herself I'm alive. Then there's Jesmin, the head physician here. He looks at me as if I have two heads.

"You must have been very healthy before your illness," he says. "We haven't had someone emerge umbertouched for years."

Rosemarked. Umbertouched. Sehmar City. Hearing these words is like seeing something through a mist. My physicians tell me about the rose plague, about the course the disease can take. Some of what they say feels familiar. The rest takes me by surprise.

The mist is uneven. I can see no pattern to it.

Late in the afternoon, Zivah visits me again. Even in these past few hours, her gentle presence has become a touchstone. I remember glimpses of her during my delirium . . . wiping my forehead, holding water to my lips . . . I even remember speaking to her. There are confusing images of a cottage in a wood.

"You really don't know your name?" she asks.

I shake my head. I can't rid myself of the feeling that I'm letting her down.

Zivah folds her hands in her lap. "When you were brought in, you wore a bracelet," she says. "I threw it in the fire along with the rest of your clothing, but I remember seeing the name Dineas on it. Does that sound familiar?"

Now that she says it, it does feel right. "I suppose that's as good a name as any."

She nods, pleased, and her smile makes me feel warm.

"Good," she says. "That's what we will call you."

# CHAPTER EIGHTEEN
## ZIVAH

Dineas recovers quickly. This shouldn't surprise me, since I'm the one who designed his illness. But the rhythms of illness and recovery are imprinted in my healer's instincts, and even though I know that he doesn't actually have the rose plague, I'm still surprised every time I find him healthier than expected. Day by day, he gains strength.

We move him to a smaller room in the hospital. After a few days, he's out of bed whenever I come to see him, either walking around or at the window staring at the ramshackle houses beyond. He's eager to be outside, but I'm not quite ready to let him. Real illness or feigned, his body is still weak. I'm firm about this, and he seems to accept my authority.

He's hungry for human interaction, anything that will help him feel less lost in this world he no longer remembers. His face lights up whenever I enter the room. It's strange to me the first few times I see it. The old Dineas would never have shown such happiness at the sight of me, but the new Dineas's smile is infectious, and his eyes are warm.

Today when I check on him, he's at the window. "Zivah," he says, and breaks into a grin.

"What are you looking at?"

I bring his herbs to him, and he keeps his gaze on the window as he sips. Outside, two women are yelling at an old man. It's too far for us to hear what's being said, though their anger is easy enough to detect. After a while, the man starts yelling back. A crowd gathers.

Dineas frowns. "This city outside. It's poor, isn't it? Not every city is this broken-down."

It's fascinating, seeing what parts of his knowledge have survived my potion. He's remembered nothing about himself thus far, which is a relief. But his understanding of the world is also haphazard. He knows bits and pieces, but he needs help stitching them together.

"You're right," I tell him. "Money and skilled workers are hard to come by in here, so the residents must make do with what they have. Once you're well enough to leave this place, you'll see far nicer cities."

It's quiet at the hospital today. One other patient is sleeping off a hangover in the corner, but other than that it's just the two of us in this room. The sheets on Dineas's bed are still mussed from the night before, and I straighten them. "Can you sit down?" I ask him. "I need to take a look at you."

He's familiar with the routine by now. I place my hand on his forehead, check his pulse, and examine his inner eyelids.

"Zivah?"

"What is it?" I cross to my herb table and close all the jars.

He hesitates for another moment. "You're a healer here, like Jesmin?"

I peer over my shoulder with an amused smile. "That, at least, I expect you to know by now."

But he doesn't return my smile. "But you have . . ." He gestures toward me, and his eyes go to my arms. I follow his worried gaze to the red splotches that decorate my skin. Of course he would notice.

I turn my face away from him. The truth of my illness is a familiar ache in my gut, but to my surprise, I find my biggest worry is how it will affect Dineas. He's so childlike in this state. I feel like I'm taking away his innocence.

"I'm a healer," I say carefully. "But I'm also a patient."

He nods slowly. "You told me that only patients whose marks turn brown will survive the plague."

I give myself time to take one breath before answering. "You were very fortunate, Dineas, to be able to beat the disease. I was not."

His eyes cloud over at this. "I'm sorry," he says.

I give him a small smile. "It's all right," I say. "I've had time to grow used to it." But the words sound empty, even to me.

I come home to the sound of harp music. It's beautiful—delicate and plaintive—yet I see no sign of instrument or player in the sitting room. The sound seems to be coming from upstairs, and I follow it until I arrive at Mehtap's open door.

Mehtap sits in the center of her chamber, a harp cradled in her lap. She's beautiful to watch, the way her arms bend delicately over the strings, and her marred skin doesn't take away from the grace of the act. As she plays, she tilts her head toward the instrument, her gaze in the distance as if she can see the music's path. Her face radiates joy.

Her father sits nearby, his hands folded and his eyes peaceful. There is genuine love in his eyes. I've seen how he comes to visit Mehtap several times a week, and I've seen how he spares no expense on her care. I'd wondered why he was so kind to me, and I think it is because I remind him in some way of his daughter.

The commander is as good a father as anyone can ask for. Yet, I look at his hands, and they are calloused from wielding a sword. His sandals are scuffed from long marches, and there are bloodstains on the straps. I've seen the scars on his body from previous battles, and I've heard of the honors he's received for his swift and thorough defeat of rebellious states. It makes me wonder if it's possible for two different men to reside in the same body.

Mehtap's song ends. For a moment, the music hangs in the air. Arxa stirs, as does Mehtap, and then they both look at me.

I realize I might have wandered in where I'm not welcome. "I'm sorry. I heard the music and—"

"Nonsense," says Mehtap. "Come in. We're having tea."

Cakes have been laid out on a small carved table. The smell of saffron tea floats overhead. I fill my own cup, then refresh Mehtap's and the commander's.

"I trust things at the hospital are well?" says Arxa.

"Quite well," I say. "In fact, one young man, a boy really, was brought in fevered from outside the walls. He's become umber-marked."

Arxa's eyes widen over his cup. "Good work. I understand that's quite rare. Jesmin can help him leave the compound when he's ready."

I drink my tea, more to fortify my courage than out of thirst. "It's not that simple, I'm afraid. He doesn't remember anything of his past."

Mehtap tilts her head. "How curious," she says. "If his memory's been burned away, and he's been abandoned with no sign of where he's from . . ."

"He's tried to remember," I say, "but there's nothing."

"Absolutely nothing at all?" asks Arxa.

"We only have two clues," I say. "He has a brand on his wrist. His body is also greatly scarred. I would guess he's a soldier of some sort."

There is a glint of interest in Arxa's eye. "A mystery patient," he says. "That is very intriguing indeed."

Please, Goddess, show me favor. "If the commander is willing, perhaps you might help us see if he has any skill with weapons. Learned skills are usually the least affected by fever amnesia, and anything you could tell us would help us decide how to proceed with him. I know nothing of these things, and neither does Jesmin."

The commander nods thoughtfully. "Umbertouched fighters are a rare thing, if he is indeed one. Let's have a look at him tomorrow."

# CHAPTER NINETEEN
## DINEAS

Zivah is nervous this morning. She hardly says a word as she unwraps the bandages around my wrist.

"The burn is uneven," she says, and she sounds unusually annoyed about it. "Parts of this will scar more heavily than the rest." Her eyes flicker irritably to my face, and if I didn't know better, I'd think she's blaming me for the burn. It's not like her to be this jumpy.

"I survived the plague," I say. "An uneven scar is the least of my worries."

Her expression softens, and a grudging smile touches her lips. "I suppose that's true." She dips her washcloth in some strange-smelling salve and wipes at the pink scar tissue.

"What's bothering you?" I ask.

She wraps fresh bandages around my wound and tucks the ends snugly. "I suppose you should know sooner than later. You know we've talked about your past, and how I think you might have been a fighter of some sort, maybe from one of the nearby tribes."

My hand goes absentmindedly to my calf, where there's the raised impression of a scar. That's the most pronounced one, but I have others all over the rest of my body. Then there are my puffy ears, which Zivah tells me only happens if I've taken blows to the head.

"I remember."

"You'll get a visitor today. Commander Arxa of the Amparan army. He'll know more about these things."

The commander arrives later that afternoon, led by Zivah and flanked by four umbertouched soldiers. Even if he hadn't been the oldest of the soldiers, there would have been no mistaking him. Up until now, I haven't met anyone who truly intimidated me. Zivah, of course, has always been on my side. But even Jesmin, who rushes around giving orders all day, is focused but mild. This man though, there's nothing mild about him. His very presence changes the air in a room. I'm on my feet before I know it, standing straight and ready.

The guards around him are closer to my age, and I can't help measuring myself against them. The closest one is big, though his slow lumbering steps makes me think he'd be heavy on his feet. The man behind him is smaller, but his eyes are sharp, and he looks at me with something like eagerness. If I really am a soldier, he'll be one I have to watch out for.

"They call you Dineas, do they?"

"Yes, Commander." I stay perfectly still as he walks a circle around me.

"I doubt you're from our army," he says. "Our barracks report all outbreaks of rose plague. You remember nothing of your past?"

"No, sir. I remember nothing since the fever."

He takes my left arm by the wrist and pulls up my sleeve. I fight the urge to wince when he pats the bandage. "Does it still pain you?"

"No, sir."

Arxa glances at Zivah, who carefully unwraps the bandage from my wrist. The commander contemplates my burn. "It's a livestock-trader mark. We can make some inquiries there." His eyes drop to the muscles of my forearm. "Are you left-handed?"

It takes me a moment to come up with my answer. "I've been eating with my right hand."

He raises his eyebrows and rolls up the sleeve of my right arm. I feel like a hunting dog presented for inspection, which then makes me wonder if I've ever owned a hunting dog. When the commander raises his head, he looks cautiously pleased. "You just might be a swordsman." He runs his thumb over the pads of my fingers. "An archer as well. And," he says, eyeing my face, "you've seen some close combat."

He backs up, dusting off his hands. "Let's see what you can do."

He spins on his heel, leaving the room as decisively as he'd entered it. The other soldiers follow him. I look at Zivah and raise my eyebrows—the man's used to giving orders. Zivah just gives me an encouraging smile and motions for me to follow. She falls in step after me.

It's my first time outside, and the dirty streets and run-down houses look even shabbier up close. I peer curiously at the rose-marked people all around, but most of them seem to be keeping their distance from us.

To my surprise, the commander takes us to the compound gates. "We're looking for some extra space," he tells the posted guards. "We'll stay close."

It's disorienting, stepping outside of the walls. Sand and brush stretch out around me in all directions. After the small hospital rooms, I hardly know what to make of such openness. The sun, too, is something fierce, sharp on my bare skin and heavy on my tunic. Sweat beads on my forehead.

One of Arxa's soldiers comes forward with a light leather chest guard, as well as arm and shin covers. After I strap them on, Arxa hands me a wooden practice sword. The names of the parts come up easily: *scabbard, blade.* I wrap my hand around the hilt. It does feel natural there. But when I try to think what to do with it, my mind comes up blank. In the corner of my eye, I see Zivah hide her fidgeting hands in the folds of her apron.

Arxa looks at his soldiers, wearing the same expression Zivah does when she's trying to choose between jars of herbs. "Cas," he says.

The small man comes out, the one with the sharp eyes, and picks up his own practice sword. He raises it in front of him, and I imitate his posture.

"Go," says Arxa.

Just like that? It's on my lips to protest, but Cas is already coming at me with an overhead swing, his sword whistling through the air. I barely get my own sword up in time to block. He's not fooling around. A crack rings over the sand, and the vibration from the clash numbs my palm. Cas doesn't stop. Before I know it, he's brought his sword around to my exposed side. Again, I block just in time, but again, I'm slow. The blow knocks me sideways, and I stumble.

A smile starts forming at the corners of my opponent's lips—smug, and I don't like the glint in his eye. He keeps attacking, one blow after another. His sword comes from above, from the side, and below. He's toying with me, and it's all I can do to keep up. I feel awkward and off-balance, like I have too many limbs and they don't work together. The worst thing is, Cas is holding back. I can tell.

"Halt," calls Arxa, and Cas lowers his weapon. I follow suit and lean over my knees, panting. He's barely winded, yet my lungs feel like they're going to explode.

I finally gather the courage to glance at the commander. He doesn't look impressed.

"Remember, Commander," says Zivah. "He's not yet recovered his full strength and balance." My insides shrivel with shame.

Commander Arxa makes a noncommittal grunt. "One more round."

Cas takes up his fighting position, and I force myself to match him. I don't dare look at Zivah—I don't want to see the expression on her face.

"Now that we're warmed up," says Cas, "we can really get started." His voice has an oily sheen.

Delightful fellow, this Cas.

He comes at me again. Strike, parry, strike. I may not know much, but I know I can't keep up with him. I'm so caught up in blocking his attacks that I have no chance to counter. When the sun shines right into my eyes, I realize he's maneuvered me to face it.

Scars, I should have known better than this.

I'm squinting now, and my eyes water from the glare. His sword comes down once, twice, and then connects soundly with my forearm. I cry out and drop my sword just as he knocks the wind from my ribs. I collapse on the ground, gasping.

Out of the corner of my eye, I see Cas wipe the dust off his sword. And I steel myself for the commander's reaction.

"You have some training," Arxa says. "We'll see if we can find anything about your origins. If we can't find anything, perhaps you could enlist as a foot soldier."

I'm not sure quite what it is—the soft grind of a footstep maybe, or a subtle change in where Arxa's looking. But before I know it, I've spun and ducked just in time to avoid getting my skull caved in by another practice sword—this one held by the big soldier. Shock runs through me, followed by a wave of rage. The man could have killed me! My body moves of its own accord. I close the distance between us and drive my fist into his rib cage. As he doubles over, I wrap his arm under my armpit and bear down on his wrist until he gives up his sword. I back away, holding his weapon at the ready.

I sneak a quick glance at the commander. His expression is inscrutable, and I don't waste any more time puzzling him out, because now there's heat pumping through my veins. I relax into a guard stance—not the same one I copied off Cas earlier. My feet want to be wider apart, my legs want more coil. Cas is watching me, his eyes wary. I give a quick nod, an invitation.

This time, when he comes at me, I know what to do. I parry his first strike and then drive back, concentrating my attack on his right. He takes one step in retreat, and then another. When he takes two more steps back, I don't follow. Instead, I back up until I'm standing over my fallen practice blade. Without lowering my eyes, I scoop it up with my free hand, and then I charge. My right blade cuts down and across, and the left one follows an eyeblink later. He deflects my first two blows, and the return blow after that as well. But my fourth strike catches him in the ribs and he falls.

Something moves in my peripheral vision and I spin around as a new soldier runs at me with a spear. I step right, trapping the spear with my crossed swords and deflecting it to the side. When the soldier stumbles, I help him along with the flat of my blade. Then I lift my sword again, scanning in all directions, but no one else attacks me.

A slow clapping rings through the air, and I turn to see Arxa watching with appreciation. "I had a hunch you were thinking too much the first time around," he says. "That was an impressive performance. Quite impressive."

# CHAPTER TWENTY
## ZIVAH

From the exuberance in Dineas's face, you'd think he'd just stumbled upon a pot of gold, not beat three men into submission. He's covered with dirt, and the fresh scratches on his hands and arms have me itching to grab a washcloth. He's also limping like an old man, but he's beaming. I've never seen him so happy.

My palms are still damp from seeing him fail, entertaining the sinking feeling that my potions might have erased more of his skills than I'd thought. I'd feared our quest was ended before it even really began.

As the party heads inside the compound, Dineas falls back next to me and breaks into a wide grin. "What do you think, Zivah? Not bad for someone who can't remember his own name."

His elation is infectious, and I smile in return. Back in Dara,

I'd believed him cocky when he boasted he'd be able to beat Ampara's best. But now that I've seen him fight, I understand. And though I had nothing to do with his skill or training, I feel a surge of pride at his victory.

Arxa walks with us to the door of Dineas's room. "You gave us a good demonstration today, Dineas." He doesn't seem to recognize Dineas from his visit to Khaygal outpost. We didn't think he would remember one prisoner's face out of hundreds, but I'd worried nonetheless. I wait for him to say something about Dineas joining the army, but he doesn't. Instead, he turns to me. "Zivah, I'd like a word with you."

"Of course, Commander." I try to ignore the tingling in my stomach as I lead him to a sitting area in the back. There's only a small window in this room, and a shaft of light falls between our two chairs. I put my hands in my lap to keep from fidgeting. "Is there anything in particular you wished to discuss, Commander?"

He leans his weight back into his chair. "Tell me everything you know about Dineas," he says. "Every detail, no matter how insignificant."

The worst thing I can do right now is to let my nerves give me away. "I'm afraid I don't know much. He was brought in by the gate guards one morning, and he was delirious with fever. When he woke, he remembered nothing. He wore a bracelet carved with the words 'For my Dineas.'"

"Do you still have this bracelet?"

"It was burned, along with the rest of his clothes."

"In his fever, did he talk about anything? Ramble about anything that might give a clue?"

I remember the time Dineas almost said my name in front of

Jesmin, before his memory had fully faded away. "He talked of battles, mostly. He called after fallen friends, or cried out that he was being attacked."

Arxa leans forward. "Any names that you remember?"

Of course he'd ask for names. "I'm sorry, Commander. At that time he was simply one of many patients. I had no reason to think he'd warrant special attention."

"Of course. I don't blame you." He falls silent a long moment. "A fighter with his talents is a rare find. And for him to just show up like this, abandoned at the colony. It's strange." He looks up at me. "You've had experience with amnesic patients, Zivah. Do they ever recover their memory? If I offer him a place in my army, I need to be sure of his allegiance."

I shake my head. "The rose plague fever burns hot. I don't know if anyone has ever regained his past." Then I see an opportunity. "There's one thing I'd like to try. Rose plague fever, when it hits the mind, has lingering subtle effects. Dineas likely has not retained his full fighting ability, and he may have trouble making sense of the world. While I think it's a lost cause to recover his past, I do have some potions in mind that might restore his physical skills and ease his transition back into everyday life. This will allow me to watch him carefully as well, and if he surprises us by remembering more of his old life, I can inform you right away."

"Yes, please do, Zivah. I want to find out everything I can about him." As he stands, he takes a rolled parchment out of his pocket. "This was sent to my estate from Dara. It's a letter from your family."

My breath catches. Leora had mentioned she would write, but

with the distance, I hadn't allowed myself to hope for a letter. I take the roll carefully by the edges, as if I might crush it with my eagerness.

"I'll let you read it," says Arxa, and leaves me.

Only after he's left do I realize I hadn't even said good-bye. But I'm already running my fingers under the edge of the parchment. The clay seal, unsurprisingly, has already been opened.

*Dearest Zivah,*

*I've no idea whether this letter will reach you, but I had to try. We miss you dearly. Alia mentions you almost daily, and I've caught Mother looking at your old dresses more than once. . . .*

The letter talks of Leora's new embroidery, Alia's goat bearing a kid, and recent repairs to our cottage's roof. Day-to-day mundane things, but I linger on every word, and I wonder if I've made a mistake by leaving them. I could be seeing Leora's embroidery for myself, advising Alia on the best feed for her goat.

The parchment quivers in my hand. Then my eye is drawn to something she says at the end.

*Things at the village are well, though there seem to be more soldiers coming through lately. When I see them, I think of you, wonder how you're faring in their land.*

A knot forms in my stomach at her words. So the number of soldiers in Dara continues to increase, and even Leora's noticed it by now. It frightens me to think of what it means.

*I don't know if there's any way for you to get a message back to me. Perhaps Commander Arxa or another umbertouched soldier would be willing to carry something back the next time they come. Kaylah assures us that if you wear gloves to write the letter and we take care to press your parchments with a fired stone, then we need not worry about the disease essence traveling all the way here. I hope to hear from you soon. Until then, we place you in the care of the Goddess.*

There's a thickness in my throat as I read the letter twice more. After I finish, I fold the parchment and tuck it into my apron, choosing the pocket that's closest to my heart.

# CHAPTER TWENTY-ONE
## DINEAS

Zivah brings news a few days later. I'm to report to Sehmar City and train with Arxa's troops. The news lights a fire inside of me. I'm still bruised and sore from my test, and I think I might have injured my shoulder, but I can't wait to get started.

"So you're happy with this?" Zivah asks.

I grin. "Just tell me when I can go. I can still come back and see you, right?" Zivah has been the only constant in the days since I've awoken.

"I'd like that," she says. "In fact I've spoken to Commander Arxa, and he's agreed that you should visit me regularly for treatment. Your mind is still fragile, and I have some potions that will help you recover."

"Fragile?" That doesn't sound good.

"Don't worry. It just means you're more likely to be confused in these first few weeks. The herbs will make it easier on you. It's nothing to worry about."

Her words are comforting, but when she fetches me that afternoon for our first treatment, she's not exactly calm. She walks ahead of me instead of beside me, and I can see her fidgeting with something in the pocket of her apron. It makes me wonder if I should be nervous too, but then, she's never given me reason to doubt her.

Zivah opens the door to a back room. It's not a patient room. There's just a few shelves, a table, and a window.

"We're doing it here?"

"It's better if we're not interrupted."

She drags a pallet in for me. I make myself comfortable on the straw, and Zivah hands me a vial.

I sniff and cough. "Do you healers compete to make the most horrid-tasting brews?"

"If it tasted good, it wouldn't be medicine," she says with a half smile.

The bad taste doesn't disappear after I swallow. There's a hellish aftertaste that has me gagging. For a while I just sit there, making faces. And then . . .

It's not exactly pain. Because it doesn't hurt. And not light either, because nothing real appears in front of my eyes. But that's what it *feels* like. Some kind of flash that hits my mind.

*Dineas.* That really is my name. And after that, the images all rush in, one on top of the other. Gatha, Monyar, my fellow tribesmen. I feel like I'm falling, and I reach out to grab something. Zivah jumps, and I realize that I'm not falling after all.

As the images settle, the last few days unfold before me.

Though my old knowledge returns, my new memories remain just as clear: waking up in the hospital, getting tested by Arxa... I go over every detail in my mind, reinterpreting them in light of my past. The face of the commander swims before me. Over the last few days, I'd admired him, but now I remember who he truly is.

"Arxa." I fling the name at Zivah. "You introduced me to him."

My words have the bite of accusation, and she blinks, confused. "That was the plan, wasn't it?"

Of course it was. I look away, trying to push down a panic I can't explain. I hadn't realized what it would be to wake up after living another life, to look at a man who's haunted my nightmares and think him a benefactor. Just the thought that I stood in front of him and shook his hand. I think over the rest of it: the fight, how I proved myself to them, and how proud I was to be invited to join the army.

My lips curl. "I guess I've made a good impression. I sure was eager to please."

"You did well," Zivah says firmly. "Better than we could have hoped."

She's right, of course. I have no reason to be upset. So why do I feel like I've betrayed everything I stand for? I want to lash out at something, and it's only with a great deal of effort that I don't. "So I leave soon for the capital?"

She relaxes a bit. "Yes, and with any luck you'll do well there. Now, listen carefully. I didn't give you much potion just now, so you'll likely fade away soon. Is there anything else we need to discuss?"

No. Not really. We just need to continue with this crazy scheme. "Just send word to Gatha that I'm in."

My head feels fuzzy already, and I know instinctively that I don't have long. I have a strange urge to wave my hands and dispel the fog, but that would only make me look like a madman. Though, I wonder, with all Zivah's done to me thus far, can I really say I'm that far from madness? I'm mulling that over when the mists drift back in to stay.

# PART THREE

# CHAPTER TWENTY-TWO

## DINEAS

After a week, I step out of the compound for the second time. Zivah gives me a waterskin and a pack of dried fruit. I have an old tunic and sandals, and a token of introduction to present when I arrive at the palace. Not exactly starting off my new life with untold riches, but it's more than any of my fellow patients will ever get.

"Do us proud, Dineas," Zivah says, clasping my hands. There's something about her smile. I'm guessing lots of pretty girls have smiles that light up their face, but Zivah's smile feels like it comes from within.

"I'll come back with all kinds of news," I promise her. The guard at the compound gates salutes me, and then I set off along the single trail leading toward the city. It's not yet noon, but the sun's rising fast. Lizards scurry across the path ahead of me, and I kick stones at them as I go. Beyond that, I don't have much company, but I'm enjoying the fresh views. The hospital walls had started to feel confining lately, and it's nice having something new to explore. It's strange to think I must have walked this trail before.

Finally tall stone walls appear ahead of me. And though I have no memory of this place, there's something in me that understands this is a true city. The grand stone walls, the stream of citizens coming in and out of the gates—this place is the center of something big. There's all kinds of people here: tall men and short men, women in jewels and women in rags. What's most noticeable though, is the smoothness of their skin. Not a single rosemark in sight.

I ask a bored-looking gate guard for directions to the palace. He gives me an annoyed look. "Just keep going up."

Up? But then I actually peer through the gates. There, on a hill in the distance, I see grand stone buildings surrounded by smooth walls and lush trees.

Fair enough.

The neighborhoods inside the gates aren't very different from the rosemarked compound, though the buildings aren't quite as shabby, and it's more crowded. As I walk though, the houses get nicer, and the people around me wear finer clothing. The roads themselves are paved with well-fitted cobblestones instead of dirt. Finally I arrive at the smooth limestone walls of the palace, where a dour guard looks at my token and points me to a small mud-brick building nearby.

"That houses the army scribe. Give your token there."

By now I'm wondering if life in the army isn't as exciting as I thought it would be. First the bored guard at the city gate. Then the grumpy one at the palace, and now the scribe in the army hut looks positively drowsy. I hand him my token of invitation, and he squints at it, frowning. "It's not the season for new recruits."

"Commander Arxa sent for me."

The scribe pulls out a long scroll, which he pores over. He shuffles to the back and comes out with an armful of things, handing them to me one by one.

"Bedding, two tunics, two trousers, cloak, sandals. Your commanders will see to your weapons."

He points to a map carved into the wall. "Barracks seven, bed five."

These are the most detailed directions I've gotten all day. I scoop up my newfound wealth and head out. From my glimpse of the map, it looks like the grander parts of the palace make up the center of the compound, while the barracks and training fields sit on the outer rim. I glance over my shoulder one last time at the polished limestone columns of the palace proper before heading to the section for mere mortals.

I run across more soldiers as I walk. Some I recognize because they're in livery. Others simply have the look of fighters, even though they're just milling around the grounds. I linger a bit by a large training field where men are working through fencing drills in pairs, and then continue on to the big rectangular barracks. I get a few second glances as I walk by, though I don't know if people are noticing my skin or my armful of new possessions. One man in particular turns his head sharply toward me. He has umbermarks like me, and I recognize Cas, the small man I fenced with at the compound. I nod a greeting.

His nostrils flare. His eyes harden, and he turns away.

So much for making a friend.

Besides soldiers, there are messengers and servants in imperial livery hurrying back and forth. Two men with slave brands on their faces clean out gutters along the barracks. People walk by them without giving them a second glance.

Barracks seven looks quiet at this time of day, and it's blissfully cool inside compared to the sunny training fields. Two men stand just inside the door. I nod a greeting and they nod back, but they don't pause in their conversation, and I continue on. Bunks line either wall, and the fifth one is the only one stripped of linens. I drape my bedding over the straw as best I can, change into the army tunic, and then I sit down and wonder what to do next. I suppose I'll get orders tomorrow, but I can't exactly sit here until then. At the very least, I'll need to find the mess hall.

I make my way back out. I'm about to step through the door when a big man comes in the other direction. We both stop, and I back up a few steps to let him through. Then I realize I know this man. He's the big soldier, the one who snuck up on me in my test.

Great. I turn my head on the off chance he might think I'm simply another new umbertouched soldier and pass me by. No such luck. He squints at me, then frowns.

"Aren't you that mystery soldier? The one abandoned at the compound?"

So much for blending in. "That's right."

The man strokes his beard. "Well, well," he says.

Behind me, the two men stop their conversation to watch.

The big man takes a step toward me, and I take a step back.

He furrows his eyebrows. "What's the matter? Shy?" He takes in my tense stance, my half-raised fists, and then throws his head back into a roar of a laugh. "You're a jumpy one, aren't you? Don't worry. I don't fight unless I'm being paid, and today's my day off." He reaches out his hand. "We've never met properly. I'm Walgash, soldier under Arxa in Neju's Guard. And you're the upstart maltworm who bruised my ribs."

I take his hand, trying not to look too sheepish. "They call me Dineas."

Walgash turns to the other two soldiers. "Naudar, Masista, you've got to meet this man. He appeared out of nowhere at the rosemarked compound with no memory of where he came from."

The two come to shake my hand, peering at me as if I were some kind of oddity, which I suppose I am. Naudar looks to be a young Amparan about my age, and Masista is a dark-skinned southerner who looks slightly older.

Walgash pats his belly. "You three had your midday meal yet? My stomach's about to turn inside out."

Naudar and Masista say they haven't, and Walgash turns to me. "You in, Dineas?"

My stomach growls in response.

Walgash keeps up a running monologue on our way to the mess hall. "We have our regular units housed here in the palace. There's battalions one through ten, then the various pet units of the commanders. We share the training fields and whatnot. Division of resources is usually equitable, unless some commander's out of favor, which happens more often than you'd think. It's all politics in here. You'd think men of war wouldn't be so petty, but you'd be wrong." Walgash continues with a rundown of all the commanders, though I'm lost in the pile of names after the first two.

Masista smirks. "That's why you're so excited to find a man with no memory, Walgash," he says. "An empty head to fill with your talk."

"I'm in favor of anything that spares the rest of us from Walgash's ramblings," says Naudar.

To be honest, my head is spinning. But I suppose they're right about one thing: I'll gladly listen to anything that will fill in the gaps in my mind.

The smell of spices drifts out of a large stone hall. There's a line of soldiers out the door, and we take our place at the end. It's loud with conversation inside. Once we reach the serving line, a cook passes me a bowl of greenish stew over rice and we continue to the tables and benches in the back. Walgash waves at someone I can't see.

"Kosru has some room down there," he says, directing us back.

Kosru turns out to be a man even bigger than Walgash, with a thick black beard and hair.

"This is Kosru, my other half," says Walgash, clasping the man's shoulder.

"His quieter half," says Masista. "The adage about lovers becoming more alike over time doesn't seem to apply to those two."

Walgash continues without missing a beat. "Kosru, this is Dineas, the soldier I told you about." Kosru gives me a firm handshake and a one-word greeting.

The stew is decent, though surprisingly spicy, and I start to relax. The men seem friendly. Masista has a wife and son in the city, though he lives in the palace when training is heavy. Walgash, Kosru, and Masista have been in the army for several years now, while Naudar joined just a few months ago.

"So, Dineas," says Masista. "Where are you serving?"

"Third battalion, I believe."

Walgash snorts. "Third battalion? No, where you want to be is Neju's Guard."

"Your unit?"

"Arxa's elite unit," he says. "Masista's in it too. Kosru is in Commander Vaumitha's elite unit, but we don't hold it against him."

Kosru lets out a long-suffering sigh. Walgash pats his hand fondly and continues speaking.

"Believe me, Dineas. You want to serve under Arxa if you can. Every unit he trains ends up fighting better. He pays attention to his men. Notices what makes them better soldiers."

Masista chimes in. "He stands up for us. A few years ago, the emperor wanted to save money by cutting our time on leave and skimping on our rations. Arxa fought him on it—spoke out in front of the court about how it would wear us down in the long run. He kept at it until the emperor gave in, and in the meantime, Arxa paid for our supplies out of his own fortune. There's many who think that Arxa would be a general now, if he hadn't offended the emperor like that."

"Neju's Guard is holding a round of tryouts starting next week," says Walgash. "Open to everyone. Naudar's trying out."

"You are?" I say to Naudar, who nods in response.

"Don't underestimate our Naudar," says Masista. "He may

have a face pretty enough to grace the temples, but he'll put up a good fight when he needs to. And he'll do it without letting a single lock of his hair fall out of place."

"At least I have hair," Naudar says between spoonfuls of stew.

"For now," Masista says, rubbing his own shaved head.

Kosru and Walgash guffaw, and my thoughts circle back to what Walgash said about Neju's Guard. "The trials are open to everyone?" Arxa does sound like a good commander. And after last week's test, I'm curious to know what else I'm capable of.

Walgash grins. "That's right. You interested?"

# CHAPTER TWENTY-THREE
## ZIVAH

I hold my blowgun steady as I try to peer through the leaves of the tree overhead. The snake I'm stalking is a master of camouflage, and its brown and green stripes confuse the eye, especially when the wind rattles the leaves. I've seen the snake a few times and I don't recognize it, which makes me all the more determined to get ahold of its venom. Now that Dineas is settled in the army, I have more time to experiment with rose plague treatments, and Central Ampara is rich with new specimens for me to study.

I draw breath to shoot, but the wind blows again and I have to wait. The next time the breeze dies down, I exhale a percussive puff. The dart embeds itself in the snake's side, and the creature's tail waves back and forth. I ready another dart in case the first wasn't enough, but the snake falls still as the sleeping potion takes effect. I reach for the long forked stick I cut for myself last night.

Carefully, I thread it through the branches and work it under the motionless body, then dump the creature into a burlap sack. A few days should be enough for me to get the venom I need, and then I'll let the creature go on its way. This serpent's markings remind me of Diadem, and I'm curious to see if the snake's venom has some of the same properties.

"Is this a common thing for healers to do?"

My heart jumps at the familiar voice. Dineas stands behind me, peering warily at the burlap sack.

"Dineas! I didn't expect to see you back so soon. You're looking well." The army has issued him new clothes, and his hair has been freshly trimmed. Plus, a few days under the sun seems to have given him his color back.

He grins. "There's not much for me to do these early days. I thought I'd come and see how things are. And"—he takes a small basket out from behind his back—"to ensure I'm still your favorite patient."

The basket's filled with candied rose petals and nuts. The sight makes my mouth water.

"My friends lent me some money until the scribes get around to paying me. I'm trying to make my way through everything in the markets, and these are my favorite so far. Try a petal."

I don't need to be told twice. The fragrance drifts up my nose as the flower melts on my tongue. "Well, it's decided. Nursing you back to health was a worthwhile effort."

"And here I thought you saved me for the pleasure of my company. Or perhaps my vast knowledge of the world."

"No. It's definitely the presents." I tuck the basket under the crook of my arm. "But tell me how your first days have been."

He brushes off his new livery. "I've settled in well. Arxa has me doing exercises with the third battalion so far, but I'll try out for Neju's Guard next week."

"Neju's Guard?" Was that the name of the battalion that fell ill?

"That's Arxa's elite unit. There's a trial for it next week, and they're open to all. They're expanding their ranks."

Yes, that's it, then. Arxa's special unit. Beyond my own experience with them, most of what I've heard about these warriors has been through fearful whispers back at Dara—rumors of villages destroyed, families slaughtered. And now Dineas says they're expanding their ranks. My spine prickles. "Dineas, do you have time for a treatment today? Since you're here, we might as well take advantage of it."

He blinks. "I suppose so."

In a short while, I have him settled in my room. If he thinks it strange that I bolt the door, he doesn't mention it.

"Are they feeding you well in the palace?" I ask as he drinks the potion.

"Well enough. I'm not—" He stops talking and his gaze goes distant. Once again, his eyes go back and forth, and he sits rapt as the memories come back. Gradually, the lines of his face harden, and a shiver of recognition runs through me. The Dineas I'd traveled to Ampara with has returned. It's the same person, the same face, but the difference is striking. He looks older, more tired.

I hesitate a moment before I speak, and when I finally do, I keep my voice low. "Have you had trouble with the army?"

He looks down, shakes off the effects of the potion, and then meets my eyes. "No," he says, his voice gruff. "I settled in just fine."

"I'm glad," I say. "But I'm troubled by the news of Neju's Guard."

Those words finally snap him out of his fog. "As am I," he says. "They had tryouts a few months ago to replace the ones lost in the outbreak, and now they're recruiting again. And they're not the only unit that's expanding. Others are as well, both the elite units and the regular battalions. I hear the most calls for skilled soldiers who can fight on hard terrain—mountains, forests, and such."

Even I can understand the significance of this. Hard terrain means that the emperor wants to go after the rebels who have retreated into the corners of Ampara, the last holdouts. "Have you heard anything about how they became ill?"

"Neju's Guard was stationed at Khaygal outpost before they came to Monyar. They arrived at Monyar thirteen days before the outbreak of the illness."

I do the figures in my head. "They were in Monyar when the first soldier became infected."

He nods grimly. "It's all rumors and speculation, but plenty think that my people infected them, or yours."

"But it couldn't have been us. They didn't get to Dara until . . ." I trail off. The battalion was out of Dara's reach the day they were infected, but very likely in Shidadi territory. . . .

A spasm of irritation crosses Dineas's face. "It wasn't Shidadi," he says. "We fight our enemies face-to-face. Gatha would have told me if she'd done something so underhanded."

"How well do you know Gatha?"

"I'd die for her," he says flatly.

It's clearly useless to press him further. "It does seem like you might learn more if you were a member of Neju's Guard. Do you think you can make it in?"

Dineas shrugs. "It's a challenge. I like challenges."

"Will that be enough?" I wonder how motivated the other Dineas would be to do well in the trials.

He looks at me as if I have no hope of ever understanding. "I'll do my best. Trust me."

I roll my eyes. "I'm beginning to prefer *his* company to yours."

I don't have to explain who I'm talking about. Dineas snorts. "Give him some time. He'll get on your nerves soon enough." But a flash of uncertainty crosses his face, and I know how he feels. It's unsettling enough for me, relating in two different ways to what should be the same person. I can only imagine what it's like for him.

In the remaining time we have, Dineas scribbles an update to Gatha. I warm a stone in the fireplace for him, and he passes it over both sides of the parchments to weaken any rose plague essence before he ties duplicate messages to Slicewing and Scrawny.

Dineas starts to drift away after the birds leave. He takes longer to respond when I speak with him, and I have him lie down and close his eyes to make the transition easier. Gradually the lines of his face smooth out.

A short while later, his eyes blink open. He groans and pushes himself to sitting.

I give him my most reassuring smile. "How do you feel?"

"Drowsy," he says. It's hard to put into words, but it's obvious to me that his memories are once again gone. Something in the way he holds himself, the openness in his expression.

"Do you remember anything from the treatment?"

He furrows his eyebrows. "I remember we were talking. But I don't remember what about."

"You're probably remembering the few moments before you fell asleep," I lie. "You napped through the entire treatment."

"Did I snore?"

"A little."

I walk with him back down the stairs. It's strange. Even when we're simply walking, being with him feels different. We're relaxed around each other, and it makes me realize how much I'm on my guard every time I'm with the old Dineas.

When we reach the courtyard, Dineas opens his mouth as if to say something, then stops.

"What is it?" I ask.

He chuckles, and runs a hand through his dark hair. "I... well, you may think this is silly, but I thought perhaps you could give me a charm. My friend Naudar... a girl at the market gave him a lock of her hair for good luck in the trials. And you're the only woman I know."

I cross my arms. "I can't say that's the most flattering request I've ever received."

"That's not what I meant!" He puts his hands up in protest. "I mean... you *are* the only woman I know, but..." He stops when he sees that I'm smiling. "You know I'm glad to know you, Zivah."

A pleasant warmth settles in my chest. Next to us is a small plot of land I've started working into an herb garden. I pluck a puzta flower and hand it to him. "I may have been able to do better with more warning, but why don't you take this. It's a puzta flower, and it's both useful and pleasing to look at. It'll crumble when it dries, but the scent stays for days. It also helps close up wounds, if you sprinkle the dried blossoms on the bleeding. I'll feel better if you have one on you during your trials, but don't lose it. I don't have much to spare."

He holds the bud to his nose. "This is the first thing you've given me that doesn't smell like something died on it."

"You sure know how to flatter the maidens, don't you?"

He flashes me one last grin. "You won't regret this. Someday, when I've made Neju's Guard, and women everywhere are begging me to accept their trinkets, I'll tell them no, because the lovely Zivah has believed in me from the beginning." He pauses. "Actually, I'd probably still take their gifts. But I promise I'll keep yours closest to my heart."

I push him toward the door. "Off with you."

He looks quite pleased with himself as he leaves.

I stare at the empty entryway long after he's gone. It's still striking to me how different this Dineas is, the way he jokes, the way he smiles. It makes me wonder what experiences made the real Dineas what he is, and the thought saddens me.

I hear the door of the house open and close behind me.

"He's fond of you," says Mehtap, coming to stand next to me. "Are you fond of him?"

"He's my first patient to recover completely. That's something special."

Mehtap gives me a sly look out the corner of her eye. "That's not what I meant."

I give her my best impression of Leora's big-sister glance. "He's my patient," I say.

"If only all patients were so pleasing to the eye. You'd think the umbermarks would mar his face, but they don't."

I kneel down in the herb patch, partly because I see some weeds that need pulling, and partly to avoid Mehtap's inquiries. Truth is, the new Dineas does seem to be getting fond of me, but it seems harmless so far. Besides, it's better for our mission if he comes to visit often.

"You know, some people do fall in love in here," Mehtap says.

I'm so lost in my own thoughts that it takes me a while to realize Mehtap has spoken. "What do you mean?"

"People fall in love in this compound. They meet here, they're drawn to each other, and they enjoy what time they have left." She speaks lightly, but behind her tone is a hollowness that's painful to hear. I feel that hollow in my own gut, and the old familiar questions come rushing back. Is there a life left for us after the rosemarks? Do we dare for happiness, or is it just asking for more pain? Is it even right to love, when you know you must leave your lover behind?

"Did you have anyone special before you came here?" asks Mehtap.

I dust off my hands. It seems pointless to continue with the weeds. "No, I was too caught up in my studies really. You?"

She shakes her head. "I kissed a general's son at a festival once. He told funny jokes, and he wasn't bad looking. But there wasn't much point in taking anything too seriously, since I would probably have been married off." She smiles sadly. "You know, I used to be so resentful of that prospect. My father and my mother barely speak, and she had no interest in raising me, even before I was rosemarked. I didn't want to live my life like that. But now, I would take that opportunity gladly. At least then I would have done some good, made some alliance to help Father, perhaps."

I've heard that well-bred Amparan women like Mehtap don't have many duties or responsibilities. Their servants take care of everyday considerations, and their husbands and fathers take on the politics. I'd assumed these women would be content to sit back and enjoy life as it passes by, but I suppose everybody wants to feel useful. I feel the same pull, the need to leave a legacy before the disease claims me. I guess in the end, it was stronger than my desire to be with my family. Why else would I be here on this mad quest?

Mehtap tugs at one of her neatly pinned braids. "Why do you think the gods make rose plague this way? Why make a disease that leaves us in this halfway place?"

Her question brings back that familiar heavy feeling. I rub the back of my neck to ease the tightness. "Perhaps it means we still have something to accomplish in this world," I say. It's hard not to wince at the triteness of my words.

Mehtap looks at me with her large eyes, and she speaks as if she's explaining something to a child. "But how do I do anything, for anyone, if I can't even leave these walls?"

# CHAPTER TWENTY-FOUR
## DINEAS

Trials for Neju's Guard start at dawn. Naudar and I climb out of bed before sunrise and march, bleary-eyed, to the training fields.

"Nervous?" he asks.

"I don't know enough to be nervous. People don't actually die in these, do they?"

Naudar purses his lips. "Not often," he says.

Not the most comforting reply, but the threat of danger feels right, somehow, like an old friend. I wonder if it's normal to feel this way. "So why did you decide to try out?" I ask him. "Walgash convince you too?"

"I've been watching Neju's Guard march out of the city since before I could grow a beard. I've always wanted to wear their colors, serve the empire as best I can."

I'm starting to see why the others tease Naudar so mercilessly. With his idealism and unrelentingly immaculate appearance, it's hard not to. "You really are insufferable, aren't you?"

His grin is unrepentant. "You're just jealous. Don't feel bad. Everybody is."

There are scribes seated at a table out front, and we take our place in line.

"Dineas, no family name," I tell the scribe.

"Neju's Guard, Dineas?" I jump. I hadn't realized Arxa was also sitting at the table.

"Yes, sir."

"You understand that the trials are hard?" he says matter-of-factly. "We make no allowance for the recently ill. Many healthy men who have been training for months do not make it through."

I square my shoulders. "I understand, sir. I want to learn my limits."

Arxa holds my eyes for a second, and then motions toward the training fields.

I take my place among the soldiers on the well-trampled grass as we wait for everyone to drift in. The hundred current soldiers of Neju's Guard are lined up at the front, facing us, wearing the black-and-silver sashes of their unit. I see a few familiar faces—Walgash, Masista, Cas. I reach into the pocket of my tunic and pick up the flower Zivah gave me. It's dried by now, and I take care not to crush it. I'm already looking forward to the next time I can make it back to the rosemarked compound. Walgash and company are friendly, but nobody listens quite as well as Zivah. I can let my guard down around her without worrying about saying some stupid amnesic remark that the guys won't let me live down for days.

Also, she smells better. Though some of her potions could rival Walgash's post-training musk. I make a silent resolution that the next time I see her, I'll tell her that her gift brought me victory.

One of Neju's Guard steps forward. "Commander Arxa of the Amparan Empire," he calls.

The slap of sandals hitting dirt echoes across the field as three hundred soldiers snap to attention. Then there's only the sound of Arxa's footsteps as he walks to the front.

"Swear fealty to the emperor," he commands.

We salute a portrait of an older man with a silver crown, purple robes, graying hair, and a long gray beard. "Long live Emperor Kurosh," we say with one voice. I look at the emperor's face with interest. So this is the man we all serve. I wonder if he deserves it.

Arxa sweeps his gaze over us, and we all stand a little straighter. "There are one hundred men in Neju's Guard. We will take fifty more with this trial. You may drop out of the testing at any time and return to your current posts without shame. Every soldier in Ampara is a priest of Neju, and every soldier carries the pride of the empire. But if you decide to put up your sword to be tested, then do your best at the tasks set before you. Neju will be watching, as will I."

We answer his words with a stomp and a shout. Then one of Neju's Guard takes Arxa's place. "We will divide you into units, and you will complete the task at each station."

We disperse then. Naudar mouths "Good luck" to me as he goes off with another group. I'm in a set of sixty men, all strangers to me, and we're led to a corner of the training field.

A lanky soldier barks directions at us. "This is a footrace

around the border of the field. You will don your armor and carry your sword and shield. Races will be run in groups of ten."

A knot of worry forms in my stomach. I don't need Zivah to tell me that I'm still weak from my illness. I shuffle forward, and we watch the first group take off. My gear is heavy, and I'm already sweating underneath it. I'm glad we drew this station first instead of later when the sun's higher in the sky.

Then they call my group to the starting line, and we're off. Three of the men shoot out at a speed I can't possibly match, but everybody else takes it slower. There are four sides of the field, and I manage to stay with the pack as we round the corner. My lungs burn though. My feet feel like stone, and by the second turn I start to lag behind. I'm dead last at the third corner, and still flagging. I urge my legs to move faster, but they don't respond.

Scars, I can do better than this, can't I? I sense someone watching me, and I glance up to see Cas looking on from the side, smug in his Neju's Guard sash. I don't look at him long, but I can feel him smirking. It's enough to give me a burst of strength. I shoot forward, passing one man and then two. I overtake a third as I round the last corner, and I see him lift his head in surprise. I fix my eyes on the men in front of me and give one last burst of speed, overtaking a few more before I fall across the finish line. Four men stand panting on the other side. I'd come in fifth. Right in the middle.

Several stone-faced soldiers jot notes onto clay tablets. I have no idea what they're writing. "The next station is archery," one of them says.

At the archery field, I'm surprised to see Walgash running the trials. He has us each take position in front of a target and gives us each a bow and quiver.

"Ten arrows at the target," he says. "Fire at will."

I sling the quiver over my shoulder, feeling pretty confident. I've had a chance over the past days to come to the archery fields. After some trial and error, the skill came back to me. I'm pretty good.

I step through the bow to string it, bearing down, but somehow, the bow won't bend enough for me to loop the string over the end. I release the pressure and try again, but the bow just won't cooperate. That's strange. Has my earlier trial sapped me of strength so completely?

Around me, arrows start thudding into their respective targets. Everybody else is doing just fine, and I can't even ready my weapon. A flush starts to creep across my face.

"Having trouble, soldier?" Walgash says from behind me.

"Yes, sir," I mutter. I can't bear to look at him, and simply continue to struggle. What in the world is wrong?

"Well, you'd better hurry. Everybody else is finishing up."

"Yes, sir," I say, more sharply this time. I don't know how much longer I should even keep trying. I'm getting tired, and the bow is not getting any more cooperative.

I hear a curious sound behind me, and I turn around to see Walgash keeled over with suppressed laughter. I look at him, puzzled, and then I take a closer look at the other men around me. Their bows are different. Mine is bigger and much sturdier.

Walgash wipes the tears from his eyes. "Oh, you should see

yourself, sweating over that bow like a beardless boy." He pauses. "Can you even grow a beard?"

A sneaking suspicion forms in the back of my mind.

"Oh, come now, Dineas. You didn't think I would let you get away so easily with that show of swordsmanship at the rose-marked compound, did you? My ribs still ache, for heaven's sake." He takes the bow from me. "This is my personal bow. It's not for everyone." With those words, he strings it as easily as if it were a child's weapon. Then, with one fluid motion, he takes one of my arrows and sends it straight into the center of the bull's-eye. "Just remember, my talented friend. You're not the best at everything around here." He grins and hands me a new bow. "Try your luck with this one. And you'd better hurry. At least I shot the first arrow for you." He leans close conspiratorially. "And watch your shoulders. You tense up with each successive arrow." And with that, he leaves me with my jaw hanging open.

After a few moments, I come back to my senses. This bow behaves as it should, and soon I'm loosing arrows one after the other. A few match Walgash's shot, while others hit the bull's-eye but don't hit the very center.

After I finish, Walgash returns. "Not a bad recovery," he says with a grin that splits his face in half. "On to the next station before you get in trouble."

I can't decide whether to thank him or punch him.

The next stations are fencing and bare-handed fighting, and after the disastrous last trial, they are a breeze. They pair us up with other candidates, and I win my fights easily. After we finish, the observers pass me a waterskin. The water's hot from sitting in the sun but no less sweet.

"Take two hours for lunch and rest," a soldier says. "You've finished the warm-up portion of the trial. The real test starts this afternoon."

After lunch, they gather us at the city gates and load us into wagons. We're allowed to bring nothing but the clothes on our backs. The sun beats down on us as we roll out of the city, and I wish I'd had more to drink before we left. Different wagons peel off as we go, and when a handful of carts are left, we stop at a seemingly random point in the desert.

They give us each a bag. I'm thrilled to see a waterskin inside, and then realize from the weight that it must be empty. There's also a map, a knife, and a piece of flint.

A soldier speaks. "On your map is marked our current location, your final target, and checkpoints you must hit along the way. Your job is to get there by tomorrow evening. May Neju watch over your journey."

With that, he taps one man on the shoulder and tells him to go. A short while later, he taps the next. And then it's my turn.

I set off quickly, scanning the map as I walk. The marks are easy enough to follow, and I'm confident I can find my way. But our path doesn't cross any springs or rivers until well into our journey. It's not a pleasant thought.

The sun is hot, and the air is gritty with dust. I realize now that my amnesia puts me at a disadvantage for this part of the trial. The others have lived here for years. They know this land and how to survive in it. They have a better idea of what's in store, how to pace themselves and where to rest, while I just have the markings on the map.

My mouth is uncomfortably dry when I reach the first checkpoint—a cliff perhaps three stories high. Several candidates cling to its face.

A member of Neju's Guard stands in front and checks my name off his tablet. "Climb up," he says, gesturing toward the cliff.

Well, it's a change of pace at least. I swing my sack over my shoulder and take a closer look. The sandstone is not nearly as smooth as it looks from afar. I dig my fingers into a crevice, find the foothold, and haul myself up. Step, pull. Step, pull.

A shadow crosses my vision. There's a sound of beating wings, and suddenly a large crow flies right past my head. I almost lose my grip.

Crows? In the desert? When my heart stops pounding, I crane my neck for a better look. The bird's still flying back and forth around me. It's bizarre.

I hear a yell, and debris fills the air as a man to my right skids down the cliff face. I pull myself closer to the wall, holding my breath as I hear the crunch of his landing. His screams tell me he's alive, but I don't look. The crow flies away at the noise.

By the time I pull myself over the top, I'm shaken and covered in dust. My mouth is even drier than before, and I scour my map desperately. I need to find a spring, and soon. I walk quickly, using the sun for navigation, and finally I hear a soft gurgle of water. It's a tiny spring, just a trickle announced by a spray of greener grass, but I bury my face in it and drink for a blissfully long time, then fill my waterskin. With my thirst sated and my belly sloshing with water, some of my strength returns.

But it's not long before I remember that water's not the only thing I need to keep me going. By nightfall, my stomach feels like it's stuck to my spine. I pass a few plants with fruit, but the cursed amnesia means I don't know if they're edible or not. As it gets darker, it also gets colder, and I'm walking as much to keep warm as to cover distance. I fall into a dreamlike state—just one step in front of the other.

I stumble into the second checkpoint just after dawn, where we're tasked with stacking a wall ten stones long and four stones high. As I heave the first rock into place, I'm surprised to see Arxa.

"You look haggard, Dineas," he says. "Have you eaten?"

"No, sir." I grunt and pick up a second rock. "I don't know which plants are poisonous, and I've had no luck hunting with a dagger."

"You still have a long way ahead of you. Hard on an empty stomach. Are you sure you want to continue? There's no shame in stopping."

He's so hard to read. Quitting sounds pretty good right now, to be honest.

I hear a fluttering of wings again, and just as I'm putting the second rock down, a crow lands on my shoulder. I shake it off. The bird squawks and takes wing, only to land a few paces away. I swear it's staring me down.

"Shoo!" When yelling at the bird doesn't help, I aim a good kick at it. The crow jumps out of the way with an outraged caw, and finally flies off. I stare after the bird, dumbfounded for a moment, and then go on to pick up the next rock.

"Just say the word, Dineas," Arxa says, "and we'll get you to food and a soft bed."

Gods, I wish he hadn't mentioned the bed. It's on the tip of my tongue to take him up on it, but something stops me. I've already marched through the night. I have less ahead of me than I do behind me. And yes, I'm tired and miserable, but I can keep going. I'll regret it if I don't.

"Thank you for your concern, sir, but I will keep going."

"As you wish, soldier."

I finish my wall a little before midmorning. I've made good time through the night, and I decide I can afford some rest. I worry briefly about sleeping too long, but something tells me I won't. A shady spot near a boulder seems as good a place as any, and I settle down. Closing my eyes is pure bliss. I doze for a while before I'm awoken by small scratchings next to me. I pry my eyes open. There's a lizard sunning itself on a rock nearby, a big one.

My stomach growls.

Slowly, keeping my body entirely still except for my arm, I reach for it, one hair's width at a time. The lizard blinks and pumps his head up and down. Finally, my hand hovers just behind it. Just a little bit more . . . I pounce. The lizard makes to bolt, but it's too late, and I break his neck with a snap of my thumb. The creature is as long as my forearm. I waste no time making a small fire.

It's the best roasted lizard I've ever had.

I eat every last edible portion of that creature, finally spitting out the bones when there's absolutely nothing left. I could easily have had more, but this is enough to give me a jolt of energy, as well as some new ideas for feeding myself. I catch a few grasshoppers after that, collecting them as I go, and roast them when I have a full spit.

As the afternoon lengthens, I see the last checkpoint up ahead, a river crossing. There is a whole crowd of soldiers here, next to a single log serving as a bridge. My feet are killing me by now, and I double-check on the map that this is the end. Almost there, but the look of the last station worries me. Why are there so many soldiers here?

The scribe crosses me off and then tells me to cross the river. He's eating a fruit that matches the ones on some bushes lining the bank. If he's eating it, then it's good enough for me. I pick one for myself and take a big bite. It's amazing—sweet, juicy, and just a little bit tart. I eat two, and it's enough to perk me up.

Sated now, I turn my attention to the log bridge. It's about as wide as the length of my hand and forearm combined, and looks sturdy, with bark that gives a bit of traction. The water below is murky and looks cold. The log wobbles under my weight, and I stumble like a drunken mouse before finally catching my balance. The water flowing underneath makes me dizzy, and I keep my eyes on the opposite bank as I make my way forward. I'm about a quarter of the way across when one of the soldiers on the opposite bank steps onto the log. It's Cas. He smiles, and it's not the friendly kind. Somehow, I doubt he's here to help me across.

I watch him now, flexing my fingers as we get closer together. I grab for him at the same time he grabs for me. A mad scramble for control, a shift of weight, a throw of my hip. He falls off the log, sending a splash of water up around us. I nearly follow, but wrap my arm and leg around the log to catch myself. Thank the gods for the long sleeves of my tunic, or bark would be embedded all over my arms. Still, I'm pretty sure I picked up some nasty bruises. Groaning, I haul myself back up, regain my footing, and keep on going.

I'm halfway across when the next man comes. I'm smarter about it this time. Just as he's about to reach me, I shake the log. The movement is slight, but enough to toss him off-kilter, and I give him some help over the side.

I'm not surprised at all when a third man comes as I'm nearing the end, but I do swallow a lump of sheer disbelief when I see him. This man is a giant. He's a head taller than me, and his arms look like tree trunks. I half expect the log to snap in two when he steps on it, but no such luck, and he's heavy enough that my earlier trick of shaking the bridge won't work. I sink lower, thinking maybe I can get his legs or trip him up, but I misjudge my reach. He grabs my shoulders, and the next thing I know I'm flying through the air. I hit the water with a slap, and the cold stuns me a moment before I regain my senses and paddle toward the surface. My feet find the bottom at the same time my head breaks through the top. Thank the gods, the water is only neck deep. I spit water out of my mouth as the big soldier grins down at me from the log.

"Your mother's ugly," I shout at him. He just grins wider.

Humiliation's the least of my worries. Does falling off the log mean I failed the trial?

Someone grabs me from behind and pulls me below the water. I swallow a mouthful in surprise and lash out at the person behind me, but there's no force behind my underwater blow. My lungs start to spasm, and I'm fighting the instinct to breathe water. They're not actually trying to kill us during these trials, are they?

Then cold realization hits me. They might not be instructed to kill us, but accidents do happen, and at least one person in this river was not fond of me to begin with. I resume my struggles with renewed strength. I try pinching my attacker, and finally reach back and grab him squarely between the legs. He lets go.

I burst through the surface, gasping, and strike out blindly. My fist connects with something head-shaped, and someone with Cas's voice curses my mother. I don't waste time looking behind me and swim as fast as I can to the far shore. Then I'm clambering up the other side, and collapse sopping wet before a scribe. He looks down at me and then crosses my name off his list.

"You're finished," he says. "You may rest."

# CHAPTER TWENTY-FIVE
## ZIVAH

Mehtap's words about being useful stay with me. They echo in my head as I go about my day, and the walls of the compound feel even more restrictive than before. I think constantly about how Dineas is out in the capital while I'm trapped in here, and how these next years are but one stage of his life, whereas for me, they'll be my last.

My only consolation is my time in the hospital, where I continue my work with the abandoned plague patients. I'm gratified to see two patients after Dineas come out of the fever umber-touched. It seems that having another healer to shoulder the work does make a difference.

One morning, I'm with an old man, Marzban, who's emerged from his fever rosemarked. He's to be settled in the compound, but he's half-blind from a clouded eye, and Jesmin has offered to treat him before he leaves. I sit with the two of them and listen with interest as the head physician describes what will happen. Surgery is beyond the knowledge of Dara medicine, and I'm eager to see Jesmin work.

"The window of your eye has clouded over," Jesmin tells the old man. "I can push it aside, to clear the path for light. It won't restore your sight perfectly, but you should be able to see more than you can see now."

Marzban shifts nervously. "Will it hurt?"

"Less than you think," says Jesmin.

When the man grants his permission, Jesmin fetches a set of curved needles. He gives Marzban a flask of strong spirits to drink from, and bids him sit in a special chair with straps to secure his arms and his head.

"Now, hold still," Jesmin says.

I can't help but cringe as the needle moves closer to Marzban's eye. My eyes start to water in empathy, and I'm glad both men are concentrating too hard on the task to notice my horrified expression.

Just before the needle touches, Marzban jumps.

"It's imperative you hold still," says Jesmin. "Otherwise, I could damage your eye."

The second try is no better. Jesmin looks at me. "Zivah, can you hold his head?"

The thought puts my hair on end, but I do my best to look confident as I approach the chair. I've never thought myself squeamish. I deal with the sick all the time, but this is different. Marzban grabs the chair nervously as I come closer. Jesmin shows me how to brace my arms around his head to keep him from turning. Marzban's forehead is cold and damp.

"Try again," says Jesmin. He raises the needle. Marzban tenses under my grip.

"Wait," I say.

Jesmin stops.

I step back from the chair. "I have some herbs that might help."

Jesmin's face sharpens with interest. "What kind of herbs?"

"It depends. Do you need him awake? Something for pain? Can he be asleep?"

"He needs to be awake to tell me what he sees. But I need him calm."

I think through my remedies. "I have some smoke bundles that dampen pain and render a patient pliable." I turn to Marzban. "You'll still be awake. You'll be able to speak to us, but you'll be in a trance, and you won't feel as nervous."

Jesmin mulls this over. "Do you use this often on your patients?"

"We offer it to women in childbirth, and patients with bones that need setting. It doesn't seem to cause any other harm."

Jesmin nods. "I'm curious to see this, if Marzban agrees."

The old man nods, and I fetch two bundles from my store. They're dry and ready to burn, but there's the question of where to burn it. The smoke is very strong. I've built up some tolerance to it, but I certainly don't want Jesmin to suffer its effects if he's going to be wielding that needle. I take Marzban into the supply room, where I light the bags and lay them at his feet. Sweet smoke drifts up. Marzban leans forward to inhale, and I wave my hand.

"There's no need. It's very potent."

After a while, I start to feel light-headed, though the effects are much more pronounced on Marzban. His pupils dilate, and his entire body relaxes, quite unlike before. I smother the flames and take him by the elbow.

"Come. It is time."

He rises placidly at my urging, and I guide him back to the room where Jesmin waits. The physician looks with interest as I settle the old man back in his chair.

Jesmin approaches cautiously. "How do you feel?"

"Drowsy," Marzban says. His eyes don't focus.

Jesmin nods. "Let's try this again."

This time the man doesn't flinch but simply sits still as Jesmin does his work.

"Tell me when your vision becomes brighter," he says.

After a few seconds, Marzban says, "Now."

Jesmin removes the needle, holds a cloth to the man's nose and instructs him to blow. "This drains the phlegm," he says to me. Then he binds the eye well with bandages.

A few hours later, Marzban is back to normal. He has newly washed clothes to wear, and a small amount of money. Jesmin and I see him to the door, where a rosemarked woman named Estir waits. She's here every time Jesmin has a new patient to settle in the compound.

Jesmin nods a greeting. "How are things with your people, Estir?"

Estir is a strong-looking middle-aged woman with a stern mouth. "Well enough. Lost a few recently, but we're doing fine for food and shelter."

"Marzban will have to tend to the eye until it fully heals," says Jesmin. "But I trust you can get him settled."

Once the two have left, I turn to Jesmin. "Is Estir some kind of official?"

"Just one of the leaders of the myriad groups that form in this lawless place. Estir leads a band of settlers along the north wall. They distribute supplies equitably among themselves and defend each other against the unsavory. I may not be able to control much here, but at least I can keep my patients from falling into the wrong hands."

"If Estir leads a good group, who leads the bad groups?"

"That changes as well, since the population shifts so quickly. Right now there's a gang led by a woman named Anahi. Many of the injuries that come in the mornings are from run-ins with her people."

The name sounds familiar, and I think back to the one time I wandered the compound at night. "Is she older than Estir, with a slight limp?"

"Yes. Have you seen her?"

"I have," I say.

Thankfully, Jesmin doesn't ask about the circumstances. "The gods strike without prejudice when it comes to the rose plague, but if you survive, your status in this world still matters. Mehtap, like the other aristocrats who fall ill, lives in a nice villa with personal guards. The less fortunate have to be shrewder about their survival."

For a moment, neither of us says anything. Then Jesmin turns to me. "But let's not dwell on the negatives. That incense of yours was impressive. Easiest surgery I've done in a long time.

We should be sharing knowledge, seeing what we can learn from each other. That was the original plan, wasn't it? I lost sight of it in the day-to-day business. Forgive me."

"There's nothing to forgive. And it's something we can easily remedy." In fact, I'm excited at the thought. As uncomfortable as the surgery was this morning, it was still fascinating.

He peers at me thoughtfully. "I hardly know where to start. Where do your interests lie? What parts of medicine excite you the most?"

"To be honest," I say, slightly self-conscious now, "over the past few months I've been mostly preoccupied with rose plague."

"Understandable. What aspects of it?"

"Better treatments, mostly." It seems too presumptuous to say I've been looking for a cure, and too embarrassing to tell him of my numerous failures.

"Rose plague seems an apt place to start our discussions. I'll see what I can procure in terms of scrolls from the academy. We can go over them together, and you in turn can tell me what your people have learned about the disease."

A smile pulls at the corners of my lips. "I would like that. Very much."

Jesmin is true to his word. Tablets of medical records soon arrive, as well as the occasional scroll. He apologizes that he can't get me more, but we're limited by my disease. Tablets can be passed through the fire and returned to the imperial library, but any parchments, once they enter the rosemarked compound, must stay here. In addition to these records, Jesmin shows me the detailed logs he's kept of every person who's come into the compound. Jesmin's painstakingly noted each patient's date and circumstance of infection, entry, and the day they finally died.

In the few hours I can spare away from my patients, I pore over the material. The Amparan view of medicine is quite interesting. While Dara healers view the body as a set of systems (sustenance, air, and mind, among others) that become weighed down with disease essence, the Amparan physicians focus much more on anatomy and the individual organs. I suppose that's why their surgeons have been so successful, but their insistence on breaking down the body into parts means they sometimes miss the subtleties of herbs and potions, which by their nature infuse the body as a whole.

The information in these records is valuable for other reasons as well. Over the past weeks, I'd been so preoccupied with placing Dineas in the army that I'd lost sight of Tal's charge to find out how the Monyar soldiers fell ill. Now though, as I read over these texts, it's clear that there might be useful information here.

There's at least one physician in the Imperial Academy with an interest in rose plague. Several of my tablets are reports made by a physician named Baruva to an Imperial Minister Utana. In each of the reports, he details his findings about the way rose plague can be spread. Much of what he writes, I already know—that the disease is spread by touch and bodily humors, that fire destroys the disease. Beyond the basics though, he goes into painstaking detail about other circumstances—for example that strong sunlight over the course of several days cleans the essence from a surface. Also, there's a warning to keep the blood of a rosemarked patient from mixing with weak vinegar, as it seems to make the disease essence stronger.

The minister Utana's name strikes me as familiar, though for a long time I don't know why. I ask Jesmin if he knows of him and the physician.

"Baruva is still a well-respected scholar in the Imperial Academy," Jesmin says.

"Is he umbertouched?" I can't imagine anyone doing this kind of research who is not immune.

Jesmin's mouth quirks humorlessly. "No, but he's very careful. And he has many slaves to help him with the more dangerous aspects of his work."

My stomach flips. There's no forgetting that I'm in the middle of Ampara. "And what of the minister Utana?"

"Utana fell ill with rose plague a few months ago. One of the hazards of being a minister of health, unfortunately. He was not as careful as Baruva."

And I realize that's why Utana's name seemed so familiar. I'd seen it in Jesmin's ledgers for the compound. "Is he still alive?"

"He lives with a servant on the east side of the compound. The emperor was quite fond of him, so he provided well for Utana after he fell ill."

"I see." A former minister of health, here in the rosemarked compound. I wonder what secrets of the court he was privy to, and if there is some way to meet him.

That night, I'm milking Diadem in my room when I hear unusual sounds from the hallway. I'm fairly sure it's muffled crying, and it's coming from Mehtap's quarters. For a moment, I stand outside her door, uncertain what to do. Though I've lived under her roof for some weeks now, I still don't exactly know how to relate to the commander's daughter. Perhaps it would be better to let her cry in peace. Still, it doesn't feel right to walk away.

I knock hesitantly on her door. "Mehtap?"

A shuffling of skirts. A sniffle. "Yes?"

"May I come in?"

There's a long pause before I hear her footsteps. The door opens a sliver, and then she steps back and motions for me to come in. She's either a dainty crier or quite skilled at cleaning herself up. Other than a slight reddish tinge to her eyes, she looks put together. Her dark blond hair is neatly combed back, and her dress is smooth and unrumpled. The sheets on her bed are piled into a small nest, and she climbs on, pulling her feet up after her. "Is there anything you need?"

"Is there anything bothering you?" I ask her. "Anything you'd like to talk about?"

Mehtap looks down and lets out a wry chuckle. "You heard me, didn't you? And here I thought I was being discreet."

"If you'd rather I leave it alone . . ."

"No, it's all right." She wipes the back of her hand across her eyes. "It's silly, really. I was just reading a letter from my good friend. She's . . ." She gestures helplessly toward a tablet nestled in her blankets. "She's getting married."

Understanding comes quickly. I think back to the day Leora came by my cottage with her bridal veil, and I feel that familiar twinge in my chest.

"I'm happy for her," Mehtap says. "I really am. It's just . . ." She bites her lip.

"I know," I say quietly.

Apparently, my words give Mehtap the permission she needed, because tears start to stream silently down her face. "She'll have a beautiful wedding. Her betrothed is a good man. And she'll have children. . . ." And here she stops herself and laughs a little. "I don't even like children."

Her words bring a rush of memories. Leora's eyes sparkling as she tells me about her betrothed. Alia's animated recountings of village feasts, her arms akimbo as she imitates the wildest dancers. Mother and Father, speaking sensibly about the harvest and plans to rotate the crops over the next years. I craved the news they brought, the window they offered into what I'd left behind. But the stories came with a bitter aftertaste. I missed my family dearly between visits, but my moments with them were poisoned by my illness as well.

"It seems unfair sometimes, doesn't it?" I say. "That life goes on outside these walls. We get put inside, but everyone just continues without us."

Mehtap wipes at her eyes. "I just want to know what I did wrong. What did I do to offend the gods so?"

She looks at me with something close to desperation, and my words tangle in my throat. There are so many things I could say. That the gods' ways are mysterious. That it makes no more sense to question our misfortune than it does to question our good fortune. That it would be arrogant to think we deserve not to suffer when plenty of others share our fate.

There are many things I could say, but they crumble like ashes in the face of our reality. They do nothing to lessen the pain.

"I don't know" is all I can say. My skin prickles, and I rub my forearms. It's the threat of a flush, the fever's ever-present promise to return.

Mehtap pulls her blankets close around her and she seems to shrink into them. "The way they throw us in here and leave us to our own devices. It's as if we've already died."

# CHAPTER TWENTY-SIX

## DINEAS

The list is posted three days later in the training yards, and I push my way to the front of the crowd. I see Naudar's name, then mine near the bottom of the list. And I can't help the smile that spreads over my face.

The next morning, Walgash gives me a hearty clap on the back as we head over to the riding fields for training. "Must have been your archery skills that pushed you over the top."

I make a mental note to put lizards in his bed.

"You know," Walgash muses, "Arxa gave an interesting command at the trials. Seems he ordered the men at one of the stations to snack on wild fruit when the candidates were coming through. Curious, isn't it?"

And that's the thing about Walgash. He always follows up

something annoying with something interesting or useful. Makes it hard to pull pranks with a clear conscience.

Commander Arxa stands outside the stables, adjusting the saddle on a roan stallion. "Dineas," he calls as we pass.

"Good morning, sir."

"I'm pleased to have you in Neju's Guard," he says. "You don't give up, even when you're at a disadvantage. That's something I value in my soldiers."

"Thank you, sir."

Arxa's stallion paws the ground. He's an impressive beast, five hundred ingots of solid muscle.

"Anything on your mind, Dineas?" asks Arxa.

"No, sir. I was just admiring your steed."

The commander nudges the horse to keep him looking ahead. "He's a recent addition to our stables. Rovenni breeding stock. We've been trying to get ahold of some for years, and the law's finally come down on our side. Are you a horseman, Dineas? I had my men ask around the markets, but none of the traders there recognized your brand. We'll try again later in the year, when new tribes pass through."

"I honestly have no idea, sir. But I do like the look of that stallion." I rub absentmindedly at the scar on my wrist. If all Rovenni animals are like that, I'd be ecstatic to claim a past with them.

Arxa jerks his chin toward the stables. "The stables will match you up with a good steed."

When I tell the stablehands I don't know if I've ridden before, they pair me with one of the gentler mares. The Neju's Guard old-timers spend the morning testing our riding ability. When it turns out I'm comfortable leading my horse through all the gaits, I'm told to join the soldiers practicing formations.

At one point, I see a man standing with Arxa by the side, watching us. The stranger looks familiar, but I can't place him.

"Who is that?" I ask Masista.

He looks over his shoulder. "That's Prince Kiran, the emperor's heir. He spends a lot of time at the training fields."

And that's why he looks familiar. The prince bears a clear resemblance to the portrait of the emperor. The prince's beard is black and trimmed shorter than his father's, and his nose is sharper, but he has the same wide mouth and heavy brows. From the way he stands I can tell he's a soldier himself.

The day's training goes by quickly. Hard work, and I know I'll be sore the next day, but I come out with the feeling I've made a good day's effort.

When Arxa finally dismisses us, Walgash gathers everyone up.

"Tonight we feast in the city," he says, "courtesy of us old-timers. Meals and drinks on us!"

The announcement is met with cheers, and we stream out the palace gates. Our mob of soldiers attracts quite a few curious looks as we move through the streets. It feels good to be here, in a group where I've earned my place.

"Do you know where they're taking us?" I ask Naudar, who's distracted by a merchant girl smiling at him from the side of the street.

"No idea," he says, when he realizes I've spoken.

"For gods' sake, Naudar. Next time you drift off I'll walk you into a wall."

We follow the crowd into a large tavern that looks like it's been reserved for us for the night. The drinks start flowing immediately, and food follows soon after. It's good fare, even better after a long day.

Several games of dice start up in the corner, though I stay at the main tables with Naudar. A serving girl brings us each a goblet of wine.

"Are you the soldier with no past?" she asks.

"That's probably me," I say, studiously ignoring Naudar's smirk.

Her smile has a spark to it. "Maybe you could tell me about it later." Her hips sway from side to side as she walks away.

Naudar claps me on the back. "Well done, my friend! And the night is yet young."

I take a deep gulp of wine. The girl *was* pretty—red lips, and round in all the right places. But I don't know, something about her seemed off. Maybe she was too flawless. Her skin was too smooth.

Over the course of the evening, a parade of new faces rotate through. Mostly I just eat, drink, and listen to battle stories. There's a native of Sehmar who tells how he fought off ten bandits with only his horse for backup. Another soldier was captured by the Shidadi for three days. I'm guessing there's a good bit of imagination mixed into these stories, but they're entertaining. I soon start losing track of which tale belongs to who.

In fact, my entire head starts to feel fuzzy.

A grizzled soldier looks my way. "Enjoying yourself, Dineas?"

"Yes, but I need some fresh air," I say, standing up. My legs wobble underneath me, which is strange because I haven't had that much to drink. I stumble and catch myself on another man's shoulder.

"Sorry," I mutter.

The soldier who was captured by the Shidadi looks over. "First one down?" he asks the man I fell on.

"Looks like it."

"Careful," someone adds. "Arxa will have our hides if any of them hit their heads."

And that's the last thing I hear before my legs give out.

The first thing I notice is my splitting headache. It's relentless, and it makes me want to shrink back into unconsciousness.

Then I notice how cold it is. The wind blows over every inch of my skin, raising goose bumps. After that, I start hearing voices and murmurs below me.

Groaning, I force my eyes open. The sky above is just turning light. That's why it's so cold. I'm outside. Also—I look down—I'm not wearing a single stitch of clothing. That's when I jump, and realize that I'm tied to a pole.

Now I'm wide-awake. I blink, casting around for any hint as to what had happened. Naudar's to my right, naked and trussed up just like me. He's still unconscious, and I can see in the growing light that someone has drawn rude symbols on his face, as well as written "Ampara's Best" on his chest. I looked down to see "Ampara's Finest" written on me.

And then I remember the voices I heard earlier. Oh no. I'm afraid to look, but there's no avoiding it.

We're on a rooftop above a crowded marketplace. Vendors

are setting up their stalls, and already, a crowd has gathered to gawk up at us.

"Naudar," I whisper, my voice tinged with panic. He doesn't stir. "Naudar!"

He groans, pries one eye open, then closes it. A moment later, both eyes open wide and nearly pop out of his head. Then he lets out string of curse words that capture my feelings exactly.

"Gods," he says. "I knew we should have been suspicious. The old-timers are never that generous."

"Naudar, what's going on?"

"Let's just say that Neju's Guard has a long tradition of elaborate welcomes for their new recruits."

If this is a welcome, I never want to get on their bad side.

The crowd below is growing larger with men, women, and children of all ages. A young umbertouched woman covers her mouth and giggles. My face flushes to the roots of my hair. There's even a few priestesses of Mendegi in the crowd. Mendegi, the goddess of women. Shouldn't they be looking somewhere else?

"They're not going to leave us up here forever, are they?" I tug desperately at the rope around my hands and go faint with relief when they start to loosen. It takes a bit of finessing, but eventually I work my way out. Naudar's not far behind, and we clamber down the side of the building. A commandeered oilcloth from an unattended booth restores some of our dignity, and we run as fast as we can back to the palace. We were supposed to be in the training fields at dawn.

At the barracks, we find our clothes folded neatly on our cots. But try as we might, we can't scrub the markings from our skin.

"It's no use," moans Naudar. "We just have to go train like this."

Arxa, to his credit, doesn't crack the barest hint of a smile when he sees. He just takes one long look at us and waves us in. "Ten-man formations," he says.

Walgash is the first to greet us as we stumble onto the field. "Fun time last night?"

His grin only widens at our stony glances.

"Oh, come on, don't be so glum. When I first joined, the old-timers rolled me down a hill in a barrel. At least you came out without bumps and bruises. And really, they did you a favor. What young woman of the city will resist you after that display?" He tugs on his beard. "Though I suppose the chilly morning did you no favors."

Naudar makes a sound like a choking cat. I give an incoherent groan. And we shuffle into place to do our drills.

# CHAPTER TWENTY-SEVEN

I try not to laugh when I see Dineas, I really do. He's so embarrassed standing in the examination room with markings all over his face and arms that it seems cruel to prolong his misery. My lips twitch, and I turn my head. But a chuckle escapes, and from there it's a lost cause.

"I'm so sorry," I choke out between gasps. "I really do feel bad for you."

Dineas gives a martyr's sigh. "I suppose I should be used to it by now."

I step in for a closer look. I can't tell what kind of dye his fellow soldiers used, but it has a while to go before it disappears. A surprisingly artistic sketch of a well-endowed woman disappears beneath the sleeve of his tunic.

I gesture toward his torso. "I'm curious . . ."

He pulls his tunic over his head. "The rest of Sehmar's seen it. You might as well too."

"Ampara's finest," I read. I force the corners of my lips down. "Let me see if I have anything that might take it off quicker."

I rummage through my drawers and settle on a root soap that I rub onto a rag. I take a firm grip on his arm and start scrubbing at the woman's legs. He flexes his bicep at my touch, and I smack his shoulder.

"Stop showing off. I'm just here to clean."

"Walgash says I might have more luck with the maidens after this. Think he's right?"

"I don't know, you'll have to ask them."

"*You're* a maiden."

"I'm a healer."

"Are healers always so hard to impress?"

"You're not dying of fever, you're not oozing blood or pus, and you're not jaundiced. So yes, I'm pleased with how you look today." Despite my words, my gaze drifts over the rest of him. The past weeks of good food and exercise have filled out and defined the muscles of his chest and shoulders quite nicely. It's hard to ignore.

He sees me looking, and the edge of his mouth quirks up. I quickly redirect my gaze to a bruise on his stomach. "How did you get that?"

"Spear butt to the ribs." The pure delight in his smile makes me think he didn't quite buy my change of subject.

I cluck my tongue. "Seems you have some new injury every time you come in."

"Ah, but you should see my sparring partners."

You could almost say we're flirting. The thought strikes me mid-scrub and I turn away for a moment. I fold up the rag and take it to the water basin for a chance to gather my thoughts. No, it's just friendly banter. Though it would do no harm to change the topic, or things will get uncomfortable when the other Dineas comes back.

"The soap doesn't seem to be working," I tell him. "I'm afraid you'll just have to wait until the dye wears off on its own. But shall we start with your treatment for today?"

He pulls his tunic on as I fetch his potion, but just then I hear yells from the window. There's someone weeping outside—no, weeping is too weak a word. These are harsh, desperate sobs, the sound of someone whose sorrow threatens to strangle them.

I look at Dineas, and then we both run out the door.

We follow the sounds to the compound gates, where a small crowd has already gathered. As we come closer, a rosemarked woman glances at Dineas with distaste. "What are you doing here, umbertouched? Come to gloat over your good fortune?"

Dineas looks at her in shock. Before he can react, I take his hand and pull him around the edge of the crowd. "Don't listen to her," I say. "She's just one bitter woman." Though the glares from others around us belie my words.

Finally, we get close enough to see through the gate. There's a parade outside led by two women in dark flowing gowns. They carry bowls of incense, and their cheeks are streaked with soot. I know enough about Amparan gods to recognize them as priestesses of Zenagua, the goddess of death. Both these priestesses are umbertouched, and I wonder if a priestess of the goddess of death would consider it an honor or a snub from Zenagua to survive a bout of rose plague. Behind the priestesses are four umbertouched soldiers wearing cloaks of loosely woven red fabric, like plague veils dyed red. And marching under their guard are three rosemarked: two older men and a boy of perhaps eight. The boy's plague veil is too big for him, and he gets tangled up in the cloth every few steps.

The wailing comes from a woman trailing the procession. There's a man holding her around her shoulders, and three children at her side. All of them wear coarse homespun robes covered in patches.

As I watch, the woman lunges toward the condemned. "Who will feed him? Who will look after him?"

Her husband grabs her around her waist, even as he himself stares after his son. The woman's other children look terrified. The soldiers remain stone-faced, staring ahead as if the woman wasn't there.

My heart squeezes. This family's certainly too poor to buy any help or protection for their son. The mother looks as if she would move into the colony herself if she could.

I feel a touch on my elbow.

"Can I help?" says Dineas, strain clear in his eyes as he watches the woman. "I can go speak with her."

His words bring me some relief. "Can you go out the gate and tell the woman we'll look after her son?"

The guards remove the condemned's plague veils and wave them in after a cursory inspection. The boy walks in a daze I remember well from my first days after waking up rosemarked. He stumbles into the open space beyond the gate, looking uncertainly at the faces of illness around him. Some people look back with pity, while others simply walk away. I wonder how many scenes like this they've witnessed before, and how many it's possible to see before becoming completely numb.

I hurry toward the boy, and I see two other women doing the same. One I recognize as Estir, the woman who'd helped settle Marzban in the compound, but it's the other woman who reaches the boy first. She's older than Estir, almost matronly looking. She looks familiar, but I can't quite place her until I notice her limp. And then my steps gain urgency.

The older woman crouches in front of the boy and wipes tears from his face. "Come now, it will be all right." She hands him some kind of sweet bun. "Fill your stomach and you'll feel better."

"Don't take Anahi's food, boy," says Estir, coming to stand next to them. "You go under her roof, you'll be sold into slavery by the end of the week."

The boy jumps away from the older woman, who shakes her head in disappointment.

"I find it sad that some will throw accusations so freely." She addresses the boy. "That woman is the one who would harm you. You must be careful who you trust."

The boy has gone pale, and he clutches the sweet bun so tightly that it's all but crushed in his hands. Not for the first time, I wonder how it was that I ended up in a place such as this.

Finally, I reach them. "Leave him be," I tell Anahi.

For the first time, Anahi loses her grandmotherly glow. "You're the commander's pet healer, aren't you? You'll do better to stay in the hospital."

There's real threat in her voice, and I wonder how many of her gang are here with her. I'm tempted to look around for Dineas, but

I don't dare show fear. "You don't want a fight right now, Anahi. It would be too damaging for all involved. And don't forget that you and yours will be in need of a healer's help someday."

Anahi sneers. "You don't take the gods seriously, if you're a healer who would withhold her skill."

I give her an icy smile. "My Goddess commands me to heal, that's true, but she doesn't require me to make it comfortable for the patient."

Anahi glares at me, and I fight the urge to step back. She wouldn't resort to force in the middle of the day, would she? But then she simply turns and walks away.

I take in a shaky breath. "It's all right," I tell the terrified boy. "Estir's people are honorable. You'll be safe with them."

Estir offers a hand to the boy, looking more like a soldier greeting a comrade than a woman welcoming a child, but after a moment's hesitation the boy takes it.

"Thank you," I tell Estir.

"I only wish we could save all of them," she replies.

My pulse starts to quiet as Estir leads the boy away, but still I'm finding it hard to breathe. The mother's cries echo in my head, and her raw grief wrings me dry. It makes no sense. I see illness all the time. Why should this boy affect me so much? But I'm shaking now, and I know that I must get out of this crowd. Lowering my head, I flee to the hospital, sweeping past the front rooms and ducking into a quiet corner where I bury my face in my hands. In my mind's eye, I hear my own mother's cries as I moved into my bamboo cottage. I see Alia and Leora clutch each other in their grief. I feel sobs building in my throat, and I hold my breath to keep them in.

"Zivah?" Dineas steps around the corner.

I hastily wipe my eyes. "Dineas, I'm sorry I abandoned you at the gate."

His eyes flit over my face. "I spoke to the mother. They mourn, but we've laid their worst worries to rest." He steps cautiously closer. "What's wrong?"

"Nothing. Just the usual business of the day tiring me out."

He frowns. "I may not have your healer's senses, but I don't need them when you're in this state."

I avoid his eyes. "You're very kind, but—"

"I'm not leaving until you tell me what's wrong. What kind of friend do you think I am?"

"Friend" is not a word I'd expected to hear in Ampara. It unravels me, and I realize I don't have the energy to put up more of a fight. "Something about that woman today. It made me think of my mother and my sisters."

"You miss them," he says quietly.

"Very much." Saying the words somehow makes me feel it more deeply. I draw a breath and hold it when it hitches at the top.

"Do you wish to go back to Dara?"

Do I? "I don't know. It's not the same as it was before I was marked. The only place for me is on the outside, watching their lives from afar. Even if I were right there in Dara, I could never really go back to them."

I don't know if I've ever said those thoughts out loud. They leave me feeling empty, and I let the words drift and settle around us.

Dineas steps closer, and I feel his hands on my shoulders.

"I'm sorry," he says softly. Then he puts two fingers under

my chin and tilts my head up, as I've done so many times to him when checking his pupils. It catches me off guard at first. The feel of someone's skin against mine is rare enough, much less a touch given solely for comfort. I'd forgotten how much I missed it.

"I wish I could do something," Dineas says, his frustration plain in his voice. "But I can't."

"It's all right," I say. "You've already done more than you know."

For a moment, we stand facing each other. I watch his chest rise and fall, and I'm aware of him, the smell of leather and root soap on his skin, the heat radiating off his arms.

A jolt of realization hits me. I back away, perhaps a little too quickly, because his eyes widen slightly.

I smile, trying to smooth over the moment. "Thank you, Dineas. You're a good friend."

I'm not sure if I imagine the flash of disappointment in his eyes. "Of course," he says. "As you are to me."

My hands feel awkward at my side, and I can't quite look him in the eye. I clear my throat. "We haven't done your treatment yet today. Shall we try again?"

He's slow to respond, but finally he nods. "Yes. Yes, we should."

# CHAPTER TWENTY-EIGHT

## DINEAS

I'm getting more used to the transition now, that feeling of memories washing back, realizing I'm more than what I thought, much more. That waterfall of understanding that paints my recent days in a different light.

As usual, the first moments overwhelm me. All I can do is hold my head in my hands as the fragments of my life come together. I see Zivah sitting in the corner, her hands in her lap and her face tight with strain, but it's one image among a thousand. Only after the flood slows down can I finally look at her.

"Eventful day," I say.

She sweeps up her skirts and walks to the table. "Yes, it was." I can't tell if she's avoiding my eyes on purpose, or if she's holding herself more stiffly than usual. She's probably embarrassed by her show of emotion this morning. I do feel bad for her, and I suppose it's good that my other self cared enough to comfort her.

I think back to the conversation, and my thoughts linger over the last few moments. The tense silence, her backing away. *You're a good friend, Dineas.* A slight sting of rejection still lingers.

Wait, were we . . . ? No, I'm just imagining things. This is Zivah. Anything between us would just be too bizarre.

"Are the crows around? I have things to report."

She puts on gloves, fetches me a pen and ink, and opens a window to whistle for the crows. As I watch her cross the room, I realize that I don't notice her rosemarks nearly as much as I used to. Instead, I notice how large her eyes are, and the bow of her mouth. Gods, my mind is more muddled from the potion than I realized.

I shake it off as the crows fly in. Slicewing struts back and forth just out of my reach, clicking her beak.

"What's wrong, crow?" And then I remember what happened at the Neju's Guard trials. "Oh. I'm sorry."

She ignores me.

"Zivah, do you have bread for the birds?"

She glances at me, confused, but fishes out some scraps from her apron pocket.

"Thanks. And you should introduce me to the crows when my memory's gone. Prevent any more confusion if they find me again."

Slicewing tries to ignore me, but she can't resist the bread for long. Soon she's on my shoulder again, and I turn my attention back to Zivah.

"Things are moving faster with Neju's Guard than expected,"

I say. "We're going on a mission next week, escorting Prince Kiran on a tour of the northern territories."

Zivah straightens. "North? Will you go to Monyar?"

"No, we'll stay south of the strait." For that I'm extremely grateful. "I have a feeling this mission is part work and part training. Arxa's eager to get us battle ready, and I'm guessing this is practice for something bigger. I'll try to keep my eyes and ears open while I'm gone."

She nods. "Be safe on your journey."

I grin. "Try not to give the other me too warm of a send-off. Don't want to give him the wrong message."

I meant nothing by it, but she stiffens. "I wouldn't do that. It wouldn't be right."

I put up my hands disarmingly. "Just joking."

"Don't."

I whistle out of the corner of my mouth. "Prickly today?"

She doesn't respond, and I start to pen my report.

# CHAPTER TWENTY-NINE

## ZIVAH

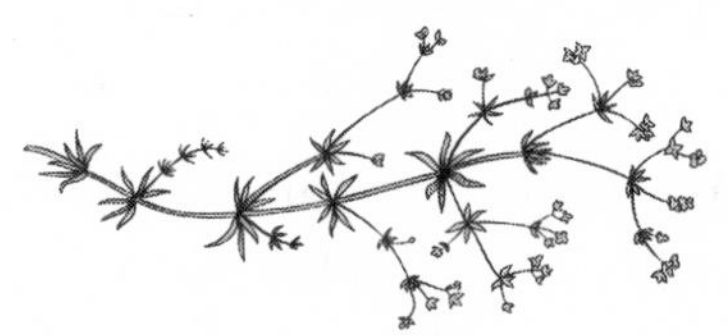

One good thing comes out of seeing the rosemarked boy enter the compound. It spurs me to write Leora back. I'd read her letter countless times, but I'd resisted writing a reply. Somehow, I feared that doing so would undo the tourniquet I'd pulled tight around my thoughts and feelings about home. Tonight though, I'm ready.

It's not as hard as I fear. After the first few greetings, the words flow easily. Though Leora doesn't know about my mission, there's still plenty to describe. I tell her about Mehtap's villa, the harp music that floats from her room every night and the passersby who linger outside her window to listen. I describe the rows of the sick inside Jesmin's hospital, the constant scramble for clean blankets and bandages. I tell her about the screams I hear outside the villa walls at night, and how helpless it makes me feel. I even tell her about Dineas, though to Leora, he's just a patient who was abandoned at the compound wall.

*Spending so much time with Dineas has made me think about the experiences that make us what we are. What would any of us be like without our past? If I could no longer remember my years growing up with you and Alia, if my training as a healer was erased, would I still be me? If I started a new life, made new friends, fell in love, decided to apprentice in farming instead of healing, which version of me would be real? Would it matter?*

I put down my pen and think of Dineas this morning, the one who chased me down and wouldn't let me go until he knew why I was upset. The one who was frustrated that he couldn't take away my pain. And I think of the other Dineas, the one who carries a shadow with him, whose remarks always have a caustic edge.

And I wonder.

Jesmin's medical texts give me numerous new ideas for cures. Unfortunately, none of them are any more effective than the attempts I'd made in Dara, and their side effects are just as unpleasant. Several times, I get sick at the hospital and have to duck into a back room to lie down or run out the back to be ill.

I think I've kept my experiments secret, until one day Jesmin walks past me as I'm reading and looks pointedly at my latest attempt—a poultice-soaked bandage that I've wrapped around my arm.

"There are several schools of thought regarding self-experimentation," he says. "Some say it is the noblest of endeavors. Others say it's brash, foolhardy, and a good way to kill yourself."

The mildness of his voice makes it hard to know which particular school Jesmin subscribes to, though I suspect it's the latter.

"I was reading about Baruva's theory of rose plague settling in the skin," I say. "I thought the right poultice might draw it out. It seemed harmless enough." At least I'm not vomiting up my breakfast.

Jesmin lifts the corner of my bandage to reveal angry red streaks on my skin, darker and bolder than my rosemarks. "Are you sure?"

As if on cue, my skin starts to itch and burn. I exhale my frustration and retreat to the water basin. The bandage comes off in pieces, and the poultice leaves a chalky residue on my skin. The itch is maddening, and I have to fight the urge to scratch as I rinse off. Finally, everything's clean, and I smear some spineleaf sap on my abused skin. As a cool numbness spreads over my arm, I breathe out one more time. At least by now, I've had so many failures that I no longer feel any great disappointment.

Jesmin looks up from his desk when I return. He doesn't speak, and I walk quietly to the table where I'd been reading. Just as I think he will let the incident go without comment, I hear his voice.

"Perhaps searching for a cure is too great a leap," Jesmin says gently. "Perhaps it would make more sense to pick a more tractable goal first."

The words on the scroll blur in front of me. It's easy for Jesmin to say so. He's not the one whose days are numbered. The instinct to argue with him is overwhelming, but he's right about one thing. As loath as I am to admit it, my cures are based more on leaps of reasoning than any real knowledge or experience.

"And what do you recommend?" I ask.

"We could focus on the spread of the disease. There, at least, we have a body of knowledge to work off of. You've told me that the Dara keep their rosemarked under far less isolation. We could pool our knowledge and try and codify a better way to treat the afflicted."

My mind goes back to the boy abandoned at the compound a few days ago, and his mother's grief. Jesmin and I could indeed make his last years more bearable for both him and his mother. It wouldn't take much effort to come up with ideas, and they'd likely be much more successful than my cure attempts.

"Very well," I say, though I add a silent "for now" at the end of it. I roll up my scroll and turn my chair to face Jesmin. "Shall we start with the terms of quarantine, then? I've already told you the limitations that were placed on me at Dara. I could still receive visitors, as long as we were careful about what they touched."

He nods, acknowledging my easy acquiescence. "Yes, I remember. And I see how that might work in Dara, but in Sehmar City and the rest of Central Ampara, we have a problem of scale. In your village, the people are spread out and there are simply fewer rosemarked. The likelihood of a mistake, and the cost of any one outbreak, would be much smaller than here. Could we trust all thousand rosemarked within this compound to be as careful with their disease as you were?"

His words make sense, but I refuse to be so easily discouraged. "Perhaps some of Baruva's reports would help. He's listed many ways to minimize the spread of the disease. A distance of five paces when speaking, bright sunlight . . . Even if visits could only be conducted occasionally, under the strict supervision of soldiers who could make sure that the healthy stayed a good distance away from the sick... and all water drawn from near the rosemarked colony should be boiled thoroughly, of course."

"Most Amparan citizens already boil their water," says Jesmin. "Everyone at court is required to, as is the army."

"The army?" I ask. This surprises me, though I don't immediately comprehend why.

"Yes. Every soldiers boils his water when on a mission. It's deemed the best way of keeping the soldiers safe."

Still, that doesn't sound right. "Every single one?"

"It is a universal practice of the Amparan army. I helped draft the recommendation myself."

My mind is spinning. I'd not yet come up with a completely satisfactory theory for how the Dara battalion had been infected with rose plague, but part of me had always assumed it was through their water. I simply didn't see any other plausible way to infect so many soldiers at the same time. I suppose it could be done through food, but rose plague essence thrives on moisture. Once it dries, its potency decreases manyfold.

"If the army boils their water," I ask, "then how did the Dara battalion get infected in such great numbers?"

"That," says Jesmin, "is the question we've all been asking."

Mehtap looks radiant when she comes down to dinner a week later, and it takes me a while to figure out what it is. She smiles at me, a mischievous gleam in her eye, and I finally see it.

"Your rosemarks!"

Her skin is smooth and unblemished, and I can hardly believe my eyes. Only when she steps closer can I see the chalky finish of whatever ointment she's smeared on her skin.

"It's pretty convincing, isn't it?" she says. "At least from a distance. I mixed it with clays from the garden."

"You're not planning to go out like this, are you?" She knows as well as I do that it's a capital crime to cover up rosemarks. Not even Arxa's status would protect her.

"I won't leave the house with it. I just wanted to be able to look into the mirror and not see the marks for a while." Mehtap looks at me and scowls. "Oh, don't look so stricken, Zivah. I just wanted to look healthy for an evening. And I won't let Father see me like this. He's a man. He wouldn't understand."

I relax a little. "You do look very nice."

"I can make some for you too," she says. "I'd have to adjust the clays a bit, but our complexions aren't so different."

"It's all right," I say. "It looks like it'd be hard to wash off."

She grimaces. "That it is. But I have plenty of free time. Probably too much, since all I've done this past day is worry about Father's mission tomorrow."

"It's just accompanying the prince to some northern cities, isn't it? Surely it's not as dangerous as other trips that your father has undertaken."

"Yes, that's true." But her voice falls away, and she doesn't meet my eyes.

I wait, hoping she'll say more.

She heaves a sigh. "Why can't I be useful like you, Zivah? I just sit here in my house all day, alone with my thoughts."

"Nobody's useless by nature. It's just a matter of finding something to do."

Mehtap purses her lips as a servant fills her plate. "So what can I do? If I were out of the compound, I'd be married to some official's son. And then I'd have children. Perhaps, if I'm extra energetic, I'd pick some fashionable cause to work on with some of the other wives. Providing scarves for beggars or whatnot," she says wryly.

"There are beggars here too," I point out.

"You're right. It's far worse in here than in the poorest parts of the city. It almost seems too much to tackle."

"It does seem overwhelming," I say. "But I wonder if things could be better if the rules were a just a little different. If the emperor assigned just a few more soldiers to guard the place, for example . . ."

She looks at me thoughtfully. "Or if they allowed everyone to send letters out instead of just those who can afford their own messengers. Things would be so much better if they just treated us like people. The sickness here runs deeper than our marks. It's a sickness of spirit."

I'm impressed at her insight, though perhaps it's unfair of me to underestimate her so. "I've been speaking with Jesmin about the quarantine. I'm not convinced it has to be so strict."

Her smile fades a bit. "Do you think it could be changed? But that would be much more complicated than simply handing out scarves in the city. If we want to change rules, we'd need to get the ear of the emperor, or at least the imperial advisers. If I were healthy I could try to get to know some of their wives, but I'm in here. . . ."

Her words give me an idea. "There are those within the compound who have some influence, don't they? Utana, the former minister of health, is in the compound. Do you know him?"

"I've met him once or twice. He's always been very kind."

Mehtap thinks for another moment, then gives a deliberate nod. "Very well, then. I'll request an audience with him for the two of us."

That went so easily I feel almost guilty. She's cheery for the rest of the meal, and we spend the remaining time talking about some volumes of harp music Arxa had ordered for her from the Eastern Provinces. As we finish up though, Mehtap once again drifts into contemplation.

"You're from Monyar, Zivah," she says. "Have you seen the Shidadi before?"

It's a rather jarring change in topic. "I've seen them from a distance," I say carefully. "They stay hidden mostly."

"Are they really as dangerous as they say?" she says.

"They do have a fierce reputation, but I wouldn't know."

She nods, as if that was the best she could have expected, and then she stands abruptly. "Well, I should get to bed." She smiles apologetically. "It's been a long day."

Later in my room, I think about her cryptic question about the Shidadi. It could have been simply idle curiosity, but that combined with her worry about her father... A frightening possibility occurs to me. Could Dineas have been wrong about where Neju's Guard was headed? Perhaps they mean to cross the strait after all. I have nothing to back up my suspicions, but Mehtap's discomfiture stays with me.

What would happen if they crossed the strait? What would Gatha's forces do if they knew that the emperor's heir was with them? Would they attack the Amparan forces, knowing Dineas was in their ranks?

I pace the length of my room until Diadem starts to get

restless. It's only a suspicion, but what if it's true? Finally, I whistle for the crows and write a brief message to Gatha and Tal, emphasizing that I have no evidence to back it up, but suggesting that they should keep an eye out. I pause once or twice in my writing, well aware that if I'm right, I could well be handing Arxa and Dineas right over to their enemies.

"Forgive me," I whisper, and I'm not sure whether I'm speaking to Dineas or Mehtap. It saddens me how often I say those words now that I'm here.

# CHAPTER THIRTY
## DINEAS

The ride north with Neju's Guard is exhilarating. The scenery's always changing, and I can't get enough of it. First we ride across desert, our horses kicking up dust and pebbles, flattening patches of brown grasses as we go up and down the hills. Gradually the air gets cooler and the grass gets longer and greener. The hills flatten out. All along the way, we stop at outposts and strongholds so Kiran can meet with the local rulers. I'm always glad for those stops, because it means we can sleep in the great hall instead of our tents.

I keep an eye out for the prince during the early days of our trip, mostly because I'm curious about royalty. Kiran is older than me but younger than Arxa, with sharp eyes and a fighter's build. He doesn't pay us common soldiers much mind, but he gets along well with the commander. They confer often as they ride, and whenever we visit an outpost or stronghold, the commander goes with the prince as he tours the grounds. Kiran's two bodyguards are also always at his side.

"The prince seems to favor the commander," I say to Walgash one evening.

Walgash nods sagely. "Kiran served under Arxa during his military service and holds him in high esteem. Certainly thinks more highly of him than the emperor does."

As we move deeper into grassland, I start seeing little orange flowers dotting the landscape. It's the puzta flower, the same herb Zivah gave me as a keepsake for my trials. Except instead of the tiny patch in Zivah's garden, these flowers paint giant swaths of color on the hillsides. The pounding of our horses' hooves release their fragrance into the air.

I pick a few blossoms to amuse myself, and then I remember what Zivah had said about not having much of this plant to spare. It occurs to me that I could easily gather up a bunch to dry and take back. Once I decide to gather the flowers, it's very easy to do. Every time we stop, I simply reach down and pluck a handful. Nobody comments on my impromptu herb collecting until Cas sees me laying them out on the ground that night to dry.

"Flowers, Dineas?" he says. "You are a sensitive soul, aren't you?"

I'm not in a mood to respond.

"Oh, I see," Cas says. "These flowers aren't for you, are they?" When I still say nothing, he snorts. "Maybe you're onto something, bedding someone like that healer. No complications, no trouble. You have your fun, and she'll remove herself from the picture in a few years."

The flowers scatter across the floor as I lunge for him. Cas barely has time to widen his eyes, and then my fist meets his cheek in a painful but satisfying crack. Before he can recover, I sit on his chest and follow up with more. Chaos erupts around us. Some men are shouting my name, some are shouting Cas's, but I pay them no mind. The world shrinks down to the two of us, throwing punches and getting a few in return.

Suddenly, arms drag me backward. "It's not worth it," Masista hisses in my ear. I strain against his grip, but he's remarkably strong for his small size. I see that someone else has Cas pinned as well, and he's about as happy about it as I am.

"What is this?" Arxa's shout cuts across the din. Everyone falls silent. I stop struggling, and Masista lets me go. I touch my lip as I straighten, and my finger comes away damp. I can feel my eye swelling.

The crowd parts for the commander, who strides in like an avenging god. He rakes his gaze over us both. There's bits of dried flowers on my shirt.

"What do you have to say for yourselves?" Arxa's voice is a low growl.

I stare straight ahead. "No excuse, sir."

Cas says the same.

"I expected better from both of you," Arxa says. "You're both on equipment duty for the rest of the mission."

"Yes, sir."

Nobody moves until Arxa is back inside his own tent. Then the crowd slowly disperses. Cas shoots me one last dirty look before someone urges him away. Slowly, I bend down and clean up the flower remains. They're dirty and crushed beyond use. I sweep them together and stare blankly at the pile. And I can't help but think how easy it is for a thing of this world to be destroyed, and how quickly something beautiful can disappear.

The aches and pains that greet me the next morning are almost enough to make me regret last night's fight. Almost.

"Your eye is blue, Dineas," says Walgash as we shiver over mugs of hot water.

I grunt in reply.

We saddle up as usual, but around midmorning, Walgash starts sniffing the air.

"Salt water," he says.

"What?" asks Masista.

But Walgash just falls silent, deep in thought.

A short while later, the hills in front of us fall away to reveal a rippling, gray body of water that stretches as far as I can see. The ocean.

"Looks like we have a change of plan," Walgash says cryptically.

"By Neju's snot rag," says Masista, "just tell us what you're thinking."

But Walgash looks to Arxa, who's ridden forward to address the group.

"As some of you may have guessed, we are deviating from our announced plan for the tour. We'll leave our horses at the docks and cross over to Monyar Peninsula, where Prince Kiran wishes to get a closer look at the terrain. As you know, this is dangerous territory. The Shidadi tribes are not to be underestimated. The prince will dress as one of the soldiers and march in our midst. From here on out, you will refer to him as Pisinah. It's your job to keep him safe."

There's a buzz of excitement among the men as we all dismount and repack our bags for the journey ahead.

Masista frowns as he tucks a clay tablet into his bags. "Would have mailed this at our last stop if I'd known," he says.

I look over his shoulder. "Letter home?"

"Boy stops minding his mother if I'm away for long. He takes too much after me." Masista shrugs. "Let's just hope we can do what we need to and get out of there quick."

I squint across the water. "What they say about the Shidadi, are they really that dangerous?"

"They're better than your everyday foot soldier," he says. "But Neju's Guard is more than a match for them."

I flex my fingers, trying to imagine what such fierce tribesmen would be like.

By afternoon, we're loaded into longboats and rowing across the strait. The wind across the water is bitterly cold, and the boats lurch on the waves. My fingers are frozen into claws by the time we get to the other side. We take off our shoes and roll up our trousers before wading onto the opposite shore. The water on my bare skin sends jolts through my bones, but it's better than marching on in wet clothes.

Arxa has us hide the boats in a sea cave, and then we continue into the forest. I see signs of settlement once in a while—well-worn paths, some wells... Walgash tells me there are peaceful villages in the lowlands, though it looks like we're avoiding them. I wouldn't say we're marching in secret—there's far too many of us to not be noticed—but we're not announcing our presence either. Kiran confers with Arxa about everything—the layout of the land, the consistency of the ground we march on, the edible vegetation on the mountainside, the flooding patterns of the waterways.

After a few days, we start marching uphill, making for the mountain pass that connects this valley with the rest of the continent beyond. According to the commander, this section of road is the most dangerous by far. The narrow path, with its bottlenecks, provides plenty of ambush opportunities. Also, there's the constant threat of landslide. Because of that, Arxa takes every precaution. He sends a constant rotation of scouts ahead, with one reporting back every quarter hour.

The path starts out wide enough for four men to walk abreast. As we climb, it gets steeper and narrower. Gray granite rises around us on both sides. The trail is rocky, and I'm constantly dodging pebbles dislodged by the men in front of me. I find myself gasping for breath, even though we're not going quickly.

"It's the mountain air," says Masista when he sees me wheezing. "Makes it harder to breathe."

Halfway through the morning, we start seeing snow on the peaks around us, and we're commanded to march in complete silence so we don't trigger an avalanche. The entire march becomes quite ghostly, just the whistle of wind and the crunch of our feet. Kiran marches a few rows in front of me, and sometimes I catch a glimpse of scouts coming back and forth.

Suddenly the column slows. A message is passed back. *One of the scouts has not returned. Be vigilant.* I feel for my sword at my side, though it's hard for me to see how much fighting I could really do out here. The path is ridiculously narrow, with the mountain rising up on one side and a steep drop on the other. At least my limbs are warm from all our marching.

Suddenly, I catch a movement on the cliffs above us. I turn to look, but all I see are rocks. I squint for a better view. It could simply be my imagination, but the hairs on the back of my neck are standing on end.

A crack rends the air.

At the front of the line, Arxa stiffens and then raises a red flag above his head. *March faster.*

A second crack sounds, so loud as to make my ears hurt. And then the whole mountain comes down on us.

A sheet of rocks and dirty snow dislodges itself from the crag above. As dust explodes around me, I lunge for a steeper section of the cliff wall and press myself against it. I can't see a thing, and the ground vibrates from falling stones.

When the dust finally clears, I feel as if I've been thrown inside a drum and rattled around. My ears ring, every part of me is covered with dust, and I can barely see straight. Coughing, I finally push away from the wall. It seems our section of the trail escaped the worst of the landslide. Rocks and snow cover the ground, but we're all standing. When I turn though, my heart sinks. The trail behind us has been completely buried. The dirt is piled higher than my head, and there's no sign of the soldiers who'd marched behind me.

Ahead of me, Arxa coughs and pulls Prince Kiran to his feet.

"Dineas," Arxa says. "Is the trail completely blocked?"

"Completely, sir." I'm frantically trying to remember who was marching behind me. Naudar and Walgash are in front near Kiran. But where had Masista been?

Then a battle cry splits the air. Armed men and women rush at us, some from the trail ahead, and some falling on us from above. It's my first look at the rebels. They're wild looking. Their clothes are mismatched, but there's something in their eyes that chills my blood. I know, in my bones, that they're kindred spirits, born fighters like me. But we're on different sides.

Two of them attack me. I barely manage to get my sword up in time to avoid getting my head sliced off, and the force of impact nearly knocks me down. Thankfully the wall of dirt behind me catches my fall. I cut down the first man when he loses his balance, and then his comrade as he looks at his dying friend.

"To Pisinah!" Arxa shouts.

He means Kiran. Where is he? It's hard to spot him since he's dressed like the rest of us, but finally I see him on the steep slope below the trail. He's fighting back-to-back with his two bodyguards, surrounded by attackers. As I watch, one of his bodyguards falls to the ground. Arxa's trying to make his way down to the prince, but two rebels cut him off. Farther up the hill, Walgash is exchanging blows with a wickedly fast swordsman.

I run toward Walgash, though he dispatches his opponent before I reach him. We look at each other, and then both of us sprint toward the heir, running, sliding, and jumping down the mountainside. The thought crosses my mind that I'll tumble a long way if I lose my footing. Kiran's other bodyguard has fallen now, and the prince is backed up against a bush, fending off two men. I run one through from behind as Walgash gets the other. The heir looks at us with recognition, and then we both turn at the sound of someone running toward us. It's Arxa, with several Shidadi in pursuit.

The commander points toward a spot where two giant boulders form a crevice. "Over there!"

We converge in front of the rock, and Arxa pushes Kiran into the crevice as Walgash and I turn to face our attackers. We're shoulder to shoulder, two sides of a triangle. I'm aware of the clash of his weapon next to me as my world shrinks to the simple acts of blocking and striking. The ring of steel echoes in my ears, and my arms move of their own accord. One man falls at my blade, and then another.

"Ampara!" Naudar's battle cry drifts down.

Out of the corner of my eye, I see Naudar inching his way down the hill. He's locked in combat against a muscular Shidadi woman. She's shorter than him, and much older, but she drives him farther and farther back. I don't dare take more than a few passing glimpses in his direction—I have my own enemies to fight. But I do see when the woman snakes her blade past Naudar's guard and into his chest. I see the spray of blood, and I see Naudar stumble and fall onto one knee.

A roaring sound fills my ears. "Naudar!"

The Shidadi woman straightens and looks right at me.

A rebel tries to strike me down while I'm distracted, but I parry and run him through. No one steps into his place, and

Walgash and I look around, panting. The closest rebel is the Shidadi woman who'd been fighting Naudar. She's still watching me, and my vision clouds over with rage.

"Rebel scum!" I charge up the hill, forgetting my orders to protect the prince, forgetting everything but revenge.

"Dineas!" Walgash shouts behind me. "Dineas, fall back!"

I ignore him. The Shidadi braces herself for my charge, and then our swords clash. It's like striking a rock. I attack furiously, looking for some opening, but she doesn't leave any. Then our swords lock, and the woman's boot connects squarely with my ribs, sending me flying.

I roll head over heels twice before skidding to a stop. I can't breathe, and I feel the throbbing imprint of sharp rocks on every limb.

Someone drags me up by the collar.

"You imbecile!" Walgash shouts in my ear. He points up toward the ridge, and I see more rebels coming down the hill. "Help me get Naudar to safety."

Naudar's just a few paces away, pale and clutching his wound. Walgash and I grab him under his arms and drag him down toward the others.

"Watch out," Naudar whispers, his eyes on the soldiers coming down. His feet leave trails in the dust. All this jostling can't possibly be good for his wound. We've barely laid Naudar down by the boulder when we're set upon again. I turn to fight, but I can tell I'm weakening. My muscles feel heavy, and I'm slow to react. When I lock blades with one man, my feet slip out from under me. The rebel's sword comes down, and all I can do is hold my breath.

Another blade stops its descent with a clang, and then the rebel drops. I scramble backward as Arxa takes my place.

"Tend to Naudar," he shouts as another rebel moves in. "Now, soldier!" he adds when I hesitate.

I climb to my feet and look at Naudar. He's even paler than before, and there's a puddle of blood underneath him. He barely reacts when I pull him further into the crevice.

"Stay with me, Naudar. We'll get you bound up."

Kiran is there, though I don't have the time or the desire to pay him the proper respect. I'm too busy cutting Naudar's tunic away, trying to get at the wound. There's too much blood, and all my bandages are with my bags, somewhere on the side of the mountain.

Naudar's eyes drift closed, and I slap his cheeks to keep him awake. "Don't you dare sleep, you lazy bastard." It's hard to speak over the lump in my throat. "Don't you dare."

Kiran thrusts something under my nose. It's a stack of handkerchiefs, expensive ones. I stare for a moment before mumbling, "Thank you, Your Highness," and pressing them to the wound. If only Zivah were here right now. She would have some magical herb or poultice to stitch Naudar back together. I reach into my pocket, hoping for some leftover puzta flower, but all I find is dirt.

"Dineas," says Walgash softly behind me.

I shift to make room for him. He's dusty and uncharacteristically grim, and he reaches out to grip Naudar's hand. "Well, Naudar, that rebel really sliced you open, didn't she?"

Naudar smiles, though it turns into a grimace. He opens his mouth as if to speak, but then seems to change his mind. Walgash and I exchange another glance. It doesn't look good, and we both know it. I stop fussing with the bandages and squeeze Naudar's arm. There's nothing more I can do. My eyes burn, and I don't bother to wipe away my tears.

A few moments later, Naudar lets out a rattling breath, and then he falls still.

My chest caves in on itself.

Walgash reaches over and closes Naudar's eyes. "We'll get them back for you," he says. Then he lays a heavy hand on my shoulder as I struggle to breathe. "We'll get them," he says, this time to me.

And that's when I realize—if Walgash is here, who is defending the entrance?

I turn toward the opening, but Walgash speaks. "There are no more rebels. Arxa's watching the entrance."

And indeed, I see Arxa at the mouth of the crevice, his back toward us. At the sound of his name, he calls over his shoulder. "Walgash, report."

"Naudar is dead, sir. The prince is unharmed. Dineas and I have minor scrapes."

Arxa's shoulders tighten. "Lay him to rest," he says. "The rebels have pulled back, but we can't stay long."

It kills me to leave Naudar's body here in the middle of nowhere, but there's nothing to be done. We fold his arms over his chest and make our way out.

Wind hits my face as soon as I step into the open. We survey the damage. Bodies litter the hillside, and their blood stains the ground.

"Rebel dogs," Walgash growls under his breath.

Arxa turns to Kiran. "I don't think that was a natural landslide, Your Highness," he says. "It was too small. There's a good chance we have soldiers alive on the other side. I advise that we try to find our way to them."

Kiran nods his assent. He steps out and looks over the bodies and raises his hand high. "May Neju guide you into Zenagua's arms and grant you your rich reward," he says. We bow our heads.

Arxa takes the lead when we head off again, while I bring up the rear. The entire mountainside is steep, and we end up using our hands as often as our feet to keep from sliding down. Thankfully, Arxa proves right about the landslide. The trail soon emerges above us, and we climb back up to it. There are signs of fighting here as well. The ground is red and trampled by many feet. There are bodies, but only a handful.

"It looks like the fighting moved that way," says Arxa. "Be on your guard."

An enemy archer materializes on the hillside below us.

"Commander, watch out!"

I act out of instinct, grabbing the closest rock and hurling it at the archer as hard as I can. It knocks him in the shoulder, and the arrow goes awry. I sprint down the cliffside again, thinking only to get to him before he can let off another shot. We collide and fall in an explosion of painfully jagged pebbles, skidding down the mountainside, snapping branches and bouncing off rocks along the way. I splay my limbs out, trying to stop our fall, but I have to pull in my arms to fend off the man's blows. Finally, we come to a firm stop with him on top of me. He pins my arms with his knees. Through the spots dancing before my eyes, I see him pull a knife out of its sheath. He's an ugly man, with one eye missing. I struggle to throw him off, but he's got me pinned solid.

He raises the blade. I grit my teeth.

Arxa's boot connects with the man's head, and he falls off me. I push myself onto my elbows, grimacing, and Arxa offers me a hand up.

"Thank you, sir," I say.

"Don't thank me yet," he says.

As if by magic, more rebels appear on the cliff below us.

"Back up to the trail," Arxa says. "Regroup with Pisinah and Walgash."

I do my best to scramble up the mountainside, but going up is much harder than coming down, and my feet can find no purchase. It's like I'm running in place.

Suddenly, shouts sound from above. My heart lifts to see twenty—no, thirty or forty—of Neju's Guard coming up the trail.

"For Ampara!" comes the battle cry. The rebels turn to flee. A volley of arrows chases them, followed by our troops. When the dust settles, the only remaining rebels are the ones who are too wounded to get away.

Arxa scans our surroundings, then slowly turns to address the troops. "Check the fallen," he says.

The troops around me rush to work, bandaging our injured. We check the surviving rebels as well. The only one in good enough shape to take prisoner is the archer I tackled. Everyone else, we finish off.

It's gruesome work. Arxa points to a young fighter on the ground who'd been hobbled by an arrow to the hamstring. "Dineas, take care of that one."

"Yes, sir." The Shidadi looks up at me with pure desperation, and he starts to hyperventilate. A chill goes through me. It's one thing to cut down an enemy in battle, but to kill someone who's been rendered helpless . . .

"Quickly, Dineas," says Arxa.

I grip my sword and drive it through his heart. The rebel shudders, and falls still. I wipe my blade off on his tunic and back away. Thankfully, Arxa doesn't call on me to take care of any others.

After all is done, Arxa calls for the troops. "Fall in tight. Weapons at the ready. We march back the way we came."

# CHAPTER THIRTY-ONE
## ZIVAH

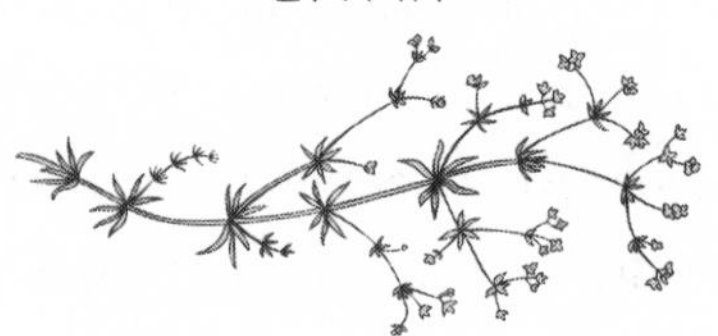

Mehtap knocks on my door as I'm getting into bed. She looks fragile in her sleeping gown. Some of her hair's escaped her nighttime braid, and candlelight illuminates the stray strands so they glow. "There's been news," she says. My heart stutters at her words. Panic, guilt, worry, and fear hit me all at once.

"They're alive," Mehtap hurriedly adds. "My father, Dineas, Prince Kiran, they're all alive. At least they were when my father wrote this letter, but the prince's trip was cut short. They were ambushed and lost a number of their men."

"Ambushed? Where?"

She hesitates a split second. "Southern Monyar. In the mountains."

And now the guilt settles in thick around me. An ambush in the southern Monyar mountains. The attackers would have needed time to prepare, make plans. They could only have done it if they'd had warning. . . .

Mehtap wipes hurriedly at her eyes. "I'm going down to the shrine to burn some incense. I know you don't have the same gods, but will you come with me? I don't want to be alone."

"Of course." I grab a robe to drape over my nightgown.

The shrine is a simple alcove tucked into the downstairs courtyard. On the wall hang images of the seven High Gods of Ampara. Neju, god of war, and Hefana, goddess of healing, take the honored center spots in this household, and it is in front of these two that Mehtap kneels in turn, mouthing silent prayers. She lights incense sticks and places one in front of each as I stand a respectful distance away.

When she finishes, she comes to stand next to me. In the orange glow of the incense sticks, she looks nothing more than a frightened child. I could almost convince myself that we're sisters in our worry and grief, that I'm not the cause of her current troubles.

Mehtap dusts the residual incense from her fingers. "To be honest, I don't concern myself much with the gods unless something goes wrong," she says. "They don't seem all that real to me, though it seems unlucky to say so right in front of the shrine."

"I'm sure the gods forgive a bit of doubt," I say.

Mehtap looks at me. "And what about your Goddess? Are you devoted to her?"

It's on my lips to reply with a simple yes, but something stops me. Perhaps because I'm so far from home, or because Mehtap herself has been so honest.

"I used to think I was touched by the Goddess," I say. "She

has a special place for healers. We're not priests exactly, but we're in her service nonetheless." A wind blows, and the incense sticks flare brighter for a moment. One blows out. "I was a very good healer. My teachers always said I would save many lives."

"But now you're rosemarked," says Mehtap. "And you don't know why your Goddess has let this happen, if you were one of her chosen." I can tell by the way she speaks that she's asked similar questions. We all wonder the same things. Of course we must.

"Perhaps the Goddess's plan will become more clear with time," I say. Or perhaps I wasn't chosen at all. Perhaps the Goddess doesn't care.

In the distance, somewhere at the other side of the compound, people are shouting. It's a fight, or a celebration, or both. Just another of the senseless things that happen in this compound.

I wonder if the people out there have made their peace with the gods. I wonder if the healing priestesses of Hefana feel betrayed, as I did, when they fall ill. The Amparan gods don't seem to be very concerned with mere mortals. From the tales I hear, they're often preoccupied with their own divine politics. With the Goddess though, it's different. We're taught that her spirit permeates the world, that she's everywhere, and always watching. Which makes it all the more perplexing when she turns away.

After a while, the shouting dies down, and Mehtap and I are once again alone with the gods. For a brief moment I think about what the afterlife might be like. Will Mehtap and I end up in the same place? Will it be quiet, like now, or will it be crowded with the cries of those who went before us? The questions send a shiver over my skin, and I shrink away from them.

Mehtap shifts her weight and then reaches out to take my hand. "Perhaps it's selfish of me," she says, "but I'm glad your Goddess sent you here."

As Mehtap waits for her father to return, she throws herself into her quest to remake the rosemarked compound. Once again, she surprises me with her intelligence and drive. She listens as Jesmin and I discuss how to keep the rose plague from spreading and compiles a list of ways the rosemarked could stay in contact with their healthy relatives. She asks questions about how the newly rosemarked are brought into the compound. When I tell her about the boy who nearly fell into Anahi's hands, Mehtap insists on visiting Estir's people by the east wall. She tours their houses, exclaims over the apprenticeships they've set up to share skills, buys jewelry from their makeshift marketplace, and promises to send them what supplies she can.

Her enthusiasm gives me some much-needed hope. I write to Kaylah of everything that's happened here, of Mehtap's efforts for change, and of all I've learned from Jesmin.

*I know you've had concerns about my coming here,* I tell her, *and what it would mean for my vows and duties as a healer of the Goddess. But now, with all that's happening, I'm more convinced than ever that my presence here is doing more good than harm. I'm glad I came, and I hope these reports assuage your misgivings. For the first time since I've fallen ill, I feel like a healer again.*

I also promise to send Kaylah tablets with more detailed notes via an official courier. I hang the parchment above the fire to weaken the disease essence, and then summon the crows. Scrawny gives me a cheerful caw before taking off with the letter.

Soon after, Mehtap gets her own letter—from Utana, granting us an audience. The night before we go, Mehtap stays up late, assembling her thoughts and rehearsing what she will say. I finally have to go to her room and force her to get ready for bed. The next morning, when I wake up, Mehtap is already dressed and ready to head out.

Utana's home in the rosemarked compound is not as extensive as Mehtap's villa. There's no courtyard, and only one or two rooms, though it's sturdily built and well furnished with fine furniture and rich tapestries. When we knock on the door, a grandfatherly-looking man opens the door. His robes, embroidered with blue and gold threads, do not have a single wrinkle. His hair, beard, and fingernails are immaculately groomed.

"You must be Mehtap and Zivah," he says with a kindly smile. "Do come in." A servant brings us tea, which Utana pours for both of us. His gnarled hands have a slight tremor. "And to what do I owe the pleasure of your visit?"

Mehtap glances at me, and there's a spark of excitement in her eyes. "Zivah and I have been talking about conditions in the rosemarked compound. I'm sure you know by now how poor they are. We have ideas for improvements that could be made."

Utana listens as Mehtap talks animatedly about schemes to allow visitors and systems for sending messages. He nods thoughtfully as she proposes appointing responsible people to protect the newly rosemarked.

"I see you have your father's keen mind," says Utana when she finishes. "And how might I help?"

"I don't think it would take much to make a difference," Mehtap says. "We simply need the emperor's attention, and just a little bit of money could go a long way."

"There are many good people in the compound who already do their best to help," I add. "If they had extra resources, they could do much more."

Utana sits back, thoughtful. "You would have me write to my old friends at the imperial court about this."

"Only if it's not too much trouble," says Mehtap, though the hope in her eyes would be hard for anyone to resist.

"I can certainly try," Utana says. "I've not heard from my fellow advisers in a while, but I like to imagine that they still think of me from time to time."

Mehtap's smile brightens the room.

Just then, one of her soldier escorts steps through the door. "Lady Mehtap, a message has arrived for you."

Mehtap gathers her skirts. "Please excuse me."

In the silence that follows, Utana reaches to pour my tea, but I beat him to it. "I'm surprised I haven't seen you in the hospital thus far, Your Excellency."

He watches me shrewdly over his cup. "And tell me, young Zivah. Do you say this because I seem like the type of man who enjoys hospitals, or because your keen physician's eye has seen something?"

I bow my head, acknowledging his meaning. I like how he gets right to the point. "I wouldn't say it takes a keen eye for a healer in a rosemarked compound to recognize the final stage of rose plague." It had taken me a while to look past his careful grooming, but now I see the frailty of his limbs beneath his robes, the strain that pulls at the corners of his eyes.

Utana sets his cup down. "The tremors started a fortnight ago," he says soberly. "The headaches are mild, but I hear they'll get worse soon enough. I have no desire to waste away my last days on a hospital pallet. I've lived a full life, and I'm comfortable here." He's admirably calm when he speaks of his impending death.

"There are still ways we could help," I say. "Ease the pain even if you are not at the hospital." I don't mention that I'm surprised to see the fever return so soon for Utana, since he only entered the compound a few months ago. I suppose sometimes the elderly succumb more quickly.

"That is kind of you. It's bearable for now, but I will remember your offer." He straightens. "But why speak of such things before they happen? I would rather hear about your time at the hospital."

I put up my hands in a matter-of-fact gesture. "I wish I were better able to care for my patients. I'm quite limited in supplies, and I have many more people to take care of than I'm used to." I'm glad he's taken the conversation to this topic, and I search for a way to steer it further. "But I'm sure you know all of this. I imagine as minister of health you dealt quite a bit with rose plague."

He chuckles. "That I did. Perhaps a bit too much, seeing my current condition."

"I'm very sorry. Did you become infected while performing your duties?"

His smile stiffens slightly on his face, though it relaxes just as quickly. "It's hard to tell with these things," he says. "I took as much care as I could, of course."

It's a small lapse on his part, but I'm suddenly sure he's hiding something. I'm deliberating whether to push for more when Mehtap comes back through the door, her entire face alight. I find myself rising halfway to my feet, even though I don't know why she's so happy.

"I have wonderful news," she says. "Father has returned."

# CHAPTER THIRTY-TWO
## DINEAS

It's hard to describe the emotion that hits me as Sehmar City finally appears on the horizon. When I left weeks ago, I didn't have a home, but now I come back as a blooded soldier. I've fought beside my brothers-in-arms and lost friends to Ampara's enemies. And now, at the sight of Sehmar's tall walls, I'm reminded of what all of this was for.

Next to me, Masista kisses his fingers and puts his hand on his heart. I follow suit, and a fierce pride in my empire consumes me. The city walls gleam like a polished version of the desert sands. As we pass through the gates, citizens line up by the road to pay their respects. And for the first time, I claim them as my people.

As soon as Arxa releases us at the palace, everyone disbands in search of loved ones. Kosru catches Walgash in a bear's embrace. Masista goes to find his wife. Even Cas has a lady to welcome him, though I have serious doubts about her intelligence or sanity. All these reunions make me think of the rosemarked compound, but it's too late in the day to leave the city. I promise myself I'll go first thing in the morning and head to the bathhouse instead. I figure Zivah would appreciate me going there first before seeing her. I wonder if she's received news about our mission yet, and if she's been worried about me.

A few hours later, I get a summons from Arxa. "The commander would like to see you in the interrogation rooms," says the messenger.

"The interrogation rooms?"

"In the prison," he says.

I suppress a shiver. That's not the place I would have wanted to go on my first night home, but Arxa had mentioned he might need to speak with me about the prisoner.

The dungeons are much as I might have guessed—dank, with smells of mold and rot. It's unpleasant, but there's a strange feeling of familiarity about it. I suppose, if I had been a soldier before the plague, I might have spent some time guarding a prison like this.

I follow the guard down one level to a doorway lit by torches. The smells wafting out here are more fresh—blood, sweat, fear. A sour taste forms at the back of my mouth.

Arxa stands in the center of the room, his back toward me. Chained to the bloodstained wall is the man who almost killed me on the mountainside. The Shidadi opens his one eye and looks at me, pleading, and for a moment, I feel like I should know this man. I look away.

"Dineas," says Arxa. "Good. You came." He gestures toward the prisoner, who looks as if he's been freshly abused. "This prisoner will be questioned thoroughly about his rebellious activities. He's committed a grave crime against the empire, and it won't go unpunished."

A strange sensation is going through my limbs. I can almost feel shackles around my wrists, and my heart is starting to pound against my rib cage. The walls around me close in, and I find myself wishing for a window.

Arxa turns to me. "This prisoner claims to be an outsider, that he was a simple villager conscripted against his will a month ago. You remember fighting him. Would you say his skill matches his story?"

The entire day was a blur, but I do remember that desperate roll down the mountainside. I remember him pinning me down and raising his knife to strike me. In my mind he turns the knife hilt-first as he prepares to bring it down on me.

No, that can't be right.

"He's a veteran soldier, sir. He gave me quite a bit of trouble."

Arxa nods at a guard standing near the prisoner, who strikes the man across the face. The prisoner coughs and spits blood.

"And that is how Ampara rewards liars," says Arxa.

I don't know what's wrong with me. I've seen much worse on the battlefield, but nausea is starting to rise in my stomach. Spots dance before my eyes. One of the guards in the room coughs, and I startle at the noise.

Arxa speaks again. "Dineas, you are to be commended for your actions on the mountain. Prince Kiran wishes to recognize you, Walgash, and me at the spring festival, for guarding his life."

It takes me a few moments to understand what he's saying. "I'm honored, Commander."

"As you should be," says Arxa. "Kiran does not bestow honors lightly. But he is well pleased with you, as am I."

I don't say anything because my stomach is clenching in painful spasms.

Thankfully, Arxa turns his attention back to the prisoner. He waves me away. "That's all I need you for."

"Thank you, Commander."

I make it ten steps out the door before I throw up.

# CHAPTER THIRTY-THREE
## ZIVAH

I'm tending a patient in the front room one morning, and Dineas is there when I look up. He's thinner than he was when he left. His cheekbones are more prominent, and his hair is longer. When he catches my eye, that familiar smile lights up his face. A warmth spreads through my limbs.

"Dineas!" I barely remember to pull off my apron before I'm running across the room. I throw my arms around him, and he laughs when I squeeze him tight.

"I think you've been taking lessons from that snake of yours."

I just squeeze tighter. He smells of sand and soap. "I don't know how Mehtap does it, waiting all the time for her father to return home." I step back and hold him at arm's length, taking in every piece of him. He has new bruises and scratches. The faint remnants of a greenish spot colors the side of his face. I scan the patient room, and then take his hand. "Come. The helpers should be able to keep everything under control for a while."

He comes readily, and I can tell he's just as eager to catch up as I am. There aren't many places to stroll outside the hospital, but we walk along one of the narrow dirt roads. The only other people around are a group of children playing a game involving a stick, several large stones, and large wooden hoops. Their laughter rings like birdsong.

"Tell me about your journey," I say.

His eyes go distant for a moment. "Ampara is vast," he says. "And awe-inspiring. I wish you could have seen it all with me." He starts talking of the dusty desert strongholds where they slept at night, the grasslands dotted with early spring wildflowers, the cold ocean spray of the Monyar sea caves. I drink it all in, captivated as much by his enthusiasm as the pictures he conjures. "I'm not doing it justice. I wish I could paint it for you. I'm not boring you, am I?"

"Not at all. I like seeing things through your eyes. I'm glad you're making new memories for yourself."

"Good memories and bad," he says. Pain flashes across his face, and I realize that there's a shadow to him now that hadn't been there when he'd left on the mission. Not as much as the old Dineas, but more than before. I suppose there was no avoiding it, but it still feels like something rare and good has been lost.

"Not all your friends made it back," I say.

He nods, looking away. "Naudar's gone."

"I'm sorry."

Dineas fixes his eyes on the children at the end of the street. They've finished their game now and have settled down to share some snacks and catch their breath.

"Everything's so fleeting, isn't it?" Dineas says. "People come in and out of our lives so quickly. It's not just memories that vanish."

There's not much I can say. Instead, I take his hand, and for a while we walk in silence. He's a warm, solid presence next to me, and I can only hope that I lend him the same comfort.

Finally, Dineas looks up to the sky, and I'm surprised to see how far the sun has moved. "I don't want to keep you from your work," he says. "I just wanted to see you. Do you think I need a treatment today?"

The space around me seems to grow cooler at his words. I'd known this was coming, though I'd tried not to think about it. I don't know what will happen when Dineas comes back to himself and realizes what he's done.

"I can come back another day if that's better," he says.

"No," I say. There's no point in avoiding it. "No, it's better to do it now."

I motion him back toward the hospital. As much as I try to pretend nothing's wrong, I can't keep the tension from my stride. He picks up on it, and we're both silent as I usher him into the back room.

I hesitate briefly before I hand him the potion. "Settle down," I say. "It might be rougher this time around, after such a long journey."

# CHAPTER THIRTY-FOUR
## DINEAS

When the memories come back this time, they carry me straight to hell. Each new recollection is a fresh piece of agony. I don't want the knowledge coming back into me, the realization that relentlessly transforms the lawless rebels I'd so earnestly cut down into friends, kinsmen.

I frantically search my memories of the battle for familiar faces. I'd fought Gatha. Was she among the bodies? I don't remember seeing her, but I do recognize others. And the prisoner I captured... Dear gods, that's Tus they're torturing in the dungeons. Tus, who turned his blade hilt-first so he wouldn't kill me on that mountainside.

I clench my head in my hands. If my fingers were sharper, they would dig holes in my temple.

"Oh gods." It's a prayer for mercy in whatever form. Even Zenagua's underworld would be better than what I feel now.

I hear a shuffling of skirts, soft footsteps coming toward me. I feel the breeze as Zivah crouches down beside me. I don't want her here.

"I'm sorry," Zivah says softly.

Sorry? Sorry is a word for a stubbed toe, a keepsake gone missing. Not the betrayal of your soul.

"Gods, forgive me," I whisper.

"It wasn't your fault."

"I'm a traitor." It's not just that I killed my own kin. It's the patriotic fervor I felt for Ampara when I came back. It's the shameful fact that of all the deaths in the battle, the one I feel most cruelly is Naudar's.

Naudar, dead by Gatha's hand. I never thought I'd be able to hate Gatha, but I do. I feel like I'm being split in two.

"It wasn't you who did these things," she says.

"That doesn't make Pouriya any less dead." Ridiculous Pouriya, who would repeat his own jokes until I wanted to knock him over the head, but who would always lend me an extra weapon in a pinch. I'd cut him down as he lay wounded on the mountainside.

This wasn't the mission I agreed to. I was supposed to be in Sehmar City, far away from my kin. Once more, I bury my face in my hands. When did it become such a tangled mess?

"I need to know how much Tus knows," I say abruptly.

Zivah looks at me, confused.

"Arxa captured one of my tribe. They have him in the dungeon."

She raises a hand to her throat. "They'll be questioning him."

The image of Tus chained to the wall flashes through my mind. Shame curls through me as I remember how I simply looked away.

"Does he know the truth of your quest?" Zivah asks.

"I think so. He didn't try very hard to kill me, up on that mountain." I grab fistfuls of hair at my temples and try to think. "There's a lot of guards in that prison. Four at least at the door, and then others that patrol the corridor."

"Could you rescue him?"

Oh, Zivah, you are so naive. "Rescue's impossible in a fortress like this. I'd be lucky if I could put him out of his misery."

She falls still. "I'm sorry."

"Not as sorry as I am." But now I'm going through what I can remember of the prison in my head, and the reality of it settles like coals in my gut. "I'm not even sure I can get in to kill him. It might run a higher risk of blowing my cover than leaving him there. This should be Gatha's decision."

Zivah slips on a pair of gloves and grabs a pen and parchment. "We'll send a crow, then. What else do you have to report?"

I want to laugh at the way she simply moves on. Of course, I'll ignore the sufferings of my kin and report now like a good soldier. "I fought well. People noticed. Arxa praised me." My self-loathing sits lodged in my chest.

She doesn't respond, just keeps looking at me, and it's the pity in her eyes that finally makes me grit my teeth and pull myself together. I don't need her pity.

"You know we went north. We stopped at some strongholds,

but then we took a surprise turn to Monyar. Kiran kept making notes to report to his father. They were looking at everything there. Anything that might matter strategically."

Zivah's pen hovers above the parchment. "If the heir himself is looking at Monyar, then this isn't some border skirmish they're planning. This is a major campaign."

"The emperor turns sixty next year, and the Amparans like to commemorate these things with new conquests. What better way to do that than subjugating Monyar Peninsula, maybe even launching through the pass into the rest of the northern continent?" I consider what I just said. "Of course, that gives us an obvious way to stop the attacks, or at least greatly delay them."

She looks at me blankly.

I speak slowly. "If the emperor never turns sixty."

She pales. "An assassination?"

I hide my own fear with a nonchalant shrug. "I'm here. We might as well use me." But I wonder . . . could I even do it? Get past the emperor's entourage and bodyguards? And then there's the issue of getting out alive afterward.

Zivah looks as if she's having the same doubts. "We'll see what Tal and Gatha say. Will you be all right, going back into Sehmar City? Can you keep earning their trust?"

"Apparently I can become any kind of monster I wish."

There's poison in my voice, and I see her tense. "If you've become a monster, let me share the blame. I gave you the potion."

"Dear gods, do you ever raise your voice?"

"Would it help?"

Yes, it would. I want to argue, I want to yell, but she's

unflappable, and I don't have the energy to keep knocking my fists against a wall.

"I'm still determined to do well..." I tell her. "My other self, I mean. But I also have misgivings about Neju's Guard. I trust Arxa, but there were things that I saw... that I did... on the mission that really shook me." I stop, because my next request feels like the worst betrayal yet. "Ask me about it before I leave. You have to convince me what I'm doing is right. You must tell me to keep doing my best for Arxa."

Zivah's forehead creases at my request, and I feel a perverse satisfaction. She's finally getting a taste of what it's like to act as Ampara's arm. "I'll do my best," she says.

"I'll listen to you," I tell her. "I trust you...."

I break off as I think back over the past few weeks. The other me does indeed think highly of her. Maybe too highly. I suppress a shiver. It's wrong, living two lives. The whole thing feels unstable.

Zivah meets my eyes, and I know she knows what I'm thinking. She opens her mouth, though it takes her a while to find words. "Dineas," she says. "I know I've grown to be close friends with you in your other state. But I want you to know that I would never take advantage—"

I cut her off with a shake of my head. "I don't want to talk about it. Just do your part, and I'll do mine."

# CHAPTER THIRTY-FIVE
## ZIVAH

The conversation with Dineas leaves me completely drained. As the potion begins to wear off, I have him lie down and close his eyes. I watch him toss and turn on the mat, his eyes squeezed shut as he waits for his burden to fade, and my heart breaks for him, for what he had to do, and the guilt that he must forever endure.

Gradually, he loses his agitation. The weight that was there just moments ago lifts off. I realize, an instant before his eyes open, that I need to calm myself as well. I'm deeply shaken by our last encounter, and I can't quite quell the sense that we're courting disaster. Thankfully, Dineas is too disoriented upon first waking to notice anything wrong. By the time he sits up, I've wiped my palms on my apron and wiped my face blank.

"How do you feel?" I ask.

"Groggy... and heavy." He shakes off the potion and stands up, rubbing his forehead.

"Dineas," I say, a bit too loudly.

"Yes?"

"You know you can talk to me, don't you?" I say. "If there's anything you don't feel comfortable discussing with the other soldiers, or with Arxa."

For the first time, he betrays a bit of tension. "What do you mean?"

I pause, hoping that I'm taking the correct approach.

"You seem bothered by something. Is it the campaign? Something afterward?"

He looks at me, stunned. "I hadn't realized I was so easy to read."

"I don't think you are. But I've been trained to pay attention."

He takes in my words, wrestling with some decision, then abruptly starts pacing back and forth. "Can I trust you? No, I'm sorry. Of course I can. You're probably the person I can trust the most."

If only he knew the layers of lies that surround us.

"It's just that... there were parts of serving in Neju's Guard that were... hard. The fighting, I could do that. But what we did to the wounded afterward. We killed them all, you know. Just ran them through." His voice falls to a hush. "And there's the way Arxa treats prisoners. The way he questions them." He runs his hands through his hair. "I'm probably being foolish. I'm sure the rebels deserved every punishment the emperor deemed appropriate. What do I know of the world, right?" His self-deprecating smile is strained.

And here's the point where I take the guileless soldier I've created and mold him into something ugly. Dineas might betray his people without full knowledge of who he is, but I must do it with my eyes open. The words don't come easily, but they do come. "It reflects well on you that these punishments weigh on your conscience, Dineas. It shows you have a good heart. Soldiers must do unpleasant things sometimes, but it's for the good of the empire."

He grasps at my words. "Do you think so?"

I think of my own village, about the humiliation we've suffered at Ampara's hands, the constant threat of destruction if we refuse their ever-increasing requests. Of Dineas's own time as their prisoner that left him so damaged.

"Imagine what would happen if the rebellions were allowed to continue. The empire would fall apart, and chaos would take its place. It's taken years to build up Ampara to the great empire it is today. Nothing is worth that. Criminals must be made an example of."

Dineas nods uncertainly. I wonder if saying something with enough conviction makes it true. I wonder if being forced into a lie makes you less of a liar.

"Arxa has been very generous to you. Do your best to prove yourself to him. Show him your gratitude, and he will take care of you."

Once again, he nods, more sure this time. "Thank you, Zivah. I think I just needed someone to talk some sense into me."

The trust in his eyes makes me want to take it all back, to undo the damage I've done. But by some miracle I force a smile. "You're a good man, Dineas. Ampara is fortunate to have you."

Dineas returns to Sehmar City that evening flush with the new confidence I've instilled in him. As for me, I return to my duties and do my best not to dwell on how complicated things have become.

The next day, Scrawny brings me a letter from Kaylah, which I eagerly open. As I expected, she's very interested in what I've learned from Jesmin thus far. She's also glad to see circumstances improving in the rosemarked compound. Still, I've not completely won her over to my mission.

*It does make me feel better to hear about the good you're accomplishing there. Perhaps that was the Goddess's plan for you all along, though I would urge you to still be mindful of the vows you took the day you earned your healer's sash. It's a tricky thing, when one starts making choices, weighing the good and the bad, and deciding the best balance point. Those judgments are the Goddess's domain. Better to strive solely for the good. That is the purpose of our vows, to keep us firmly in the mortal world.*

It's good to hear from Kaylah, but her letter does nothing to dispel my unease. I wish I could scoff at her simple view of things, but given what I have just lived through, I'm no longer sure. Could Kaylah be right? Have I crossed into the domain of the gods, with all I've done to Dineas's mind? And yet, what was my alternative but to let our village be crushed under Ampara's heel? If I couldn't trust the Goddess to save me from plague, how could I trust her to protect Dara?

It's a question that smacks of hubris, the type of thinking that in the Amparan stories of old would cause a man to be crushed for his insolence. Perhaps Dineas and I will be punished for what we're attempting. Perhaps we already have been.

Utana sends us another invitation to tea a few days later. Mehtap rushes to my doorway, clutching the invitation. "Do you think he's met with any success? How wonderful would that be?"

She's in high spirits as we walk over, chattering about everything from the warmer weather to her old memories of court. My own mood is more mixed. I'll be glad of anything that can help the sick, but I remain convinced that Utana's hiding something, and that it has to do with the rose plague and his work as minister. But despite my attempts to coax information out of him, Utana has proven remarkably discreet about anything having to do with the imperial court. It's a valuable virtue for a minister to have, but unfortunate for me.

When Utana answers his door, I know the news he bears is not good. Mehtap senses it too, and she takes worried glances toward me as he pours our tea.

"I wish I had better news," he says. "I've written to my old friends. Some didn't write back, and the ones who did sent their regrets. The emperor has big plans for next year, and that leaves few resources to deal with other concerns."

Mehtap's delicate mouth opens in surprise. "Nothing? But surely they could offer some help."

Her disappointment is hard to see, perhaps even harder to face than my own. I hadn't truly pinned my hopes on Utana's efforts, but Mehtap clearly had.

Utana turns his palms up in an apologetic gesture. "I will

keep writing and keep trying. Perhaps donations could be collected from the citizens. Any little bit would help, wouldn't it?"

"Yes," echoes Mehtap quietly. "Every little bit. Thank you, Your Excellency, for your efforts on our behalf. We are grateful."

But as we walk home, Mehtap takes my arm and speaks her true thoughts. "They've forgotten us, haven't they? To the healthy ones, we don't exist anymore."

Mehtap is noticeably quieter over the next few days. She makes some attempt at conversation when I'm around, but her eyes drift off, and her words sometimes stop midsentence. When I try to ask what's wrong, she says she doesn't want to talk about it and makes an excuse to leave the room.

It's a full week before her spirits rise again. One morning, she runs to my doorway. "I've news," she says, leaning in and hanging on the doorjamb with one arm. "Good news!"

"From Utana?"

She frowns. "No, not that. Never that. But come. Dineas is waiting in the courtyard."

Dineas? Conspiring with Mehtap?

Mehtap bounces alongside me as we make our way down to the courtyard. When I get to the doorway, I come to an abrupt stop. Dineas is standing in the courtyard. He's in full ceremonial attire—black conical helmet and silver-and-black-embroidered tunic. The bronze of his shield shines, as do the buckles on his fine leather belt.

Mehtap giggles. I quell my unease at seeing Dineas standing so proud in full Amparan regalia.

I dust my hands off on my apron. "I'm underdressed for the occasion, apparently."

He bows deeply, his eyes full of mischief. Then he pulls out a parchment and starts to read. "On behalf of Emperor Kurosh of Ampara, I hereby extend an invitation to Mehtap, daughter of Arxa, and Zivah, daughter of Ruven, to attend the Spring Equinox Festival in a fortnight's time in the Imperial Palace Gardens."

"The emperor's gardens," says Mehtap in a singsong voice. "It will be so beautiful."

That can't be right. The garden is in the city.

Dineas continues reading. "Three soldiers of the empire will be honored at the feast for their bravery in service of the empire. Commander Arxa, son of Asina; Walgash, son of Frada; and Dineas, son of the gods."

Has everyone gone mad? "Dineas, the festival's in the palace. In the middle of a city full of people."

Dineas drops the formal act and breaks into a boyish grin. "The emperor's made allowances. You'll be taken to your own marked area in the gardens, separate from the other guests."

Mehtap adds, "But we'll still be able to see the festivities, hear the music, eat the food, sit in the gardens."

Their enthusiasm starts to rub off on me. The emperor's gardens are said to be beautiful beyond compare, but I never thought I'd see them for myself.

Mehtap is still chattering. "You'll need a dress, of course. You can borrow one of mine. A dark blue one would look lovely with your hair."

"Are you sure it's a good idea?" I'm still having trouble believing this.

She lets out an exasperated sigh. "You don't understand, do you, Zivah? You must go. One of the honored guests at the feast has specifically requested your presence. Father has asked if I could be there, and..." She looks significantly at Dineas, who nods.

"You really must see the gardens, Zivah," he says. "I couldn't share the rest of my journeys with you, but this I can. And besides, you're the closest thing to family I have."

Warmth spreads through me at his words. I imagine the scent of spring flowers drifting on the wind, and the last of my resistance crumbles. "In that case, I would be honored."

# CHAPTER THIRTY-SIX

## DINEAS

"Don't come to the equinox festival." I blurt out those words as soon as my memory returns.

Zivah's taken aback. To be fair, it hasn't yet been an hour since I read her the invitation and pleaded for her to come. But that was before she pulled me away for another treatment. Before I remembered who I was and regained my senses.

She speaks slowly, as if addressing a temperamental child. "Why do you say that?"

I don't want to tell her why. "I think it's a bad idea. It'll be a good chance for me to see the emperor's bodyguards up close, but there's nothing for you to do. You can make some excuse to stay away."

"I can't simply change my mind. It would offend Mehtap,

Arxa, and the emperor. It will offend *you*, once this potion wears off."

Part of me knows she's right, but I don't want to admit it. "There must be a way. Are you really thinking about our mission, or do you just want to spend a night in the gardens?"

A spasm of irritation crosses her face. "What's wrong with you? I do want to go, but that's not the point. If you want me to back out of this festival an hour after agreeing to go, you have to give me a reason."

I grit my teeth. "The reason . . ." I stop. Breathe. Force myself to spit out the words. "The reason is because I'm falling in love with you."

And finally, one of us has said it. Zivah's jaw snaps shut. She knows I'm not declaring my devotion to her. No, my words are an accusation.

I never thought I'd live long enough to speak of love. I've been one of Gatha's elite since I turned fifteen, and that meant an early death on the battlefield. Killing Amparans was far more important than chasing women. How I got here to this point, sitting on a mat in the rosemarked hospital, sorting through the heartsick adventures of my other self, I do not know. It's like my other self was a lovesick puppy, and now I'm left to clean up the mess on the floor.

"I know that you're—he's fond of me," she says carefully. "But you overstate things."

"Do I? I see him getting more hopeful every time he sees you, daydreaming about you all hours of the day. And he's thrilled that you'll be at the feast. More thrilled than he should be."

"You can't blame me for his infatuation. He doesn't have many friends outside the army, and I've helped him through a difficult time. If it gets to be too much, I'll set him straight."

She brushes a hair from her eyes, and I notice the curve of her cheekbones, the graceful arch of her wrist. Her rosemarks, strikingly bright against her skin, accentuate her features. Though they disgusted me just a few months ago, they now seem to give her an otherworldly beauty, the beauty of someone who's seen life and refused to back down. It's something *he* would think, not me, and it just makes me angrier. What madness is this, being possessed of someone else's eyes? I feel as if I've just climbed out of a swamp. I want to be myself again, the real me, but the other Dineas clings to me like a film of mud. Stubbornly, I dig up my oldest impressions of Zivah. The timid Dara villager, too fearful to devote herself to war. The plague victim, covered with the marks of death. Yet those impressions no longer feel right. They're faded and awkward, like a piece of leather that has shrunk after the rain.

I shake my head. "Don't lie to me about pushing him away. Do you think I don't see the way you look at him? The way your eyes light up when he surprises you? The way you threw yourself into his arms when he came back from Monyar? I was there, Zivah. I remember everything."

She stiffens, and I can almost see her wrapping invisible tendrils around herself and pulling herself together, that maddening self-composure. "I was happy to see him safely back. I was happy to see *you* back."

She speaks so softly. I remember that was my first impression of her, and remember how I thought she was weak. But I can no longer dredge up that reaction either. What was once weakness now looks like quiet strength, and a capacity for compassion that I've never seen in anyone else.

And she's so maddeningly calm. It drives me crazy that she can wear such a mask when I've basically thrown myself at her feet these past weeks.

I surge to my feet. "I'm tired of being your plaything."

She takes a cautious step back. Neju's sword, she's hard to read.

"Look, Zivah, I know it's hard to be rosemarked. It must be. And maybe it's too tempting to have the other Dineas throwing himself at you, playing out your fantasies of a normal life, but—"

The blood drains completely from her face and she makes a faint choking sound. She takes another weak step backward.

I walk toward her, but she stops me with a word. "Stay away from me." The raw emotion in her voice throws me back.

"Zivah, I didn't mean—"

"You have no idea," she whispers. "You have no idea how it feels to be locked in here like a living corpse. To be cut off, reviled, unable to touch another human being unless it's someone who's also slated to die."

I open my mouth to speak, but she silences me with a look of pure steel. "I won't deny it," she says. "I've enjoyed the moments I shared with y—with him. And there have indeed been times when I was tempted to let it go further than it should. Times when I couldn't be as distant as I needed to be." She shakes her head. "But don't you dare mock me, or paint me as some manipulative, self-serving temptress. I've given up too much, and I've suffered too much to take any more abuse from you. I may not have much dignity left, but may my Goddess strike me down now if I let you be the one to trample what's left to me."

She throws a pen and a piece of parchment at my feet. "Your memory will fade away soon. Write your report for Gatha." And then she turns deliberately away from me and sits down at her herb table.

Her words fade away, but the tension stays in the air. I scoop the implements off the floor. I do have things to report, but I can't concentrate. Instead, I keep sneaking glances at Zivah. I can sense every breath she takes, the rigid strain of her muscles. Her back is straight as a spear, and her face has been smoothed of all emotion. But though she's gazing at the herbs in front of her, I know that she's not truly seeing them. In fact, I know many things. I know the truth of what she's said, the extent of her loneliness and pain. I know because Dineas knows. The other Dineas, who's taken the time to look. And he won't let me ignore it.

"I'm sorry," I say.

The glare she shoots me could light kindling, but I continue.

"You say you have no dignity left, but that's not how he sees you. Not how I see you." The words are hard to get out, but I'm rewarded by a flash of puzzlement across her face. "He admires you for the things you've done, for your kindness and your strength. He thinks highly of you for good reason, and it isn't because you've been making false promises. I know this. I was just too much of a horse's ass to admit it."

She searches my face, and I'm not sure what she sees there.

"I would never toy with him," she says.

"I know."

The silence between us is a bowstring about to snap.

"I should go to the feast," she says.

I let out a long breath. "I know."

Another silence, and then she looks away. "Finish writing your report."

# CHAPTER THIRTY-SEVEN
## ZIVAH

Mehtap goes into a whirlwind for the equinox celebration. She takes out all her dresses and implores me to try them on. At first I do so because it's easier than refusing, but her enthusiasm is contagious. At times, she reminds me of Alia, the way she exclaims over a particularly lovely gown or giggles over one that doesn't fit quite right. When she tries on her dresses for me, she poses like officials' wives she knows, or dances across the room. After we've chosen our clothes, we try different ways of braiding our hair and experimenting with rouge and kohl. Here too, there's a good deal of laughter when one of us employs too heavy of a hand or lines the other's eyebrows in red. It's been a long time since I've had such a chance to be carefree, and it does help to distract me from everything else surrounding the festival.

On the day of the equinox, we spend the morning getting

ready. When we're done, Mehtap pirouettes in front of her polished bronze mirror and smiles in delight. I've braided a fat strand of her dark blond hair into a crown on the top of her head, while the rest hangs loose. A single green jewel adorns her forehead, matching the green embroidery of her white silk gown.

"I've done well, don't you think?" I tell her.

She beams at me and then pushes me toward the mirror. "Your turn."

I'm nervous as I approach the mirror, but the woman that stares back still looks like me, just grander and more refined. My dark blue gown is similar in style to Mehtap's—loose fitting with gathers at one hip and the opposite shoulder. Rather than a jewel though, Mehtap has woven ribbons through my hair and pinned up the braids. My eyes linger on the skin of my face and my arms, on my ever-present rosemarks. They make me look older than I am, wiser to the world. It's hard to remember what I looked like without them.

We meet our umbertouched soldier escorts at the door of the villa. There's laughter and chatter in the streets as we make our way toward the gates. People have put up bright-colored cloths in their windows, and mill around outside, talking with their neighbors. At one corner, an acrobat does flips and somersaults to the applause of an appreciative crowd. I pull at Mehtap's sleeve to point him out, and she smiles. "Just wait until we get to the palace."

Even the soldiers guarding the compound stand up straighter today as they wave us through. Outside, there is a palanquin waiting, lavishly decorated with red-and-gold cloth. Our escorts bow and motion us inside, and the litter jerks as they lift us onto their shoulders. The soldiers bear us at a leisurely pace. The roof of the palanquin shades us from the afternoon sun, and Mehtap pulls open one of the curtains to let in a breeze. It's the perfect spring day, crisp and not too warm.

"We must make the most of this night," she says, gazing out over the horizon. "Who knows if we'll ever have an opportunity like this again."

As the walls of Sehmar City loom near, one of the soldiers bearing our litter calls out to us. "Now is the time to lower the curtain, Lady Mehtap." She doesn't seem surprised, and quickly undoes the ribbon securing the drapes. We're suddenly illuminated in reddish light. It makes sense, as we enter the city, that we would be kept from view. Still, I feel a bit of regret that I won't be able to see it.

"I think we can peek out," Mehtap says. "As long as they don't see us."

That's all it takes to convince me, and I lift a corner of the curtain. The first thing that hits me is how crowded it is. Shacks and sheds stand shoulder to shoulder along the street. Slaves in rags weave between free servants wearing household uniforms. The occasional carriage or palanquin lumbers down the street, parting the crowd as it passes. The crowd gives our own litter a wide berth, though I don't know if it's because they know what it carries, or if they simply fear the soldiers.

I watch the mix of humanity until we leave the noisy outer sectors behind. As we're carried uphill, the sheds give way to giant stone temples and mansions, walled gardens with cypress trees arching over the stone. The palace, as we approach, is unmistakable with its gleaming white alabaster walls and gold inlaid gates.

Instead of going down the main promenade though, our bearers take us along the perimeter walls until we finally pass through a side entrance.

The fragrance of flowers and fresh green leaves flows through the curtains as soon as we turn in. Compared to the busy city outside, the gardens are an oasis. Elegant women stroll the paths escorted by men in tall hats and grand court robes. Servants weave among them, bearing platters of delicacies, and the mouth-watering scent of cardamom and mint wafts over to us. Our litter bearers carry us away from the main crowd into a quiet corner of the garden, where we're finally lowered to the ground. One of the soldiers pulls aside the curtain, and we climb eagerly out.

It's every bit the paradise Mehtap had promised. We're on a raised level separated from the rest of the grounds by a low hedgerow. There are polished stones under our feet, and flowering trees to provide shade. From here we also have an unhindered view of the geometric squares and rectangles that make up the gardens, as well as the dozens of small pools among the foliage. Our enclosure is still a cage, I know, but it's a beautiful one.

A fragrant steam drifts by me, and I turn to see umbertouched servants laying out trays of flavored rice, rabbit pudding, spiced squash, and lamb skewers on a low table. Moments later, they set up reclining chairs. I lean over the food, overwhelmed by the selection laid out before me. Mehtap comes up behind me and reaches for a plate.

"Better not wait too long," she says, "or I will eat it all."

I consider that fair warning and dig in. The lamb bursts with fragrant juice, and the pudding is creamy and smooth on my tongue. It's by far the most delicious food I've ever had, and yet I find myself thinking about my mother's goat milk stew.

A flute melody drifts over as we eat, and we look down into the garden to see a group of minstrels playing. A crowd gathers to listen, swaying along to the music in colorful gowns and sparkling jewels.

Finally Mehtap tugs at my arm. "It's time," she says.

Indeed, the musicians are putting down their instruments, and I see Arxa, Dineas, and the soldier Walgash step in front of them. They're led by two men in rich purple-and-gold robes that can only be Emperor Kurosh and Prince Kiran.

The crowd quiets as Kiran starts to speak. We're too far away to hear everything, but I catch bits and pieces. "Quick thinking . . . skilled and dedicated soldiers . . ."

Mehtap glows with pride, eyes fixed on her father. As for me, my gaze keeps drifting to Dineas. His dark brown hair is washed and trimmed, and his crisp, ankle-length robe almost makes him look like nobility, though it doesn't hide his strong arms and broad shoulders. As I look on, Kiran places large purple sashes over Arxa's, Dineas's, and Walgash's shoulders. The crowd cheers, and then a lute player starts a lively tune.

As the sun begins to set, servants light paper lanterns along the paths. It gives the entire place a magical feel, especially where the pools reflect their glow. In the garden, a flute and dulcimer begin a duet, and I take in a deep breath of night air.

Mehtap raises her hands in a lazy stretch. "That was perfect," she says. "I'm going to rest a while inside the palanquin."

"Are you unwell?" I wouldn't have expected her to retreat on a night such as this.

"I'm quite well, just tired." She glances toward the festivities, then gives me a conspiratorial wink. "Don't come with me. You wouldn't want to miss any visitors while you're gone."

Our palanquin is just outside our enclosure, along the path. Mehtap steps around the hedge, and I can hear her telling the soldier outside that she'd like to rest. I'm wondering if I should follow her, when I see a familiar figure walking toward our corner of the garden. The guards salute Dineas as he enters. He smiles when he sees me, and clasps my hands.

"I'm glad you came," he says. He looks even more handsome up close, and he smells faintly of cedar.

"I am grateful for the invitation," I say. "This whole night has been wonderful."

"You look beautiful." He says it without guile, and the look in his eyes sends a pleasant tingling through my chest.

Though I'd worried about seeing him here, he's so genuine that it's hard to put up walls. "It's very sweet of you to say so."

"May I join you in whatever you were doing?"

"I was simply enjoying the sights."

"That sounds delightful," he says.

"Shouldn't you be holding court among the adoring crowds?"

"I find I don't care for their company."

I shouldn't encourage such sentiments from him, but I gesture toward a chair. "Sit, then." There's a pitcher of wine on the table, and I pour a cup for each of us. Down in the garden, three young men start an elaborate dance that involves the juggling of lit torches. The flames rise and fall in hypnotizing patterns.

"I almost forgot," he says. He presents me with a handful

of berries wrapped in a linen handkerchief. "These grow in the garden, and they're delicious."

I tilt my head. "Are you sure they're safe to eat? I'm not sure I trust your herb lore."

"Ha! Well, I haven't dropped dead yet, have I? Here, I'll eat one with you. Then we can be poisoned together."

We each take one. The juice is rich and sweet, and my eyes widen with delight.

He smiles and pushes the rest toward me. "Have your fill. I've been sneaking bites all afternoon."

I don't need any more encouragement. When I've finished a handful, he looks at me and grins. "You have berry stains on your face," he says, and he wipes the corner of my mouth with his thumb. His hand is gone before I've even fully registered what he's doing. Still, his touch leaves a tingle on my skin.

"We might make a forager of you yet," I say.

"At least now I've brought you some useful plants," he says. "I did try to gather some puzta flowers for you on my trip north, but they spilled."

I laugh. "I can forgive you dropping my precious flowers during an ambush."

His smile fades a bit. "Actually, they spilled before we even went up the mountain."

"They did? How?"

He shakes his head. "Just a silly thing." He pauses again, and it's clear that he's reliving some moment. "Some people can't see past the surface. I think it's their loss." There is a conviction in his voice that I can't quite understand.

"You're being cryptic."

Again, he struggles over his words, only to shake his head again. "You're an extraordinary woman, Zivah," he says. "You're one of the bravest and kindest people I know. You're more than the marks on your skin, and don't let anyone tell you otherwise."

I still don't understand what happened to the flowers he gathered, but I do understand what I see in his eyes. A heaviness settles in my stomach, and I know what I must do.

"Dineas." I place my hand gently on his arm. "I'm fond of you, you know I am. But it's as a brother and a friend. You must know that."

A long silence follows. I see his chest rising and falling next to me. Finally, I can't stand it anymore, and force myself to look at him.

He's studying my face, though he looks more puzzled than hurt. "If you say so, but..."

"But what?"

He lets out a quick breath, and then squints at the dancers in the distance. "I'm starting to get a good idea of the parts of me that survived the fever. I don't have my memories, and I don't know much about the world, but I still have my instincts. It's not just the fighting. I can also sense an enemy hiding around a corner. I know when it feels like rain. And I can tell when somebody..." He stops and looks at me. "I guess what I'm saying is that I don't believe you. Not when you say that I'm just like a brother to you."

He doesn't say it as an accusation. In fact, he's almost apologetic, but still I can feel my heart pounding against my rib cage. "I wouldn't lie to you. Why would I?"

"I don't know," he says quietly. He catches my gaze, and he doesn't let it go. "Why would you?"

My mouth goes dry, and my mind races with the answers I could give him. I could tell him he's naive and delusional, that what he thinks are his instincts is just his own wishful thinking. I could tell him that he knows so little of the world, that there are many women out there and he shouldn't stick with the first one he's met. I could tell him that I have no wish to tie myself to a man.

"Because you deserve better," I tell him.

He frowns. "I don't understand."

Once the words start coming, they rush out in a torrent. "Look at me, Dineas." I wave my arm, gesturing hopelessly toward myself. "Look at the marks on my skin. You know what that means, don't you? It means that in some number of years, months, or even weeks, the fever could return for me. Is that what you want? To love someone who might not be here tomorrow? To set yourself up for grief? Because the fever will come back. The fever always comes back." I stop as abruptly as I started, struck with the realization that I'd just spoken truths long buried, fears I hadn't even admitted to myself. Even if I haven't told him the truth of his double identity or the complications of our mission, it doesn't matter, because I've just bared my soul.

Dineas stares at me, eyes opening in comprehension. "That's the reason, then? That's why you won't let me close?"

I could try to take it back, but he wouldn't believe it. No one with eyes or ears would.

He turns away, his brow furrowed as he studies the ground in front of him, as if he's trying to figure out some puzzle. Finally, he lets out a breath and turns back. "I *have* looked at you, Zivah, and I see you. Now I need you to look at me."

When I don't, he touches my cheek gently and guides my gaze toward him. "What am I?"

I don't answer.

"I'm a soldier," he says. "I just came back from a mission where we were ambushed by barbarians. My comrades and I were honored by the emperor tonight because we were the only ones stranded with Kiran who survived. You say you might die in a year, well, I might have died last week." He runs a hand through his hair. "Nothing's promised us by the gods. Isn't that all the more reason to love while we can?"

I can't speak. My eyes are burning and I can hardly breathe.

Dineas lets out a frustrated sigh. "Zivah . . ."

He reaches up a tentative hand and grazes the back of my neck with his fingers. His touch is warm, but it sends a shiver down my spine nonetheless. I'm rigid, frozen.

It's unclear which one of us leans in first. I don't know if we draw closer of our own volition, or if we do so simply because there's no other way to go. But I do know the exact moment our lips touch, and the jolt of it sweeps everything else away.

His breath warms my face, sending a heat through my limbs and thawing me out. His lips are soft, and his arms are wonderfully solid. I marvel at how long it's been since I've touched someone with any tenderness at all, and I'm parched for it. I lean into him, burying my hands in his hair. And though I know I should stop this, it would be as futile as ceasing to breathe.

I'm not sure when I start crying. At some point, even as I'm lost in the scent and feel of him, a tear escapes, and then another. And in the end, it's Dineas who pulls away. Who looks into my eyes and then at my grief-moistened cheeks. And the look he turns on me is both a plea and a question.

"Dineas," I whisper. "Please."

His face twists briefly, but he gathers himself and steps away. His gaze lingers on my eyes. "Promise me you'll think about what I said, at least."

I can't answer. I don't know how.

Mehtap finds me a short while after Dineas leaves, as I stare at a wall of trimmed cedars without really seeing them. My first instinct when I hear her coming is to dry my eyes, but I resist the urge and simply hope that the darkness is enough.

"Zivah?" she asks cautiously. "What are you doing?"

I force a smile. "I'm just lost in my thoughts. How do you feel? Did you rest well?"

"I did," she says. "It's good to have some time alone, once in a while." She smiles, and I wonder if she saw more than she's letting on.

Arxa drops by later that night and sits a while with his daughter. The celebration winds down. The crowd clears from the garden, until only scattered clusters of guests remain. Their chatter carries crisply over the garden's numerous pools.

Finally, long past midnight, Mehtap and I climb back into the palanquin to be carried home. Mehtap lies back on a pillow, smiling dreamily. "It's like being alive again, isn't it?"

She closes her eyes, and her breathing becomes slow and steady. I lie awake for a while longer, and once we're out of the city I open the curtains to take in the sights and sounds of the desert.

It was indeed like being alive again, the heady illusion of possibility and hope. My only regret is that such a thing could never last.

After the feast, life continues as normal, though normal has a duller cast to it after the bright colors of the celebration. In some ways, I'm glad to numb myself in the routines of the hospital.

A letter arrives from Leora two days after the festival. It's a godsend to hear from her now, and I eagerly take the letter to my room. Leora's steady handwriting easily conjures her rich voice, and I soak in her words.

She's married now. The wedding took place on a sunny morning, with much of the village in attendance. Alia carried the incense, and Mother and Father gave their blessing. She and Gil have moved into a cottage a short distance away from my family. Leora describes both the festivities and her new home in great detail—the sun shining through the bamboo groves, the goat that wandered into the wedding dancing. I know she's doing her best to include me, and I am grateful.

*I find it fascinating to hear about your mystery patient*, she writes. *How strange it would be, to be wiped blank. I do see, as a new bride, how much our past can affect who we are. Gil gets terribly moody on rainy days. He lost his younger brother to a flood during a hard rain, and every time the skies darken, the memory comes back to him. It's hard for me to see him like this, but I suppose life leaves its imprint on all of us, good or bad.*

*I do think, though, that there are parts of us that would be the same, no matter what our lives are like. You, my dear sister, would be compassionate, hardworking, and intelligent, whether you were a healer, a seamstress, or a goatherd. I'm sure of it. Perhaps, with your Dineas, you get to see a version of him that is unmarred by time. Be good to him, for his sake. Not all of us get the chance to start our lives anew.*

I wonder what Leora would think if she knew the whole story. That not only do I have the new Dineas, but I also have the old Dineas with me, and that they hardly ever agree. That I've become too close to one, and soon I'll have to face the other. He'll be angry with me, and rightly so. I've broken his trust, and I'll have to answer for it.

But it's more than his anger that I fear. I revealed too much in that garden, thoughts and fears that I hadn't even quite acknowledged to myself. It was hard enough to share them with the Dineas who loves me. For the other to know as well... I don't know how I will bear it.

A few nights after the feast, a messenger comes for me from Utana. "His Excellency is in great pain and requests your help."

"Headaches?" I ask.

"Yes, Healer."

Worsening headaches over time are a common symptom of the fever's return. There's not much that can be done, except to numb the pain when it happens. I grab a few supplies and head to his house. I find the old man sitting on his bed, drenched in sweat.

I rush to his side. "Is it bad?"

He nods, squeezing his eyes shut. "It normally comes and goes, but it's been bad today."

"I have some herbs bundled I can burn for you. It takes away pain, but it also puts you in a trance. You'll be awake, but more trusting and obedient to others. You'll remember your time being treated, but it will have the quality of a dream. Would you like me to burn it for you?"

He nods, rocking back and forth with the pain.

I move quickly, requesting a plate from the servant and then sending him outside. I tie a damp cloth over my nose and mouth, then hold a flame to the herb packet until it starts to smolder and a thin stream of smoke snakes up toward the ceiling. Carefully, I help Utana lie down on his bed. After a few moments, he lets out a deep sigh.

"Better?" I ask.

"Very much."

I sit with him for a while. He closes his eyes, but I can tell by his breathing that he's not yet fallen asleep. After a short time, he speaks again, and his voice has a dreamy quality. "The fever usually doesn't return so soon, does it, Zivah?"

Typically it would be hard to answer a question like this, but there's a freedom in talking to someone in this state. "Not usually," I say.

He breathes in deep through his nose and then lets it out. "I know why it has," he says. "I know why."

The shadow in his words stirs a feeling of foreboding in me. "Why is that?"

"Guilt."

My breath catches. I have an opportunity here, one I should not take. The Goddess's commands are very clear. Herbal knowledge is for healing. The tools we're given are not meant to be used for our own agendas.

But it would be so easy.

"Why do you feel guilty?"

"A minister of health is supposed to protect the people. But I didn't say anything. I stayed silent, and Hefana punishes me now."

There's a tingling at the base of my neck. Whatever lingering doubts I have, I smother them. "What did you see, Utana?"

He tosses back and forth on his bed. "Baruva. Kiran. The soldiers. It wasn't right to turn the plague against their own people."

Kiran? "What do you mean?"

"Just the right amount of weak vinegar... to sicken the troops..."

Weak vinegar... Baruva's method of strengthening the rose plague essence. "What troops?"

"Troops for Monyar. It was just what Kiran needed to start a war...."

My heart knocks against my rib cage. "It's Kiran who wants the attacks?"

"The emperor was happy to rest, but the son wanted more.... But it wasn't supposed to be his mentor's battalion. It wasn't supposed to happen so soon."

The smoke in the room suddenly feels impossibly thick. I have trouble breathing, and I feel an overwhelming compulsion to get out. "Rest, Utana." I don't wait for a reply before I leave the room.

The servant waits outside.

"He should be fine to sleep with no danger," I tell him. "If you need to enter for some reason, cover your face with a damp cloth and open the windows to disperse the smoke."

My mind spins as I make my way home. It was the prince, all

along, who'd sickened the troops, and he meant for our people to take the blame. My stomach rolls as I think of everyone back in Dara, of Leora and her new husband starting a life together, of young Alia, of my parents—all of them unaware of the machinations against them, of the punishment heading toward them for a crime they knew nothing about. I need to tell Dineas. We need to tell Gatha.

But first thing I do when I return to my room is take off my healer's sash. I run my fingers over Leora's embroidery, remembering the day I received it. The test and the feast all feel like they happened years ago, though it's only been months.

I hold the sash to my temple, conjuring up images of the day I took my vows. Then I put it down and take out my knife. The sash makes a horrible rending sound as it tears, and I let it fall into two ragged pieces on the floor. I stare at them, barely able to breathe, and wonder if I've made a grave mistake. But I know in my bones that I haven't. The sashes are for those worthy of the Goddess's trust, and after tonight I no longer count as one of their number.

The next morning, I fashion myself a new sash made of plain brown fabric. Mehtap notices right away, and I tell her I'd caught the other on a nail and will have to take time to mend it. All day at the hospital I think about Utana. Does he remember that he confessed his secrets to me? Will he tell me more, or will he hate me for betraying his trust? What would Kiran do to us if he knew?

That evening I send a messenger to Utana's residence, requesting an audience. I don't know what I'll say to him, whether I should ask his forgiveness or ask to know more. Either way, I need to see him again.

The reply comes a few hours later, via the servant that had tended Utana the night before. He looks shaken, and he stumbles a few times on his words.

"I'm sorry, Healer. It was very unexpected for all of us."

I take one look at him, and I know what's happened. Even though it's far too soon, I still know. "What is it?"

"His Excellency was feeling better after you left yesterday, but this afternoon he took a turn for the worse." He takes a deep breath and swallows.

"What is it?" I ask again.

"He died, Healer Zivah. His Excellency has passed away."

# CHAPTER THIRTY-EIGHT

## DINEAS

Zivah is bent over a patient when I step through the hospital door. She lays one hand on the old man's arm, her eyes soft with compassion as she speaks to him. She's back in her everyday clothes now, a long plain dress and an apron stuffed with herbs. But I can still see hints of the radiant woman at the equinox festival—the ribbons braided through her hair, the soft silk of her gown hinting at subtle curves in the wind. Either way, she's beautiful.

Finally, she stands up. Her eyes scan past the door and settle on me. It's a moment before either of us does anything.

"I'm glad to see you, Dineas," she says. There's some strain around her eyes when she speaks.

"And I, you."

She leads me wordlessly down the hall to the back room. A

cloud of silence surrounds us, thick enough to touch. There are things I could say, but the cloud muffles it all.

We know what to do by now. I fetch a pallet for myself while she mixes her herbs. As I put everything into place, I'm aware of every one of her movements, the grind of her mortar and pestle, the clink of the bowls.

She seems to take extra care as she carries the bowl to me—the water inside doesn't sway at all. For a brief moment, we're both holding the bowl, though our fingers don't touch. And I know she's already put up a wall between us.

"I would still like to be friends," I say. "If we can."

"I would like that," she says.

Her words bring some relief, but the tension she carries doesn't go away. I don't understand, but over the past months, there's been many things I don't understand. I take the bowl from her and drink.

There's no pain, but it still feels like a splitting headache. The images chisel at my brain, and my world expands. The night of the festival still sits foremost in my mind—I can feel Zivah's lips, smell the scent of herbs in her hair. But now, other details come back, filling out the picture and making it so much more than the simple kiss it had been before. She's not who I think she is. I'm not who I thought I was. I understand now, why she pushed me away.

More memories come flooding back—an argument, a promise that she would keep her distance. I look up at her, see the guilt written on her face, and I'm angry.

"I'm sorry," she says.

The torrent doesn't stop. I see her again, her eyes as she broke away from our embrace, the hunger in them. And I understand the flicker of loneliness, and the desperation that haunts her. I see her life through her eyes—being cut off from her family, gaining the chance to heal again, to matter again, but paying a grievous price for it.

"I should have listened to you," Zivah says. Her back is rigid, her shoulders tight. She expects me to explode. "I shouldn't have gone to the festival. Forgive me."

I still want to be angry, but the anger feels hollow now. The words on my tongue drain away. Anything I say would be like twisting a knife that has already gone too deep. I stir on the pallet, lift my head like a man stepping out of a quagmire. "What's done is done. Let's not dwell on it."

And now she stares at me. She doesn't understand my reaction, and neither do I. The silence stretches between us. The sound of a delirious patient's screams drift through the door.

I clear my throat. "I had a chance to see the emperor's guard." I speak deliberately, willfully putting the events of the festival behind us. "There's five of them with him, plus the crowd of courtiers and officials following him around. He keeps to the palace most of the time. I don't know how I could get to him."

Another long silence, and finally she follows my lead. "Don't go after the emperor, then. It's not him that's the problem."

What follows drives thoughts of the festival out of my mind completely. Zivah tells me how Kiran was the main force behind the empire's plan for expansion. And she tells me what she's learned about the sickened troops at Dara. I start to shake my head as she speaks. It doesn't make sense. Kiran, the warrior prince, raising his hand against his own troops?

"I can't believe Kiran would do this."

Yet is it really that hard to believe? He's always been enthusiastic about expanding the empire. Not many in his position would have taken it upon himself to scout out Monyar Peninsula. But his friendship with Arxa seems real. "Kiran wouldn't poison Arxa on purpose."

"Utana mentioned something about a mistake. That it wasn't meant to be Arxa's troops."

A last-minute change of assignments? Or a reshuffling of supplies? As I continue to think about it, my anger builds. I think of Arxa, with his unwavering loyalty to the empire, and Walgash, who could well have died from that plague. They may be Amparans, but no soldier deserves such depth of betrayal from his superiors. And then to throw that blame to my kinsmen...

"If Arxa knew..." I say. "Or if the army knew..."

"But we have no proof," says Zivah. "No one would believe us, and we don't know the specifics."

"We must tell Gatha and Tal, at least."

Zivah hands me a parchment. "There's something else you should know. Gatha sent us a reply about Tus."

Gatha's message is short, but clear. Tus knows who I am, but she doesn't think he'll reveal it under torture. If it is too risky to go in after him, I'm to leave him there as I wait for a better opportunity. It's a weight off my chest not to have to kill him, but my relief only means that Tus will suffer more. Once again, he carries the brunt of my failings.

A knock sounds on the door. Panic flickers across Zivah's face, and she gestures for me to lie down.

Her soft footsteps pad across the room. The door creaks open.

"I'm with Dineas," she says softly. "He shouldn't be disturbed."

"You need to hear this." I recognize Jesmin's voice. "It's important."

"What is it?"

I fight the urge to fidget, breathe as silently as I can.

"News has come in from Sehmar City," says Jesmin. "The emperor is ill with rose plague."

# CHAPTER THIRTY-NINE
## ZIVAH

It's as if the air becomes thicker at Jesmin's words. I step out of the room and close the door behind me. "What happened?"

"He manifested spots yesterday morning. Fever set in that afternoon."

Though I know that the emperor is as mortal as the rest of us, it feels irreverent to be talking about his illness with the same terms we use to discuss our other patients. "Thank you. You were right to interrupt us."

I turn back to the door, but Jesmin speaks again. "Zivah."

The urgency in his voice gives me pause.

"He manifested spots yesterday," he says again.

And finally, I understand. Yesterday was eleven days after the equinox festival. Rose plague takes ten days to show itself.

My head swims, and I grab the doorknob for support. We

weren't even near the emperor. But if Jesmin has suspicions, others will undoubtedly come to the same conclusion.

"Jesmin. You must believe me. I would never—"

He raises two fingers to stop me. "You are a consummate healer, Zivah. You've taken vows to guard all life, and I don't believe you would turn your arts against another living being, even the ruler who has conquered your people."

If Jesmin's earlier talk seemed irreverent, this feels downright dangerous. We've never spoken of politics before, and now of all times, I do not want attention drawn to my origins.

Jesmin lays a hand on my arm. "Settle your patients here, and go back home and rest for the day."

"Thank you," I say again, and then retreat back into the room.

Dineas is lying on the mat with his eyes closed. I'm not sure if he's still awake, or still himself for that matter.

"I'm alone," I say.

He opens his eyes, and I can tell by the chiseled set of his face that the old Dineas is still here.

"How much of that did you overhear?" I ask.

"Kurosh has rose plague," he says.

I nod.

"It'll be bad if he dies," he says. The irony is so plain that neither of us see fit to say it. A week ago, we would have been overjoyed at this news. Now it's a disaster.

I don't mention that it's been eleven days since the equinox festival.

My skirts are heavy around me as I turn toward the shelves. "Your memory will fade soon. Let me get you another dose, and then we can relay the news to Gatha."

I mix him more potion to keep him with me as he scribbles out a report. When he's done, I tuck the parchment away to send later. "I'll likely have to invent some excuse to get you back here in a few days, once we know whether the emperor will survive."

"Perhaps you could make something up about a new potion," he says.

It's strange. Today of all days, we're cooperating better than we ever have before. And now that the message is written, our earlier unfinished conversation comes back to settle around us. I'm still not sure why he hasn't taken me to task for what happened at the equinox festival.

Dineas meets my eyes and then looks off to the side. For a moment, it seems as if he's about to speak, and I steel myself. But he simply returns to his mat and lowers himself down.

"Be safe," he says, and then he closes his eyes.

It's only a short while before the new Dineas returns. I send him off quickly, pleading fatigue, and then hurry home.

The sights and sounds of the street press on me as I walk. I do my best to push them aside and get my thoughts in order. It still seems impossible that Mehtap or I could have infected the emperor. We were kept to such a small space, and we were never even within shouting distance of anyone else.

A thought crosses my mind, and I stumble. *I* was in the enclosure the whole time, but how much did I see of Mehtap that evening?

The courtyard is empty when I get back to the villa. I push through the front door and call Mehtap's name. She's not in the dining room or the sitting room. I'm climbing the stairs when I finally hear her.

"I'm here," she says from her room.

Mehtap is sitting by the window, gazing out over the compound's dusty streets. She has a scroll in her hand, but she's not reading.

"Did you hear about the emperor?" I ask.

"I did. It's a terrible thing."

She speaks almost as if in a trance, and I don't know what to do or think. I stand at the door, struggling with my doubts, when Mehtap looks at me again. "Is something wrong?"

"At the equinox festival. You were in our enclosure the whole time, weren't you?" It feels like a breach of trust even to ask.

Mehtap blinks a few times. "Of course I was," she says. "Where else would I have gone?" Something about her expression sends chills over my skin, and yet, my suspicions make no sense. Mehtap is the daughter of a respected Amparan commander. She has no reason to harm the emperor.

"Of course," I say. "Forgive me. I'll leave you to your reading."

I can feel Mehtap's eyes on me as I walk out the door.

# CHAPTER FORTY
## DINEAS

The emperor's illness casts a shadow over the palace. At the training fields and in the barracks, everybody's talking. Everyone's wondering what will happen.

"A rosemarked emperor, can you imagine?" says Kosru over dinner one night.

"He'd have to step down," says Walgash, emphasizing his words with a swig of watered wine. "How would he see dignitaries? Would he have to move into the rosemarked compound?"

Masista chuckles at that, though he catches himself and looks around nervously.

I stir the chickpeas around in my stew. "They have good healers looking after him, don't they? He could yet live."

"True that," says Walgash. "If a scrawny thing like Dineas can pull through, who's to say the emperor won't?"

Kosru frowns at his bowl. "Let's hope he comes out with more of his wits than Dineas did."

"Ha!" Walgash punches me in the shoulder, and I wince. "In all seriousness though. It's strange, isn't it, that the emperor would just fall ill like this? Him and no one else?"

"You think someone got to him?" asks Masista. "A minister? An assassin?"

"If you're wise, you'll stay out of the talk," says Kosru. "Dangerous, to be feeding rumors at a time like this."

We fall silent, each lost in our thoughts.

Two days later, we're out in the training fields when things inexplicably go still. I lower my practice sword to see a palace herald at the entrance. Instead of his usual gold robes, he wears a rough garment of pale brown cloth—mourning clothes. Little by little, a wave of silence overtakes the field. Only then does he speak.

"I announce this news with the deepest grief. Emperor Kurosh, seventh emperor of the House of Katana, has passed this morning into Zenagua's arms."

At least three fights break out in the barracks over the next few days. Had they kept the training fields open, things might have been different, but we're forbidden from training during the mourning period. So instead, we sit in the barracks or wander the city, wondering what the emperor's death means for us. Rumors abound. One day we hear that Kiran will disband five battalions. The next day, that he's launching an expedition across the Great Sea.

After the week of mourning is over, there's a call for all

Sehmar's troops to assemble on the training field. It's the first time I've seen all the units lined up, over fifteen thousand of us shoulder to shoulder, from elite units up front to new recruits at the sidelines.

Though not a particularly warm day, it's sunny, and there's not much of a breeze with so many men around. The air smells of armor oil, and an ache starts to build in the center of my forehead.

Suddenly, the energy shifts, and Prince—no, Emperor Kiran steps onto a wooden platform at the front of the field.

"Hail, Emperor Kiran," shouts a voice. "May his reign be long and prosperous."

"Hail, Emperor Kiran," we echo.

The new emperor lifts his hands to receive our praise. His voice rings out over the fields, echoed by heralds who repeat his words farther down.

"These are hard times in which I address you," Kiran says. "My father was taken from the world too soon, and we mourn his passing. But you, my soldiers, the lifeblood of our empire, you give me confidence in the future. You have served my father well, and I trust you will do the same for me.

"In a few short days, I will be crowned, and I will start to make changes as befits a growing empire. I will be appointing two new generals: Commanders Vaumitha and Arxa." Next to me, Walgash nods appreciatively. "I will start my reign by securing our empire. My father had long been too soft on the rebels to the north. Reports from these regions tell of increasing aggression that threatens the very fabric of Ampara. They go so far as to poison our soldiers with disease. My father had been slow to bring them to justice, but I will not allow a danger like this to stand. We will subdue the Shidadi and Monyar Peninsula once and for all."

He pauses and peers over our heads. "Be proud to be part of Ampara. The empire is fortunate to have you." He raises his fist. "To victory!"

His words are full of fire. I feel energy gathering around me, and my own spirits lift as well.

As one, we raise our fists, and our response rumbles like thunder. "To victory!"

# CHAPTER FORTY-ONE
## ZIVAH

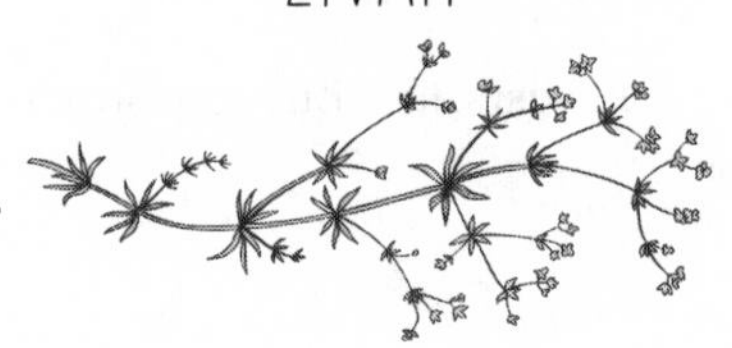

When I restore Dineas's memories this time, urgency overtakes him right away.

"How much have you heard?" he asks before the cloud of recollection has even cleared from his eyes. He scrambles to his feet and casts around for the writing implements I've laid out on the shelves, then nearly knocks over the ink bottle when he grabs for it.

"Be careful," I say, though his panic sets my own pulse racing. "What happened?"

He grudgingly sits down. His fingers tap incessantly on the pen. "They're mustering an attack on the Shidadi," he says.

I blanch. "How soon?"

"It will take a few weeks to get everything together."

"Any news of Dara?"

He gives up on sitting still and starts to pace the room. "Nothing specific, but it won't be pleasant for your people either way. We need to get word to Gatha and Tal right away. Any reply from them yet?"

"No, nothing."

He writes out two copies of his report. It's too crowded outside to risk calling the crows, so I call them to my window as soon as I return home that night. Scrawny pecks at my table as I tie the message to his leg, and Slicewing sneaks glances at Diadem's cage.

"Fly fast," I tell them. "Don't dawdle."

I count every passing hour over the next days. In good weather, the crows can cover in two days the distance it took us a month to hike, but still there are storms and predators. And that's simply how long it would take for the message to get there. After that, Gatha and Tal need time to decide on a response.

Six days later, I come home to see Scrawny and Slicewing on my windowsill. I fling myself at them and unravel the parchment from Slicewing's leg. I read the note once, and then again two more times as equal parts anticipation and dread take hold. Perhaps the crows sense the change in my mood, because they stop hopping around. I fold up the parchment and tuck it into the secret pocket of my apron.

Scrawny comes to perch on my shoulder.

"Do you miss the old Dineas?" I ask him. "He may be coming back soon."

I can see Dineas's jaw working as he reads. I'd summoned him back to the compound with some odd story of how the last batch of potion had used improperly dried herbs. Now, with his memory restored, Dineas reads the note several times over. I fidget with my mortar and pestle as I wait for him to speak, but he simply stares at the parchment.

By now I've memorized the contents of the letter. We need to stay in the capital, get proof of Kiran's wrongdoing, and expose him. But before we can do that, we must buy time by delaying the invasion of Monyar. Meanwhile, our peoples are making preparations for the worst. Tal is directing construction of shelters in the mountains, while Gatha is sending messengers to Shidadi warlords in nearby lands, in hopes they might join the fight.

"An army can't move without its supplies," Dineas says. "That's the most obvious way to delay things. I'll have to find some way to destroy their supply wagons and food stores." He looks up at me. "Unless you have something up your sleeve. Can you do anything useful with your potions? Poison the army or something?"

My pestle falls still. "I can't."

He lifts an eyebrow.

"I took vows when the Goddess's knowledge was passed to me. I can use my skills only to heal, not to harm." I wonder if I can still justify this refusal, after all the compromises I've already made, but deliberate infection feels like a clear step too far.

I'm prepared for Dineas to argue, but he simply nods. "I've always thought wars should be fought face-to-face. None of this poison or backstabbing."

"I can give you sleeping potions. The kind I use in my blowgun for capturing animals, if you promise not to harm your victims after they fall asleep."

"That's a complicated set of rules."

Is there anything about our situation that isn't complicated? "Believe me, there's little precedence for the decisions I'm having to make."

That gets a chuckle from him, though there is not much mirth in it.

I pour water into my bowl and give it a stir. "You'll be going back with your memories intact, then. Will you be able to live and train in the barracks like this?"

His shoulders stiffen. "I'll have to be." He looks at the bowl in my hands. "Will I be taking potions with me?"

"Twice a day, as before." I pause, wondering about how he'd hide the vials from the others. "Or, if you prefer, I can restore your memories once and for all."

He doesn't answer right away, and a haunted look creeps into his eyes. "No. If I'm caught, it's better if I'm unable to tell them anything."

A bitterness on my tongue, though I've drunk nothing.

There's no point in delaying things longer. I portion out the contents of the bowl into clay vials and wrap them carefully. After he tucks them in his bag, Dineas brushes the dust off his sandals and adjusts the sleeves of his tunic.

"Think I can pass for him?" he asks.

"Your eyes look ten years older."

The corner of Dineas's mouth lifts in a grin that's tinged with sadness. The air around us feels heavier. "Until next time, then, Zivah. Take care." They're simple words, but he speaks as if he means them.

I don't pretend to know what Dineas is to me. At different times, in different states, he's an infuriating ally, a friend, a patient, a missed chance for love. But I do know that I'll feel his loss deeply if he fails. I take his hands.

"Be careful," I say.

And then he's gone.

# CHAPTER FORTY-TWO
## DINEAS

As I head back to Sehmar City, the many times I've walked this path compete for attention in my mind. The very first time had been with my memories intact, trailing Zivah to the compound. That had felt dangerous, a mission through enemy territory. But since then, this land has become my home. The contrast is enough to make my palms sweat and my head hurt.

Slicewing and Preener fly above me, and their shadows cross my path from time to time. After a while, I start looking for them. It's nice to have friends with me, even if it's friends with feathers and a beak.

My skin crawls as I pass through the city gates. I recognize the guards from all the times I've come and gone, but now, as the noise and trappings of Ampara surround me, I remember more. Images of being driven through Khaygal Outpost in chains, guards aiming kicks at my ribs when I stumble, dust from the road caking onto my wounds. Mixed in with these pictures are newer memories of trips to the market, tavern outings with Walgash, coming home after visiting Zivah. I feel as if I've lived two lives, and I suppose I have.

At the palace gates, I walk through the three sets of guards. I tell myself not to black out, not to lose track of reality. One step after the other.

And then I'm in. Up ahead of me are the ornate buildings of the palace, and I turn right toward the barracks. Soldiers pass by me. A spearman from Neju's Guard nods a greeting, and I return it. My blood pounds through my veins. I'm all right. I'm here.

"Dineas!"

My chest constricts.

"Dineas," Arxa calls again.

Sweat breaks out over my skin. I take a deep breath and turn around. "Commander, sir."

"Your helmet's been looking the worse for wear. Report to the armorer tomorrow for a sturdier one."

It seems impossible that he can't see my thoughts, sense my fingers itching for my dagger. I could run him through right here, and he wouldn't think to stop me.

"Yes, sir," I say. "Thank you." I should cut off my tongue.

Arxa furrows his brow. "What's bothering you, soldier?"

It's maddening that part of me actually feels grateful for his attention. I scramble for a lie, something close to the truth. "Nothing of importance, sir. Just personal matters." I let my gaze flicker in the direction of the rosemarked compound, let my thoughts go to Zivah. It's not hard to summon a flash of confusion across my face.

Comprehension crosses Arxa's eyes. "A good farewell is just as important to a mission as a good sword," he says. "Weigh your words carefully, and say nothing you will regret. Remember that we fight for those we love. That is what lends us strength on the battlefield."

Is Arxa capable of love? I see him with his daughter, and then I see him torturing Tus. I lower my head. "Thank you, Commander."

He walks away. It's a while before I can do the same.

# CHAPTER FORTY-THREE

## ZIVAH

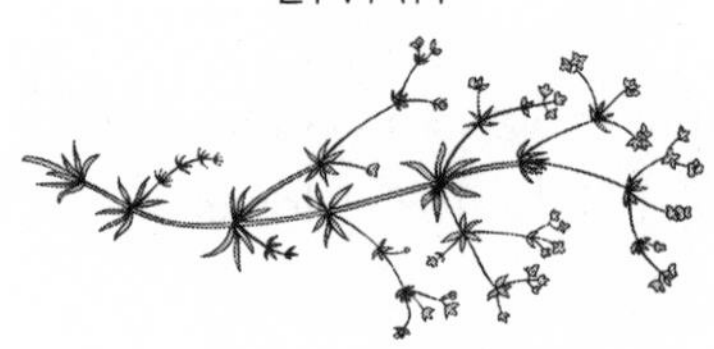

I know something's wrong when I return to the villa this evening. Two umbertouched soldiers stand at the door, and they're not our usual guards.

"Are you Healer Zivah?" the closest soldier asks.

"Yes," I say.

He holds up a clay tablet. "I have orders to take you under guard, to face accusations of poisoning Emperor Kurosh."

My mouth goes dry. "You are mistaken."

He reaches for my arm, and I step back. Every instinct tells me to run.

"It's not wise to resist, Healer," the soldier says. "We're instructed to use whatever means needed to bring you in."

I'm shaking where I stand, and all around me people have

stopped to watch. But the man is right. I'm not Dineas. I can't fight two soldiers, and there's nowhere for me to run. "Very well."

The soldier looks relieved and calls to someone inside the courtyard. "We have both of them. Let's go."

I've barely taken in his words when two more soldiers step out, escorting Mehtap between them.

"Mehtap!" For some reason, I'd assumed all the suspicion would fall on me.

She walks stiffly, and her cheeks are flushed. Our eyes meet briefly.

"Mehtap, does your father know about this?"

Her lips press into a line. "He will." She jerks her arm from her escort and marches out ahead.

As they throw plague veils over us and march us out the gate, my mind flies in all directions. I have no idea where they're taking us, or what lies in store. Diadem is in her cage in my room, and there's no one to care for her if I'm gone. And what will Dineas do when he finds out? If he finds out?

They lead us to a small mud building outside the city walls. It looks like some kind of old outpost. The dim interior has tables and chairs for guards, and three dusty cells. The soldiers push us inside one of the cells and slam the door shut. The sound rattles my bones.

I press up against the bars of the door. "What are you going to do with us?"

The man who'd been escorting me signals to the others, and they all file out. I pound my fist against the door, though it does nothing except bruise my hand.

"That won't help," Mehtap says quietly.

I turn around, surprised to finally hear her speak. She's crouched near the wall, on the straw pallet that's supposed to be our bed.

"You must talk to your father," I say. "Let him know that we couldn't have done it. We'll lay out our side of the story. They must believe us."

Still she doesn't look straight at me. And suddenly, I know without a doubt.

"You killed the emperor," I say.

Something shifts in her eyes. "How could I possibly have infected him? I was with you the whole time."

"No, you weren't. I never checked if you really were inside the palanquin. Somehow, you got past our guards and found your way to the emperor's servants. A drop of blood in his food or drink. That's all it would take."

The slightest flicker of regret passes across her features. "I didn't wish for harm to come to you," she says.

It's like swallowing a stone, hearing those words coming out of Mehtap's mouth. Sweet, gentle Mehtap. "Why?" I whisper.

Her shoulders fall, and for a moment, her mask comes off. "Look at me, Zivah. I'm useless. It was nice to pretend for a while that I could make a difference, but really, the world doesn't care about us. The emperor doesn't care about us. Now my father's a general. He'll be a good one too, and he'll bring glory to Ampara." She looks up at me with desperate eyes. "That is my gift to him, if I can do nothing else."

The sense of horror is growing in my chest. "Mehtap, you killed your emperor."

"He doesn't mourn our deaths. Why should I mourn his?"

It's too much to look at her, and I turn away, pacing the room. "I can't keep quiet about this. I have to say something."

"You wouldn't." For the first time, there's a hint of panic in her voice. "What proof would you give? I'll tell them that I saw you disappear as well."

"Your father is an honorable man. He would want to know the real reason for his good fortune. This is not the way he would have done things."

Mehtap reels back. "Don't presume to know him," she says. "I'm his daughter. And he wouldn't believe you even if you told him."

I stare at her, and the final pieces fall into place. "And what if I point him to the cream you made to disguise your rosemarks, or the fresh scar on your palm?"

She snatches her hand closer to herself. "Don't," she whispers. "Please."

"Why shouldn't I? Shall I just quietly doom myself alongside you?"

"Please don't," she says again. There's real fear in her eyes now, and she's gone deathly pale. "He's all I have. I can't—" She stops, and her eyes brim over with tears. She looks young again. Young and lost. "Please, Zivah," she says, and in her plea I hear the quiet desperation of one utterly without hope. "You're right. He'll despise me if he knows, and I won't be able to bear it. I beg you. Let him love me when I die."

# CHAPTER FORTY-FOUR
## DINEAS

Training sessions are scenes straight out of my nightmares. Amparan uniforms fill my vision. Practice swords cut through the air and clash against each other. I'm drenched in sweat, clinging to the repetitive strikes and parries of the drills, trying desperately to keep my sanity.

"Whoa, Dineas," says Walgash. "We're warming up, not going for blood."

I realize that I have him backed against the fence, and I'm still driving like a madman. Neju's sword, I need to take more care. "It'll take more than warm-up exercises to lighten those brick feet of yours," I grumble. Only after I say it do I realize I shouldn't have.

Walgash stares, and then bursts out in a deep belly laugh. "He's getting surly with age."

It's a good thing Walgash is so mild-mannered, but I shouldn't have slipped like that. Still, I can't help it. My body won't let me forget I'm in enemy territory. My nerves are on edge and I can hardly sleep. I don't know how long I can keep up this ruse, to pretend to be normal around Walgash and the others. And I don't dare think about what they would do if they knew the truth.

After training, I claim a headache and slip off alone to walk the grounds. At least it's easy to scout enemy territory when you've been living as one of them. I already know where the food stores are and where the equipment is. Now I just need a closer look to see how I can destroy them. The problem with my mission is that the numbers don't work in my favor—me against a palace force of thousands just doesn't look good. There's only one way for one person to cause the damage we need, and that's fire. I need oil, lots of it.

I find a quiet corner and whistle for Slicewing. She flies down immediately, but she's agitated, hopping and ruffling her wings.

"Calm down," I say. She squawks, and I toss her a piece of bread. "I'll need your help soon. Can you do it, or have your brains been fried by all this sand?"

She ruffles her neck feathers and looks away. It's strange how jumpy she is, but I can't exactly go into the desert to figure out what's rattled her. All I can do is give her some more bread and hope the problem sorts itself out.

It's only at dinnertime when I learn what's wrong.

"Did you hear the news?" says Masista over dinner. "They've arrested Commander Arxa's daughter and the healer Zivah on suspicion of poisoning the emperor."

I stop mid-bite as everyone around the table turns toward me. I was just with Zivah yesterday. How could this have happened?

"You know anything of this, Dineas?" Masista asks.

My mind races. I try not to look worried, but then I remember that I'm allowed to be worried, because the other Dineas cares about Zivah as well.

"I hadn't heard," I say. "What else do you know?"

"There's to be a trial," says Kosru. "The commander's not happy about it happening so close before we have to leave and all."

Murmurs of acknowledgement all around, as my food loses its taste. What now? Do I continue with the plan? Will they harm her? Certainly, they'd treat her better than the war prisoners, wouldn't they?

"Enough," says Walgash, cutting over the conversation. "Show the commander more respect. No more discussion of his daughter over dinner."

The chatter dies down, and men return to their food, chastened. Walgash sneaks a glance at me, and I know that he stopped the conversation for my sake—or rather, for the other Dineas's sake. Guilt twists in my gut. I don't want to be indebted to him.

Don't do me any good turns, Walgash. Because if you stand in my way tomorrow, I will still have to kill you.

# CHAPTER FORTY-FIVE

## ZIVAH

Mehtap and I don't speak the rest of the day. It's hard, because we are in such close quarters, but somehow we manage. An umbertouched guard comes in several times a day to bring us food or change our waste bucket. Otherwise we're alone.

Arxa finally arrives the next afternoon.

"Father!" Mehtap runs to the door of her cell.

The general takes her hands. "Have they mistreated you?"

Mehtap shakes her head. "They've mostly left us alone."

"And you, Zivah? How do you fare?"

I'm aware of Mehtap's eyes on me. "I'm unharmed as well."

Arxa turns back to Mehtap, his face tight with anger. "The nerve they have to make accusations like this. I'll speak to the emperor and see what can be done."

He doesn't even ask Mehtap if she's guilty. Why should he?

The idea of Mehtap doing such a thing is unthinkable. I do wish I could get a better sense of whether he suspects me, but even if he does, I don't think he would confront me in front of his daughter.

He continues to talk to Mehtap for the better part of an hour. Mehtap's words echo in my mind. *Let him love me when I die.*

Finally Arxa readies himself to go. "I'll do my best to end this soon," he says to Mehtap. "Until then, conduct yourself in such a way as to bring honor to our house."

I imagine a needle sewing my lips shut. I feel the prick of every stitch.

After he leaves, Mehtap turns to me. "Thank you," she says quietly.

I look at the naked relief in her eyes, at the childlike face that can do no wrong. And there is nothing to say.

# CHAPTER FORTY-SIX
## DINEAS

The news about Zivah makes me wonder if I should delay my plan, but in the end, I can't see the good of it. Waiting won't help her, and the longer I wait, the more likely that supplies will be under greater guard. It's best for me to continue as before and see what I can do for Zivah after that.

First order is figuring out how to set a good fire. I don't know where the palace keeps its supply of lamp oil, but I do know that slaves come by the barracks and refill the lamps every evening. So I shadow one of the slaves—a young, pretty one so I have an excuse if I get seen. She makes the rounds to ten buildings, and I actually start feeling worried for her by the end, seeing how many catcalls she gets. Give the girl a knife and a few months with Gatha, and maybe those same catcallers would think twice about bothering her.

The slave girl makes it back to the main palace unscathed, and she takes her oil jar to a servants' closet. There's a steward waiting who unlocks the door for her. I duck into a corner to watch. Slicewing and Preener, who've been trailing me, settle on a window ledge nearby. A few more slaves come by to drop off their supplies, and then the steward locks up the closet.

Slicewing ruffles her feathers when she sees him drop the key ring in a pocket of his robe. Keys are one of her favorite things.

"Yes, we want that," I tell her. "Just let me figure out how."

I follow the steward as he heads back to the central part of the palace, weighing my options. I can't exactly hit him over the head and pick his pockets, and sending a crow to snatch the key out of his hands seems too obvious. I need some kind of distraction.

Then a servant rounds a corner with five hunting dogs on leashes, and an idea pops into my mind. Not exactly subtle, but might be worth a try.

"Preener." I point at the dogs. "Drive, that way." And then I point in the direction of the steward.

The crow takes off eagerly—he'd happily harass dogs even without orders from me. One moment he flies high, and then he dives straight into the middle of the hounds. It's only a moment before they break free of their hapless handler, and then they're all charging down the path after a black blur—right toward the steward.

The shock on the steward's face is priceless. As he braces himself for the canine stampede, I turn to Slicewing. "Get the keys."

The dogs converge around the steward in a glorious tangle. Their handler chases after them, yelling for help rounding up the creatures. The steward makes a halfhearted grab at one hound, then seems to decide against it and backs up along the side of the pathway—not a dog lover, I'm guessing. In the midst of it all, Slicewing flies through and plucks the key ring out of the man's pocket. The steward doesn't seem to notice the crow at all.

"Hurry," I mutter, as Slicewing races back toward me. The dog handler's joined the fray now, shouting apologies as the steward yells accusations back. The hounds start to howl.

Finally Slicewing drops the keys in my hand. There are a few of them on the ring, but I've been around long enough now to know that the closet key is the smallest one. I take that one and its neighbor. I give the ring back to Slicewing and the neighboring key to Preener, who's returned as well, looking quite proud of himself.

"Drop it there. Fast."

The crows take off one last time and deposit their loot back along the side of the path. By the time all the dogs are rounded up, we are long gone.

Walgash stops me that night on my way into the barracks. "What's bothering you? You haven't been yourself."

I shrug him off. "Mission nerves."

"You sure? Is it about that healer?"

"It's nothing." I push past him to my bunk.

I lie in bed that night, feigning sleep. At least there's no worry of accidentally dozing off. My nerves are so raw, I doubt even one of Zivah's sleeping potions would knock me out. The hours tick by. I hear the men from first watch returning and climbing into bed. When there's nothing but steady breathing and snoring, I slide out of my blankets, grab my weapons and armor, and sneak out.

Slicewing lands on my shoulders as soon as I step outside, while Preener flutters nearby. They probably guessed from my nerves earlier today that I was planning something tonight. I run a quick hand down Slicewing's back, then shoo her off my shoulder so I can put on my gear. Then I'm on my way, with the crows following silently behind.

There's not many people out tonight. The few times I run across someone, I simply walk as if I have somewhere to be and no one stops me. Soon I'm back at the storeroom. There's a nervous moment when the key doesn't turn, but then the lock gives, and I'm in.

Jars as tall as my thigh are lined up along the floor. I break the seal off one and the sweet smell of lamp oil floats up to my nostrils. I take two of them, one in each hand, and stagger under their weight. Scars, these are heavy—those slave girls are stronger than they look.

Slicewing hovers around me as I stumble out the door, as if she's wondering why it's taking me so long. I shoot her a dirty look—I'd like to see her carry one of these—then stash one of the jars behind a bush. That one, I'll use to burn the food stores, but first I'll deal with the supply wagons and chariots.

The better vehicles are stored in a giant warehouse past the training fields. I carry the remaining jar until I'm almost in view of the building. Carefully, I peer around the corner. There are two soldiers standing guard by the door—I recognize them from my time in the third battalion. They shouldn't be much trouble, though it'd be better if I can get them one at a time.

Very carefully, I put down the jar and tie a scarf over my face. I have two other scarves, which I give to each of the crows. Then I remove the jar's lid and dash it against the ground. It breaks into three pieces.

Voices drift around the corner. "What was that?"

As footsteps come my way, I shrink into the shadow of a doorframe. One guard steps around the corner and accidentally kicks one of the broken pottery shards. He watches it skid across the ground, puzzled, then scans the ground for more.

The soldier doesn't see me until I'm on him. His mouth drops open. A punch in the ribs doubles him over before he can talk, and then I follow up with a knife hilt to the base of his skull. As he sinks to the ground, I scratch him with the blade so he gets a dose of Zivah's sleep potion. Never hurts to be careful.

"Baran?" a new voice calls, and more footsteps head toward me. The steps are measured, more cautious this time. I retreat back into the doorframe.

There's the slink of a sword being drawn as he nears. This guard won't be as easy to surprise. I whistle low under my breath.

The soldier steps around the corner. He sees his comrade on the ground, then looks up and sees me. His eyes widen.

"Attack," I hiss.

A flutter of wings, then Slicewing drops a scarf onto the soldier's head. He grabs at it, and I close the distance. My sword opens a shallow scratch across his chest. He swears and clutches at the wound as Preener drops his scarf. As the soldier bats at the second cloth, he sinks to his knees, then falls to the ground unconscious.

I hit him over the head as well. No reason to let on that there was a sleeping potion involved.

I'm surprisingly relieved that the fight ended the way it did, and that I didn't have to kill men I'd seen around the training fields. I look for a place to hide the sleepers, and settle for some hedges off the path. Then I pick up the oil, grab a torch from a nearby pathway, and hurry into the building.

Inside, it smells like old, polished wood. Wheeled shadows loom in the light of my one torch. There must be at least two hundred chariots here, and an equal number of supply wagons. I put the torch in a wall sconce and run between the vehicles, pouring oil. I don't have nearly enough to get at all of them, but hopefully the flames will spread on their own after a while. As I make my way farther in, I try not to think about what would happen if it all goes up in flames while I'm in here.

Finally, my jar is empty. I'm at the wall, taking down my torch, when the door opens and three men walk in.

I freeze. The torch flickers in my hand. The men array themselves between me and the door. I can't make out their faces, but their shadows are disturbingly familiar, especially the large one that steps now to the front.

"Stop there." Walgash steps into the light and looks at me—the torch in my hand, the shiny trail of lamp oil leading away from me. "What are you doing, Dineas?" His voice sounds more dangerous than I've ever heard it.

My stomach feels like it's been weighed down with stones. Behind Walgash, I see Kosru and Masista. "I was sent to check on the chariots. There was a commotion by the gates. . . ." I trail off. What's the point of spinning stories when we're practically drowning in lamp oil and I'm holding a torch?

Walgash shakes his head, bewildered. "I want to think I've misunderstood something, but I don't see how."

The flame wavers in my hand. I only have to lower the torch a bit to start the whole thing ablaze. "This whole place is going to burn," I say. "I don't want to hurt you. Save yourselves while you can."

"Who sent you, Dineas?" Walgash asks, advancing toward me. "Who do you serve?" The disbelief in his voice makes me feel lower than a worm.

"Stay back!" I lower the torch just a bit. He stops. Images of my training sessions with Walgash flicker through my mind. Memories of lazy evenings relaxing over a skin of wine.

Walgash shakes his head. "I don't pretend to understand this. But if you surrender now, you might still get a merciful death."

He's lying. I know it, and he knows I know. If they capture me now, they won't let me die until they've dragged every last piece of information from me, bit by excruciating bit. My only comfort is that in a few hours I won't remember anything worth telling them. Behind Walgash, I see Kosru trying to sneak around behind me. I wonder why there's only three of them, and why Walgash didn't bring more people with him when he clearly had suspicions about me sneaking out at night. And I suspect that it was because he was still hoping he was wrong. That he hadn't wanted to think the worst of me.

Such is war, I tell myself. Sacrifices must be made. If only believing something were as easy as saying it.

And I know there's no point in delaying the inevitable.

"I'm sorry," I say. And I lower the torch.

The oil catches fire quickly. I draw my sword and dagger, charge for the exit—and find myself face-to-face with Masista. I block his strike, then slash at his arm with my dagger. I can't tell if I drew blood, but I don't have time to check because Kosru is rushing me from behind. I duck to the side and give him a push as he careens past me, and he has to scramble to keep out of the flames. We face each other, panting. Somehow, in that scuffle, they've managed to stay between me and the door.

It's starting to get hot in here. Beads of sweat run down my skin. The smoke is thick in the air now, and it's clear we can't stand here forever. The others are sneaking looks at the door as well, edging closer to the fresh air. They're no longer attacking, and I realize they're just going to wait it out.

The smoke is getting to me now. My head feels stuffy, and I'm wheezing—I'm running out of time. Masista and Kosru stand side by side in front of the door, and I charge them, at the last minute ducking to the left. Kosru's caught off guard. He turns, but he's off-balance, and I easily deflect his sword. I'm close enough to the door now that I can feel the fresh air coming in.

Something big and heavy collides with the back of my head. My knees buckle, and black creeps in on the edge of my vision. Someone drags me out the door by the collar.

"I'm smart enough by now not to try and match your fancy moves," says Walgash. I struggle and try to stand, but he simply throws me to the ground and pins my arms together. Rope twines around my wrists and digs into my skin. As I lie there, hacking my lungs out into the dirt, I hear Walgash yelling for help with the fire. Finally, he drags me up by one arm.

"The general will want to see you," he says. There's a mournful cast to his eyes. I wish I could tell him the whole story, but who am I fooling? That wouldn't change anything.

We track soot the entire way back to the barracks. They drag me into a shed, and Walgash pushes me into a chair. I crumple into it, sending a silent apology to Gatha and Zivah for my failure. In my mind, I count the hours since I took Zivah's last dose of potion. I don't have to hold out for long. Another couple hours at most, and I'll fade away. Then they can torture me all they want.

The others in the room jump to their feet, and I know Arxa has come. By habit, I almost stand as well, before I realize there's no longer any point. An hour or two, I tell my beating heart. That's as long as I need to last.

Arxa might as well be Neju himself, the way he strides in. He looks at me, and then at the others.

"I've never seen such depth of treachery," he says, and his voice is as low and dangerous as a snake's. "Who are you really, Dineas?"

I stare at the ground in front of me. I am stone. I feel nothing.

Arxa looks at Walgash, who comes forward, his forehead creased as if pained. Reluctantly, the big soldier takes hold of me by the shoulder, and drives his fist into my gut. Scars, that man can pack a punch. My lungs feel like they've collapsed. Several more of those and I'll be coughing up blood.

"Judging from your timing," says Arxa, "you're Shidadi. Who else is working with you? Are there others in the city?"

I can't talk. All I manage is a small cough.

Another punch. I gag and thank the gods my stomach is empty.

I spit on the ground. "Zenagua take you all."

Walgash pulls back his fist, but Arxa shakes his head. "No, he won't break easily. We'll have to be careful not to kill him before he spills his secrets. Take him into the interrogation rooms, then secure the grounds. Triple the guard and scour everything to see if anything else has been tampered with."

The general looks at me, and the deepest disappointment is written on his face. "Then I'll come back to him and see what he has to say."

The first thing I notice is how cool it is, and how everything hurts. When I try to shift my weight, hard metal restrains my arms. Stone presses against my back. I'm chained to a wall.

I push my eyes open, but it's almost as dark in this room as it was behind my eyelids. I'm in some kind of cell. The prison?

My head feels as if it's been crushed between two boulders and filled with sand. How did I get here? I wrack my brain. I was in the rosemarked compound with Zivah. She'd given me a potion. After that, nothing.

Time ticks by, though I have no way to measure its passing. I do know I have wounds that need tending. I feel as if I've been fighting, but I don't remember any of it. Did the city fall under attack?

"Is anyone there?" The walls absorb my voice. It's just me, in the darkness, with the sound of my own labored breathing.

Just as I think I've gone mad, I hear footsteps coming down

the hall. I pull at my chains, unsure if it's friend or foe approaching, but the shackles hold tight. The door opens, and my eyes water at the torchlight flooding in. Then I make out Commander Arxa's features, and I melt in relief.

"General Arxa." I do my best to stand up straight. "What's happened..."

I trail off at his expression. The only time I've seen him look this cold was when he interrogated the Shidadi prisoner. And now he's looking at me in the exact same way.

He sets the torch on a wall sconce. "I'm disappointed, Dineas. Disappointed in you for throwing my trust back in my face, and disappointed in myself for giving you that trust. But we'll right things now. You will tell me how you came here. How you ended up in my army. You'll tell me who sent you, what you learned, and what information you sent back. Once I'm satisfied, then you can die."

I understand the words coming out of his mouth, but they make no sense. "General, what's happening? Why am I..." I trail off in horror as another man enters the cell. I recognize him as one of the prison interrogators, and my skin erupts in cold sweat as he starts setting out strange implements on a table.

"Don't try my patience," Arxa says. "You've made a fool of me already and caused untold damage."

Perhaps this is a nightmare, some dream brought on by the potion. "General, I swear I'm not playing games. I have no idea how I got here."

Arxa grabs me by the throat and slams me against the wall. Pain explodes at the back of my head.

This is a nightmare. It has to be, but the pressure against my windpipe is real. I thrash against my chains. "I swear on Neju's sword, I woke up here after seeing Zivah this morning, and I don't know how. I know it makes no sense, but I'm telling the truth." It becomes harder and harder to speak. My vision starts to blur around the edges. But then Arxa releases his grip. I crumple over, coughing.

"Look at me, Dineas."

I'm aware of the torch being moved closer to my face. The heat feels sinister against my skin, but I meet his eyes.

"Tell me again what you just said."

I cough. "I left this morning to go to the rosemarked compound for my treatment. I took a potion, as I always do, and then I woke up here."

"You didn't go to the rosemarked compound this morning. You were in the training fields with the rest of Neju's Guard."

I shake my head. "That can't be. We had the morning off today." Arguing with him will just bring another blow, but I'm so confused I no longer care.

Arxa continues to stare at me, his face hard with suspicion. I try not to think about him shoving the torch into my eye.

"How often have you been seeing Zivah?" he says.

I hesitate. Perhaps I shouldn't have brought her up, not to this monster with Arxa's face. "Twice a month for my treatments, as you commanded. More often recently."

"More often? Why?"

"She said she'd had a batch of bad herbs recently."

"When did the visits pick up?"

"Only this past week, maybe a little longer. It's nothing, sir, I didn't mean—"

Arxa silences me with a glance. "Since Kiran came to power . . ." he says under his breath. He storms out of the cell, only to return a few moments later. He holds up some clay shards for me to see.

"We found these vials among your things," he says. "Did Zivah give them to you?"

I can see that they are the remains of shattered vials. "I don't remember anything like it," I say. And I steel myself for another blow.

But Arxa simply curls his hands over the shards. "If you are lying to me," he says, "you'll soon learn what a grave mistake that was."

He signals to the interrogator, and they both leave.

# CHAPTER FORTY-SEVEN
## ZIVAH

Mehtap runs to our cell door when Arxa enters the building, but he shakes his head. "Not now."

As she steps uncertainly back, Arxa looks at me, and I know that something has gone horribly wrong. Over the past months, it's been easy to think of him as a generous patron, the father of my friend, but not at this moment. He regards me with the flint-hard gaze of an Amparan general, and I once again remember what a dangerous man he is.

"We captured Dineas last night," he says. "He set fire to a building full of valuable chariots and supply wagons. It's likely he would have done even more, had we not stopped him."

My bones go soft. It is just as I feared.

The general continues. "When he awoke, he claimed not to remember any of what transpired," he says.

My heart clenches at the thought of Dineas waking up blank in the dungeons, not knowing how he got there.

And now Arxa's eyes lock on me. "The last thing he remembers is visiting you and drinking one of your potions. He claims to have no memory of what happened after that, even though it's been days."

My mind races for a response, but there's nothing I can say. Nothing he would believe.

Arxa doesn't seem surprised at my silence. "I've heard rumors that your type can manipulate the mind. It seemed far-fetched to me, but you've certainly accomplished your share of miracles in our hospital. I can't decide, though, whether you simply manipulated Dineas with your potions, or if he's been with you from the beginning. He did arrive soon after you."

Goddess help me. "Dineas is innocent. I gave him a potion to render him suggestible, and I told him to sabotage the effort. I couldn't stand by and watch while my people bore the burden of another prolonged battle campaign."

Arxa's lips curl in something that isn't quite amusement. "The first confession is never true, not when it comes so quickly. He's been your ally from the beginning, then." Once again he shakes his head. "I've misjudged you, Zivah. Gravely. To think I brought you so close to the emperor, and that you would have let my daughter take the fall for his death."

Behind me, Mehtap draws a sharp breath. I could deny Arxa's accusation, but what would be the point? He wouldn't believe me, and it wouldn't change my fate.

Arxa pushes away from the bars. "I've failed badly, though I will remedy my errors. The campaign will continue as before, but we will not be nearly as kind to Dara now. If they've thrown their lot in with the Shidadi, then they will die with them."

A guard comes in and opens the door to our cell. I shrink to the back, but Arxa simply takes Mehtap's hand. "Come," he says to her. "You are no longer under suspicion."

He lays one hand protectively on his daughter's arm, and once again looks at me. "I'll return to deal with you."

Mehtap doesn't look me in the eye as they leave.

After they're gone, I crumple against the cell wall, gasping for breath as the reality of my situation finally strikes me. I'm alone, imprisoned in a foreign land. My one ally is in prison awaiting torture and interrogation, and soon I will join him. Spots dance before my eyes, and I fight a wave of spiraling panic. This is not the way I would have chosen to die.

I gouge trails into the sandy floor of my cell, thinking about soldiers coming down on Dara, burning our houses and taking my sisters captive. It will happen because of me—Arxa made that plenty clear. Sand forces itself under my fingernails, but the pain seems fitting. What do I do when Arxa comes back to question me? Do I try to stay silent and hope I have the strength? Do I confess everything? Tell him what I learned about Kiran and hope he believes me? Hope that buys something for my people?

In the corner of my eye, a tiny movement catches my attention. A lone scorpion crawls along the edge of my cell. It's a small brown variety, not as poisonous as some we have in Dara, but with a formidable sting nonetheless. Every few steps, it scrabbles at the wall, as if trying to get out. The bricks are laid tight though, and there are no cracks for it to disappear into, but it keeps going. It doesn't give up.

I look at the curve of its tail, the deadly needle at the end. I'm not ready to give up either.

Gathering my skirts, I creep toward the wall on my knees. The scorpion continues to move forward, and then freezes when it senses my presence. I stop crawling and send my hand closer, little by little. Then I grab for it, pinching right behind the stinger. It scrabbles its legs. I dump it into my lunch bowl while I tear off a part of my skirt to fashion a makeshift bag. And then I drop the tiny creature inside.

Over the next day, two other scorpions join the first. It seems a small number of creatures to entrust with my fate, but I can't afford to wait to see if any more will show up.

That night, when I leave my empty dinner tray by the cell door, I drop one of the scorpions in the bowl. The creature crawls around, exploring the space, but the sides of the bowl are too steep for it to escape.

Finally, the building door opens and the late-night guard comes in. He's a gruff umbermarked soldier, and he growls at me to stand against the back wall as he takes out the keys to my cell. In my apron pocket is my bag with the two remaining scorpions. The cloth twitches almost indiscernibly.

He opens the door, and I keep my head bowed, my breathing even. I wonder if he can hear the rapid beating of my heart.

I can feel the man's eyes on me, not the tray, as he lifts it off the ground. I wait until my bowl is close to his face before crying out, "Be careful! There's a scorpion in the bowl."

He looks down. Jumps. Almost drops the tray. I push off

of the wall, dumping the other scorpions into my hand. One of them stings me, sparking a burst of pain in my palm. I raise my open hand long enough to make sure the guard sees the contents, and then throw the creatures onto him. He drops the tray, and I snatch the keys from his belt as he brushes desperately at his clothing. Then I run out the cell door and lock it shut behind me. The guard shouts in outrage.

"Demon!" he snarls at me. But he doesn't run for the door or try to reach through the bars. He's still too busy shaking his clothes off.

"Stay still," I say to him. "They won't attack unless they're provoked. You can survive one bite, but it's doubtful you can survive two."

A string of curses trails behind me as I run for the prison door. I know that the next change of guard doesn't come in until tomorrow morning, so with any luck, my absence won't be found out until then. The door is heavy, and I brace my feet to pull it open. Cool air rushes in. I stumble outside—and nearly run straight into a second guard.

It's a wonder we don't collide. He's the one who jumps back, windmilling his arms for a couple of steps before he regains his balance and draws his sword. I stumble back against the wall.

Two guards. Why hadn't I realized there were two guards watching us? And then I see the smooth, unmarked brown of his face and realize the answer. He's never had the plague. The shifts must be arranged so that an umbertouched guard was always here for closer contact with us, while a second unmarked guard provided backup against outsiders.

He steps squarely in front of me, blocking my way to freedom. "Where's the other guard?" he asks.

The man is bigger than me, stronger than me, and he has a weapon. I can't outrun him. I hold back a frustrated sob.

The guard takes a threatening step toward me. "Get back in the building."

He's blocking my escape, but he keeps his distance. Why hasn't he attacked me yet?

And then I understand. I remember the whites of his eyes as he jumped back to avoid colliding with me. He's afraid of getting too close. A skilled soldier might be able to subdue me at sword point without touching me, but this man is clearly not ready to take that chance. He's a big man, and I've no doubt that he's brave in battle. But bravery comes in many flavors, and years of tending the ill have taught me that sometimes the most fearless soldiers on the battlefield will quail at the thought of a long, wasting death—an enemy that cannot be defeated with a sword.

In a split second, I make a desperate decision. With the keys in my hand, I score the underside of my arm as hard as I can. Blood wells out, and I let it pool in my palm for him to see.

"Your friend can't help you," I say. "You'll have to put me back yourself. And when you do, your life will be forfeit."

He wavers again. "The commander will have my head if I let you escape."

"And Zenagua will take you if you don't. Or you could let me go. The guard doesn't change until morning. You have many hours to concoct an excuse to save your skin. Maybe I released scorpions on you like I did to your friend."

He blanches.

"Or you could run. You can make it far away from the city before dawn. With the campaigns about to march, they won't spare the men to come after you."

Still he hesitates. I back away from him, holding my arm between us like a talisman. "I'm leaving."

He doesn't stop me.

It's a cold night, and I hurry across the sands. I check behind me for pursuit, but none comes. My arm stings, and I pick up my pace.

I know I must return to Mehtap's villa. My potions are there, as is Diadem, and I'll have a much better chance of making it through anything if I have them both with me. Beyond that though, I don't know what I'll do. I can't leave without Dineas, but I have no idea how I can help him.

The shadowy walls of the rosemarked compound materialize in the darkness. Not for the first time, I wish more of Dineas could have rubbed off on me. I've never broken into anything in my life, and my gown isn't suited for scaling walls. Still, I've seen him climb the compound walls before, and I remember some windows at the villa that never fully closed.

I skirt the compound at a distance, trying to catch a glimpse of the guards. I've walked a quarter of the way around when I'm set upon by a flurry of wings. I bite down on an exclamation as a familiar weight settles on my shoulder. It's Scrawny. Preener lands on the ground in front of me. And on my arm is . . . Slicewing?

"Slicewing, where's Dineas?"

She stretches her wings at the name. I don't know what that means.

"Slicewing, find Dineas."

She takes off without hesitation, angling toward the city, and I call her back before she goes too far. And now, I start to feel a spark of hope. If her confidence is any sign, then perhaps I'll be able to find him after all.

A guard rounds the corner of the compound, and I freeze. He is not in a hurry, nor does he look particularly alert. My heartbeat quickens. If I want to scale the wall, then this is my opening. I gather my skirts as he nears the next corner. When he disappears from view, I run for it. The three crows take flight silently behind me. I whisper for them to scout, and they fan out to the sides.

The wall is as high as my head, and my first jump isn't enough for me to get a good grip. I back up and try again, and the second time I clamber over, scratching my already wounded arm in the process. In a few moments, I drop down onto the other side. There's nobody in view, though I hear the occasional shout in the distance. I take off again, and the crows fly back and forth around me. At one point, I hear a caw to my left, so I turn right and continue that way for a while before circling back.

Finally, I see the walls of Mehtap's villa. I know there are guards at the door to the courtyard, so I circle around to the kitchen on the other side. There's a window here with broken shutters that don't completely close, and I feel around the edges for the telltale opening. It's there. I give the entire shutter a push. It pops open with a crack that sounds impossibly loud, and I freeze, my heart in my throat. But no one comes running, and I scramble inside. I can hear the snoring of servants sleeping next door. I waste no time hurrying up the stairs.

The door to my room stands ajar, and I see right away that

someone has been through my things. My trunk is open, and my clothes are scattered all over the floor and bed. I go first to Diadem's cage and breathe a sigh of relief when I see the moonlight reflecting off her scales. She stirs when I open the cage, and she crawls up my arm before I even whistle. I'll have to feed her soon.

But first, I turn my attention back to my belongings. Everything's in disarray, although it doesn't look like much has been taken. I find my bag next to my bed, as well as my blowgun and darts. My vials of potions have been moved around, but they haven't been poured out. I'm stuffing it all in the bag when the creak of a door in the corridor catches my attention. I freeze and look around for a place to hide, but there's nothing large enough to block me from view.

I definitely hear footsteps now, and they're getting louder. The glow of lamplight leaks under the door, and then my doorknob turns. Light floods in and I find myself face-to-face with Mehtap.

She is still in her sleeping gown, and her hair is plaited for the night. Her mouth opens.

I pull her in and close the door. "Make no sound, Mehtap. I have Diadem on my arm and I have nothing to lose."

Mehtap stares at me with a mixture of grogginess and surprise. "Zivah, how did you get out?"

"Quiet." I can't have her alerting the guards. I'll have to tie her up until morning. I must have rope somewhere. . . .

Mehtap looks at Diadem on my arm. "Would you really kill me, Zivah?" she says evenly. "Were you never a true friend at all?"

Her words strip bare my hypocrisy. For the last days, I've been horrified at Mehtap's betrayal when I've done worse to her, using her friendship and her trust against her father and her empire. "I'm sorry," I say, and the words are heavy on my tongue. "We could have been friends, I think, if things had been different."

She searches my face. "But why? Why would you do this?"

It's a question that's hard enough to answer in the light of day, much less in the middle of the night, surrounded by enemies. "The rosemarked are not the only people Ampara treads on," I say. "I didn't want to lie to you, but I had to help my people."

"And what will you do now? Are you going back to your people? Will you take Dineas with you?"

I don't answer. I've already told her more than I should have.

Mehtap sets her jaw. "Answer me one thing. Why didn't you tell my father that I killed Kurosh?"

And here my breath leaves me. I'd wondered the same thing. "I don't know. I suppose I just couldn't do it."

And finally she falls silent. The urgency of our situation presses upon me once again, and I look around for something to use as a rope.

Mehtap's voice is sad when she speaks again. "If you're trying to tie me up, I have cords in my room," she says. "Or you could trust me, and I could help you."

I falter at her words. "Why should I trust you?"

"You didn't tell my father, and so I am indebted to you." She lets out a frustrated breath. "Do you think I care whether you're loyal to Ampara? Swear to me that you won't hurt my father, and I'll show you how to get into the palace, where Dineas is imprisoned."

Given what she's done, I've no reason to doubt her lack of patriotism. Still, I can't make that promise. "There's to be a war, Mehtap. People will die on both sides."

"Yes, I know what happens in war," she snaps. I wonder if she's guessed my role in the Shidadi ambush, and if she blames me for it. "But swear on your Goddess you won't raise your hand against my father, or let your friend Dineas harm him. Promise me that you'll leave the city as soon as you can."

"And why would you trust me to keep my promises?"

Mehtap lets out a sad laugh. "You're the only friend I had in here," she says. "I must trust you, otherwise I have nothing else to hope for."

I stare at her, and something twists within me.

"I haven't screamed for the guards yet, have I?" she says quietly.

She falls silent, eyes fixed on Diadem as she awaits my response. And I realize that I understand what she means. It might not be the wisest thing to accept her help, but it is as she said. We were friends during my brief stay in the rosemarked compound. And if I can't believe that bond was real, then I don't know what else I could trust.

"I swear on the honor of my Goddess," I say. "If I can get to Dineas, we will leave the city. And I won't harm your father, nor will I allow Dineas to do so."

There's a space of one breath, and Mehtap nods. "Come with me to my room."

When I don't move, she lets out a huff. "By the gods, Zivah. Put that snake on me if you must."

In the end, I don't put Diadem on her, though I stay close to

Mehtap as we file silently down the corridor. Once we're in her bedroom, I close the door and lock it.

Mehtap rummages through a box in front of her mirror and takes out a small jar. "It's not exactly your skin tone, but if you use it at night, it should disguise your rosemarks just fine." She drops it into my outstretched hand, and then she fetches the gown I borrowed from her for the equinox festival.

"On the north end of the palace gardens is a small gate with a faulty lock. They don't fix it because the young aristocrats use it to sneak in and out. The guards turn a blind eye toward the occasional nighttime adventure. They won't give you trouble if you look the part." She presses the gown into my arms. Then she takes my hand in hers. "Please don't remember the worst of me, Zivah," she says. "I wasn't always like this."

She pushes me into the hall and closes the door before I can respond.

I stand outside the palace walls, staring at the wrought iron gate. It's short and narrow, obviously a side entrance for gardeners or servants. If I hadn't known better, I wouldn't even have thought it was in use.

A breeze blows by, and I pull Mehtap's cloak closer around me. The silk of her gown brushes my skin. I can almost pretend that it's the equinox festival, except this time it's the middle of the night, I have a bag full of potions on my shoulder, and I feel the silk of my dress through a sticky layer of clay and oil. Mehtap was right about the ointment. Though it doesn't match my skin completely, no one will notice at night. And now I must decide whether to believe the rest of her advice.

Scrawny lands on my shoulder and sticks his beak into my hair. It pulls, but I don't stop him.

"I didn't ask for this, Tal," I whisper. But then, I suppose it was foolish to think I would simply come to Sehmar City and stay in the safety of what I know. I smooth down the folds of my cloak and don a pair of silk gloves. "Ready to go?" I ask the birds.

The gate sticks a little, but then something gives and it swings open. I duck my head and glide through, telling myself that I'm not Zivah, rosemarked healer on a suicide mission, but a great Amparan lady, poised and self-possessed, on my way to a midnight rendezvous. As I pull the gate shut, I see a guard's shadow in the corner of my eye. But nobody stops me.

The gardens are magical at this time of night. I walk through clouds of fragrance, and the moon lights my way, both from its place above me and through its reflections in myriad pools below. I whisper to Slicewing to take me to Dineas, and she leads the way, a spot of ink cutting through the night. I follow her until the gardens give way to grand buildings—forests of stone columns and facades with bas-relief carvings that hint of men and animals. I pass the occasional slave or soldier and even a well-dressed official, but none of them give me a second look.

After a while, I pass through to what looks like an outer circle of the palace. The buildings here are built of mud, and I see soldiers walking around. Slicewing slows here and flits from rooftop to rooftop until she finally alights on a squat building. It doesn't seem much different from the others at first glance, though then I see that the walls are stone, and the windows are narrow. Two guards stand in front, and through the windows I see others in the anteroom beyond the door.

This must be the prison. I duck out of view, shuddering at the thought of Dineas inside, and open my sack. I have five bundles of smoke herbs to burn, as well as a jar of fine wine laced with sleeping draft. Diadem is wrapped tightly around my upper arm.

I will myself to think. There's one good thing about this prison—the thick walls and small windows make it hard to air out. There's a chimney near the front, most likely connecting to a fireplace in the anteroom. I take out two strips of cloth and wet them thoroughly. The first, I tie around my neck. The second, I hold out to Slicewing.

"Slicewing, take this to the chimney." I point as well as I can. Slicewing obediently grabs it and flies toward the prison, but simply drops the cloth onto the roof before circling back to collect her praise.

I shake my head. "No, Slicewing, bring it back." The bird cocks her head to the side and fetches the cloth again. I frown, trying to think how better to give the command. "The chimney, Slicewing. Take this to the chimney."

Again Slicewing takes flight, but this time, she drops it on the other side of the roof.

I sigh, and order Slicewing to fetch the cloth back. Perhaps it's too much to ask. I'm about to tuck the cloth back in my bag when Scrawny digs his claws into my arm.

"What is it?"

Scrawny stretches his wings in reply. I shrug. "If you want to give it a try . . . Scrawny, take this to the chimney."

The bird takes wing, flying high above the roof. I hold my breath, and then he drops the cloth right on top of the chimney.

I almost laugh with relief, and scratch his neck when he comes down. "We don't give you enough credit, do we? If only you three could fight guards."

But they can't, and the rest is up to me. I take out two herb bundles, place them on small plates, and light them on a nearby torch. The leaves immediately began to smolder and smoke as I adjust Mehtap's gown. The gown is light and airy, like those of the priestesses of Zenagua. It's also more layered and ornamented than a priestess habit, but my cloak covers much of it and I'll just have to rely on the darkness to hide the rest.

"Goddess help me," I whisper. "Let this work."

I circle the prison, stopping in front of every corner of the building with the smoking plate, making up some nonsense gestures, and speaking words into the air. I can sense the soldiers watching me, and I hold my head high as befits a priestess of Zenagua. I continue my stately march up to the door, praying that the soldiers do not notice my shaking hands.

"Good evening, good soldiers. The gods smile upon your service."

They look at me quizzically as I lay the herbs on each side of the doorway. Perhaps the Goddess is with me, because there's no wind, and the smoke from the herbs rises straight up around us. The smell is quite strong.

The soldier on the left waves his hand. "What is this? It stinks."

"It is for the consecration of the palace," I say. "It has been a month since the late emperor passed into the underworld. Tonight we bless the grounds."

The guard narrows his eyes. His suspicion is clear, but I also see his pupils dilating in response to the fumes. He shakes his head as if to clear it. "Under whose authority is this?"

"The temple of Zenagua and Emperor Kiran."

The other guard steps to the side, probably to avoid the smoke.

"Sir, wait," I say. "I have something to ask you." He stops, albeit unwillingly. "I..." My mind goes blank. The herbs are affecting me too.

The first guard rubs his eyes. "I'll have to check with my commander," he says. But as he steps past me, he stumbles against the wall.

"You're not well, sir." I take out my jar of wine. "Drink this. It will counteract the effects of the incense."

He takes the wineskin and drinks, though he stops mid-swallow, as if he's remembered not to take drinks from strange women in the middle of the night. I quickly take the wineskin back and give it to the other guard. "Your friend feels better. You should do the same."

I use the same authoritative voice I've honed over years, but this guard steps back. "No."

He looks around as if to sound an alarm. Without thinking, I grab a dart from my pouch and scratch him on the arm.

"What did—" he says. He stumbles against the wall and slides slowly to the ground as his friend topples over as well. I drag them into the doorway. They're heavy, and the walls only partially hide them, but it's the best I can do.

The front door opens into a dimly lit room. Three guards sit around the table, and there is a fireplace on the far end. The guards stand when they see me, and I pull the door shut before they can notice that their friends outside are gone.

The soldier closest to me wrinkles his nose at the smoking bundles. "What is this?"

"Incense to bless the palace. To commemorate one month of Emperor Kurosh's passing."

"Give me those. They stink," he says. He grabs the dishes out of my hand and pushes them across the table, farther away than I'd like. Then he takes a closer look at me.

"You're not dressed like a priestess," he says.

Curse the room's numerous oil lamps. If he looks carefully enough, he'll see the ointment covering my rosemarks. "And who are you to say what a servant of Zenagua should wear?"

"A lone priestess like you, wandering the grounds at this hour?"

"My sisters are doing the same as we speak."

He glances out the window. "I don't see them."

One of the soldiers at the table coughs. "Farbod, the smoke is foul," he says, and grabs the herbs. I tense, thinking he's going to take the dish out the door, but instead he puts them in the fireplace.

Farbod glances back, then resumes his interrogation in earnest. "What order are you? Who is your mother priestess?"

"I will not be questioned like a common criminal," I snap.

The soldier who'd moved the herbs into the fireplace coughs. "Chimney's blocked." He picks up the plates and carries them toward the door, but then he falls to one knee. One herb bundle rolls, still smoldering, onto the ground.

Farbod's eyes open wide, and he grabs me by the arm. His fingers dig into my cut. "Who are you?" he demands, and he drags me toward the door.

"Let go of me!" But he's too strong. I might as well be a sack of rice. Panic thrills through me, and I kick at his shins. He swears, and throws me against the wall. Lights explode in front of my eyes.

"Vicious wench." He grabs me by the collar.

A slithering up my arm, a flash of scales, and then Farbod screams and grabs his hand. I had forgotten about Diadem.

Farbod keeps screaming. The sound is like claws gouging the underside of my skin, and I stare in horror as he slowly sinks to the ground.

"Stop there!" shouts the third soldier, and he runs toward us. My hand moves of its own accord, pulling my blowgun out and fitting it with a dart. I shoot him in the neck and barely duck out of the way as his momentum carries him into the wall.

And then I'm the only person left standing. My head spins, and I pull the damp cloth over my nose and mouth. Farbod is still moaning from the snakebite. I see all the signs of the poison moving—the rash making its way up his arm, the bloodshot eyes. I could still save him with an antidote, but I don't have one.

Bile rises in my throat. I've delivered dozens of people from the bite of the purple-crowned serpent. Tonight is the first time I've killed someone with it.

"I'm sorry," I whisper. I take out a dart, and he watches with wild eyes as I scratch his skin. It will put him to sleep and save him from the worst of the pain when his organs begin to fail. "This is the best I can do."

I feel ill. Using the herbs against Utana was nothing compared to this. But I've no time to linger. There will be other soldiers coming soon. The herbs I brought in are still smoking, and I leave them there. On the belt of one of the men is a ring of keys. I take them, along with his dagger, and run toward the holding cells.

The cell doors have sliding panels, and I run from door to door, checking each in turn. As I finish checking the third room, a guard emerges from the stairwell at the end of the corridor. He pauses, puzzled at the sight of me, and I shoot him before he recovers.

I keep going, finishing with this floor and then moving down. Finally, I slide open a panel to see Dineas's familiar profile. I can hardly hold the keys steady as I try them one by one on the door. The lock turns.

He's chained to the wall. His eyes are closed, and he doesn't react to my coming in.

"Dineas!"

He's still—frighteningly so. I run to him and turn his face toward me. His skin is warm and covered in sweat and grime. He's marked by bruises and scabs, but he's alive.

"Dineas," I say, more insistently this time, and he groans. I take my keys again and work at the shackles around his wrists. The first one gives way, and then the other, and he sinks to the ground. It's all I can do to slow his fall.

I sit down next to him and cradle his head in my arms. "Dineas." My voice breaks. "Wake up, please."

# CHAPTER FORTY-EIGHT

## DINEAS

Zivah visits me in my dreams. She holds me close and whispers my name.

"Wake up," she says, but I don't want to. Because if I open my eyes, I'll be back in my living nightmare, and she'll be gone. The past few days have been bad enough. Just give me a moment of peace.

But she keeps calling me, and a cold cloth passes over my face. I groan. "Don't make me go back."

"I'm so sorry," she whispers.

If she's really sorry, she wouldn't be trying to wake me up. But it's no use. I'm drifting back to reality. I open my eyes, and the hateful walls of my cell appear around me, the jail I don't even remember entering. Gods, how did this happen?

I expect Zivah to waver and disappear, but she's solid, holding me close even though I'm covered in grime.

I don't understand.

"Did they arrest you too? If I've gotten you in trouble . . ."

She shakes her head. "I'm here to get you out," she says. "But we don't have much time. You must come with me now, and I need you whole."

"Whole?"

Zivah rummages in her bag and takes out a vial. "I need you to drink this."

In my mind, I see the vial fragments Arxa had shown me. "What is it?"

"It's a potion to help you remember."

I pull away from her. "They say you manipulated me with your potions. That you made me lose my mind."

Zivah glances at the door, and when she looks back, her eyes are sad. "I can't prove anything to you. You have to decide whether to trust me."

She unstoppers the potion and puts it in my hand. It smells foul as always, and I wrinkle my nose. Can anything good come from something that smells so bad?

She's getting restless now, her eyes continually drawn to the door and the corridor beyond. "Please, Dineas. You need to trust me, and you need to do it now, or we'll both die."

I stare at the potion. I've been missing pieces of my past for months now, and I suppose I've learned to trust my instincts. My instincts tell me that Zivah doesn't mean me harm.

And with that, I drink it down.

I'm back in the place I never wanted to be again. The cursed stone walls that haunted my dreams and even now make my soul shrivel inside of me.

"Are you back?" asks Zivah.

I look over my arms, my shoulders, the angry welts on my wrists. They haven't yet had time to do much damage. "I didn't think you'd come for me."

She'd started to offer me a hand, but now she hesitates, and something like hurt flickers across her face. "Is it really that hard to believe? I wouldn't abandon you here."

Briefly I wonder if the other me would have been so surprised. "How long will my memory stay this time?"

"Forever. I gave you the permanent antidote."

Strange that I feel a sense of loss at her words. It's almost as if I'd lost a friend. Well, that's another thing I can mull over when I'm no longer in a dungeon full of Amparan soldiers.

She hands me a dagger. "We need to go."

"What's out there?" I ask.

"Most of the guards are asleep. One's dead."

"You killed him?"

"Snakebite." She doesn't look at me.

I head for the door, then stop. "Wait, there's Tus. We have to go get him."

She's silent for a moment. "Other guards will be coming soon," she says. But she says this as a warning, not an argument.

The walls press in on me as we go. I grit my teeth and try not to think about suffocating as I run from door to door, peering in the small windows. Finally I see Tus, almost unrecognizable with his hair matted and the rest of him covered in filth. Zivah hands me a key.

At the sound of the door opening, Tus snaps awake. He shrinks away from me, almost animallike in the way he moves, and it feels like a dagger to the gut.

"Tus, it's me. I'm back," I say in Shidadi. He looks at me, uncomprehending. I take the key and start working on his shackles. "I'm sorry." I shake my head at how inadequate the words are. "I'm so sorry." I repeat the words over and over, though the mantra does nothing to absolve my guilt.

Tus's bloodshot eye darts frantically to Zivah, and then back to me. "This is the healer who took away your memory?"

"Yes, but it's back now. And I'm getting you out."

"I can't," he says.

"If I can get out, so can you." I throw his arm over me and haul him up, suppressing a gag at his smell, but he lets out a sharp cry and collapses. He muffles the rest of his moans against his arm.

"Dineas, his leg," says Zivah. She reaches out to unwrap a dirty bandage from around his calf. If I thought he smelled bad before, what pours out from under the bandage is ten times worse. Zivah gasps, stricken. Even I know what this means.

"It's badly infected," Zivah says quietly. "Very badly. Even with the best treatment, in the best of circumstances..."

I drive my fist into the floor. Curse them. Zenagua strike them all. Tears of frustration build behind my eyes.

"Dineas, we can't take him with us," Zivah says softly.

Tus quiets abruptly, then turns wild eyes to us. "Go," he

says. "Go back to Gatha. Finish your mission. Tell her I gave the Amparans nothing."

"We're not leaving you here."

He grabs me by the wrist. "Then don't. But the only way out for me is through Zenagua," he says. "Help me find her."

It's like a boulder has been dropped on my chest.

Next to me, Zivah shudders. "I can give him a sleeping dart and a bite from Diadem. He shouldn't feel pain that way."

Her words snap me out of my stupor. "No. A Shidadi should die by his own hand." Tus is a warrior, the man who cared for me after my father died, who protected Shidadi secrets to the very end. That's who he really is, not this quivering broken thing in front of me. My hands tremble as I give him my dagger. "May Neju carry you straight to Zenagua's paradise."

He's so weak that the dagger dips toward the ground before he musters the strength to lift it. "Go," he rasps. "I'll make peace with the gods alone."

My last glimpse of Tus is of him leaning against the wall, staring at the blade. As Zivah and I flee down the corridor, we hear a muffled groan and a soft gurgle. I lift up one last prayer for him. That's all I can afford to give.

❋

The first floor looks like it's been worked over by assassins. Bodies lie sprawled everywhere, and a smoky haze lingers in the air. I give her a sideways glance. "You did this?"

"Hurry" is all she says.

"Neju help me if I ever insult a Dara maiden again."

She's right that we need to hurry though. I scan the soldiers and strip the livery off the one closest to my size. Zivah turns her back as I change, though I'm fairly sure she's seen me bare plenty of times by now. I lift a sword and a new dagger off the same man, and then we're out the door.

"How did you get in?" I ask her.

"There was an unlocked gate in the garden. Nobody challenged me in this dress."

True, many soldiers will look the other way rather than confront a powerful lady. "Let's go that way. I'll pretend to be your bodyguard."

She walks ahead, and I trail behind her, though it's hard to play the menacing bodyguard when everything hurts. There's also a question of how often noble ladies walk around the barracks at night. The hair on my arms stands on end every time we pass another soldier, and she gets her fair share of looks and knowing grins. Still, no one stops us.

A short distance out, I'm enveloped in a cloud of feathers as all three of my crows try to land on my shoulder. There's quite a bit of jostling and my head gets buffeted by wings several times. Still, the crows are a welcome sight. "Good to see you too," I say, "but I can't have you attracting attention. Scout."

They take off again, though Slicewing manages to shoot me a reproachful look before taking off. "I know, I'll make it up to you," I mutter.

I find myself counting our steps, measuring the distance to freedom. We're a third of the way to the gardens. Halfway there.

A bugle splits the night. Zivah tenses, and I swallow a curse. Someone's discovered the mess at the prison.

Immediately, the barracks come to life around us. Soldiers

stream out of the buildings, and I know more will follow. I catch up to Zivah. "Quick, off to the side."

We duck into a corner shadowed by bushes. More soldiers are coming out, reporting to their commanders. Everything is chaotic at the moment, but the confusion won't last.

"We won't get to the gate in time, will we?" says Zivah. She's right. The entrances into the aristocratic portions of the palace are likely already locked down.

"Probably not," I admit. Then the wind changes, and the distinct smell of horse manure reaches my nose. It's an intriguing thought.

Zivah must smell it too, because she turns to me. "Will they be checking the stables?"

"Yes, but we might be able to get there first. You in?"

She pauses a moment, then gives a deliberate nod.

The stables have already started to stir by the time we get there. A stablehand stands in front of the door, scanning in all directions. I hear horses stomping inside. I walk straight up to the door, doing my best to exude authority.

"What are you doing out here?" I snap. "Get back in. Someone might be after the horses."

The boy stumbles, his mouth falling open, and he rushes back through the barn door. I'm right on his heels, and as soon as we're inside, I whack him over the head with the hilt of my dagger. The poor fellow slumps to the ground.

"What's going on out there?" a voice calls from the back.

I suppose it was too much to hope that a clueless stable boy would be the only person sleeping here at night. "Just making sure the stables are secure," I call. "A prisoner's escaped."

A man steps into view on the other side of the barn. He looks suspicious . . . and very muscular.

"Where's the boy?" he asks.

"The boy?" I need to work on my innocent face.

He puts up a hand. "Stay right there," he says. "No one's allowed in here."

I hold out my hands, but I keep walking. Maybe ten more steps until I can get to him. "No harm intended . . . Just passing along the news."

"Stop. I mean it." He reaches behind the stall and picks up a stout-looking club. I brace my feet and reach for my sword as the man comes at me. I hope I can still fight after my stay in the dungeon.

The man grabs at his neck and falls over.

I turn to see Zivah holding a blowgun. "Get us a horse," she says.

Right. I look through the stalls and see the roan stallion Arxa had identified as Rovenni breeding stock. The fences at the far end of the riding fields are the farthest and hardest to guard, and this creature should be able to carry both of us there with no problem. Plus, I'm guessing a certain Rovenni tribe would be glad to see this horse again.

That is, if this stallion will mind me. His ears flick back and forth as I come closer, and he paws at the ground. I think back to what I saw the Rovenni do, holding up the brand on my arm so he can see it.

"Easy, there," I say. "I'm a friend."

To my surprise, he calms down. I saddle him up, haul the

unconscious stablehands outside, and tie the horse to a post, leaving Zivah out there as I run back and start opening the other stalls. Two horses come out right away, but the others stay put.

No, that won't do. We can't have all these horses around when the Amparans muster up pursuit. I gather a handful of straw at the back of the barn and hold it to a candle flame until it catches. Smoke curls through the air. A few horses stomp their hooves and whinny.

Neju help them, these horses are too calm for their own good. I put my fingers to my lips and whistle for the crows. A few moments later, Slicewing and Scrawny dart through the door. They give the smoking straw a wide berth before landing on the wall of the nearest stall.

I point to the mare nearest the barn door. "Drive." This better work, because my eyes are starting to water.

The crows take off, screaming and diving at that poor horse until she bolts out the door. Another horse follows, and then it's a full-on stampede out the barn. I follow, coughing at the thickening smoke, and then I realize that the crows' calls have changed. They're no longer screaming to scare the horses. They're giving warning calls....

Zivah.

I run outside. Zivah stands in front by the stallion. The stablehands are nowhere to be seen. Cutting off Zivah's escape are five soldiers, two of whom are archers with bows pointed at her. And leading them is General Arxa. As I come out, one of the archers shifts his aim to target me.

So much for sneaking up unnoticed. I raise my hands and

move to stand next to Zivah. She has her blowgun pointed at the general, which is probably the only reason they haven't captured her yet. He must not know that it would only put him to sleep.

Arxa's face is a dark cloud, and he doesn't look surprised to see me at all. "To think I trusted both of you. Will you still hide from me who you really are?"

The fire of the barn is catching now, and I hear the screams of fleeing horses in the distance. And I decide that I'm tired of all this deception. "I am Dineas, son of Youtab and Artabanos of the Shidadi, warrior under Gatha." My voice gets stronger as I continue. "I spent months in an Amparan dungeon until I was stricken with rose plague and the guards threw me out to die."

"Shidadi, of course," says Arxa. "You're cold-blooded, to fight your kin like that." I shift my weight, and Arxa puts up his hand. "Don't tempt me, Dineas. You know what our archers can do." He turns to Zivah. "Dineas disappoints me, but it's you who shocks me the most. It's hard to believe that someone so seemingly selfless can foster such deception. That's my daughter's dress you're wearing, isn't it? Have you no shame?"

Zivah's voice trembles, though her weapon remains steady. "I love my people. It pained me to deceive you, to steal Mehtap's clothing and break your trust, but I had no other choice."

The fires continue to crackle, and I can feel the sweat pouring down my skin. It's only a matter of time before the soldiers take their chances with Zivah's blowgun. I look again at the two archers with arrows pointed toward us. Does their aim have to be quite so steady?

"I met a minister named Utana in the rosemarked compound,"

says Zivah. "He told me that Emperor Kiran betrayed you. He was the one who poisoned your troops."

I see shadows flitting behind the soldiers, a flash of feathers. As Zivah continues to speak, I whistle low under my breath.

"Lies," says Arxa. "You'll tell me the truth in the dungeons. Don't think your rosemarks will protect you."

"Get the arrows!" I shout. Preener and Slicewing swoop down and snatch the arrows from the archers' bows. As everyone gawks at the crows, I cut the rope securing our stallion and all but throw Zivah on, then clamber up behind her and kick the beast into motion. The creature needs no coaxing with the fire so high, and he bursts into a gallop as the soldiers in our path throw themselves out of the way. And then we are off, racing down toward the riding fields and into the darkness beyond.

# EPILOGUE
## ZIVAH

We have several close calls—a short skirmish with guards at the city gate, and two more encounters with riders on our tail. Several times, arrows pass perilously close to my head, but our horse is fast and agile, and finally we're riding alone in the open desert. Dineas urges the horse north until finally we come to an abrupt stop in the middle of nowhere.

"What is it?" I ask as he dismounts.

"Help me," he says. He grabs a large rock and starts digging. After a moment, I drop down to help him. The dirt we clear away grows moist under my fingers as we dig deeper.

"Got it," Dineas says. The dirt falls away as he pulls out a long oilcloth-wrapped packet. He lays it on the ground to unwrap it, and reverently lifts out one of his swords. The moonlight reflects off the blade as he draws it. I watch without speaking as he squeezes his eyes shut and takes a shaky breath. I don't know what thoughts are running through his head, but I sense that he needs this moment.

Finally, he opens his eyes. "We should go," he says.

We ride more slowly after that, hour after hour. When we pass by a lone cottage, Dineas sneaks off alone and returns with half a loaf of bread, though we don't stop to eat. We keep going until my entire being becomes numb with exhaustion. When the sky finally starts to turn gray, Dineas speaks again.

"The crows haven't called out pursuit for several hours now." I can hear his fatigue in his voice. Our horse's head hangs low, and his steps begin to lag. I know we can't go much farther.

We stop near a small spring. Dineas untacks and waters the horse, then spreads an oilcloth near some boulders to sit on. He hands me a piece of bread. It's dry and hard to get down, but I gnaw on it nonetheless. Now that we're no longer moving, the cold night air seeps into my bones and I shiver.

Dineas looks at me. "We'll have to sit closer without a fire. It was often the only way to stay warm in the mountains."

I'm too exhausted to be self-conscious, and I scoot next to him so our shoulders touch. He takes his cloak and covers both of us, and slowly his warmth starts to creep over. Still, there's a wall between us. We've been through so much in the past months, but I don't know this Dineas—the real Dineas—much better than I did when we came. I only know the illusion.

"Will you miss him?" he asks, almost as if he'd read my mind.

I hesitate, unsure if he's mocking me. But there's genuine

curiosity in his voice, and I find I don't want to lie to him. Whatever our differences, we share things now that no one else will ever truly understand.

"I will," I say.

The wind whistles over our heads. It's a lonely sound.

"I can't believe he's really gone," Dineas says.

"Everything he's gone through is still with you," I say. "You've lost nothing of his."

"Nothing except peace."

And I know that I'm not the only one who's lost. I adjust my arm so I can hold his hand, and this time it doesn't feel so awkward.

"Do you think we can make it back in time to help them?" I ask. "Have we done any good at all?"

Dineas's eyes go flinty with determination. "We'll go back. We'll prepare our people for battle. We won't let Ampara take us without a fight."

His words sadden me, though I accept their grim inevitability. The winds have shown their direction, and though I may not like it, it's time to prepare for war.

"I don't know if I can do this," I say.

"You can. You're one of the bravest people I know."

I look up at his words and scan his face, half expecting to see a hint of the Dineas we left in Sehmar City. But the eyes of the man next to me are old beyond his years. Dineas catches my reaction, and the corner of his mouth quirks just slightly. And he gives my hand a squeeze that says more than words ever could.

The wind blows, and the crows chatter to one another. Dineas pulls his cloak closer around us. I lean my head on his shoulder, and together we wait for dawn.

END OF BOOK 1

# ACKNOWLEDGMENTS

Once again, my editor, Rotem Moscovich, shepherded every aspect of this story: from idea, to draft, through revisions, to publication. Heather Crowley provided valuable assistance and a great tagline, and ninja publicist Cassie McGinty guided the book's big debut. My gratitude as well to the rest of the Hyperion team.

My agent, Jim McCarthy, offered key advice on an early version of the manuscript, and support throughout the publishing process.

My critique partners Amitha Knight, Jennifer Barnes, Rachal Aronson, and Emily Terry once again read over those messy first draft chapters.

Beta readers offered their take on later drafts: Lauren James, Andrea Lim, Jenna DeTrapani, Emily Lo, Rebekah Greenway, Lianne Crawford, Lisa Choi MD, Faye Matuguinas, Nicole

Harlan, Summer McDaniel, Bridget Howard, Kelsey Olesen, Rachel Andrews, and Anya Johnson.

Several readers also provided their expertise on specific topics. My former grad school classmate Retsina Meyer discussed with me the latest neuroscience on erasing and restoring memories. (The novel is firmly based in fantasy, but I couldn't resist working in what brain science I could.) Chris Lenyk gave me many tips on military strategy and psychology. And finally, Al Rosenberg gave crucial insight into the experience of people with terminal illnesses. A shout-out as well to the Writing in the Margins Database for connecting me with Al.

My husband, as always, was a supportive presence throughout the ups and downs of the novel-writing process, as were my parents and extended family.

And a thank-you, finally, to my daughter, who grew her major organ systems as I wrote the first draft, kicked her way through revisions, and kindly waited until copy edits were finished before making her grand entrance into the world. I wouldn't say you made any part of this process easier, but all the same, I couldn't ask for a better writing partner.

Turn the page for a sneak peek
at the sequel to *Rosemarked*,

# CHAPTER ONE

## DINEAS

You can tell plague guards by their fear. Some hold their sword hilts as if trying to crush them to dust. Others jump at the slightest brush of wind. Still others look fine from a distance, but up close, you see how wide their eyes are, how their gazes jump from bird to grass to stone.

You'd think that guarding a quarantine of civilians would be easier than fighting a battle. I mean, you're not staring down a line of archers or charging into a wall of spears. But somehow it's worse. Maybe it's because there's no fighting to heat up the blood, or because you can't kill a fever with a sword. Whatever the reason, every soldier guarding the walls of Taof is terrified, and the citizens pay the price. This morning, a woman strayed too close to the perimeter and ended up with seven arrows in her back.

Which is why I stay low as I creep forward in the knee-deep grass outside the city, cutting as narrow a path as I can through the sharp, scratchy blades. Taof sits at the edge of the northern grasslands, where the plains start giving way to hills and shrubs. A road of flattened weeds and wagon ruts runs past the city gates, though I don't walk on it—it's far too easy to be seen.

It's sundown, and the light is fading fast. My crow Slicewing circles around my head, ready to call a warning if anyone draws near. The other two crows are back in the hills with Zivah. Since the entire empire is looking for an umbertouched man traveling with a rosemarked woman, it's safer for me to scout alone.

It's been a month since Zivah and I barely escaped Sehmar City with our lives. A month since Commander Arxa unmasked me as a spy and Emperor Kiran started amassing an army to invade our homeland. We should have returned by now, but instead we've doubled back one league for every three we've traveled. We've gotten lost, run in circles, and huddled, starving, in caves as soldiers camped within steps of finding us. Finally, we managed to get as far north as Taof, only to run straight into a rose plague outbreak. Emperor Kiran's declared a quarantine, and the river crossing ahead of us swarms with plague guards.

If we don't find a way through soon, we'll have to double back and follow the river for days upstream or downstream. Even the thought of doing that is maddening. Every day we lose makes me wonder if this will be the one that lets the Amparan army overtake us, that leaves our kin in Monyar to fight without our help.

"Lies!"

The shout sends a jolt through my entire body. I freeze, then realize that the speaker is too far away to have anything to do with me. Peering over the grass, I see a crowd of people outside the wall dressed in travel leathers. They look familiar. A big, grizzled man seems to be speaking to an official on their behalf.

"Lies," the man says again. "We've been camped outside the city the whole time, and the horse market was across the river from the outbreak. None of us are a danger. If you put us within the quarantine, you might as well murder us all."

Horses. Now I see the herd of them a short distance away, and I realize why these people look familiar. There's no mistaking the elegant lines and long silky manes of Rovenni steeds. I had a run-in with this tribe back in Sehmar City. It wasn't exactly a friendly visit, but Neju knows I don't wish the plague on them.

I sneak closer.

"It's Emperor Kiran's decree," the minister says in an oily voice. "You must be kept in the city because of new plague laws."

"Lies. The emperor wants us all dead so he can take our stallions for his army."

I remember this man. His name is Nush, and he once accused me of being a horse thief.

"Think carefully before refusing a direct order from the emperor," says the minister.

It seems now that the soldiers guarding the gate all turn to watch.

Finally, Nush speaks again. "Keep us here if you must, but put us outside the walls. If you try to force us in, we'll fight, and we have nothing to lose." There's enough threat in his voice that any smart man would take heed.

I don't think the minister will bring in soldiers, but I can't afford to wait and see what happens. Grass bends and crunches under my feet as I hurry away, and soon the ground starts to slope downward. The river is a thousand paces wide, swollen from the spring rains, and the water splashes and froths as it rushes past. It's deep too, judging from the boats I saw earlier in the day. I don't know what I'm looking for. An abandoned boat? A secret log bridge? Stone jutting up from the river at convenient intervals? It really isn't the type of river to ford or swim, even for those as desperate as me and Zivah, and the only proper bridge is currently the centerpiece of the Taof quarantine.

Slicewing caws. I freeze. A lone soldier walks the grass toward me with wide, swaggering steps. He's not looking in my direction, though, and I duck down into the grass. With any luck, he'll walk right past. But since we've been short on luck lately, I wrap a hand around the hilt of my knife.

As he comes closer, I see he's a typical Amparan sentry in standard armor. Not as scared-looking as the others now that he's farther from the city, but I'm not impressed with the way he's keeping watch. He looks like he's daydreaming rather than scanning for fugitives. I notice he's rubbed mud on his skin to look like umbermarks. It's not the first time I've seen someone try to fool the plague that way. Zivah says it doesn't work. I guess she should know.

The soldier swivels his face in my direction. His eyes widen.

Maybe not so much of a daydreamer after all. I tense my muscles to spring.

And then his face shifts. His skin darkens. His eyes grow more wide set, and his cheekbones more pronounced.

My knife falls from my hand. "Masista?"

The man's face shifts back to that of a stranger. Gods, what was that? I grab on to my confusion and use it to propel myself into the man. For a moment, we're a tangle of limbs—his neck is slick with sweat, and he smells like swamp mud—and then I catch his ankle with mine and throw him down. He hits the ground with a grunt as I sprint away.

"Halt!" he shouts.

What self-respecting fugitive has ever halted? I double my speed, plunging blindly through the grass. The soldier screams for reinforcements. I flinch as an arrow flies past my head, and I swerve toward the hills. Once I get there, I can disappear into the shrubs, but it's at least a quarter league away. Hooves thunder behind me now, sending vibrations through the ground, and I bite back a curse, reaching for any last bit of speed.

It's not enough. I skid to a stop as a soldier on horseback cuts me off, his warhorse kicking dirt into my face. Two other horsemen take their places behind me. That's the problem with Amparans. They never want to give you a fair fight.

"Halt," said the soldier in front of me, "or we'll grind you into the mud."

This time I halt.

I call myself all sorts of names as I put my hands up in the air. If the Amparans don't beat me senseless, I'm tempted to do it for them. What kind of good-for-nothing fighter mistakes an enemy for a friend and drops his knife? There are toddlers in my tribe who could have done better.

The soldier who'd threatened to trample me dismounts now and raises his sword. He's an ugly brute with a scar that makes his eyebrow look crooked.

"Who are you?" he asks. "What is your business out here?"

A sliver of an idea. Since I dropped my knife, that first soldier might not even know I'd drawn a weapon. "Sirs, there's been a misunderstanding. I was just out to gather wood for our cooking fire."

"You run pretty fast for someone with nothing to hide."

It's not hard to fake a nervous laugh. "I was afraid I'd be cut down on the spot."

"You might be cut down yet."

"I'm umbertouched, sir." I reach for my sleeve, and Crookbrow raises his sword. "I'm just rolling up my sleeve," I add. "I'll move slowly."

He doesn't relax, but he doesn't skewer me either.

"I have no reason to fear the plague," I say, pulling up the fabric to reveal my skin, "but my fellow Rovenni do. We must boil river water if we want any chance of surviving, and wood from the riverbank burns hotter than grass."

Crookbrow stares at my arm. In the moonlight, it's hard to see the dark splotches that mark me as someone who survived rose plague and emerged immune, but you can find them if you're looking. Crookbrow's gaze moves from my umbermarks to a scar on my wrist. "He bears a Rovenni brand," he tells the others.

If he were more observant, he would see that my brand is unevenly applied, the work of an amateur rather than a Rovenni elder. But I don't bring that to his attention.

"Please," I say. "I don't want any trouble. Perhaps this evidence will be more convincing." I detach a small bag from my belt and toss it at the soldier's feet. He picks it up, his eyebrows rising at the heft of its jingling contents. My fingers curl into claws. It's hard not to snatch the pouch right back out of his hand. That's the last of our money, the leftovers of a purse I lifted from a traveling priestess of Mendegi. Maybe this whole thing is the Goddess's wrath for stealing from her.

Crookbrow frowns as he weighs the bag in his hand. I wonder if he's going to take the money and kill me anyway, but then he slips the pouch beneath his cloak. "We'll escort you back to your kin, but if you leave again, we'll shoot you like any other plague fleer, umbermarks or no."

"Thank you, sir."

Truthfully, though, I don't know whether to be worried or relieved as the soldiers march me back toward the city. On the one hand, they didn't recognize me. Still, I'm now at the Rovenni's mercy. A word from them, and this entire charade will be over.

Outside the city gates, some haphazard wooden fences have been set up to form a corral. Several large square tents have been erected inside, and a handful of Rovenni mill beside them along with their horses. I see men and women, young traders and old. Amparan soldiers stand sentry outside the fence. As my guards bring me closer, the Rovenni gather around the gate, looking warily at my escorts and then at me.

The man Nush stands closest to the gate, legs planted wide as if he were still astride one of his steeds. I catch his eye. "I told you it was folly to send me out there, brother," I say loudly. "Brother" might be too much, but I don't exactly have time to send a subtle message. "Almost got me killed."

Nush's eyes are intent on my face, and his thick beard does nothing to hide his frown. I can tell he finds me familiar, though I'm not sure he can place me.

Crookbrow jerks me toward the gate by the sleeve of my tunic, rattling my bones. "You are all to remain inside this enclosure. Even the umbertouched."

Nush stares at me, and I stare right back. If only we could send thoughts through our eyes.

Finally, the Rovenni grunts. "Kill this one if you want," he says with a noncommittal shrug. "I won't shed a tear."

The soldier guffaws. "Your friend doesn't seem overly fond of you," he says. But he pushes me through the gate and returns to his horse, probably eager to go count his money. I stand next to the fence, painfully aware of all the traders' eyes on me.

Nush clamps a large hand on my shoulder and pulls me toward the center of the enclosure. "Good to see you safely back, *brother*." His arm is so heavy it's a wonder I don't sink into the ground. He steers me between tents until all Amparans are blocked from view, then whips me around to face him. "Who are you? I've seen you before." He furrows his eyebrows again, and a flicker of recognition flashes in his eyes. He grabs the lapel of my tunic and yanks me closer. "You're the umbertouched horse thief!"

I grab my tunic to keep the fabric from choking me. Do I look like a good target to push around? I used to cut a more intimidating presence. "I never stole any horses from you." I pick my words carefully. Even though I never stole their horses, I did steal something else. To be fair, I was in some pretty desperate circumstances at the time.

Nush's eyes flicker down to my wrist. "What is . . ." He grabs my arm and then runs his fingers over the brand. It tickles when he brushes the edge of the scar tissue. Comprehension dawns on the Rovenni's face. "Why, you scoundrel," he says. He holds my arm up for all around him to see. "This is the man who stole our branding iron," he says.

I grit my teeth as murmurs sound all around. Everyone stares at me, and not in a friendly way. I cringe to think how far Nush's voice might have traveled.

I step closer to him and lower my voice. "I can explain. And I can be useful to you. Just hear me out." I don't actually know how I'd help them, but I'll say anything at this point.

Nush's gaze doesn't soften. "Our brands are legacies from the founders of our tribe. Our men and women train for years in horsemanship to make themselves worthy of the mark. It's core to everything that makes us Rovenni, and you stole the iron as if it were no more than a horseshoe."

I have a feeling that more lies will get me killed. "You're right. I did steal your brand. I was a spy in Sehmar City and needed it to throw Arxa off the scent of who I really was."

There's a brief silence as Nush puts together my words. "You're the Shidadi spy the emperor has been trying to capture."

Disconcerting how quickly he figured that out.

"Where is the healer you travel with?" he asks.

"She's in a safer place than this," I say. "But there's no need for us to be enemies. I know you have no love for the empire. I can help you get out of the quarantine."

The Rovenni man snorts. "Help us? You're locked in here just like we are. You have no weapons and no horse."

"I can help in other ways. Not all weapons are made of wood and metal."

"You Shidadi might have a fearsome reputation, but you

think too highly of your skill if you think one man can make a difference."

I wrack my brain. "My companion the healer has some... unconventional tools. She'll be able to help you." *Prove me right, Zivah.* "We also stole a Rovenni stallion from the palace stables. You can have him back."

Nush's fingers spasm around my wrist. "You have Natussa?"

"If that's the name of the roan stallion the emperor forced you to sell to the army, then yes."

A change comes over Nush at the mention of that horse. Now he looks at me as if I'm a bug to brush away, rather than a bug he wants to squish. "Say your friend can help us. That means we'll be raising arms against the empire's soldiers. We'd become fugitives."

"You can't avoid it," I say. "Kiran's already forced you to sell your breeding stock to the army, and you know he's trying to sicken your people. Unless you want to hand over your life's work and the legacy of your ancestors, you'll have to start fighting him soon, whether you want to or not."

Murmurs erupt around us again. I hadn't realized that the others had come closer.

"Help never comes free," says Nush. "What do you want from us in return?"

This I can answer. "Create enough of a distraction so Zivah and I can cross the river without being seen. Help us flee north to Monyar."

Nush glances around at the others. Perhaps what he sees is encouraging, because he looks back at me. "Tell us more about what your healer friend can do."

Discover More

# Livia Blackburne!

@LETSTALKYA